Born in 1928, RICHARD VASQUEZ worked for several newspapers, including the *Santa Monica Independent*, the *San Gabriel Valley Tribune*, and the *Los Angeles Times*. In addition to *Chicano*, he published two other novels, *The Giant Killer* and *Another Land*. He died in 1990.

CHICANO

• A NOVEL •

RICHARD VASQUEZ

With a Foreword by Rubén Martínez

An Imprint of HarperCollins*Publishers*

HarperCollins books may be purchased for educational, business, or sales promo-
tional use. For information, please write: Special Markets Department, Harper-
Collins Publishers, 10 East 53rd Street, New York, NY 10022.

This book was first published in 1970 by Doubleday & Company, Inc.

RAYO FIRST EDITION, 2005

Designed by Stephanie Huntwork

Printed on acid-free paper

Library of Congress Cataloging-in-Publication Data is available upon request.

ISBN-10: 0-06-082104-3
ISBN-13: 978-0-06-082104-3

05 06 07 08 09 DIX/RRD 10 9 8 7 6 5 4 3 2 1

To my wife Lucy

. . . without her this would not have been written . . .

Foreword

BY RUBÉN MARTÍNEZ

In the early 1970s, my cousin Mario Castaneda often visited my family's home in Los Angeles along with his wife and young children. He'd arrive, as usual, unannounced (Chicano style, Mario would say), and my parents would hastily prepare a snack and bring out cans of pop for the kids.

I looked forward to Mario's visits because he was the only member of our extended family with long hair and who wore bell-bottom jeans. He also spoke in a tongue largely foreign to our household, one that connected us to a particular culture— Chicano radical chic, let's say—that my parents could never indulge. *"Qué pasa,* homes?" Mario would greet me. "How's my little *primo* doing in *la escuela?"* He delivered lines like these while cocking his head back slightly to emphasize his Chicano-cool detachment.

I understood, and I didn't understand. Mine was a bilingual family, but our tongues were separated by clear and present borders: my parents spoke formal Spanish to each other, used English with us kids, who in turn spoke solely in Spanish with our grandparents. Mario was the only one to speak both languages *at once*. In fact, he was the first person I ever heard utter the word *Chicano,* because that's what he considered himself.

The thing is, Mario was not a Chicano, at least not in the narrow sense (a Mexican born in the U.S., that is, a Mexican-American). Mario was a Salvadoran-American, born in Los Angeles to parents who'd emigrated from Central America in the 1940s and settled in the Pico-Union neighborhood west of downtown. When Mario was growing up Pico-Union was a largely Chicano barrio, and at Belmont High School he was weaned on the dominant culture of the neighborhood. (Years later, ironically, Pico-Union became the hub of Salvadoran L.A., receiving hundreds of thousands of refugees from the civil wars of the 1980s.)

As for me, growing up with a Salvadoran mom and a Mexican-American dad in largely Anglo neighborhoods, I never knew what the hell to consider myself. In elementary school, I invoked "Spanish" to avoid being a "dirty Mexican." In middle school, I said I was Mexican to avoid questions and jokes about Central America. In high school, I wanted to eschew race and ethnicity altogether and play rock 'n' roll (I suppose I just wanted to be "white," or better yet, British). Later, I undertook "roots" journeys and tried to reclaim my Mexican-ness and Salvadoran-ness to the exclusion of my American-ness. Today, I'm just your typical Salvadoran-Mexican-American.

I always had trouble claiming the term Chicano for myself, though. I clearly recall my Salvadoran grandfather admonishing me, after one of Mario's visits, to never "speak like *that*" and to not be "confused" like my cousin about who I really was (according to *abuelo,* simply a Latin American lucky—or perhaps unlucky—enough to be born in the States). Then there was the issue of who other Chicanos would recognize as a Chicano. Could a Mexican-Salvadoran-American be a Chicano? My cousin Mario certainly seemed to evidence that this was a possibility, but when I was coming of age as a writer in the 1980s, I shuttled frenetically between East Los Angeles (the ultimate Chicano barrio) and Pico-Union, between Chicano art gigs on Brooklyn Avenue (now César Chávez Avenue) and Central American solidarity meetings on 7th Street. I earnestly tried to "belong" in both realms, wanted to inhabit them simultaneously in fact. Largely from this tension came the words that I wrote back then and indeed, the words that I write today.

With luck, middle age grants belated answers to the existential quandaries that torture the young, and in recent years I've been given the simple gift of this idea: that I was Chicano all along, precisely because I was Mexican and Salvadoran and American all along as I grew up between Spanish and English, on the political and cultural border that divides—and yet does not separate—the U.S. from the Southern lands that reach to Tierra del Fuego. Mario—who went on to become an activist-teacher, fulfilling the basic Chicano tenet of giving back to the community that formed you—taught me that Chicano-ness has less to do with nationality than it does with the deconstruction of the very idea of a fixed identity. Chicanos and Chicanas are always trespassing across territorial divides, linguistic and political and even historical markers. It's an exhilarating space to inhabit, and also a very troubling one, because it seems that many, if not most, people in the world still cling to the notion that their lives have singular meanings in the cultural, or national, sense. There is nothing singular or unitary about being Chicano.

Conservative commentators in recent years have feasted on a caricature of Chicanos as crazed nationalists hellbent on *re-conquista*. And while it is true that separatist notions were popular in the early days of the *movimiento* (notions that owe as much to Malcolm X as to firebrand Chicano nationalists), Chicanismo was always a much larger realm, one that could never be completely circumnavigated by its theorists. Indeed, the movement was in many ways merely retracing the path of an epic journey across generations, the evidence of which was in the language, music, food, style, and even religion of the millions of pilgrims who'd undertaken that journey. Yes, Chicanismo was and is a political movement. And it was also always a way of being in which a culture not only flowed from history, but made it. So if you're looking for Chicano history today, you can find it in an activist manifesto as much as in an East L.A. homegirl's slang, the chrome-gleam of a Chevy Impala's rims, a rapper's bilingual rhapsody, or even in my Salvadoran-American cousin Mario's sense of place in the world.

Maybe in the end there is something essentially American about being Chicano. Wasn't it our great bard that said "I am large, I contain multitudes"? Walt Whitman: the first Chicano.

Perhaps more than any Chicano writer in his time, Richard Vasquez made a herculean attempt not only to "explain his people" to others, but to reconcile the contradictory signs clashing in the soul of Chicanismo itself. And of course he failed in this regard. When the novel was published, Chicanos were not magically re-cast in the white American imagination, nor were Chicanos suddenly relieved of their identity questions. But it was an important failure, maybe even a magnificent one, in that Richard Vasquez mapped out an essential territory of American cultural, social, economic, and political geography: the relationship between white and brown in the American Southwest, particularly in the city of Los Angeles.

An American of Mexican descent whose grandfather had pioneered the city of Irwindale on the outskirts of L.A., Vasquez was a WWII veteran, boxer, grape picker, construction worker, cabbie, newspaper man: he lived his time and place intensely, inhabiting spaces that took him in and out of varying, and often contrary, points-of-view.

Richard Vasquez the writer was in the right place at the right time. By the late 1960s, after decades of ignominy, Chicanos had finally arrived on the national stage. Robert Kennedy sat with César Chávez in the San Joaquin Valley shortly before his assassination. Chicano students at several East L.A. schools led "blowouts," walking out of classes to protest blatantly inferior educational resources in the barrios. And the music of Carlos Santana (born in Mexico but an honorary Chicano if there ever was one) played constantly on the airwaves.

Chicano the novel had been ten years in the making and it hit the bookstores in 1970, the very year that activist energy converged in what was then called Laguna Park in East L.A. for the Chicano Moratorium against the Vietnam War. It was a hot and smoggy day in late August, the kind that used to leave my young lungs aching on the school playground. The crowd that turned out was estimated at between twenty and forty thousand, grandparents to tots, and especially young people in their late teens and early 20s, the generation that took the very word Chicano—which historically had been used by snobbish Mexicans to put down working-class Mexicans, the kind likely to emigrate to the States and become "Mexican-American"—as its badge of rebellious honor.

At the time it was considered the largest Chicano demonstration ever held (that distinction now goes to the hundred thousand-plus that marched in 1994 to protest California Governor Pete Wilson and the immigrant-bashing legislation he championed). It was to be a day of music and poetry and fiery speeches, a day to say ¡basta! to the war in Vietnam and the disproportionate toll it was taking in the barrios.

That innocence and idealism was transformed into a bloodbath by hundreds of Los Angeles County Sheriff's deputies, who charged the crowd with nightsticks and worse. Vasquez's colleague and friend Rubén Salazar, a journalist who straddled the English- and Spanish-language media with jobs at both the *Los Angeles Times* and at KMEX-TV, was killed when a tear gas canister fired by a deputy tore through the swinging doors of the Silver Dollar Saloon on Whittier Boulevard and struck him in the head.

Salazar had been a pioneer—the first Mexican-American columnist to appear in the pages of the *Times,* and upon his death that mantle fell upon Richard Vasquez, who also covered the Moratorium that fateful day. With the death of his friend Salazar, Vasquez was alone in more ways than one. Although he'd already "pioneered" at several regional papers beforehand, arriving for his gig at the *Times* must have been both a heady and deeply perturbing experience. I can imagine him receiving assignments at the news desk of the *Times.* How about some copy on those illegals, Vasquez?

Vasquez, like Salazar before him, was expected to be the "spokesperson" for "your people." *Your people:* the phrase sums up the very distance and uneven balance of power in the brown-white relationship in media, in politics, in the labor economy. *The lusty señorita. The Latin Lover. The mañana peasant. The Greaser, the Wetback, the Dirty Mexican.* Vasquez winces. Takes the assignment on.

The critique of representations of race, class, and gender as battlegrounds for power has become a cornerstone of postmodern literary criticism. But by and large, we still don't bat an eye when Salma Hayek re-embodies the same colorful, slightly ditzy, and fulminantly sensual characters that Hollywood has typically employed reaching back to the silent era. Nor do we blanche when, on the local news, it is obvious that we see Latinos more often as gangbangers, "illegal aliens," and drug runners than as state senators or even cabinet members.

These representations not only have social and political and economic effects, they are also rooted in social and political and economic relationships. The relationship between Mexico and the U.S., for example. Or between America's vast "service sector" (which jobs are largely held by immigrants from Latin America) and the largely white middle class: the relationship between the urban American commuter couple and the Guatemalan nanny who raises their kids. The stereotypes are deformations, like looking through shimmering heat waves, of what we cannot otherwise utter in public. They serve to cover up, to deflect, to keep the conversation from happening—the conversation about whether this is just the way things are or whether there is another way to imagine one another and, thus, another way to live with one another.

And so for the Chicano or Latino writer in America, the question was, and is: *how do we represent ourselves?* Embrace the Carmen Miranda or Che Guevara templates? Go for gritty social realism? Become flamboyant bilingual poets? Speak to ourselves, speak to the Others? (We've done 'em all.) Can one speak to one's "people" and to the broader audience at the same time?

In 1970, the challenge for Richard Vasquez was particularly daunting. There had been only one— ONE—novel by a Mexican-American released by a major publisher beforehand, Jose Antonio Villarreal's *Pocho*, a poignant effort long before its time that was barely noticed in the literary world (although it wound up surviving through academic course adoptions, that form of affirmative action for the "minority" writer). The manuscript for *Chicano* arrived on the desk of Luther Nichols, editor at Doubleday's West Coast office in San Francisco. A Californian and a liberal, Nichols saw the obvious opportunity the book represented. "It was fresh territory," Nichols, now retired, recalled recently. "Vasquez was opening a door."

Nichols also remembers the honchos in New York scratching their heads at the idea of a novel from a Mexican-American in Los Angeles, but headlines about brown militants on the streets probably convinced them to take the risk. (Although the publishers must have been disappointed when they realized that there were no brown militants in the book.)

Chicano's debut was not the smash Doubleday had hoped for, although sales were respectable, especially and predictably so in Southern California. National publicity bookings, however, were hard to come by. And contemporaneous reviews broke along ethnic lines: white reviewers were generally positive while many Chicano critics were scathing—certainly a bitter pill for Vasquez to swallow. Much of that criticism has to do with the fact that there were and are several currents within Chicanismo, contraries that to this day inspire heated debate.

When the novel was first published, the strategy of cultural

nationalism was reaching its apotheosis in the Chicano movement. A corollary to Black Power, Chicano cultural nationalism celebrated "indigenous" over "Euro-American" roots. At
its best, cultural nationalism returned pride to working-class,
brown-skinned Mexican-Americans about their heritage. (But
it could also be easily critiqued as an inversion of white racism,
and a denial of the complex mestizo—mixed-race—history of
the Americas.) The nationalists—and there was more than one
faction among them—were confronted by Marxist-oriented
activists who played down the importance of race and ethnicity
to focus, of course, on class struggle. Chicana feminists began
to apply their critiques as well (although these would only
come to the fore later; the early *movimiento* was by and large a
classic "gendered" space).

The irony here is that Richard Vasquez, author of *Chicano*,
was not a Chicano by the youth activist standards of his day. He
was older than the radical generation (he was forty-two in
1970), and in cultural and political temperament he mostly belonged to the so-called "Mexican-American" generation that
preceded Chicanismo. The radicals considered their elders to
be tepid reformers, or perhaps even *"vendidos,"* sellouts in the
assimilationist vein. Chicano critics focused on Vasquez' tendency towards didactic passages—whose obvious purpose is to
explain the Chicano experience to a mainstream white audience—as a sign that he was more of an apologist for barrio
pathologies (the notion of the "culture of poverty," promoted
by Daniel Patrick Moynihan and others, was gaining momentum at the time) than a champion of *la causa*. Thirty-five years
later, some of that critique can be written off as the heated rhet-
oric of the political moment. And it is also clear that many
righteous Chicano artists themselves indulged didacticism in an

attempt to explain Chicanismo to Chicanos. We've been explaining ourselves to ourselves and to others for a long time.

Chicanismo raises aesthetic questions that are largely taken for granted in other realms. To this day, young American writers are told by many of their mentors, "if you write *your* story well, it will be universal." But the fact is, if one reads, say, a García Márquez in translation and without even a basic knowledge of Latin American history, one is likely to enjoy a "colorful" and "magical" story without realizing how closely García Márquez is following the contours of Latin American history itself. But we don't want to know about *that*.

And so the Chicano, that internal exile (so far from García Márquez and so close to John Updike), faces a strange frontier indeed. Not quite exotic enough to be Latin American, too particular to be understood as American. It is that very border which Richard Vasquez faced in writing *Chicano*.

Chicano is a multi-generational family saga that begins with the Mexican Revolution, which sent millions of refugees northward to baptize the 20th century's Mexican-American barrios—what we might call the birth of Chicanismo.

Whether reading it for the first time or returning to it after many years, the book adds priceless depth to Chicano literary history and enhances our reading of what has been written since. In the early 70s, a flurry of novels burst through the door that Vasquez helped to open, including Rudolfo Anaya's *Bless me, Ultima*, Tomás Rivera's *Y no se lo tragó la tierra*, and Oscar Zeta Acosta's *The Revolt of the Cockroach People* and *The Autobiography of a Brown Buffalo*. Books which in turn opened the door for Chicanas like Gloria Anzaldúa *(La Frontera)*, Sandra Cisneros *(The House on Mango Street, Woman Hollering Creek)*, Ana Castillo *(So Far from God)*, Alicia Gaspar de Alba *(Sor Juana's Second Dream)*, Denise Chávez *(Loving Pedro Infante)*, Cherríe Moraga *(Loving in the War Years)*, Demetria Martínez *(Mother Tongue)* and others to rewrite the canon from the other side of the border of gender and even sexual orientation in the 80s and 90s.

Because of Vasquez' experience as a journalist and the novel's essentially social-real style, we also have a quasi-documentary work of enormous value. *Chicano* is in the vein of Steinbeck and especially of Henry Roth, whose *Call it Sleep*, the stark novel about Jewish émigrés arriving in early 1900s New York, is perhaps *Chicano*'s most direct American literary forebear.

The book follows the Sandoval family through four generations, beginning with the Mexican Revolution and ending on the streets of East Los Angeles more than half a century later. Héctor Sandoval and his wife Lita begin the journey north from the aptly named Mexican village of Trainwreck, crossing the border and joining the migrant stream from picking field to picking field (" . . . the Thompson Ranch in May, the Gibson place in August, Selma in October . . ."). The family quickly splinters. Héctor succumbs to alcoholism; Lita returns to Mexico with an old beau; daughters Hortensia and Jilda are forced into prostitution and son Neftalí, suddenly alone in America, decides to try his luck in Southern California, where he pioneers what will become the city of Irwindale (as Vasquez' own grandfather—whose name in real life was Neftalí—did).

It is not the only family disintegration in the book. Each generation suffers its own shock, has its own casualties. The "trainwreck" never really stops, although there is a semblance of upward mobility when Neftalí's son Pedro works his way up into a union job as a cement pourer and makes more money than either Héctor or Neftalí could possibly have dreamed of as migrant workers. Here, as on many other occasions where he writes of physical labor, Vasquez' descriptions approach a kind of proletarian modernism:

> In the brightening morning light he could see the huge earth-moving machines abandoned at quitting time the previous day lined up on the dirt right-of-way. A few men were appearing here and there, starting the little auxiliary engines which, when warmed up, would turn over the main engine in each machine. He heard one start, blatting like an outboard motor. In the relative quiet the engine's raucous sound sputtered and coughed, then steadied to a high-pitched whine, then the pitch suddenly slipped as the clutch was thrown to engage the main engine, and in a few moments the boom . . . boom . . . boom, boom of the diesel engine's thunder drowned out the outboard sound.

Although Vasquez often affords his characters dignity on the job, by and large their "work" is decidedly undignified. Day laborers clamor for work on street corners, ready to sell their bodies as readily and as cheaply as Hortensia and Jilda. It is only late in the book (the third generation) that anyone comes remotely close to finding the American grail of middle-class living. But when Pete Sandoval whisks his family off to the suburbs, it ends up a short-lived experiment in integration; the white neighbors band together against the brown menace invading their neighborhood.

The latter half of the book—set loosely in the post-WWII years—concentrates on Pete's children Marianna and Sammy, the fourth generation. Marianna appears primed to be the first child of the clan to "succeed" in the American sense of finding a permanent home outside the barrio, which Sammy, who has the "monkey" of heroin on his back, will never leave. It is in these latter pages where clearly the most is at stake for Vasquez.

Perhaps feeling trapped between the contrary impulses of *movimiento* nationalism and liberal notions of integration, Vasquez tried to engage the ambivalence directly with the romance between Marianna Sandoval and one of the whitest of white boys in Chicano literature, David Stiver. Son of a business scion and a student of sociology at USC, Stiver is all liberal awkwardness, in contrast to Marianna's class, grace, and street smarts. She knows more about his world than he'll ever know about hers, though that doesn't stop him from trying to "save" the brown-eyed children of the barrio when he witnesses a classic Chicano encounter with the LAPD. The relationship between Marianna and David, driven to melodramatic climax, is not one of the stronger points of the book—but it does betray the hard truth that Vasquez lived in his day. Despite his mixed-race marriage and living in an "integrated" neighborhood in real life, despite his work for mainstream publications, brown and white did not come together for a fairytale ending at the end of the 60s. And, of course, the war in Vietnam ground for another few bloody years, claiming many more Chicano lives.

As a writer, Richard Vasquez seems to me to embody what is best about the feature journalist—the one who trusts that an accumulation of detail will create a living, breathing representation to be reckoned with. One that will make us pause and ask questions, reconsider old positions, imagine a new relationship

across the borders of representation itself. The details bring
characters to life. We begin to love them or hate them, understand them, and perhaps most importantly, trust the writer
who's giving us those details.

In re-reading *Chicano*, I came to trust the writer who de-
scribes construction work as only someone who's been a construction worker can write it. I trusted the Richard Vasquez
whose own grandfather was among the founders of Irwindale,
that bizarre, typically Southern Californian meeting-ground
between natural beauty and the industrially-refined landscape.
I knew I could trust Vasquez writing about the LAPD and its
infamous methods in the barrio because he was a crime-beat re-
porter for several years. And I knew I could trust him writing of
the encounter between white and brown because that's what he
himself lived in the most intimate way possible: his second marriage was to Lucy Wilbur, a concert pianist with whom he
raised his daughter Sylvia (a "mestiza" several times over, that
is, a Chicana), whose efforts made it possible for this book to be
reprinted. (In a scene that played like an L.A. version of *Guess
Who's Coming to Dinner*, Richard's initial courtship of Lucy
was rebuffed not by her but by her parents, who refused to let
their daughter marry a Mexican.)

We cannot read *Chicano* today without realizing that for all
his efforts, Vasquez could not completely rise above stereotype.
But then, encountering *Chicano* today is necessarily a multi-
layered experience. We are reading a novel penned more than
thirty years ago and cannot avoid doing so without a revisionist
eye. The book's white characters are often cartoonish, serving
as villainous foils that in turn weaken the Chicano portraits.
And although Vasquez was obviously concerned with explor-
ing the divide of gender, how he makes his brown heroine pay

back all the accumulated historical debt of the brown-white narrative cannot help but jar the reader.

This does not diminish *Chicano*'s importance, however. *Chicano* is a brave and pioneering attempt to create dialogue across a terrible divide, the kind that has opened up on so many occasions throughout our history when "foreigner" meets "native." It is happening again today. Nearly one hundred years after the Mexican Revolution created the first Mexican-American generation, millions more migrants have arrived, relocating Ellis Island to the U.S.-Mexico border.

Like the first and second generations in *Chicano*, there are countless migrant families today that follow the picking seasons across the country. There are new Mexican barrios in places like Georgia, Arkansas, Wisconsin, Iowa. There are workplaces today that are not very different from the ones described in the early pages of Vasquez' novel, or, for that matter, in Upton Sinclair's *The Jungle*. And there are young people today—much like Marianna and Sammy—facing the challenges, and the glories, of growing up in that Chicano world of contrary signs.

In the age of the global, those signs are becoming the world's. There will be many more Chicanos—and not all of them will be Mexicans. They will also be from Asia and Africa and the Middle East and Eastern Europe. They will exist wherever journeys of necessity bring together, and draw apart, distinct peoples to summon new identities. This is a novel about such journeys—Chicano, American, human.

For the last decade, Americans have debated immigration with increasing intensity, resurrecting impulses of both nativism and tolerance embedded deep in our history. As I write this, a group calling itself the "Minutemen" has staked out a portion of the U.S.-Mexico border in Arizona in a bid to prevent "illegals" from crossing over. They have been met on the line by a like number of activists that seek to humanize our immigration policy—and especially the representation of the people most affected by it.

As always in our history, there is also a third narrative. Already, we have begun to hear the voices of the newest immigrants and especially those of their children—in the workplace, in schools, in our neighborhoods—as we decide, once again, who we are as a people. And there will again be a need for—and there will be—more books like *Chicano*.

April 2005
Velarde, New Mexico

A Note from Sylvia Vasquez

My father, Richard Vasquez, was about thirty years old when he decided to become a writer. At that time, during the late 1950s, he worked construction and drove a taxicab. By chance, he once saved the career of a drunken newspaper editor by whisking him home in his cab and in return asked for a chance to try his hand at journalism. Thus began his first weekly column, *The Cabby*, which consisted of humorous stories depicting his experiences as a cab driver and life in general.

My mother, a concert pianist and extraordinary musician, taught day and night, probably so my father could write. As the youngest child in our family I spent much of my time at home with him. His modus operandi was to think for a few hours, then pound the keyboard for a few more. It took him ten years to write *Chicano* on an old typewriter; he used carbon copies, making it necessary to plan each sentence carefully.

My father drew much of *Chicano* from his own family history. My great-great-grandfather Gregorio Fraijo came to the

United States from Sonora, Mexico, sometime during the 1850s (possibly earlier), eventually settling in what is now Irwindale, California. Today there is a plaque in honor of him at Irwindale City Hall.

My grandfather Neftali Vasquez (who inspired *Chicano's* Old Tony) was the resident engineer on many bridges built in and around Los Angeles during the middle decades of the twentieth century. Although he was by far one of the most experienced engineers around, he was told he would never get a promotion because of his name, Vasquez. He replied he could do anything they asked—except change his name.

Although briefly, my father did spend time picking crops. He and five siblings served in the military, some during World War II. He drew from these and other memories to write the story of the Sandovals.

Chicano's publication in 1970 coincided with the offer of a new job at the *Los Angeles Times*. My father replaced columnist Rubén Salazar, who was covering the Chicano anti-Vietnam War Moratorium in East Los Angeles when he was killed by a tear gas projectile fired by a sheriff's deputy. I can remember going to the grocery store with my dad, watching him explain to other shoppers why they shouldn't buy grapes. As a child who did not yet fully understand my father and all he stood for, I was a little embarrassed by his strong opinions, but a big part of me was left in awe of his courage and convictions.

In writing *Chicano,* he delved into aspects of human nature with an honesty that he carried with him always. He knew his opinions were controversial, but he had to put them out there anyway, maintaining that controversy sparked intelligent thinking.

My father said the job of a novelist is not to resolve problems, but to present them; he couldn't solve the problems *Chicano* portrays, but felt a responsibility to articulate them. It is my hope that new readers or those returning to the book in its beautiful new edition will ask this relevant question: have things changed over the last thirty-five years since *Chicano* was first published? More to the point, have things changed enough?

My father passed away and left me his works—a bittersweet and unique treasure. While I still miss him and yearn to laugh with him and feel the gusto with which he embraced life, I am blessed to have been bequeathed his legacy. Since embarking on this journey to reissue *Chicano,* I have been heartened and humbled by the enthusiasm and support I've received from those who knew or knew of my father. I would like to thank my uncle, James Vasquez, for his unfailing love and support, and Luis J. Rodriguez for his inspiring encouragement. Also my heartfelt thanks go to my agent, Stuart Bernstein, and to René Alegria at Rayo/HarperCollins, both for recognizing the value in republishing *Chicano.* Finally, I would like to thank Rubén Martínez for his expertise in writing an introduction that gives insight into what *Chicano*—the book and the term—represents. Now that *Chicano* will once again be available to the public, I am even more proud to be my father's daughter.

Sylvia Vasquez
June 2005

Shortly before the turn of the century a railroad was built across the deserts of northern Old Mexico, against the advice of those who were familiar with the characteristics and inhabitants of the continent's arid western region.

PART ONE

The locomotive roared out of the narrow stone canyon and for a few moments quickly gathered speed as the tracks dropped sharply to meet the level terrain of the valley of desert stretching ahead. The men in the cab strained their eyes and briefly, just before the tracks leveled to the valley floor, they caught a glimpse of the engine and two flatcars carrying the protective troop detachment far ahead. Then, in the valley, the shimmering heatwaves cut vision to a few miles, although the tracks stretched out in an arrow-straight path for many miles.

The men glanced at one another, nodding faintly, a little of their anxiety abated at the reassuring sight of the train with soldiers ahead.

The noise of the locomotive steadied to a monotonous pounding as they settled down for the long stretch of unbroken ground before they would climb into the next low range of stone mountains.

The wheels of the fifty boxcars and cattle cars, all full of cattle, were among the first to christen this one-hundred-mile stretch of track through nothing but desert and mountains.

This was northern Mexico, where the sun rose with hideous vengefulness each day, allowing only the martyred cactus and low brush to survive on the sandy plains. One of the men pulled his head from the window into the cab, wiped away the tears caused by the torrid wind and shouted above the roar of the firebox, steam, wheels, and rushing air, "They should stay closer to us."

His companion wiped his grimy face with the sweat-soaked kerchief around his neck. "No, amigo," he hollered back, "they must have time to warn us if they run into a blockade . . . or something." It was the "or something" that made the two men's eyes hold an instant.

A third man, through shoveling coal for the moment, joined them. He was fat, wore greasy overalls, as did his companions, had an enormous mustache and his hair almost covered his ears. All wore shirts with sleeves torn off at the shoulder.

"It was a mistake, making this railway here. If the Yaquis don't get us, the bandidos will. No law, no city for two hundred kilometros, no nothing. I think I quit and go to the Estados Unidos," he said.

"Don't kid me," said an engineer, "they don't let Mexicans drive locomotives in the United States. And besides, they have bandidos there, too."

"Not like here. Here we have fifty little generals each with his own little army, claiming to want to free Mexico, when really they just kill and steal and rob," the fireman said.

With squinted eyes, watering from the sweat and hot wind, the men passed a cloth water bag and each drank deeply, splashing some on the face and hair. Then the vigil at the windows was resumed, and the fat fireman went back to shoveling coal, and the train sprinted on into the heat waves.

More than an hour later they were stirred from their near lethargy by the slight slowing of the rhythm of the engine and tracks, and they knew the sloping climb out of the valley had begun. The engineer pushed the throttle forward a little, and the engine steadied for a while, then again started to slow its rhythm. Again the throttle was pushed forward, and soon the fireman was shoveling rapidly and the train was moving slowly, smoke trailing, as it lumbered up the incline into the mountains. They wound through a wide, low canyon, climbing, then abruptly picked up speed as they neared the summit. Over the top, the engineer put reverse steam to the driving wheels to check the train's speed, and the descent was almost as slow as the climb. For a moment coming around a curve the floor of the vast valley ahead was visible, and the tiny train carrying the troops could again be seen.

The train had almost reached the next valley floor when the engineer, looking out the window, shouted and applied the brakes. The others looked. There ahead, dust still rising, was a rockslide piled high on the tracks, small stones continuing to fall from the cliff alongside the tracks. Shouting, the men threw open the door on the cliff side and jumped, rolling over and over in the dirt by the ties, and the next moment the engine was tearing into the slide, leaving the tracks, and pulling the fifty cars behind as, miraculously, it remained upright and churned into the shallow ravine away from the cliff. The steel wheels and undercarriage bit deep into the earth as the fifty cars, like a giant hand, pushed it relentlessly along, until the wheels of all the cars, too, sank deep into softer footing, and the entire train came to a jolting stop against the far bank of the ravine.

Only the sound of the desperately bellowing cattle, some injured and dying, all frightened, could be heard. Smoke poured from the locomotive, which was tilted at a crazy angle against an earthen bank, as though it were injured also. Two of the trainmen were on their feet, looking up in fear at the crags and bluffs overhead. The third, the fat man, lay on the ground cradling his foot, moaning.

The others approached him. "Hurry! Get up. We better get out of here."

The injured man groaned. "My foot. It's broken. Don't leave me. Stay here."

"We can't stay here. Whoever caused the rockslide will be coming now. We have to start after the troop train."

"They're gone," the injured man said, gesturing. "They won't be back."

"Yes, they will. As soon as they realize we're not behind them, they'll come back to help us."

The man on the ground gave a laugh of pained irony. "As soon as they realize the bandidos wrecked this train they will go to the garrison where it is safe."

The third man spoke. "Maybe it wasn't the bandidos. Maybe the indios."

The man with the broken foot thought a moment. His voice was surprisingly calm. "You two better go. Maybe the train will wait for you. If so, maybe you can talk them into coming back for me. I can't walk. I'll have to take my chances with whoever is up there." He indicated the reaching cliffs and mountains. All three looked about, but there was no sign of life.

One of the men who was unhurt looked at the other. "We would be foolish to go on. At least here in the canyon we might find food and water."

"We might also find Indians."

"But we could only live several hours crossing that desert. The troops might have kept going."

Finally it was decided the two would walk after the train carrying the troops and see if the latter would return for the fireman.

And Hector Sandoval gently rubbed his swelling ankle as he watched his companions, each carrying a waterbag and a shovel for protection, climb the mound of rocks and start toward the shimmering valley below.

Hector Sandoval realized he was lying in the blazing sun. The cattle, still trapped in the wrecked cars, were beginning to quiet down. He crawled on his hands and knees to the ravine. He made his way down the slope to a clump of hardwood brush. Carefully, crawling along, he selected the right bough and took a pocket knife from his pocket and began cutting it. Soon he had it free. He trimmed the small branches from it, leaving the top in a large fork. He fitted the fork under his arm, whittled a little more on it, and soon had an operable crutch. He found that his injured foot could support none of his weight.

He made his way painstakingly to the locomotive. With a great deal of trouble he climbed in. The fire still burned, the steam still hissed and the cattle still bawled. But the sound diminished as he waited. The long afternoon progressed slowly, the pain of his leg increased as the hours dragged by.

Presently he saw a man coming up the ravine on horseback. At first he was fearful it might be one of those responsible for the train wreck, but then he recognized the working attire of the vaquero, the chaps and pointed boots, the ancient, heavy single-shot pistol at the hip. The rider was approaching slowly, disbelief on his face as he examined the wreck.

Hector Sandoval hailed him. "Ho, amigo! Here in the cab." The rider directed his horse to the engine.

"Madre de dios," he exclaimed. "What has happened here?"

"We had a wreck. I'm hurt. My foot I think is broken. Can you help me get away from here?"

"To what? I work on a rancho ten kilometros from here. How did this happen?"

"Bandidos. Or Indians, I don't know. There are two others. They left, walking, to seek help. Do you think bandits did this? Or Indians?"

The man shrugged. "Quién sabe? Such a shame. But it was a bad idea to put a railroad through here. It is too wild. Now I guess the railway will be abandoned."

Sandoval made his way to the ground with the help of the cowboy, who introduced himself as Lalo. He made himself comfortable and then examined his injured foot.

"It's badly broken. I can't walk, or ride a horse. Is there a town nearby?"

"Yes. By the rancho where I work. I'll go send them. But what about the cattle here?"

Sandoval shrugged. "Many are injured. They should be turned loose, I guess."

"No," the other replied, "the village near here is called Agua Clara. They should have the injured cattle. And mi patrón, Señor Domínguez, he will want to keep the uninjured cattle until their rightful owner can claim them."

Sandoval gave an amused laugh. "Ha! It's my guess nobody will ever show up to claim anything. Tell you what. If you get the villagers to come and get me, tell them I will give them the injured cows. And the train, too, if they want that. The company will not risk sending another train to collect them."

CHICANO

Soon Lalo rose to leave. "I will carry word of the train wreck to the village. And to my patrón. Try to rest comfortably. I'm sure the villagers will care for you when they get here in the morning."

In the morning they came. Don Francisco Domínguez leading his vaqueros, and behind them the subservient villagers. The ranchero directed his men to free the cattle, shouted instructions as to how to get them out of the tilting cattle and boxcars. His delight was apparent as he counted the dozens of uninjured cattle herded together. Before noon he had what he wanted. "I will keep them safe until an owner claims them," he said in a loud voice, and he drove them to his ranch.

The men, women, and children of Agua Clara swarmed over the tilted train. Knives were unsheathed, throats of the cattle were cut, and blood was caught in earthen jugs. Fires were lighted, spits were improvised, pieces of carcasses were handed to the women. Hector Sandoval watched as an entire village ate all it wanted for the first time. Some women roasted meat, some fried, some ground it, some set to work drying meat for carne seca (beef jerky); some had brought pans and rendered fat. A festive air of a once-in-a-lifetime occasion prevailed, and the men sang and laughed as they stripped and scraped hides, sawed horns and hacked off hoofs.

"Come, taste this, taste this!" one man would shout as he cut a steaming morsel from a roasting haunch that dripped red. With perhaps a half hundred cattle left to them, they knew there was more than several times their number could eat. Almost frantically some went about preparing meat for curing.

And in the midst of the labor and gorging, a chill settled through all as they observed a large group of Indians watching, half the men mounted, women behind with babes in arms.

The villagers beckoned, addressing the newcomers in Spanish. "Come. There is plenty for all." And the Indians joined. Some wore leather leggings and no shirts, some wore the tattered remains of fine vests, many wore what had once been fine dress hats and coats; all had their hair in long braids past the shoulders, and the men were conspicuous by their lack of facial hair. The group of villagers with whom Hector Sandoval was eating was approached by one of the Indians.

"Our jefe would like to speak with the alcalde of the villagers," he said ceremoniously.

One whom Sandoval had learned was the village spokesman, Estorga, arose, stifling a pained expression at the formality of the Indian chief in sending a messenger some twenty feet to summon him. Estorga approached and shook hands with the Indian leader.

"Good afternoon, jefe," he said.

"Good afternoon, jefe," the Indian returned. "I would like it known that my people are not to blame for the train wreck," he said in perfect Spanish. "Should the federales come to punish those responsible, I know you will tell them we did not do it."

Estorga nodded politely. "Should the authorities come to the village to ask, I will say there was nobody here when we arrived, that you and your people came after we did."

"You may say we encountered the bandidos who did this as they climbed down the back of the mountain to circle around and claim these spoils. When they told me what they had done, I was angered, as were my people. Not only may we get the blame, but we wanted the railroad here, that we might develop trade with los mejicanos as other groups of poor Indians have. When the bandidos saw our anger, they left."

Estorga's face brightened. "They left? Or perhaps you killed them."

The Indian smiled broadly. "No, they saw my angry young men looking with desire at their fine horses and saddles and guns, and they left."

Estorga spread the word that the Indians had driven off a group of bandits who had derailed the train, and the feasting continued throughout the day.

Later in the afternoon the villagers prepared to go home. Burros were loaded with meat, hides, and other loot. A sled was made for the injured train man. The next morning Hector Sandoval awoke in the village of Agua Clara.

Estorga had offered his shack to Hector Sandoval, and the train man had said he planned to leave for the city as soon as his foot was well. He saw that Estorga had a crude hammer and attempted to do a little iron work, but was hampered by lack of tools.

"At the train," he told his host, "there is a fine hammer, tongs also, and bellows. You will find them in the tool box in the cab. Here, I have the key." And a few days later Sandoval suggested that the villagers take a door from a boxcar and with the burros drag it back to the village to make a roof. Within a week or so he was able to ride to the wrecked train himself, where he showed the villagers how to disassemble parts which might be useful in the village.

He noticed a girl. She was slim, dark, and typically sad-eyed. He had made no mention of his wife and children in the big city, who no doubt now thought him dead, and daily he thought about how hectic life had been in the city, how fat and demanding his wife had become, how she gave every extra little bit of money to the priest, to help heal a sick child, to bring good luck to a widowed sister looking for a husband, or to buy forgiveness for sins committed by a member of the family. Taxes, double because he couldn't pay all of last year's, rats killing the family cat in a fight over scraps of food, the cramped heat and stifling smell of the city slums. Yes . . . even though he'd been in Agua Clara only a few days, he noticed the sad-eyed girl looking at him as she passed to get water at the little stream that went by the village.

"Good morning, how is your foot today?" she asked as she went by one day, and his decision was made.

"I have decided to stay here in your village," he told a spontaneous meeting of village men one evening when his foot was almost well.

"Good."

"You will not regret it."

"We welcome you as one of us."

"And to earn my living I will catch and train wild burros. I did much of that when I was a boy near Texas. But it takes two to make a burro-catching team, as you know. Yet, I don't think the enterprise will support two men."

Straight-faced, the others agreed. What solution?

"If you could take a wife, then you could follow your chosen profession," a villager offered.

"Yes," Sandoval replied, "but there seems to be small chance of that. Unless, that girl, what's her name? Lita, I think—if she could be persuaded to be my bride . . ."

"Yes, my daughter, Lita," one villager put in. "She is getting old. Almost seventeen. She had been seeing that worthless boy Eduardo, but I stopped that. Were you and she married, she could go off with you to help."

"The priest will be here next week. He comes every month from the city. He will marry you."

Sandoval set about building a house. From the cab of the train he took the sheet metal roof, and had the finest roof in the village, with little rain gutters on each side—although it rarely rained. Boxcar doors served as walls, and from the caboose he took the little pot-bellied stove, and had the only factory-made stove in the village. Right after the marriage ceremony they left, on two borrowed donkeys, with a third loaded down with supplies and equipment.

Hector Sandoval had questioned the natives and learned the lay of the land well. By nightfall of the first day he was making his honeymoon shack beside a waterhole. The shack was mesquite boughs propped up, with a piece of canvas stretched over. And that night in the middle of a wild valley beneath a moon whose brightness hurt the eyes Lita became his wife.

The next morning he set out on a burro, leaving Lita by the waterhole. He rode fast for hours until he came to another waterhole. He built a crude fence around it and stuck poles into the ground and tied cloths to the poles, so that the fabric flapped in the breeze. Then he returned to his bride.

He explained his actions. "That one is ready. Unless the wild cows tear up my work. Sometimes they do that."

The next morning he again rode off, this time in the opposite direction, until he found the watering place he was looking for. Again he built a crude fence and erected waving banners. Again he returned to Lita.

"Now," he said, "we wait." And he moved his honeymoon cottage downwind to a small ravine where they would be out of sight.

"Too soon," he told her the next day, and he would only let

her show her head above the ravine bank. "We must hide carefully. They can see a man many miles away."

She patiently waited with him in the ravine, shaking her head in wonder as he told her he now had all waterholes within burro range blocked off, and soon the animals would have to come here.

On the fifth day he saddled his burro, taking great pains to be quiet and remain out of sight. Then they sat, the two lovers, waiting, looking out over the shimmering plains.

"See?" he said quietly, looking toward the horizon. She strained her eyes and finally saw movement.

"The burros?"

"No. The wild cows, with the great horns. They too have been kept from water. They will be the first to come, as they have less fear. Then, if we are lucky, the donkeys will come to drink. Then after that maybe horses."

"Will you catch the cows or horses?"

"No. These cows are too dangerous. They will kill any man they see. To catch them requires lots of good riders, expert horsemen with lariats, and fine horses. The same with the wild horses. But I can catch the burros, I think." He crossed himself.

It took the wild longhorns two hours to make their cumbersome way to the waterhole. There were not more than a dozen, and one middle-aged bull stopped and stared suspiciously at the water as they approached. The cows leading calves brushed past him with unconcern. The animals watered at leisure and several times the bull stared in the direction of Lita and Hector. It was the first time she had ever seen these huge wild cattle up close and she was frightened by their massiveness and the size of their horns. They were crouched near the top of the little gully, heads just above the rim, peering from beneath shrubs. The bull was drinking, then suddenly he raised his head and seemingly looked right at them. Then he walked toward them, his huge blank eyes unblinking. The animal stopped within two dozen feet of the pair and stared, ears bent forward like large hearing horns. Lita and Hector held their breaths. One of their burros tethered behind them suddenly stamped its foot and brayed. Immediately the bull, satisfied it had identified the object of its suspicion, wheeled and joined the other longhorns.

"Gracias, señor burro," Hector breathed lightly.

The next day the wild burros came. Lita and Hector watched silently as they finally got up enough courage to overcome their natural suspicion and approached the waterhole. The burros drank and drank and drank, as though they might not see water for another five or six days. There were a stallion and two fine mares, each with a colt. Hector waited with his saddled and gagged burros until the wild ones were actually staggering under the weight of the water taken on. Then he mounted and spurred his donkey up over the shoulder of the gully at full speed.

The wild burros fled, but were slowed by weakness from days without water and by stomachs now sloshing like water-filled balloons. Hector's mount, bigger and stronger than the wild ones, quickly overtook one mare. His rope sang out and jerked her from her feet. The colt snorted in terror as its mother was quickly and securely tied. Then Hector went after the other mare. Even though she had a head start, he caught her within a few miles. He didn't bother with the stallion.

A few days later, when the wild mares were rope-broken, Lita and Hector rode into Agua Clara with what he announced was the embryo of his new enterprise.

Young Neftali Sandoval awoke and silently rose from the rag-stuffed mattress which served as his bed at one side of the small room. His mother and father still snored over at the other end of the room which served as a kitchen for the family. Against the opposite wall his two older sisters huddled, arms entwined, like lovers, for warmth, although there was only the smallest chill in the air. Neftali quietly crossed the room and pushed back the rough, woven blanket that was the door to the home and stepped out into the growing dawn.

The family dog raised his head on hearing Neftali emerge and wagged his tail. The mongrel stretched, yawned hugely, and got up to follow. Neftali picked up a wooden bucket with a leather thong for a handle and started for the stream. Any moment his mother would be getting up, starting breakfast by patting the cornmeal dough into round, flat tortillas, heating the boiled beans, and water would be needed to make hot chocolate, sweetened with sugar syrup squeezed from sugar cane grown nearby.

Neftali wound his way through the little village. The worn footpath took many unnecessary turns, leading by each shack, but he stayed on it, as there were fewer sharp rocks and brush stubble to hurt his bare feet. He wore white cotton trousers and a loose white cotton shirt, nothing more. In the heat of the day he would wear a wide sombrero "because the sun makes you black like an Indian."

The boy's route took him past the Rojas shack, where six girls and two sons slept in a single room made of loose stones and boards. Soon the girls would arise to begin the day's sewing. They made hand-stitched infants' and children's gar-

ments, which their father periodically took on his back to la ciu-
dad, whence he returned after a several-days drunk, with not
much more than a bolt of cloth for his daughters to begin
sewing once more. The two sons labored for Estorga, the
smith, or took turns watching the family's flock of chickens and
driving them to fresh scratching ground daily, retrieving an egg
or two a day, waiting for the young roosters to mature enough
to be eaten or sold.

The next shack was that of Estorga, who had years before
looted the wrecked train of items different from those taken by
other members of the village. He still had the tools, the large
hammer, and the bellows used to start the fires in the engine. He
had taken all the metal he could pry loose or unbolt, using burros to haul load after load of metal from the wreck. As a boy Estorga had briefly been apprenticed to a blacksmith, and he
recognized the value of the metal and tools. He had begun his
smith shop, making hinges and iron stakes, which the ranchero
Domínguez across the valley liked to buy. He could fashion
iron hoops to hold barrel staves in place, and together with another villager who carved wood, they sold buckets and barrels.
Yes, the train wreck had done the most good for Estorga, Neftali thought. He himself carried a knife with a razor edge which
Estorga had hammered from a piece of metal from the train.
Neftali had watched as Estorga heated the metal to a glowing
red color and then, holding it with a pair of tongs the train had
yielded, hammered it into shape, after which he made the fire
intensely hot with the bellows, heated the knife until it was
nearly white, and then just at the right instant, as the knife
cooled, Estorga plunged it into cold water. That made the cutting edge hard, the smith had explained to the boy, so that it
would not become dull easily.

Nearly all of the shacks had a dog, and as the boy wound through the helter-skelter pattern of the village homes, many mongrels came out to sniff his dog, and the animals occasionally growled at one another. Neftali passed through the village and less than fifty yards to the east he came to the stream. The inhabitants of the village had scooped out a little reservoir, which caused the water to deposit its silt and foreign matter on the bottom before resuming the journey to the valley below. Neftali went to the little pool and filled the bucket. The brook made only the tiniest of sounds, and all else was quiet. The jagged song of a meadowlark suddenly filled the air. The boy saw the sun beginning to redden the eastern sky and realized he could already feel the precious chill in the air dissipate.

He let his eyes wander up the mountainside, over the harsh rocks and shrubs which rose higher and higher. On the other side were los indios, who would come occasionally to trade or buy, their women walking silently behind the mounted men. When would they come again? High overhead large birds circled deliberately. Hawks or vultures? He could not tell from here.

He saw Doña Pura the Hag emerge from her lean-to where she lived alone, a widow for many years. She wore a burlap garment that covered her to her knees. Neftali was always uneasy in the presence of the old widow. She seldom spoke to anyone. Whenever an animal was killed, rabbit, goat or fowl, she would appear at the fortunate family's door to beg the entrails. She had no income, lived on animal entrails and beans, occasionally sewed or washed in exchange for cornmeal.

Now she came toward Neftali, bucket in hand to carry water, her steps very slow but deliberate. Neftali stood uncertainly as she approached, her eyes fastened on something out in the valley.

"I saw it hours ago," she said as she dipped her bucket.

Neftali's eyes followed hers, and he gasped as he saw a great pillar of smoke ascending from leaping flames at the Domínguez ranch house. The ranch was several miles across the valley and he could see no activity other than the flames. He stood transfixed in disbelief at the sight.

"Soon they will be arriving here," the hag continued. Neftali broke into a run as he sprinted toward his home, water forgotten, the dog yapping excitedly at his heels.

His father and mother were just rising as he burst in, out of breath. "Mama! Papa! The rancho is burning. Quick, come see."

Hector Sandoval slept in his clothes, as did his wife, and no dressing was necessary. He looked shocked as he lurched out the door and looked across the valley. Then he wheeled, looking grave, and shouted, "Ortiz! Estorga! Manuel. And you others. Hurry, come see this."

Within minutes all two hundred members of the village were gathered, watching the distant flames and smoke. A few made fearful comments. All mentioned the name Guzmán.

The old hag, who had been watching silently, raised a hand and pointed. "See. On the road from the ranch. They are coming here."

Silently, the villagers watched a little dust cloud near the burning ranch house as it moved toward them down the dirt road that bisected the vast pastures of the rancho. They watched as the dust cloud moved, seemingly inches at a time. Breakfast and children were forgotten, and soon the dust cloud took the shape of many mounted men leading spare horses and a few cattle. The group followed the dirt road out of the valley to the foothills, and began climbing the winding road to the village.

"Who will do the talking?" Estorga the smith asked, the worry in his voice as well as on his face.

"They will," the old hag said with a cackle.

Ortiz the woodcarver was nervous. "Our young men and women . . . They should run."

Señor Sandoval smiled grimly. "Why? So that they can be dragged from the hills at the end of a rope? It is best we stay here and talk."

It took nearly an hour for the mounted men to wind their way up the mountainside to the village. The last five minutes seemed the longest as they strung out around a sharp curve. Their voices could be heard as some of the riders doubled back to urge on the pack animals straggling behind. Then they rode, thirty of them, Neftali counted, into the village.

A man who was apparently the leader rode up to the villagers, who were grouped at the edge of the town. Wide-eyed, Neftali marveled at his appearance; two huge pistolas, one on each hip, two rifles in scabbards near the horn of his saddle; a wide straw sombrero added heft to his short, stocky body, but did not hide his hair, which came just below his ears and met his great mustache and full beard. Two cartridge belts crossed his chest, meeting a wide belt about his waist that was also full of fresh cartridges. A large hunting knife hung near one pistol behind one hip. His shirt was of some smooth, lustrous fabric, although dirty and smoke-stained. He wore loose cotton trousers, faded, but his boots shone like new, and Neftali recognized the handiwork of the cobbler whom the rancher Domínguez employed to make his family's footwear.

The rest of the riders reined up. All were heavily armed and unkempt, looking tired but wary. The leader dismounted and walked to the villagers. He gestured dramatically at the burning rancho.

"It is yours, what is left. We took what we need."

Neftali's father stepped up and cleared his throat before speaking. "And Domínguez? And his family? And the vaqueros?"

The man made a gesture to emphasize the insignificance of those at the rancho. "I am Guzmán. They had their choice—to stay and be killed or flee. Those who lived are by now halfway to the next state." He looked around, fierce but friendly. "Who here is a smith? Our horses need attention." Estorga came forward. Guzmán indicated the horses. "Some of these mounts need shoes. We have a long way to travel over rough roads. We must be on our way quickly." He glanced nervously across the valley where the road that ran from the village past the ranchhouse disappeared into the distant mountain range. Then he barked at his followers, "Pelón! Chico! Macho! Take the barefoot horses and follow this man. All of you will behave while here. These people will have enough trouble when the federales get here tomorrow or the next day."

The rest of the riders dismounted, offering to pay for fresh tortillas and beans. The three men Guzmán had addressed led the horses to Estorga's shack, where the smith began heating and fitting horseshoes. One pack animal was brought forward and Guzmán took several bottles of liquor from the pack and opened them, offering the contents to the villagers.

"Ha!" he laughed. "I'll bet in all the years you've been here you've never had Domínguez liquor offered you."

Neftali's father accepted the bottle. "You're right, Señor Guzmán. In fact, since coming here I have never tasted strong liquor. Muchas gracias." And he drank deeply. The other men of the village came closer, talking to Guzmán and his henchmen, yet never daring to ask for more information than Guzmán offered.

The sun was rising swiftly and the heat began soaking into the mountainside as the outlaws and the villagers mingled in friendly talk in the center of the village. One of the riders took a fine guitar from a pack mule and began strumming. Before long two village men were singing, each taking a separate harmonic part without so much as discussing the songs or verses. All found seats either next to a shack or on one of the boulders strewn about, while Estorga labored mightily, shoeing the horses and mending the stirrup chains.

Those in the village center were divided into two groups; some singing with the guitarists and those gathered around Guzmán as he talked.

"The Domínguez rancho was number sixteen for us," he said laughingly, draining the remnants of one bottle and pulling another from a pack mule. He passed it to those nearest him. "But it was the first one in this state. The federales are still looking for us two hundred miles from here, where we last struck. Now with these fine horses they will never catch us."

Estorga, sweating profusely, had finished and called to Guzmán. "Señor. The horses are ready. And fine horses they are. Domínguez knew how to breed animals."

Guzmán rose heavily. "Yes," he said with an air of significance, "he took good care of animals. But not such good care of his neighbors, I think. Ha! Anyway, he now has no use for horses. He has a better method of transportation. He now has wings." All the outlaws laughed heartily and started rising to take to their mounts. Guzmán faced the villagers. "And now," he said, his voice taking an edge, "who will go with us?"

The people of the village stood still, pleading looks on many faces. Guzmán and his men looked around. For a moment nothing moved. Then a hide was pushed back from the doorway of a shack and a young girl, perhaps fifteen, pretty, flashing eyes, dressed in rags, stepped out with what was obviously her personal belongings wrapped in a shawl. All eyes traveled to her as she haltingly made her way until she stood before the bandit leader. The girl's mother rushed to her.

"No! No!" the woman screamed, embracing her daughter. "Not my baby. No. Hija, you don't know what you're doing." Guzmán gently but firmly pushed the older woman back. Her husband joined her and tried to lead her away.

"She wants to come with us. Mexico is free. Almost, anyway," Guzmán said. He strode to a nearby pack mule and untied a pack. In a moment he pulled out expensive women's garments. He sorted through them briefly and then found a lady's riding habit, which he threw to the girl. "Here," he said. "You will never regret coming with us. There is much more, waiting to be wrenched from the rich who have kept you dressed worse than an Indian."

The girl went wide-eyed as she examined the clothes. Then she hurried to the shack to change. Guzmán walked to a spare horse, already saddled in fine silver-inlaid leather. He untied the lead rope and put the bridle on the animal, and led it back to the center of the group just as the girl emerged, her face somehow changed and beaming as she looked at herself in the finery she wore.

"Here," Guzmán said, offering her the reins. "This horse will be yours as long as you ride with us." He looked around at the people again. "We need fighters," he said flatly. His eyes traveled around until they rested on Neftali. Señora Sandoval rushed to her son's side. "No!" she hissed, and then her words tumbled out, "My two brothers were conscripted by revolutionaries. My father died by a bullet when the Mexican Army forced him to fight. It will not happen to my son. Never!" She put her arms protectively around Neftali. Her vehemence took Guzmán temporarily aback.

The outlaw leader went to his horse nearby and from the saddlebag he pulled a shiny leather holster with a silver-plated pistol in it. Neftali saw the large letter D inlaid on the leather. Guzmán tossed the holster and pistol to the boy, who caught it in involuntary reflex. He had never before held a pistol. "Let him decide for himself," Guzmán said with authority. Neftali examined the holster and pistol, looked at the agonized faces of his parents, and threw the merchandise back to Guzmán.

Guzmán shrugged, turning away. "Oh well, if he won't fight with me, within a few days he will probably be fighting against me, when the federales take him."

A slim dark youth, a little older than Neftali, stepped forward and silently reached for the holster and pistol, the while his eyes traveling in meek defiance to his parents, who stood nearby. The mother of the youth gave a choked sob and turned away, followed by her husband.

"Ah! One volunteer," Guzmán said with gusto. "Very well. Take a horse, joven. Get your miserable private belongings together and let's be off, before it is too late."

A quarter of an hour later as the band rode out of the village the men, women and children of Trainwreck, as their town was now called, stood watching. The parents of the youth and of the girl who had left turned and went into their shacks, griefstricken. The others began hurried preparations to loot the burned rancho. Señor Sandoval hurried to get his half-dozen burros, and Estorga took up his tools to dismantle whatever metal work could be salvaged from the corrals, doors, kitchen, beams, and shops at the rancho.

More than a hundred made up the group that left, making its way down the winding mountain road and across the valley to the ranch houses. Neftali followed his father, who led the burros. They raised a great cloud of dust as they traveled along the valley bottom over the dirt road between the pastures. Neftali recalled that the only times he had visited the rancho were during drought, when the little stream by the village ran dry. His father each summer made a few pesos by taking his burros, laden with buckets and small barrels made in the village, to beg water from Don Francisco Domínguez, whose wells were always fresh and full. Domínguez allowed him to take water, and Hector Sandoval charged the villagers for the use of his animals and his labor. With great wonder, Neftali had watched the vaqueros go about the ranch chores. Señor Domínguez always looked elegant, in wide dress sombrero, tight clean trousers and shiny boots. His mustachio was always trimmed neatly, and only occasionally did Neftali get a glimpse of Doña Irene and her daughters, who always dressed in what Neftali thought was royal fashion. He and his father, whenever they visited the rancho, were more than aware their presence was only tolerable, as far as the rancher and his workmen were concerned. His father always bowed excessively and said "thank you" too many times, and Domínguez or his wife always dismissed him with an impatient wave of the hand.

Now as they approached the smoldering ranch house, no dogs came out to investigate, and Neftali saw the bodies of the dogs strewn around the yard. No vaqueros came out to ask what they wanted, and he saw the bodies of those who had stayed to defend the rancho.

The villagers broke into a run as they neared the ruins. Then they were in the blackened rubble. "Ay! look here what I found!" "Look at this! A fine ax!" "This window has glass! I can put it in my house."

The remaining horses and cattle, the fine buckboards and wagons, all that could not be hidden, were left untouched. It would go hard with anyone who had identifiable loot when the federales arrived a few days hence, and harder yet when the rich relatives of Domínguez came to fall heir to the rancho.

Neftali took the handmade collars from the dead dogs. How handsome the family mongrel would be in a collar, he thought. Some of the men took the clothes from the corpses nearby: "Ho! one washing and they will be as good as new. Except for the bullet holes!"

Guzmán had chosen to leave behind the wine, but had loaded all the hard liquor he could afford to carry, and the villagers soon found the underground wine storage sanctum.

Estorga was feverishly stripping the house of the hand-wrought joining bands on the fallen beams, the hinges, many of which he had made and sold to Domínguez, the anvil in the corral area, the winch at the well, the pipings and fittings at the windmill.

Neftali found the master bedroom and in a nearly burned-out chest of drawers he discovered treasure. A compass, a jeweled belt buckle, a pair of gloves of the softest leather imaginable, a folding pocket knife and coins.

The women salvaged half-burned quilts, linen and wool blankets. A calf in the corral quickly met death and within minutes was roasting on a fire. This was a fiesta the likes of which the people of Trainwreck had not seen since the cattle train had been derailed more than a decade and a half earlier. And as night came they made their way back up the mountainside to the village, burros laden, arms full, and stomachs too.

"A nd you did not try to stop them!? After you saw them kill and plunder?" the lieutenant was roaring.

"How could we, teniente? We are peons, unarmed. There were forty or fifty men with Guzmán. Most had three guns."

"Now tell me this! Did any of you help them in any way?"

"No," it was Estorga, "in fact, they abducted a boy and a girl from this village. If you catch Guzmán, remember, they were taken by force and would never fight against federales."

The lieutenant spat. "We shall see about that soon. All right. You say forty or fifty men. I have thirty-five. That means I need more. Five of you had better volunteer or I will do the volunteering for you."

He looked around at the villagers gathered about him as he and his men ate tortillas and beans ravenously. Their many days on the trail had made them all lean and gaunt. His eyes traveled around as he waited for volunteers. He finished his food and wiped his mouth with a large red kerchief.

"You have waited too long. You," he pointed to a young man in his early twenties, "take the first empty horse there. Be quick about it. And you. And you." He selected those obviously young and not married. "I need one more." His eyes fell on Neftali. "How old are you, joven?"

"No, no," Neftali's mother began whimpering, "no, no, no. Not him. He is fourteen, no more, you cannot take our son."

But Teniente Ramos remained adamant. "I'm sorry. I have to catch the bandits. It is for *you*, all of you, that we are making Mexico safe. Everybody wants law and order, but no one is willing to fight for it." He looked at Neftali. "Ándale. Take a horse. You will return to the village when Guzmán and his pirates are dead, and they shall be dead by the end of the week."

With great force Hector Sandoval pushed his near-hysterical wife into the shack, clamping a hand to her mouth as she tried to scream. Then with a roar of hoofs, the detachment thundered out of the village, down the mountainside to the road leading in the direction the bandits had gone.

The group traveled at a slow, loping gallop. Neftali had never been on a horse, but found it little different from a burro. He reached down as he rode and adjusted the stirrups to his leg length. He was near the rear of the group, and the pack animals and calves were behind him. The lieutenant suddenly pulled alongside him and threw a rifle at him. Neftali had to catch it or let it strike him across the chest. The lieutenant smiled and spurred ahead to lead his troops.

Lita and Hector Sandoval stayed in their shack all day. Periodically she would begin to wail, and he would comfort her, saying their son would be back as soon as the outlaws were tracked down. But his face showed the doubt of his own words. Toward evening she went outside and looked about, exhausted from weeping. She sat on a large rock in front of the house and sobbed softly. Her daughters had huddled silently all day, glad that neither of the conscriptors had selected them.

Señora Sandoval sat quietly until darkness came. Then, "I'd like a fire here, outside," she told her husband. Without hesitation he walked out of the village, up the hillside, and gathered wood. He returned and built a small fire near her.

Hector Sandoval felt a little guilty that his grief for the loss of his son was perhaps a little outweighed by concern for his wife. He loved this woman, who still looked like a girl after sixteen years of marriage. Fate had been kind to him, he thought, again with guilt, in that he had had only three children. Others in the village had seven, eight, even ten, and he couldn't understand how such a family ate in this land of want and poverty. A thought occurred to him that had fleetingly often crossed his mind. Los Estados Unidos. Thousands, he knew, were fleeing either tyranny or poverty in Mexico. To America.

His daughters came out to sit on the ancient railroad tie that served as a bench in front of the house. "He'll be back, Mama," one of them said. Mrs. Sandoval burst into tears anew, and Hector gave his daughters a stern look. The fire crackled mockingly.

Hector silently motioned his daughters to prepare something to eat within the house. They disappeared inside. The other villagers were peculiarly absent from sight. Soon Jilda, the eldest daughter, brought her mother a plate of food, but it was refused. The family sat and ate and only an occasional sob could be heard. A bright moon rose, and now and then a night animal gave its night cry. Hector Sandoval kept the fire supplied with small sticks.

Well after midnight the little fire leaped and flickered, making small popping and hissing noises in its preoccupation. Then Hector Sandoval thought he heard a sound. He raised his head and turned one ear toward the valley to the west, which at this time was a vast sea of blackness. He strained to hear. Then suddenly the sound burst upon them. A fast-approaching horse coming up the winding road. Now the hoofs clicked as they crossed stone underfooting; now they pounded as they hit soft dirt. The horse was approaching so fast the family felt terror, then horse and rider burst into the small circle of light, the animal slamming its feet into the ground to stop as the steel bit cut into its mouth, and then Neftali was running to his mother's arms.

A few minutes later when the cacaphony of reunion had abated somewhat and Señora Sandoval had momentarily ceased to praise the Mother of God, Neftali explained. "No, mamacita," it was the first time the lad had used the endearing diminutive and Hector Sandoval felt a surge go through him as he experienced a feeling of man-to-man equality toward his son, "God did not bring me back. I escaped. I am now a deserter from the Mexican Army. They'll be looking for me in the morning, to make an example of me."

Before his mother could begin wailing, Hector Sandoval took command. "All right. All of you listen. Neftali knows what we must do. He and I have talked it over before when we were alone working with the burros. We leave. Now. To go north. Quick. No talk. Pack our things. Neftali and I will go get the burros. We have six. We should be able to take everything and be a long way from here before another night."

Except for the boy, the others were stunned. "But, where . . . ? "

"To los Estados Unidos. Where there will be no more of all that makes us suffer. Hurry now. You women wrap up everything and bring it out here. We can leave within an hour. Or the lieutenant might return for Neftali."

2

The shrill, cold air knifed through his clothing to the flesh as Hector Sandoval drew the cowhide tighter around him and tensed his muscles, the more effectively to shiver. The railroad flatcar on which the family was riding bucketed along, swinging rhythmically, noisily nudging the car ahead, then impatiently tugging at the car behind. Jilda and Hortensia and their mother also lay flat, hides pulled around them. The last time Hector checked to see that they were bearing up under the ordeal they could hardly talk from the cold. Only Neftali sat, back to the wind, his cowhide encircling him and covering his head, but his face uncovered so that he could see. All yesterday and all night they had been riding. Dawn—and the sun—couldn't be far off. If there would be a sun. All Hector could make out of the sky was an uninterrupted overcast. He had expected California to be green country, soft pastures and farmlands, but so far he could only make out rugged, rocky hills, barren except for brush, cactus, and an occasional group of stunted trees.

Hector remembered back to another train ride, in another time and another place. That day of the train wreck, the heat had been sweltering. Which was better, he mused, that heat or this cold? With a convulsive shudder he decided the heat was better.

He closed his eyes in the darkness and drew the hide tighter about him. This hide had come from one of the unfortunate cattle the train had been carrying that day so long ago, as had those in which his wife, daughters, and son were now wrapped. These hides had been cured well and still held their shape and flexibility. How many had he had? Twenty or more at first. Over the years he had traded some to the cobbler at intervals in return for goods. The family had left Trainwreck with a dozen, but had traded all but six for lodging or food. They had served well.

He opened his eyes and saw that the sky was becoming light in the east. Odd, he thought, that merely the presence of light made the air feel warmer, more bearable, although he knew the sun couldn't possibly have warmed it yet.

The train slowed and as the wind decreased he felt warmer. Soon they were traveling not much faster than a man could walk, and he sat up and saw that the others were sitting also, getting the first good look at their new country. He saw flat land, farmed and cultivated, as far as the eye could reach, with a backdrop of near-barren mountains. Farmhouses seemed spaced about a mile or so apart, and he was struck by their apparent affluence, evidenced by the accompanying auxiliary buildings such as storage facilities, barns, corrals and sheds.

A cold steady drizzle began to fall.

The Sandoval family was riding on one of half a hundred flatcars making up the train. Several other families also rode the train, and as it continued to slow they saw a trainman approaching, walking the length of each car, then leaping to the next. Hector watched as the man came to the car immediately ahead and said something to the family riding there. Then the man leaped onto the Sandoval car.

Hector was chilled by the look of complete and intentional disrespect the trainman gave him and his family. "You have to get off the train now," he said in broken Spanish, and kept walking toward the car to the rear.

"Can't we wait until the train stops?" Hector asked.

The man turned and, as though he hadn't heard, said in a loud voice, "If you don't get off now, you will all be very sorry," and he continued on.

Hector waited until a relatively even stretch of terrain came by and then, throwing off their belongings first, he jumped. Running alongside the train, he helped off first the children and then Lita, and the train kept going. The other families aboard the train chose to ride a little farther and risk the trainman's threat.

The Sandovals walked back and gathered their belongings, each carrying a fair share, and the caboose rolled noisily past. The sound of the train grew smaller and smaller and finally disappeared and as they stood looking about there was no sound at all, even the steady drizzle was silent.

A great sense of being alone in unfriendly territory gripped the family. The land was flat. A mile or more away, in opposite directions, were two farmhouses. A dog barked somewhere far off. The gray sky blended with the horizon. A hundred yards from the tracks stood a grove of eucalyptus, and Hector saw a family camped by the stream that ran there. They approached the family to ask directions and share their fire, and were told the city was a dozen miles to the west. This family had also come by train, on the previous day, and were waiting only for a sick child to recover before pressing on to the city to look for work.

The Sandovals trudged on toward the city, laden with what possessions they had not traded or sold to get this far. By early afternoon they were entering the town, bone-weary, chilled and tired. The drizzle continued and the path beside the tracks veered and became a broad muddy road. Hector had seen many Mexicans working the fields nearby, but they had been reluctant to stop to talk to him.

The shacks were almost solid beside the road now, and an occasional store or business advertised its wares. Dios, Hector wondered aloud, was the whole city nothing but slum shacks and mud roads? He asked a man walking by. "No," the man smiled, "just the Mexican section."

A huge wagon loaded with produce came down the road, pulled by finer and larger horses than Hector had ever seen. The horses tugged mightily and the harness pressed into the shoulder flesh as the animals' strength fought to overcome the sluggish mud miring the wheels. The steady drizzle fell.

As they passed a row of shacks a woman came out and asked if they were new. She readily appointed herself their helper and showed them a brick shack next to her own. "This is vacant," she told Hector. "I think Señor Cárdenas will rent it to you. You have money?"

Hector reached into his pocket and felt the six dollars there. It was all he had after selling the burros and other things they could not carry when they left Trainwreck. It had been a much larger sum before he had converted it from pesos to dollars. "Yes, I have some."

"Good. Let the wife and children rest here with me. I'll feed them hot beans and soup. Go down this street to the cobblestone avenue, turn right, and in the tavern with the naked woman on the sign you'll find Cárdenas. Ask to rent this house. Then I'll tell you how to find work in this hell-hole."

Hector walked in the drizzle down the street. Mud squeezed through the holes in his shoes and made his feet hurt. His wide sombrero dripped water in front of his face whenever he tipped his head forward. He wore the cowhide around his shoulders like a sarape and was reasonably dry down to his knees.

The structures lining the streets were primarily living quarters. Ragged children, noses hanging mucus, barefoot in the mud, played in the street or shrieked in the shacks. Groups of men stood around at corners and on the dirt walks, talking. Some wore clothing in shreds, were unshaven and barefoot. Hector noticed a great variety of attire, but poverty was the common style. He talked with a few persons and discovered that finding work in the fields and orchards was on the minds of all. Everyone, it seemed, was almost starving, and "until more crops are ready" was the universal phrase, the thought that gave all here the determination to remain in the barrio bajo.

All the shacks, the tiny stores and businesses lining the streets for blocks in all directions had been erected, Hector saw, on a purely temporary basis, to make do, to improvise until something more substantial could be built, but all the temporary shelters and shops had become a town, a town for people who lived in anticipation of the time when "more crops are ready," and it was a town such as Hector had never heard of.

The street he was now on was the main street. He stopped at a corner and looked around. The drizzle still fell, making little rivulets on the street, which the children tried to dam up or channel. Diagonally from where he stood was a tavern, the walls of which were galvanized sheet metal. The front was open, as the large door was hinged at the top and swung upward. It was tied in place so that it afforded a little shelter to a group of men, dressed like tramps, who swore loudly in Spanish and passed a bottle among themselves. He was about to cross the street when he heard hoofs splashing in the mud.

He noticed heads turning and saw two men approaching on horseback. As they came closer he saw that they were americanos and wore badges. He noted that their horses were magnificent, well fed, large and muscular, well trained. The saddles were of rich leather, and the men wore soft hats, riding boots, and huge pistols at the hip. Their horses were coming at a casual trot. As they neared, one rider suddenly spurred his mount ahead and rode to the rear entrance of the tavern Hector had noticed. The other rider spurred to the front door. The men who had been in front scattered.

Except for the men on the train, this was Hector's first look at americanos. He noticed the lawmen were stern, fierce and unflinching.

From his vantage point Hector could see the rider sitting his mount facing the rear door of the tavern, and the other now dismounted and, feeling reassuringly for his pistol, quickly walked inside. Hector heard a few loud shouts, then something he couldn't understand in English. He couldn't see the man inside, but the door at the rear burst open and a young tattered man, bearded and wearing a sombrero, ran out, obviously fleeing. He took only a few steps before he saw the mounted man in front of him. He stopped just as the rider drew his pistol and fired. The tattered man clutched his breast and swayed, and the rider took careful aim and fired again. The man collapsed. The lawman rode up to the fallen man and, pointing his pistol almost directly down, put another bullet into the still form.

The other lawman came out the rear door, examined the body briefly, went to his mount and the pair rode off at a casual trot.

Hector joined the gathering crowd at the rear of the tavern. All looked down at the dead man. "He shouldn't have tried to run" . . . "Never run from a gringo policeman" . . . "They wanted to question him about the knife fight he had in the americano town the other night" . . . "He was a bad one" . . . "They had him in jail before and they let him go."

A young woman appeared, carrying an infant perhaps six months old and holding the hand of another child of three. Hector knew immediately, when the crowd quieted and parted to let her through, that she was the widow. She stood a long moment looking down at her dead husband, her eyes streaming, more with pity than grief, Hector thought. The infant stirred and his face sought her breast. She untied a drawstring on her blouse and, while one hand wiped away tears the hand of the arm cradling the baby guided his head to her nipple, as though she had practiced these movements.

Her other son standing beside her pulled at her skirt.

"Mama! Is Papa dead? Mama! Answer me. Is Papa dead?"

A heavy elderly woman wearing a dress that came to her ankles came forward and disengaged the child's hand from his mother. "Yes, little one, your papa is dead. Now come with me. Your mother needs to cry and you'll bother her. We'll go to my house."

"Do you have any more chicken like you had last time?" the boy asked.

"We'll see. I'll give you something good to eat, I promise."

"All I want?"

The old woman led the boy away. The young mother stood looking down at her husband's corpse, her baby suckling half-heartedly. She looked up, and Hector saw her thin beauty and grace.

"Who will help me bury him?" she asked. A half dozen men stepped forth reluctantly, some complaining the dead man still owed them money or favors, all taking in the slender body and full buttocks and breasts. Hector turned to go, knowing that when a girl like this was widowed, she usually ended up better off than before, and he suspected this would be the case.

By the time he got to the tavern with the large painting of a nude woman on the front (the tavern was called The Naked Woman), word of the shooting had spread. It was on every-one's lips as he entered.

Catching his eye first as he looked around were the young girls, gaudily dressed, sitting provocatively on a bench against the rear wall as though they were on display. There were nearly a dozen and some appeared to be scarcely into their teens. It had been many years since he'd seen working prostitutes and their youthfulness shocked him. His own girls were older, he real-ized.

Ten or twelve men were at the bar drinking, and a like num-ber were scattered throughout, drinking at tables or trying to tease the young prostitutes.

Hector ordered a mug of beer at the bar and observed. A fat man, as fat as himself and about the same age, was seated at a table near the girls. The others nearby were enjoying the con-versation between the fat one and one of the girls.

"Fifty cents! For one time! That's too much."

"Nobody's begging you."

"Besides, my wife and kids need the money for food."

"Then go home to your wife."

"Now, if you would just trust me, until the Valencia crop starts next week . . ."

"Sure I trust you until next week. Come back then. You can trust I'll be here."

Laughter from the spectators.

"I don't think you're worth fifty cents."

"You'll never know until you try, will you?"

"But you're so young. You probably don't know how to screw very well."

"It'll cost you fifty cents to find out."

"Aw, come on. I can spare twenty-five cents."

She shook her head smartly. "I'm worth fifty. Ask your amigo over there."

"Where? Who? You mean Paco? Paco! Tell me, is the little lady worth fifty cents?"

"Dios! That little lady is worth fifty dollars!"

Laughter again echoed.

Hector turned his attention to the man behind the bar.

"I'm looking for a man called Cárdenas."

"It's me."

"I want to rent the place by the bakery there. It's empty."

The man showed interest. "Fine. Three dollars a month. Pay me now for the first month. There's a water pipe running inside, and I just had a new toilet dug out in back. It's got a stove, too."

Hector gave the man three dollars and Cárdenas took a pencil and paper. He made a note of the transaction and gave Hector a slip showing $3 received. The business transacted, Cárdenas moved away to wait on customers.

Hector finished his mug of beer and ordered another. Then a swell of applause burst out. Looking to the rear, Hector saw that the fat man and the young girl had finally struck a bargain and were going through the door to the side. All cheered or clapped and returned to their drinking.

Hector struck up conversation with two men standing by. He learned this place was the starting point. Immigrants and U.S.-born migrant workers came here—at least a large number did—each year and began spreading out eastward and north-ward. This was a coastal city, and they told him there was a thousand miles of crops to be picked north and east. But things were tough. It took money to live, and to get from one place to another. So you had to work around here for a month or two, so you could buy shoes and clothes and transportation. And there were too many Mexicans here. Without luck, you could go a month or two looking for work.

Hector noticed an American come in. He was nattily dressed and in a hurry. He motioned to Cárdenas and the bar owner approached. Although Hector didn't try, he couldn't help hearing.

"I need four right now. Party. Guarantee two dollars each."

Cárdenas beckoned and his girls came to him. "Americano party. Go with him. Nothing doing here. I want my usual cut."

The girls perked up with enthusiasm at the mention of Americano party, and followed the gringo out.

The beer had an effect on his empty stomach. He ordered another, feeling guilty about spending the money, and he walked toward the rear almost without realizing it. Only five girls remained—another was still with the fat man. He stared, unconsciously going closer as he studied the girls. One in particular fascinated him. She had a low-cut dress, tight, and her full, youthful beauty sang to the eye. Her calves were exposed and shone an even brown. Black shiny hair fell to her shoulders, and her red mouth glistened. She was smiling as she talked to another man. She suddenly threw back her head and laughed, and her heavy full breasts seemed to want to explode. Then her dark eyes traveled to Hector, and he became aware of her looking at him. His travel-worn and filthy clothes, his mustache untrimmed for a week, his hair uncut and tangled, his forty-eight years showing in the gray of his beard. The girl's voice was tauntingly understanding as she spoke to him.

"Señor, go home to mamacita, get dry and warm, clean up and eat and sleep well, get a job tomorrow and get settled, and after a few paydays, come back and see me."

Hector made his way back to the shack of Doña Dora Lucero, the woman who had befriended them as they arrived in the city. The worry in Lita's face disappeared when she saw him. "We heard there was a killing." He explained what had happened and told how he had rented the place next door.

"Good," Doña Dora said. "Come, I'll show you how to unlock it." The Sandovals picked up their belongings. Hector saw the weariness on the faces of his daughters, his son, and his wife. They seemed to struggle mightily as they all lifted their packs and followed the woman next door. She led them around to the rear. The house was made of mortared stone, plastered over, and the tin roof was patched with tarpaper. Doña Dora went behind the outside toilet and took a metal rod which was hidden there. She went to the rear door and slipping the rod under the door, she pried upward, at the same time pushing on the door. It opened inward.

"There is no key for the lock, but this method works well. Just make sure no one sees where you hide the rod and you'll always be able to lock your house when you leave."

She showed them inside, chattering incessantly about the previous family that lived here, how the man had stolen chickens from a nearby farm and then the family had to flee when the police came looking for him. The Sandovals were still shivering and wet, and Mrs. Lucero went home and returned with an armload of firewood. "Here," she said, more or less assuming command as she built a fire in the stove. "Señor Sandoval, about a half mile out of town, following the creek, is a demolished house. Take some rope to tie the wood in bundles, so you can carry it back easily. Meanwhile, your son and I will carry over my bathing tub and we'll heat some water for baths. We'll have you all comfortable tonight, wait and see."

Hector started out, following her directions. He walked down the muddy street, still soaked, bones aching, past a bar where he heard singing and guitar music. He found the creek and walked along to the grove of eucalyptus Doña Dora had mentioned. In the middle of the grove, just as she'd said, was the remains of an old wooden house. Within a few minutes he had two large bundles of wood tied together and slung over his shoulders, and he started back.

He was walking along the edge of the creek on a narrow foot path when he heard someone call "Ho! Amigo!" He looked around. The sound evidently came from a thick patch of willows about fifty feet from him. Then the bushes parted and a man stood there. "What do you have there?"

"I have some firewood," Hector said uncertainly.

"You have a moment? I'd like to talk to you."

Hector hesitated, but approached the man. The man stepped back into the patch and Hector followed, not knowing what to expect. He saw a little clearing. Three other men sat around a small fire. They were incredibly dirty and unkempt. Hector saw the watery glaze in their eyes before he saw the gallon jug of wine they had. One spoke thickly. "Are you alone?"

"Sí. My family is in the town. I came to gather wood."

"Between here and the town, did you see any lawmen?"

"No, but earlier I saw two policemen kill a man," he replied. They were intensely interested, asking him to describe the victim and glancing among themselves knowingly.

"Yes, that was Juanito," they finally agreed. They told Hector to tell no one he had seen them, and when he seemed so willing to comply, they offered him a drink. He set his load down and sat, drinking from the nearly empty jug. One of the men took the jug from him and drained it. Walking to a nearby lean-to, which Hector had not noticed before, the man picked up a full jug and returned to the fire.

Hector drank more wine and soon had told them the story of his coming to California. When they heard he had just arrived, one man went to the lean-to and brought Hector two freshly killed rabbits. "We have more, they are plentiful here," he explained. Hector was delighted, and as he talked he skillfully tied the rabbits' hind legs to a tree, using some of the cord he'd brought, took a knife and skinned and cleaned them. He saw they had been shot with a small caliber gun. He wrapped the carcasses in the hide and stuffed them into his bundle of wood.

He thanked the outcasts for the rabbits and wine, promised to say nothing of them, and left.

When he got back to the house he knocked and Lita answered. She had bathed, combed her shiny black hair and wore clean clothes. She smiled radiantly. The warmth from the stove had permeated the room. Doña Dora had left, but she had given them potatoes, which were frying in bacon grease on the stove. The square house had a partitioned room, so that the rest of the house was shaped like the letter L, and they had taken the large washing tub into the room and had bathed there. Fresh cold water was in the tub for Hector, and a large kettle of water was steaming, ready to be added to the tub to bring the water to bathing temperature. He put some of the wood into the stove and gave Lita the rabbits. They all were jubilant at their good fortune. This to them was a fine house, and it seemed their hardships in getting here were worthwhile. The wooden floor of the house was a luxury none had experienced, and the cold water tap, although there was no sink, made them very aware of the availability of fresh water and each kept going to the faucet for a drink.

While the rabbits fried Hector went into the bedroom, closed the door, and undressed, experiencing a luxurious sense of privacy, and sat in the tub. Lita came in with his extra pair of clean trousers, which she had dried by the stove. He got out, dried himself, dressed, and then shaved with a worn old straight razor which he always kept in an oily rag with the sharpening strop. The family hand mirror had made the journey without mishap.

Then they ate. The only furniture in the house was a

makeshift table and some wooden boxes which served as chairs. With their bedrolls and spare things they improvised mattresses and made the beds, using the hides for blankets. Hector and Lita took the partitioned room, Jilda and Hortensia took one quarter of the remaining room to the rear and Neftali made his bed by the front door. Both doors had glass windows, but the rest of the house had only blank walls. Hector and Lita used a kerosene lantern in their bedroom, and candles lighted the rest of the house. Lita insisted on saying a prayer to the Virgin, giving thanks for the warmth, the food and house, and the wonderful feeling of well-being she felt.

Hector and Lita said good night to the children, made sure the doors were secure against intruders and went to their room. Closing the door was a new experience in their marriage, and they felt indescribably isolated.

"It's warm enough in this house to sleep with no clothes on," he said quietly to her. She looked at him and nodded sincerely. She went to turn out the lamp. "Leave it on just a tiny bit," he said. She complied. He lay back on the bed on the floor and for the second time that day became aware he was highly aroused. He compared her to the young prostitute. Lita's breasts were heavier, hung down a little more. That was because of the children. And her hips were a little wider. That was also because of the children. She came to lie down beside him and he turned to her. As he patted her into position he thought, Dios! *Either it's the wine or this country is making me younger!*

No, don't go down to the waiting place. A bunch of tramps hang out there. They gamble, drink, and have knife fights all day. Go out that road. About an hour's walk and you'll come to the ranch house. The gringo foreman there understands Spanish. Ask him for work," Mrs. Lucero told Hector the next morning when the family had eaten tortillas and the leftover fried rabbit.

He started out. A few blocks away he passed the waiting place. At least a hundred and fifty men were gathered at a corner. Some were literally in rags. Some wore the white pajama-type work clothes of the Mexican peasant. Some wore American clothes. Most wore hats, and there were many sombreros among them, and all had large mustachios and talked in Spanish.

It was still cold and drizzling, and the waiting men joked little. Doña Dora had warned him not to hang out here, and he was not enough at home to take the responsibility of going against advice. But he walked slowly past. The main body of men stood on a corner, watching an approaching wagon. They crowded to the fore. Hector saw a small, slight man who looked almost feverish. He was trying to slip in at the front. Someone roughly shoved him back.

"Please," the little man pleaded. "My family, they are actually starving. I've got to work soon." He addressed one nice-looking young man. "Just let me stand here near the front."

"Sure," the man said, "just so you don't stand in front of me," and he firmly pushed the little man back. A large, fierce-looking man shoved him farther back, and yet another man said, "Don't get in front of me. I want to work, too."

The wagon pulled up, and like an ocean wave, the men moved in on it. An American driving the team stood up.

"Twenty, that's all, twenty. A dollar and a half for the day, if you work hard." He counted out twenty as they scrambled on the wagon and then cracked the horses' rumps with a wide leather strap and the wagon lurched through the mud. The remaining men went back to pushing and shoving to get better position for the next wagon. Those at the rear, with no hope of getting on the next wagon, found seats and argued or passed bottles back and forth.

Hector walked on.

At the farm he found the foreman striding among the orange trees, a notebook in his hand as he kept track of each worker's output. "You're in luck," he told Hector in broken Spanish. "We've got to rush to finish the navel crop. It was late. And the Valencias will be ready next month. Get in there and start stripping that row. Keep up with the others and you got a job." A tired but happy Hector trudged home in the evening to break the good news to his family.

Three days before Hector Sandoval got paid the family was broke. Doña Dora next door saw to it they had beans and chocolate. She showed Lita how to make tortillas de harina— tortillas of flour instead of cornmeal.

"It's hard to get good ground corn here, and once you get accustomed to tortillas made of flour you'll like them."

They all watched as she mixed flour with cold rendered lard, water and a little salt. When the dough was the proper consistency she formed it into fist-sized balls, and then patted these out into large, round tortillas ready to cook on the hot surface of the stove.

On Friday night Hector came home with twelve dollars he'd earned. They all went to the market and bought five dollars' worth of groceries. Lita sent Hortensia next door to pay Doña Dora Lucero what they owed her, and then she set about making dinner. Hector had bought a large jug of wine, and now he sat drinking from a tin cup.

"But here's the best news," he said to all, "I asked the foreman and he said Neftali can start to work with me next week. I
said he was sixteen and can work as hard as any older man."

Neftali was impressed by the organization of the work. One
crew of men did nothing but drive a team and wagon through
the orchard loading the stacked crates of oranges. The foreman
came by keeping score of individual output. Some workers had
chosen piecework, to be paid per crate picked, but Hector and
Neftali were paid a straight twenty cents per hour. The hours
were from six to six, with a brief respite for lunch. They
trudged wearily home at the end of each day, joining the hundreds of other workers who were also leaving the fields and orchards, some carrying empty paper bags, to be used again the
next day to bring lunch. Occasionally a team pulling an empty
wagon happened by and the driver, in the unique and indescrib-
able way in which the Mexican can so quickly communicate
without spoken words, would indicate with a motion of the
brow it was all right to climb on for a free ride as far as he was
going.

The Saturday following Neftali's first payday each member
of the family got either a pair of shoes, a dress, or new trousers.

About a month after Neftali had been working with his father Doña Dora raced into the Sandoval house.

"I have friends who have this placement service. They say
they can place a girl who doesn't speak English. Which of you
girls would like to go?"

Lita and Hector questioned her at length about the job. It
paid five dollars a week, she would be required to feed and dress
two children for school and during the day to do housework. It
was a profession, Doña Dora told them, and when you learned
to be a good housemaid you were never out of a job.

H ortensia returned home on weekends.

"You should see the way the americanos eat. They have a machine that makes ice cream and they eat it every night, after they have chicken or steaks." None of the Sandovals had ever had ice cream. "And they have an icebox and every day a man comes to put new ice in it, so that the milk and butter and cheese always stay cold. They have two children I have to take care of. These kids have a set of clothes for every day of the week. La señora is teaching me how to cook all the foods. They are of an old California family and they speak pretty good Spanish. The toilets are in little closets and where you go is full of water and when you're through you pull a chain and fresh water comes and takes away all the old stuff in a pipe. I'm learning to speak English. And I have a little room all to myself, with a bed that has springs."

With her earnings Hortensia bought some new clothes and gave the rest to her mother. The family now had some furniture and mattresses and utensils. And now Jilda wanted nice clothes so that she might get a job like Hortensia.

Not long thereafter on a Friday evening Hector and Neftali were walking home, tired, but with their week's earnings in their pockets. Hector stopped at a tavern a few blocks from home.

"Go home and say I stopped to talk some business. Lots of men hang out here who know the work situation pretty well and I have to talk to them."

"Where is your father?" Lita asked when he arrived home alone.

"He had to stop off to talk some business," Neftali explained.

Lita was quiet a moment. "At the bar?"

"Sí."

She said nothing. When Neftali was in bed he heard his father come in, moving clumsily, breathing hard.

"Your pay?" his mother asked.

"I spent some. I've got to have a little relaxation. And . . . I loaned some to a guy. He'll pay me back next week, don't worry. Besides, we have Neftali's money. And Hortensia gives us some all the time. We're a lot better off than if I hadn't insisted we move from Mexico."

The stopping off became a regular thing. Hector explained his vanished wages. "They have a game. If I win I'll get fifty dollars. And I will soon, don't worry. Lots of the men play it, and you're bound to win sooner or later."

One night he came home very late. "I won," he announced jubilantly, handing Lita some money. She counted it.

"There's only ten dollars here. You said you'd win fifty."

"I did. But when you win you're expected to buy drinks for those who lost. And besides, I had to pay a guy I borrowed from. So my credit's good, and if we ever need to borrow, everybody knows I always pay back."

Neftali had fleetingly had the impression that the family had come into a giant trap. His father's words—and actions—now made this feeling more pronounced, although he could not have expressed it. And on a Sunday when Hortensia wanted to show them the house in which she worked, all except Neftali expressed enthusiasm. But he accompanied them as they walked out of the barrio, dressed in their best, into the residential area. Hortensia led them to a house with a spacious lawn with well-trimmed shrubs and trees, and with stone walks neatly circling the house and leading to the street. The house was of shingle siding with a brick chimney at each side, with freshly painted green trim around the windows and doors. French windows opened onto tiny balconies on the upper floor.

"What does the señor do to make enough money to have a house like that?" Hector asked his daughter.

"He owns some kind of business that lends people money. They also have a gardener who comes every day and does nothing but take care of the plants and trees. He's from Mexico also, and I've gotten to know him pretty well," Hortensia explained, and Neftali saw something cross her face as she mentioned the gardener.

The group began walking slowly, examining the house in detail, then they stopped as they saw a middle-aged woman come from the front door and approach them. Her ankle-length dress with lace fringe rustled about her feet. She wore a bustle, veil and white gloves.

"It's Mrs. Wadsworth," Hortensia said a little fearfully. "I hope she's not angry because I brought you here . . ."

The woman walked up to them. "Hortensia! How nice! And this is your family, I'll bet," she said in fairly good Spanish.

"Si, señora," Hortensia said. "This is my father, and my mother, and my brother, Neftali, and my sister Jilda."

"Mucho gusto!" Mrs. Wadsworth replied with an abundant smile. "I'm glad you wanted to bring them here. Come," she led the way, "I'll show you all around, and then you won't be curious any more."

Neftali noticed her eyes went to the neighboring houses with a little anxiety as she led them toward the house. He was aware of a great awkwardness in himself and his parents as Mrs. Wadsworth showed them cursorily through the house; the strained, soft-spoken politeness of Mr. Wadsworth as he interrupted his stereoscope viewing in the study to assure them he was pleased to meet them, and then it was over and she was showing them out, saying she had to get ready for some very important guests. "I'll be glad to see you again some time," she said with vitality, and Neftali thought she didn't conceal her actual feelings very well.

Mamacita, did you ever notice that when we're really broke, when there's nothing to eat, Papa doesn't drink? Then he works hard and gives you all his money. But when we have enough, and he knows Hortensia or I will give you money, he spends his pay at the bar," Neftali mused.

She had not noticed, but now realized this was the pattern. Invariably, when it looked as though they would have enough left over at the end of the week to buy a piece of furniture, or perhaps to save a little, Hector would stop at the bar on the way home and spend his week's salary. When questioned, he would explain, "This job I have now, I wouldn't have it if it weren't for a man I met and bought drinks for. It's very necessary that I keep up my contacts and that everyone knows how generous I am. Right now if I got laid off I know three or four guys I could go to work with. Keeping up contacts at the tavern is sort of insurance."

By the time Neftali was sixteen his mother was resigned to life as they knew it, in the same house, which had deteriorated considerably since they came. Vanished were the hopes of moving on to a better place. Prices were high, and only by managing to sneak and save as much of Neftali's earnings as possible, were they able to coast through the lean months, when little was being picked. And Hector's drinking increased.

Neftali now had a fine mustachio. The sun kept his skin a coppery black, and he could pass for eighteen or twenty years old.

Hortensia and Jilda had been working away from home for two years, and their visits were infrequent. They seemed well off and spoke little of their jobs. Their clothes were fine and Lita bragged and showed them off whenever they came to visit in the barrio. They always gave her money when Hector wasn't around.

Neftali walked the streets of the barrio in his spare time. He looked at the dirty streets and houses, the people caught up in this life, and he remembered back to the little quiet village where he had roamed free, alone. And he almost longed to go back. He noticed a tavern where youths about his own age gathered, and one Saturday when he was dressed in his best he entered. He ordered a glass of wine and began talking to a young man named Francisco. And soon they were talking about girls.

"I know a place across the barrio," Francisco told him, "for a half dollar you can get it. Good-looking young girls. They'll do anything and you can spend all the time you want."

Francisco said he went there often, and Neftali asked him in detail about the adventures. He begged off and went home early to fantasize in his bed. For the next few days he recalled vividly everything Francisco had said about the girls, and then he went back to the tavern to ask Francisco more details.

"I believe a man should want a good, clean girl to marry, and he should be able to respect her."

"I agree," Francisco said, "but you can't expect a man to stay away from girls until he's married. These girls, they're screwing lots of guys all the time. They're not saving themselves for marriage. If you don't get some of it, it's your own fault."

Again, Neftali went home to think. But he knew that Saturday night, when he had kept some money out for his own pleasure, he would go with Francisco to the whorehouse.

As the downtown district of the city receded, the slum confiscated the old buildings. The whorehouse was a once-fine hotel, now run down and musty. The floor inside tilted crazily and small, high windows were reluctant to admit light. Ceilings were long ago blackened by the gaslight fixtures, now unused, and the narrow stairway leading from the lobby required the passer to turn sideways.

Neftali's blood pounded as a man approached and asked for fifty cents each. They paid and he motioned them upstairs with aplomb. In the narrow hallway upstairs, lit only by a window at each end, Francisco indicated the nearest door.

"Go in. There's a girl in there. They're not too busy now, or we'd have to wait."

Neftali put his hand on the door knob but then waited and watched Francisco, who went to the next door, opened it, entered and closed the door behind him.

With only a little trembling he opened the door in front of him. The room was small, lit by a candle on a stand beside the bed on which his sister was lying.

Sí, I've been screwing here for two years, and I'm not one damn bit sorry." He had never heard Hortensia so vehement, so fiery. "You don't know what the hell this country's all about. Crap! It happened the first few months I was at the Wadsworth house. The man who delivered things to the door, he came in once and forced himself on me. I threatened to tell the patrón and he laughed, saying he would say I had seduced him. The delivery man kept returning, forcing me to do it, until the patrón caught us. He kicked him out fast, and then *he* fucked me. And that kept up until la señora suspected. She called me every name she could think of and then threw me out, owing me a month's pay. I happened to run into the delivery man again and he steered me to this place. I make ten times as much money as housekeeping, and put in half the hours. And have time to go places and do some things which you'll never do, because you pick oranges from dawn to dark."

"Hermana, if mama and papa knew about this it would . . ."

"Ha! Our good father has been here. Don't look so surprised, Neftali. He was. I heard his voice and locked that door right there or he would have been in here. Manuel, the man down in the lobby, I told him to keep papa out after that, so he doesn't know we are here . . ."

" 'We?' "

Hortensia had thrown a wrap on to cover her nakedness. She quickly left the room and he heard her walk down the hall. In a moment she returned with Jilda. Jilda looked at him defiantly. Neftali shook his head.

"So. You're shocked. Yet you come here yourself."

"It . . . it would have been better had we stayed in Mexico . . ."

"Like hell it would. Don't you remember, brother, the hunger, the nothing we had, no clothes, beans and corn every day, a big occasion when we had a chicken? Well, now I eat chicken whenever I want. Hortensia and I have a room all our own, on the edge of the barrio, where we buy things we like, that we never dreamed we could own in Mexico."

"But . . . you should have been saving yourself for marriage . . ."

"The way you were going to save yourself?"

"But it's different with men . . ."

They laughed. "Where would you men be who believe it's different for men if all us girls believed the same? Then where would you go, eh?"

He stood still a moment, then turned to go. "Please, don't let mama and papa know what you're doing."

The defiance left both girls. They came to him and hugged him and he saw how close they were to tears. "We won't. We love them too much," Jilda said, "but it's hard enough to be a Mexican in this country without being honest. You either have to be a maid and screw the patrón, or marry an orange picker and live in a shack in the barrio bajo. The gringos won't let you go to the park or the beach . . . you haven't found all this out yet, have you?"

"Yes, I have. But we've got to know our place. I heard of a little town, it's called Rabbit Town, north of here, near Los Angeles. It's a little city of mejicanos like us, and you can buy land and it's not like this. I'm going there, where I can live in our own town and still find work that only this country offers."

"Well, when you find such a place send for us. I don't believe it. Here we are trapped. Either do the white man's work, or if you're a young girl, service him, or live like an animal in Mexico."

A great chill seemed to come over him. He gave each of his

sisters an affectionate hug, squeezed back tears, and turned to go.

"Adiós, hermanito," Hortensia said. "We'll be over this weekend. Mama needs money."

He reflected a moment. "Yes," he said, and left.

Hector had felt the sudden, stabbing pain on several occasions. But this night as he stood at the bar, singing and shouting with his fellow workers, it almost caused him to double over. More wine would fix that. It always deadened the pain in his stomach. Suddenly he retched. A companion saw the bright red fluid he vomited.

"Ho, Hector! All that wine is coming up, eh? Maybe that's good. Now you can enjoy putting more back down." And they all laughed, and paid little attention when he paled a little and then staggered toward the back door to vomit outside. He knew the bright red stuff was not wine.

He was weak, partly from being drunk, but he made it to a large fig tree in the rear and emptied his stomach more. Then he sat down, feeling very tired, sleepy and drunk, and while he slept under the tree the perforated ulcer on his stomach lining again filled his stomach with blood and then filled his abdominal cavity and there was not enough blood left in his veins to keep him alive.

Neftali found him under the fig tree the next morning. Lita wailed in grief when she heard, and Neftali paid another visit to the whorehouse to tell his sisters their father had drunk himself to death. They came, the two whores, in their fine clothes and veils. They paid the thirty dollars for a casket, a hearse and a priest, and walked behind in the tracks of the two big black horses that pulled their father's corpse with lively unconcern to the camposanto del barrio bajo—graveyard of the ghetto. The horses stopped at a hole beside the grave of the tattered young man Hector had seen shot down the first day he arrived in the barrio bajo.

A steady drizzle was falling as the priest set up a portable altar and prepared to give the service, and a half dozen of Hector's fellow orange pickers lifted the casket from the hearse against a backdrop of outhouses, while the horses stamped impatiently. A small naked boy, three or four years of age, came out of a shack and approached the ceremony, stopping to stare, mouth agape as he scratched his scrotum, until his mother came scolding to drag him back, warning of the bad luck staring at a funeral could bring.

Darkness was setting in as the four surviving members of the Sandoval family arrived at the house. Jilda and Hortensia started preparing a dinner by the flickering candlelight. Lita sat reflecting, and it seemed to Neftali that his mother appeared strangely at peace, serene. As they finished eating she looked across the table at her two daughters and said, "You two had better be getting back to your work," with a knowing attitude. The girls glanced at one another, then at Neftali, who shook his head almost imperceptibly. The girls came around to their mother and put arms around her.

"No," Lita said answering the unspoken question. "Your father didn't know. But I raised you, you sucked at my breasts, I put the first spoonful of solid food into your mouths. Do you think you could ever keep anything secret from me?"

The girls said nothing, embracing her, then rose to go.

"Don't worry about me, children," she said intimately. "And please return to see me very soon. Or I might miss you." The girls glanced at one another, a little puzzled. As they left, Lita looked proudly at them. "Bless you," she said calmly.

Neftali lay in bed a long time thinking, trying to get accustomed to the idea he would never again hear his father's voice or loud belch, never again see the round rugged face or hear the heavy footsteps. He heard his mother sob gently and say something to God.

Three weeks passed. He trudged home one Friday night with his pay in his pocket. Past the bar where Francisco hung out. Yes, maybe later he would go in and find him. Maybe he would try girls once more, but in his mind he had a secret fantasy of a cream-skinned young girl, virginal beyond belief, who wanted, as he did, nothing more than to start a close-knit family, and watch babies grow, and he wanted to never look at any other woman. She would be from a small village, eager for the steady home life, wherein he could cultivate the outside relationships he desired, where he could have good family friends over every night, and have guitar music and enough to eat for all, and live where his children would never know the stinging poverty he had grown up with or the lashing temptations that had torn his family apart here in the barrio bajo. He kept picturing the girl of his dreams, and each time he thought of her he added a little something to her appearance, her manner or her interests.

His mother smiled warmly as he entered. Her delicious cooking filled the air with aroma. He realized suddenly that she was startlingly pretty, and she resembled a great deal the girl of his fantasy. She served him and chatted, took his money and gave him back some. He felt very adult as he took the large chair his father had bought secondhand, and rolled a cigarette. His mother put a big pot of water to heat so that he might bathe. There was a knock at the door.

At first Neftali didn't recognize the man. Then quickly he knew, and his surprise was enormous.

"Eduardo!" And he embraced the man, who had lived in the little village of Trainwreck as long as he could remember. It hadn't been so very long since he'd seen him, Neftali realized, but the man was ragged, unshaven and looked on the point of collapse from weariness.

Neftali turned to call his mother.

"Mama! It's Eduardo from Trainwreck. Here! He found us . . ."

His mother came smiling, and, incredibly, showed no surprise. Her face was shining as she embraced Eduardo, and Neftali saw it was more than an embrace of a casual acquaintance. His wits were reeling as he heard him say, "Lita. I came as soon as I heard."

And his mother said, "We've waited a long time. Can you ever forgive me?" And then he began to understand. His first reaction was violent emotion. *Faithless! Betrayer! Adulteress.* Then he calmed. His mother stood looking directly at him, taking in his confusion.

"I was a good, faithful wife to your father. And I would have remained so had he lived to be a hundred. But Eduardo and I knew we were meant for each other before your father ever came to Trainwreck. I did not send for him. But I knew he'd come. I have my things almost ready. I'm leaving to go back with him now." And there was no surprise on Eduardo's face.

And for the first time in his life Neftali was alone. The sound of the water boiling on the stove drew his attention. Odd how much noise boiling water made. He bathed and dressed in his good clothes and listened to the night sounds of the barrio begin. An impromptu mariachi group commenced its playing down the street. A horse-drawn wagon loaded with men returning from the fields to the barrio. Dogs barking and children screaming. From somewhere he heard a man's voice raised in drunken persistence, berating a woman. He thought of his fantasy girl. No, there would be none of that sort of thing in his house. Only harmony and affection.

He left the house, making sure it was locked and the iron rod hidden, and walked to the whorehouse where his sisters would be on Friday night. The man in the lobby summoned them and he told them of their mother's departure. He left them almost in shock and went to the bar where he'd met the man who had told him of Rabbit Town up near Los Angeles. Sure enough, Chonte was there.

"It's just a little place, maybe forty or fifty houses. That's all. And there's plenty of work within a few miles. Lots of crops. See Moran. He'll sell you a lot for a hundred dollars, complete with papers to prove you own it and you can build on it just how you want to."

When he got home from work on Monday he cooked his dinner and then lay down. He could have that hundred dollars in a few months if he saved. He'd eat sparingly and stay home, and be out of the barrio soon. He leaned back in his father's chair and tried to catch the words of a ranchero song that drifted in from a tavern a block down the street.

His fantasy girl was beginning to materialize when the door opened and Hortensia and Jilda stood there, gaudily dressed, smiling.

"Shame on you, a young man your age acting like a viejo. Come on, we're going to take you to the fights."

He was overjoyed to see them, and began to take his bath, asking about the fights, who was fighting, how much it cost and where they were staged.

"Over in the stadium. It's in the americano town, but it's all right for us, because many fighters are Mexicans," Hortensia told him.

"I was invited by one of the main fighters, who gave me free tickets. His name is Leonardo Salazar," Jilda said.

While he dressed, one of the girls ran to get a bottle of wine, and his spirits were so high he drank more than one large glass.

Then they walked to the stadium. Neftali found he was proud as the eyes of all the men went to his snappy-looking sisters as they crossed the barrio. The man at the door tore their tickets in half and handed the stubs to Neftali, who was momentarily embarrassed because he didn't understand this. They had seats near the ring.

Looking about, Neftali was surprised to see the hundreds of spectators were about half americanos and half Mexican. And he was delighted when Salazar came into the ring amid much shouting and praising from the latter, and then Salazar searched the rows until he saw Hortensia and Jilda and he waved, shouting, "Wish me luck."

Neftali had heard men in the orchards talk of the fights and when the bout began he found himself quite excited. Salazar was quicker and stronger than the gringo he was fighting, and the spirit of heckling and shouting that pervaded the spectators was contagious. He saw one americano stand up, cup his hands to his mouth and shout in terrible Spanish: "Murder him, Mason, murder him!"

The wine and excitement caught Neftali up, and he asked Hortensia, "Quick, tell me how to say 'hit him a good one' in English?" Hortensia thought a moment, then drilled him until he could say it clear enough to be understood. Then Neftali stood up and roared, "Geev eet to heem, Salazar!" Gringo and Mexican alike rocked with laughter at the pronunciation, and then another man picked it up: "Geev eet to heem, Salazar!" and soon dozens were echoing the chant.

At the end of the fight, when Salazar had thoroughly trounced his opponent, the referee grinned and announced through a megaphone: "The winner, Geev-eet-to-heem Salazar!" And even Neftali understood and rocked with laughter.

As they walked back, Neftali told his sisters of his plan, to go to the little place called Rabbit Town, the little Mexican settlement where he knew things would be different. They listened without taking offense as he talked of the pure girl he wanted, the family, how he would teach his children what things really mattered. "Hermanito," Jilda said, "you will not have to wait months for that hundred dollars. We'll give it to you now, all of it."

As the train rocked along beside the sea, sometimes climbing the stony cliffs to frightening heights, then coasting down to seashore level, Neftali remembered back to that other train ride, a few years before. How different this was. Now he was a paying passenger.

He sat at the rear of the passenger car, a large cardboard carton encircled by twine and containing his possessions next to him on the seat. He had his utensils, his clothes, some personal treasures he had collected all his life, and a few old cowhides in it.

The car was only half full of people, and when he entered he had unconsciously gone to the rear where two Negro men and several Mexican couples with children were seated. The seats faced one another and because it was convenient he sat facing the Negroes. The sight of them somewhat jarred him and he tried not to stare. He recalled having seen Negroes only once as they worked on a sewer project in the americano section of the city. They were black, blacker than the Indians he'd known in Mexico, and their hair was short and kinky-tight against the head. He had never seen anything like the flaring nostrils and heavy lips, and he was more than startled when one of them addressed him in perfect Spanish.

"You been working pretty steadily?"

Neftali fumbled for words. "No . . . yes, as steady as I want . . ."

One Negro seemed to sense his surprise. "We're from Texas. We're trying to find the right place to settle, and then send for our families. You're going to Los Angeles?"

"No. I'm going to a little town called Rabbit Town. Near Los Angeles. I've never been there, but I'm told I can buy some land and build a house of my own."

They were dressed in denims and heavy work shoes and each had two suitcases. Neftali was surprised to find they could read and pleased when they agreed to tell him when he came to the station nearest his destination.

They told him they had been farm hands in Texas but had heard jobs were plentiful in California and it was possible to buy property here. By the time the train arrived at the stop near Rabbit Town Neftali felt they were his friends and invited them to investigate the possibilities of the town with him.

It was a small station stop but there was a thriving little city next to it. Neftali was aware that the people around the station stared at the Negroes, but he found an old Mexican who knew about Rabbit Town.

"It's not called Rabbit Town so much anymore. It's called Irwindale. But that's where the only Mexican settlement is around here, outside of Los Angeles. Go out the main street here in town and keep going until you come to a dry river. Go north, toward the mountains, for about five miles and you'll come to a market at the corner of two dirt roads. That's it."

Carrying his large cardboard box on his shoulders, Neftali left with the two Negroes.

As they came to the end of the paved road Neftali saw the vast dry river bottom. Miles away on either side were green fruit orchards such as the train had journeyed through all morning, but here in the center of the valley, perhaps a dozen miles from the mountains towering in the north, was sand and gravel, scrub oak trees and giant cactus, thistles, nettles and brush. In the middle of the dry bed, which was about five miles across, ran a tiny stream, two or three feet wide, several inches deep. The afternoon heat was penetrating, but the water was cool and thirst-quenching.

Outside the small city no habitation was visible for a few miles, then a shack appeared now and then. Neftali felt an odd excitement as he was reminded of the little village in Mexico.

"Where I come from," he said to the Negroes, "the country

is much like this. Dry brush, cactus, and huts where people live."

Soon the path they followed turned into a road and before long they came to a loose gathering of shacks and stone houses surrounding a large frame building with a sign *MERCADO* on it. The rear of the store, apparently, was the living quarters of the proprietor. There were pens with chickens, goats, a cow, a few pigs, and some ducks.

Tired and dusty, the three travelers mounted the steps to the wooden porch at the front of the store and entered. Inside Neftali saw many familiar items: dried beef hanging from the ceiling, cornmeal ready to be made into tortillas, tripe, various types of chili peppers, a bin full of dried beans and flour in large cloth sacks. A heavy dark man appeared from the living quarters in the rear to serve them.

"This is the town of Irwindale?" Neftali asked.

"Sí. This is Irwindale," the man answered, eying the Negroes.

Neftali extended his hand. "My name is Neftali Sandoval. I came here because I heard I could buy some property and live in a community where there are no americanos." The proprietor looked again at the Negroes. "They too would like to find out about land," Neftali explained.

Without looking at them, the man said, "There is no Negro land here."

"They speak Spanish," Neftali informed him.

The man addressed the Negroes. "No, no land for Negroes here. But only a few miles to the north is a place where Negroes are settling. In this same river bed. Follow the same road and you'll come to it." His attitude was imperative as he pointed.

The Negroes shuffled their feet a little. They were being ejected, and their air of acquiescence showed it was not a new experience. Politely, they said good-bye, friend, to Neftali, picked up their suitcases and left. "I'll come and see you," Neftali called after them.

The proprietor introduced himself as Moran, and began telling Neftali about the land available in Irwindale.

"Come," Moran said, "I'll show you a lot that would be ideal for a youngster like you to build on." He called to his wife in the rear to mind the store should anyone enter, and he and Neftali set out on foot over the dirt roads of Irwindale.

Moran was gentle-spoken and sure of himself. He had shaggy black hair and a black mustache, although Neftali thought Moran should be getting gray. He reminded Neftali vaguely of Guzmán, the outlaw leader, but only in appearance. His speech was eloquent, and Neftali guessed he could read, write and speak English. Moran questioned him about his family, and Neftali found himself in tears when he told of how they came to the United States and how the family had disintegrated.

"My sisters," he said to Moran, "I miss them so much. Because I know they will never come to my home."

Moran nodded with understanding. "And your mother?"

Neftali brightened. "I'll see her again some day. Maybe I can send for her and my stepfather, if I ever have the money." But he knew his mother would never come, that she had hated every day of being away from the little village overlooking the pastures.

Moran led him over the winding dirt road. Huge stands of cactus were on either side. An occasional oak tree broke the monotonous landscape. The ground was made up of fine, powdery dirt and sand. They passed a house now and then and the residents waved at Moran. Finally they stopped and Moran began to tell Neftali about the history of the area.

"This rocky, cactus-covered area in the middle of the valley, it was once a great river. Long before the Spaniards came. Now it is only we who settle here, although there are those old timers living here—you'll meet them—who can remember back when our people owned all the land. See? To the left over there? Fertile orchards as far as you can see. And to the right. And in front of us and behind us. We owned all this long before the americanos came. Now we just have this rabbit town." As if to verify his words, a pair of jackrabbits darted from a clump of brush and raced away.

"How come," Neftali asked sincerely, "all the good land is now owned by the gringos?"

In a fatherly fashion, Moran put his arm on Neftali's shoulder. "Well, it happened like this. You know how the Jews are, don't you? Well when the americanos fought Mexico in the war, the americanos won. They conquered Mexico. You knew that, didn't you? But all the wealth, all the money here in California went to try to defeat the americanos. But they were too rich. They won. And all the great ranchos, hundreds of them all over California, were broke. Bankrupt. So then the americanos started pouring in. They took the land two ways. Many Jews were among the americanos. They always have lots of money. And they made big loans to the rancheros. At very high interest rates. And when the loans were due on one day, the next day the Jews were there with the sheriff to take over the land. That's how we lost all the big ranches."

"You said they took the land *two* ways."

"Sí. The other way was easier. The gringo law says if you

CHICANO

own land you must have what they call a legal description of it. Who ever shows the gringo authorities the first legal description of any land, he is the owner. Those Mexicans who did keep their land knew it had been given to them by either the King of Spain or the Governor of California. But it was not registered with the americanos. So the gringos came, moved in on the land and registered it, and when the Mexican owners protested, the sheriff said, 'Show me proof that this is your land.' And there was no proof, of course. Boundaries among the Mexicans had always been a matter of agreement between gentlemen. Not so with the Americans."

"But how do you come to own this land?"

"Ha! I was smart. I worked in a gringo town in Colorado, in the official's office. I learned how to register title. I came here and went looking for land unclaimed and unsettled. This land, here in Rabbit Town, had not been officially claimed. It was part of a big rancho once, but the owners long since were in bankruptcy. I found the records. The old Spanish land grant said the Ranchero Castillo was owner of all the land from the giant oak tree to the large boulder by the river, things like that. I had to make a survey, present the proper description, and I got title. It was a lot of work and all I have is rocks and cactus, but it will be our own community."

Neftali stood with Moran looking at the piece of property he was buying. It was situated on the main street, which was no more than a wide dirt thoroughfare from which most of the larger boulders and cacti had been removed. He had noticed the homes in the area were of mortared stone.

"You see," Moran pointed out, "building material here is cheap. There is abundant natural sand and millions of stones. Water can be carried from the little creek and all that is neces-

71

sary to build a fine house are sacks of cement and muscle. I can get the cement for you through my store. You have the main ingredients for a fine home, namely youth and strength."

Neftali looked over his property. Yes, he could see it. A nice house, wife and children, family dog, chicken coop. Within walking distance in every direction were farms and orchards. Yes, this was it. He felt excitement. "Will you show me how to register the land properly with the americanos?"

"Sí. I will do that for you. Come back to my store and we will get started. You have a hundred dollars?"

Neftali took a hand-sewn cloth money belt from beneath his shirt. He took a hundred dollars from it.

"I see that leaves you almost broke," Moran said. "Give me just seventy-five. I will order cement and tools for you. You'll have to have enough to live on until you find a job and get paid."

When they returned to the store a family was buying groceries. Moran introduced Neftali to the Mendez family.

The Mendez house was closer to Neftali's property than any other. Mendez was delighted with his young new neighbor, and while they talked Neftali made a great effort to avoid looking at a young Mendez girl about his own age.

"Look, joven," Señor Mendez said, "I have a nice shed at the rear of my lot I used for storing wood. A little fixing up and you can live there until your house is built. You can use our toilet, too."

Neftali started working at his dream. He envisioned a dynastic type of life. He would find a wife soon, have many children, who would grow up, marry and build near his house.

Within a few days he got a job in the orchards. And each evening when he came home he worked on his house. He used all the stones he could from his own lot, thus helping to clear it, and then searched for usable rocks on the surrounding land. And when it got too dark to work, he would go to the Mendez house and eat, maybe sing a little with the family while Señor Mendez accompanied on the guitar, and he would exchange sly glances with Alicia, the girl about his own age.

One Saturday night she asked him, "Are you going to work on your house tomorrow?"

"Of course."

"I'll bring you some lunch."

When she came with tacos wrapped in a cloth that had once been a flour sack, he sat on a large boulder and talked to her while he ate.

"Where I work, I'm now stacking crates. If I'm lucky, I can get on with the packing plant crew. Then I'll have a steady job year round. First I'll be loading the boxcars, but then if I work hard I can get on inside the packing plant, and it won't matter when winter comes. That's my ambition."

He told her of the plans for the house, showed her where the kitchen would be, the bedroom, and the rooms he would add as his family grew.

Every day off from work he toiled tirelessly on his house, and regularly Alicia would come to bring him food and talk. One day she noticed he had a head cold.

"I'll fix you a cure," she said, and ran home. Soon she returned with a necklace made of string threaded through cloves of fresh garlic. "Here, put this around your neck under your shirt and the cold will be gone in a few days."

At work the next day he did not need to tell his fellow workers he was wearing the cold cure. "That's the best thing," they said, "it works every time."

And when he developed a severe cough, Alicia went to the

creek and picked the blossoms from a pungent small tree. She made tea by boiling the flowers and brought it to Neftali steaming hot. He gagged at the acrid, licorice taste and heady fumes that stung his nasal passages, but in a little more than a week the cough was gone.

It took about a year, but finally Neftali's house was complete enough to be lived in. He had proudly kept Alicia informed of his professional progress, and he now worked inside the packing plant, and was thus a member of a rather elite stratum.

Neftali found that more and more he was looking at Alicia's big bottom, her strong brown legs and huge bosom, which thrust forward the entire front of her long and faded dress, making her appear even heavier than she was. She had an angelic face, her long black hair usually shone, and her bare feet were perfectly formed. Neftali's ideal fantasy girl, the one that looked hauntingly like his mother, began to fade, as Alicia had the decided advantage of being present in the abundant flesh, as well as being the only eligible girl his age in the vicinity. He felt guilty over abandoning the girl in his fantasy. Also over picturing himself lying on top of Alicia, feeling those huge breasts against his chest. Nights alone in the woodshed, knowing Alicia slept just inside a broken window fifty feet away, became an ordeal. He realized that the lewd, imagined goings-on were indecent as long as they were not married, so he began conducting the fantasy in the respectability of imagined matrimony.

The day came when he shakily called Señor Mendez to his house on the pretext of showing him his latest project.

"It's all ready," he said with matter-of-fact pride. "I just need to get some more furniture. Then it will be ready for Alicia and me to live in as soon as we're married."

Neither man batted an eye, and Mendez commented on what

an adequate house it was. They discussed the house, jobs, the community, but neither mentioned the coming marriage again.

When Mendez went home he called his wife to him.

"Have you told Alicia about what married people do to make babies?"

"No . . . I haven't . . ."

"Well, you'd better. Young Neftali wants to marry her. She's nearly eighteen, and if she doesn't get married now she may never."

Within a year Neftali and Alicia had a child. Within another year they had another. And the third year they had a third. World War I came and went and Neftali never understood much more than that they didn't take those who spoke no English or those with a family like his. The couple's reproductive pace slackened, and at the end of ten years they had six children and another coming.

Neftali was twenty-seven years old, and he began casting about for perhaps another means of earning a living.

The town's homes were furnished water by a complex but satisfactory system worked out generations before by the people of arid territories. A network of ditches originating at the stream, crisscrossed the community, and the community's only elected official, the zanjero, from the Spanish word zanja, meaning ditch, was charged with the responsibility of seeing that the hand-dug cistern at each home was kept full of fairly clear and pure water.

Neftali decided to run for public office and become the town zanjero. The present zanjero's term had several more months to run, but people were already a little disgusted with him. Neftali set about learning the job of keeper of the ditches. He saw that the job was fairly easy and the zanjero's main duty was to see that the channels remained intact, that no children played in the water, that all dead animals were promptly removed, and that each cistern was kept full, yet no water wasted by neglecting to divert the flow when a cistern was filled.

The campaign for the office was bitter, but Neftali Sandoval won out over the incumbent zanjero, who had acquired a reputation for drinking on the job. A main issue at election time was the carcass of a dead goat that had remained in the main channel for two weeks. Also a dike had broken once, flooding the main street and several homes, and the hastily summoned crew that repaired it had later found the zanjero drunk in a tavern.

Each morning at dawn Don Neftali set out on foot to tour the entire channel system. Regularly he stopped at houses to ask when they would need the cistern filled. He supervised the building of a bridge over the main channel, so wagons wouldn't get stuck crossing town. He was the best zanjero Irwindale ever had.

It was the first time Don Neftali ever had a salary by the month. Each home owner was assessed a specific amount each month for water service, and this amount was his salary. With his previous jobs, Don Neftali had been paid by the hour at the end of each day or week, or by piece work after a few days service. He was hard pressed the first month as zanjero, waiting for his payday, and when it came he promptly loaded all his children into his four-wheeled wagon, hitched up his two horses and went to El Monte, where he bought each of them—except the youngest—a pair of shoes.

The Sandoval children were the only ones in the community with shoes, and they wore them every day. They had no socks, and it wasn't long before their shoes began to smell, as the residue of perspiration accumulated. Their feet began to itch, and soon cracks appeared between the toes.

Alicia knew precisely what the trouble was.

"The European Itch," she scolded her husband. "They cannot wear shoes without socks. Go buy some."

She knew the cure for athlete's foot, if not the proper name for it. She gathered all the children together. She had a large washtub, big enough to bathe in, and, shouting orders in her shrill, loud voice, boxing an ear here, whacking a bottom there, she had all the infected children stand naked in the tub together.

"Now, urinate," she ordered. The children obeyed. She directed the boys to aim at the feet. The girls were less adept at accuracy. Soon a dozen little dirty feet were drenched in urine, and the squirting match was over quickly as the little bladders were depleted.

"Now," Mama Sandoval said, "go play. Leave your shoes off from now on unless we go someplace to visit or to church. Leave all your shoes outside in the open for three days."

When a doctor in a neighboring town heard the cure she'd used he shook his head sadly. "These superstitions," he muttered. "Athlete's foot can't be cured. But I have special powders that can arrest it." But from that day forward, cracks between the toes of the Sandoval children dried up and healed. The itching disappeared and never returned.

Then one day not too long after Neftali had been elected zanjero, progress caught up with him. The americanos, the gringos, tried to explain in their broken Spanish about collective effort, county taxes, water districts, and bond issues. He understood none of that, but he did understand they were sealing off the river and were running pipes all over.

With typical Yankee speed and efficiency, they stopped the flow of water and within days ran a huge main pipe into Irwindale, and within days after that a small pipe with a faucet was supplying each home with fresh running water. There was no more need for cisterns, for ditches, or for a zanjero.

On the day Don Neftali's job officially ended, he got up early, borrowed a wagon and team, loaded up the older children and drove to the foothills, where he knew of a huge dead oak tree. He spent the day chopping and sawing the tree. The children played and helped stack the wood in the wagon. By nightfall, Neftali was weary from hard work. He drove home the wagon loaded with wood and children and the next day he began selling wood.

There was no piped gas in Irwindale. All cooking was done on wood stoves, and his seasoned oak wood was much in demand. He had made a huge wheelbarrow—the only one in Irwindale—and for ten cents a customer could load it up and take it home—if he brought the wheelbarrow back immediately. For a few cents more, Neftali would deliver a load of wood to the customer's home at the end of the day. This now was his living. On alternate days he drove to the foothills, to the San José hills to the east, or to the La Puente hills to the south. His children scouted for seasoned timber, and he cut, sawed and hauled, and every other day he was a wood salesman in Irwindale.

Then progress again caught up with Neftali Sandoval, again in the form of iron pipes, this time carrying natural gas. He fought it for a while, as not many could afford a gas burner, but he soon saw what was inevitable.

The surrounding communities had long had piped water and gas, and Irwindale was catching up with the world. There was no fighting it.

Neftali Sandoval went back to packing oranges.

Angelina Sandoval was the eldest offspring of Don Neftali and Doña Alicia Sandoval. Her first impression of the world around her had been negative. When she was a toddler her parents made no attempt to hide their disappointment at her being born a girl. The oldest child, she came to realize, should always be a boy. When the first born was a girl, a little awkwardness was involved in overlooking her and bypassing her in favor of the first boy to be born in the family. Thank God, Don Neftali and Doña Alicia thought when their second child was a boy. Now, regardless of the sex or number of subsequent progeny, the family pattern could commence. The eldest son would be second in command in the family. He would be consulted (and only he) concerning any plans regarding building, moving or the acquisition of anything material. He would inherit, regardless of the needs of any of the other siblings. If the family could afford only one education, or only one of anything advantageous, it would be his. This was a custom, a way of life which the family accepted without question—except when a girl was born first. Then the family accepted this way of life and this custom with a tiny bit of question.

Augmenting the awkwardness of the situation were several things. First, Angelina was a very bright child, and had to go to school in the nearby Anglo community. Within a few years she was speaking and reading English, and she learned that the rest of the world didn't feel about first-born sons and daughters the way her parents felt. Her first reaction was that she had been cheated by being a girl. Her second was that the subsequent children had been cheated by having an elder brother. Another reaction was that her younger brother, who was the older brother, was extremely selfish in thinking that things were fine just as they were.

One morning when Angelina was about eight years old, and Gregorio was seven, and Victorio was six, and Luisa was five, and Orlando was four, and little Pedro was three, and Roberto, Rita, and Delores were not born yet, the family was seated at the table having breakfast.

On the large stove, which had little silica windows through which could be seen red flames eating at chunks of wood, cooked four big, round tortillas made of flour. The old wooden table, covered by a stained, torn oilcloth, supported plates of fried rabbit—Don Neftali had shot the rabbits in the back yard that very morning while the family slept—the inevitable pot of beans, and fried potatoes. The children all talked or hollered at one another, while their father occasionally raised his voice, threatening corporal punishment as the alternative to silence. In a thread-bare sweater, with nothing underneath, and cotton trousers and ankle-high heavy shoes, he dished out portions of food according to the size of the individual child. He allowed only four-year-old Orlando and three-year-old Pedro to eat with their hands. The others ate with metal utensils.

When the first four tortillas were cooked to a spotted brown and white, Alicia Sandoval took two and handed them to her husband. The other two were divided up among the grasping little hands, and four more tortillas were set to cook on the near red-hot stove top. Alicia wore an old and ragged cotton print dress and hand-stitched leather slippers. Nothing more. She wore her jet-black hair in a bun at the back. She was now heavy and solid, and commanded her children's respect in more ways than one. All who knew her were aware of her unwavering, immense mother love, which motivated her life far more than anything else, which influenced her every movement, even as her strong hand flicked out to crack sharply against a little cheek or bottom.

Several goats, kept in a pen attached to the rear of the stone house, supplied the Sandoval children with fresh milk daily and with cheese occasionally. The pen was next to the kitchen-front room-dining room in which the family ate, cooked and lived most of the time, and a small window, left open in the warm months, blocked off in the winter, looked out at the pen. A larger goat, by standing on its hind legs, could thrust its head partway through the window in the thick stone wall and bleat, begging for food, until another goat, overcome by jealousy, shoved it aside to take its place.

"Do not feed the goats while we are eating," Don Neftali had ordered many times. And while he wasn't watching, the children tossed little morsels of tortillas or potato to the goat at the window, and the goat would either snap them up or plaintively watch them fall back to the stone floor out of reach. The little window not only provided an outlook post for keeping an eye on the animals, but also solved the Sandoval's garbage problem.

The goats had had a problem too. When the leftovers were dumped into their pen through the window, the family dog, a large mongrel, would crawl under the fence and intimidate the herd, while taking his pick of the garbage. Then a young billy goat started to mature. At first there were terrific fights between the young billy and the dog. The children would shriek, fearing one would be hurt.

"Let them alone," Papa Sandoval would say. "They will settle it." And sure enough. The dog soon found that at best he was taking a terrible battering for such a small reward. And then as the billy continued to mature, the battering became even more severe, and the dog was completely outclassed by the sharp hoofs and ram's horns. The dog withdrew to the other side of the house to be content with bones, fat, gristle and sour milk.

Now the dog lay at the doorstep of the front room, peering through the slats that formed a coarse screen on a door frame, anticipating the rabbit bones and entrails that would soon be his when the family finished eating.

Little Pedro squealed in delight as he shoved a handful of beans into his mouth. Angelina took a large square white cloth that had been a flour sack, now used as a napkin by all the children in turn, and wiped the bean-and-potato-streaked face of her youngest brother. Through eating, Papa Sandoval sat finishing his coffee, rolling a cigarette, regarding first Angelina and then the family pride, the oldest son, Gregorio.

"Too bad," he said to his wife for the hundredth time, "that she had to be so light and he so dark."

Doña Alicia looked for the ten millionth time at the dark, homely, Indian-like face of her oldest son. It almost seemed to her that Gregorio's face became a shade darker at hearing his father's words. The boy was looking intently at Angelina.

"Yes," the mother said as she had so many times before, "had he been born first, he would have had the light skin."

Angelina found herself returning Gregorio's stare. She knew the parents' words did not hurt him, only remind him. It was at school. The Anglo kids. How they taunted him, left him out. There were many other Mexican children at the school, but only a few were as dark, squat-featured and . . . non-Anglo looking—she realized—as her brother. She had many times examined herself in the piece of broken mirror above the stone sink. Her olive skin—lighter, actually—black hair, black eyes with a tiny bit of what looked like smoke in the whites, her features, all combined to make her look, Mexican to be sure, but very unlike Gregorio. The other Sandoval children varied in appearance between the relative extremes of Angelina and Gregorio.

Now the other children looked at the two older ones, then began screaming at their mother, "Mama! How light am I?" "I'm lighter than you!" "Look here, Mama," said Victorio, showing the untanned underside of his arm.

By virtue of the futility of the situation, Angelina felt but little sympathy for Gregorio. She remembered his severe rebuff when, in the unintentionally cruel way of children, the Anglo kids let Gregorio know his being the oldest son meant nothing to them. Well she could understand his dislike at leaving this little community whenever it was necessary, where being the eldest son entitled him to accompany his father on adult business to other homes where his position in the family was recognized as an important one. But Angelina had heard even the friendliest, most well-intentioned of neighbors in Irwindale say, "Too bad he's so dark. Poor thing."

At the age of sixteen Angelina was told by her father to stay out of school and work in a nearby packinghouse to help support the family. Gregorio, a year younger, stayed in school. "It's necessary that he prepare himself," the old man said, but Angelina never did quite understand what he was to prepare himself for. Then when Victorio was sixteen, he also went to work beside his father in the fields, and the following year when Rosita was sixteen, she too went to work.

Don Neftali's plan was to get Gregorio started in a little cobbler shop. While modernization had defeated Neftali on different occasions in the past, "People will always need shoes," he told his family. And it was necessary that Gregorio get all the schooling he can, so that he might be a successful businessman. There was an old, old man, so old he could remember the gringos arriving around Rabbit Town in covered wagons, and he had been a zapatero, a cobbler. Neftali invited him to the house, and the three of them, Neftali, the old man and Gregorio, made plans. They would build a little shop next to the house. With the money the older children earned, Neftali would buy the necessary equipment and pay the old man—Pelón, Baldy, he was called—to teach Gregorio the cobbling trade. And within a few months Gregorio drove a large stake into the ground in front of the house and nailed a hand-lettered sign reading ZAPATERO across it.

But the year was 1941. The family for years had had delivered a daily English language newspaper. Now the children read to Neftali, translating into Spanish the news, and explaining why all the boys over eighteen had to register for the draft. Pedro was just eighteen and Gregorio was twenty-two years old, and Victorio and Orlando were in between. Together, Gregorio assuming leadership, they went to the nearest town to register, and within weeks they were all told to report for induction, except for Orlando, who was retarded. Neftali and Alicia had recognized his affliction and taken him out of school early, dubbed him Poca Luz, and had him work in the fields. To them he could be as useful as anyone else, even if the gringo schools didn't want him.

The war dragged on. The three boys came home several times, rarely together. Neftali noticed they were changing. With the exception of Gregorio, they seemed only to tolerate the family system and traditions of Neftali and their mother

Alicia. "I bought a stitching machine," Neftali proudly told them. "When Gregorio returns for good, he'll have a fine business."

On a hot, dusty afternoon as Angelina arrived home from the packing plant she found a Western Union messenger trying to make her mother and father understand they were to accept and sign for a telegram. She signed and thanked the messenger, then turned to her wide-eyed parents. She had already seen it was from the War Department. A chilling lump formed in her stomach as she kept her face calm and opened the envelope. *Which one?*

She read the brief sentences with hardly more than a glance and then said softly, "It's a death notice, Papa."

Neftali's face grew taut and white, and Alicia's head began shaking as her face screwed up. "Which one?" Neftali asked, trembling, "Not Gregorio, I know."

Angelina knew there was no kind, pleasant way.

"Yes, Gregorio has been killed." She felt as though she was in a trance as she saw her father stiffen, and her mother begin tearing her hair and screaming. It was more than an hour later before Neftali and Alicia could ask for further details, and Angelina gave them what meager information the telegram contained, that Gregorio was buried on a little island in the Pacific, that his belongings would be coming soon. She left them clutching one another and set about to inform her other Army brothers so they might be home for the services.

Pedro and Victorio came home and the family walked to the little stone church a quarter mile away. After the services, the family walked slowly back, through the fields of cactus and sand and boulders, to the stone house Neftali had built himself.

They sat around the kitchen-living room, the Sandoval

family, now reduced to ten members. Pedro and Victorio, still in their immaculate Army uniforms, said nothing. The younger children began warily to play and drift into the added stone rooms. Neftali and Alicia sat at the dinner table, palms to their foreheads, stifling sobs.

Victorio, now the eldest son, broke the silence.

"Papa, I can take over the cobbler shop. Perhaps not as well as Gregorio could have, but I can turn it into a thriving business, once I'm out of the Army. I know I can . . ."

Neftali shook his head. "No. It wasn't meant to be. There won't be a cobbler shop. I have already made arrangements with Pelón to buy the equipment and supplies. None of you has had the training or preparation to begin a business." And he continued to brood over the death of his eldest son.

They sat. Soon all the younger children were in the other rooms, away from the despair and depression. The older offspring sat self-consciously, occasionally glancing at one another, knowing sooner or later the mood would have to change. The soldiers found themselves looking at Angelina. Somehow, her face was different from what it should be. She wore a black dress, almost tight, showing off her well-shaped figure. Her long black hair was smooth and shiny. Her expression was one now of anger and impatience instead of grief. Suddenly she arose, standing straight and tall.

She spoke English, as they all did when they preferred that their parents not understand the conversation. "Well, I've had enough." She said it simply, with conviction, hands on hips as she faced her brothers. They looked puzzled. The old man looked up from the table, a little annoyed.

"What do you mean?" Victorio asked, his voice low, his attitude still one of remorse.

Angelina looked at each one a moment before continuing.

"I mean, when you guys get out of the Army you can come back here and spend the rest of your life picking oranges and using an outside open toilet, but you won't find me here."

Pedro was looking at her evenly, but Victorio seemed angered. "Angie! What are you talking about?"

Neftali Sandoval raised his voice above the others.

"Now listen! I won't have you speaking English in front of your mother and me. We have the right to know . . ."

Angelina turned to him, speaking politely but firmly.

"Please, Papa. Stay out of this. We have something to discuss. When we work it out we'll tell you about it."

Rarely had a son or daughter talked back to him, but Neftali knew this was one of the changes coming about in the younger generation raised away from the old country. He remained silent.

Angelina continued. "You, Victorio, are a gutless wonder. You won't say a word about Papa not letting you run a shop. He'd rather give it away than let one of you take Gregorio's place. Well, listen to me. I paid for half that Goddamn stuff there, and helped support Gregorio while he sat on his ass learning to drive tacks into soles. Christ, I'm twenty-three years old, and you know how many dates I've had? Not one real one, that's how many. Every time a boy came to see me papa would interview him. Or worse yet—and I truthfully couldn't stand it another time—if Papa wasn't going to be here he'd appoint Gregorio to look him over. And if he looked like a good prospect for me"—she jerked her thumb—"out he'd go. Because I'm needed to help bring in money."

Victorio was looking shocked. Orlando sat uncertainly, as usual, taking it all in. Pedro, however, was listening intently.

Victorio said, "Angie, all this was for your own good. Dad was raised in the old country. We shouldn't be talking like this about the old traditions . . ."

"Oh, crap. I'll tell you how sacred the old traditions are. If things had been really tough, he'd have married me off to the first cholo that came along when I was fifteen. But I was able to work all the time. So that makes him extremely selective in my behalf. Now there's not a guy within ten miles who'll come near me, because he'll have to give a personal history to Dad or my brother. I've had it and I'm getting the hell out of here, and if you guys are smart, you won't come back."

Victorio persisted. "But the folks. They need money. Dad makes very little and there's still the younger kids . . ."

"Good grief, Victor. I could get a factory job in the city, support myself and still send Mama and Papa more money than I make packing fruit."

"But . . . living by yourself in a city . . . it's not proper for a girl . . ."

"*Girl!* I'm practically an old maid."

"There'd be none of us to look after you and see that you meet the right boy . . ."

Angelina gave a huge shrug and turned her back. "It's hopeless. The way you're talking, I'm more than ever convinced I've got to get out of here. Now. Immediately."

Pedro stood up and spoke for the first time. "She's right, Vic. That's the way I feel, too." He spoke with more of a Spanish accent than the others, and now his voice cracked, as though he was ready to cry. "I'm tired of this way. All my life, I've had the feeling I don't matter to Mama and Papa. I helped pay for Gregorio's shop also. I'm good enough to work hard in the fields from age sixteen, but not good enough to learn to use the tools I sweated to help buy. Since I've been in the Army I've learned other people don't live like we do. Not even the mejicanos in the cities. They laugh and say we're Mexican hillbillies."

Orlando sat listening, squinting, concentrating, trying to understand. He remained silent. Neftali sat glaring, impatiently waiting to be told what the heated conversation was about. Alicia looked bewildered. She too had not understood a word.

Victorio stared at Angelina a few moments, then said, "All right. What do you plan to do?"

She faced him squarely. "Get out of here. Now. Today, quickly, so there's not the slightest chance I'll lose my nerve and reconsider for even a week."

"Where'll you go?"

"The Ornelas family. They live in East Los Angeles. Olivia Ornelas invited me to come and stay there. There's plenty of defense plant work. And I'm going."

They all looked at one another. Neftali cleared his throat.

"Okay, now tell *them* about it," Victorio said, indicating their parents. Angelina waited a long moment, sighed, then turned to her mother and father still seated at the dinner table.

"Papa, Mama, please try to understand . . ."

I don't understand," Neftali said when she'd finished. "Why? We have it good here. We've always had plenty to eat. So we all do have to work hard. The Bible says . . ."

"Don't try, Papa," Angelina said softly. "My mind's made up. I'm going to get my things together now."

Neftali's eyes were watering. "I know, this never would

have happened in Mexico. It's because you see all the gringos, who have no sense of proper behavior. No one looks after the gringas to see that every man that happens by doesn't take advantage of them. It's because you've seen them in their loose way, that you no longer want to have propriety . . ."

Angelina pressed her forefinger to his lips gently to shut off the conversation. There were tears in her eyes too as she said, "You're right, Papa."

Pedro coughed once and came to stand in front of his father.

"I have to be getting back to camp," he said, a little nervously. "I'll walk with Angelina to the bus stop and leave from there. I'd better be going. The Army is hard on you when you're late." He paused, obviously wanting to say more. Neftali waited. "And Papa, when I get out in a year or so, I'll come to see you. But don't make plans for me. I have plans of my own."

Neftali looked at him hard for nearly a minute. Then he slumped a little. "All right, son," he said. He looked at Victorio. "And you? Are you wanting to leave your family, too?"

Victorio looked at the stone floor. "No, Papa. I'll come back to stay."

Neftali regarded Orlando, still sitting silently on the couch. "And my son with the small light in his brain," he said fondly, "he'll always be with me."

3

Julio Salazar, age thirteen, awoke and stretched lazily on the stale-smelling mattress which he shared on the floor of the one-room cabin with his two smaller sisters and a smaller brother. He could hear his mother outside, under the tin roof which was really an extension of the roof of the cabin, with no walls, under which his two older brothers slept.

Only a week before the Salazar family had come here from the valley in the desert, where the family had shared a large barn with three other families of field workers. Julio liked this ranch best. He remembered it from the previous season, for his father had a regular itinerary for most of the year; walnuts in the Pomona Valley at one season, oranges nearby at another, stoop crops in the desert country at another time of the year, and the grape country of Fresno County in the late spring. He liked this place best because the family was given a cabin with running water from a tap just outside the door. When the family came here, school was just about out, so no one bothered to pester the kids about enrolling so close to the end of the term.

Out here in the middle of the vineyards there were a dozen cabins close together along a dirt road. It was like a village in the midst of the sprawling acreage of grape vines which stretched to every horizon, broken here and there by a ranch house, a barn, storage facilities, shacks for the migrant workers and a complex system of railroad laterals which allowed trains to pick up the crops in the fields.

Julio was dressed in cotton trousers, which he wore night and day until they became too dirty, which was not very often, since at every chance he climbed into one of the large concrete wareboxes which dotted the vineyards, inside of which water bubbled up from a pipe below and spilled out into troughs running to the rows of vines.

He stepped out into the hot dust and warm sunshine, listening to his mother, who was cooking on an open grated fireplace, talking in her rapid-fire, shrill Spanish: "This is Sunday. We should all be up early and go to Mass. We could get there if we really tried. We are lucky enough to have a car. At least we should spend our day of rest dressed in our nicest clothes. Hurry up, all of you, if you want to eat . . ."

The two older boys, Carlos, sixteen, and Ernesto, seventeen, were lazily getting up from their cots near the fire. Carlos poured hot water into a tin washbasin and shaved by a little round mirror tacked onto a post supporting the tin roof which gave them shelter. They both dressed in cotton dress trousers, shiny at the seat, and silk shirts, the type rodeo riders wore, and ankle-high shoes.

"Where's Papa?" the older boy asked his mother.

"Where do you think?" his mother replied with some disgust, glancing down the dirt road toward where it seemed to disappear in a mosaic of vineyards. "He will be back when he's had enough drinking and fighting."

While his mother prepared the chili and corn for breakfast, Julio's older brothers took the two family guitars and started strumming, trading new rhythms learned, or words to yet another song to be added to the seemingly endless repertoire. The younger children awoke hungry, and all ate outside, scooping up chili with tortillas, drinking coffee from tin cups. Then the older boys turned again to playing their guitars and singing. As though by unspoken agreement, the neighbors from the nearby cabins began to accumulate, some bringing their own guitars or violins.

When a dozen or so had gathered, and Mrs. Salazar resignedly cut up the last of her pork to make a big pot of chili con carne for the afternoon singfest, Julio walked casually away down the dirt road. He knew it would be a day of singing and lounging for the workers in the labor village. They would sing endlessly of love, fighting, ranch life, which none of them had ever known, and magnificent horses. In the early afternoon wine would be brought out, and perhaps by evening a small-scale fiesta would be in progress. But none of this was ever planned. It just happened.

Julio made his way down the dirt road, past the dozen little cabins like his own. On each side of the road the rows of grapevines waited with heavy burden for the hooked knife of the crop pickers. Every day of the week but Sunday the families worked in the fields—fathers, mothers, and older sisters and brothers. Each family had its own area, and stacked the crates of grapes at one particular spot, to avoid confusion of payment.

Each wooden crate of picked grapes was worth two cents to

the vineyard owner. A hard-working man could make three or four dollars a day by great effort and long hours. A hard-working wife could earn almost a comparable amount, as could older sons and daughters.

In this California of the 1930s the farm labor people knew little of the economic disaster overtaking the nation. Little of the headline news of gangsters and movie stars filtered down to them. They were perhaps better off than millions of other Americans, for through the family effort the Salazars were able to own a car, actually an old sedan with the back half of the body cut away and a wooden floor added to make a homemade pickup truck. They were able to have meat much of the time and wear clothes that were not ragged. The only evidence here of the economic straits gripping the nation was the occasional battered car with out-of-state license plates, loaded with Anglo families that came to look but usually left without inquiring for work after seeing the dark, serious faces and hearing the jabber of a foreign language.

As he walked Julio kept an eye on the vineyards. He was expected to pick the grapes also, but he had other things to do, so he had devised a scheme to raid the neat stacks of full crates of grapes at the ends of the rows picked by other workers. By being careful, he could steal large bunches off the top of a very full crate, or perhaps entire crates, if they were stacked randomly and thus unlikely to be missed. These he took to the spot where he stored the product of his own labor, and each evening at count time his father was pleased to see how much his thirteen-year-old son had picked.

This left him free during the working day to steal quietly back to the cabin and play the guitar, or to walk around to the ranch house, where the owner lived, and watch what went on in that different world, from an unseen vantage point.

He felt the hot desert air moving across his skin as he walked in the ankle-deep light brown dust of the road. A million insects buzzed, hissed or clicked. No other sound could be heard.

He followed the dirt road to where it ended, intersecting a broader gravel-covered road lined with small eucalyptus trees. Turning right, he saw his father's car, and a few other battered old cars, parked by the tavern. Sure enough, while he was still fifty feet away he heard his voice, raised in drunken argument.

The tavern was merely a large roof of corrugated metal over a counter and table and handmade benches. An old large icebox was behind the counter. The floor was dirt. There were no walls, but kerosene lamps hung from the rafters supporting the tin roof.

His father Leonardo was seated at a table with four other men. All had glasses of wine. As Julio approached the familiar and exciting aroma of alcohol came to him.

Julio loved his father, but felt guilty because of a contemptuous superiority he also felt. His father had once been a prize fighter, fighting in arenas up and down the state. His father spoke English quite well, while his mother spoke none. His father was literate, frequently quoting from Cervantes and Lope de Vega and he knew hundreds, perhaps thousands, of those little adages in Spanish with which it is possible to carry on a complete conversation.

Many times Julio had watched his father in a tavern talking with a man, then arguing a senseless point, insisting on his viewpoint; then the threats would come, then the fight and oddly, though he fought well, Julio supposed his father never really cared whether he won or lost. Afterward, either bloody and beaten, or hurrying home to await fearfully the knock on the door of the law looking for the attacker of the man beaten senseless, his father seemed gentle and satisfied.

Now he approached and stood at his father's elbow. The man didn't notice at first, so busy was he defending a foolish point. Then he looked at Julio. "Hijo! How are you? Have you come to spy on your poor father?" The men laughed. Julio stood silently, dark eyes flashing. His father raised his glass and drank deeply, leaving an inch or so in the glass, which he handed to Julio. Julio drained it in a gulp, making a wry face which again made the men laugh. Then he stood by as his father continued the argument. Julio did not push his luck. He knew as the men became more loosened by alcohol, they would give him more and more of their wine, until at last he felt that light-headed happiness which released him to sing, shout, laugh or run on the instant, whichever occurred to him.

The men at the table called to the tavern keeper, an old bent and toothless man who lived in an abandoned and wheelless boxcar behind the tavern. The old man went to the icebox and took out an earthen jug. He filled the large glasses on the table, collected five cents from each man, and resumed his silent watch behind the counter.

Two hours later, after Julio had drained an inch or so of wine from a dozen glasses, and his father was calling his opponent a dumb son of a whore, the fight started.

They were still seated and with an oath the man pulled a knife, but before it could be brought into play Leonardo Salazar leaned across the narrow table and smashed his great fist into the man's face. The man fell backward onto the floor, but rose, teeth gritted as he advanced toward Salazar. Julio was wide-

CHICANO

eyed, but stood fascinated. His father, jabbing and punching, shredded the man's face and once more knocked him to the dirt floor. Then as the man crawled toward him, still brandishing the knife, Leonardo Salazar kicked him hard in the face, and the man rolled over and lay motionless. Before he could do more, the old tavern keeper, with surprising speed and dexterity, was hitting Julio's father on the back with a club.

"Fuera! Fuera!" he screamed. Get out! Get out! "Don't ever come back here again to make trouble. You're a bad customer. Don't come back." Under the hail of blows from the older man, Leonardo Salazar ran out of the tavern to his car. Julio followed, but as his father tried to start the old machine, Julio darted back to the tavern. The keeper was helping the downed man.

"My father wants the change from his dollar," Julio said.

The tavernkeeper had already pocketed the ninety-five cents Julio's father had left, but reluctantly gave it to the boy. Julio tucked it into his pocket and started for home. His father was already driving crazily down the dirt road.

The scene in the little cabin was a familiar one. His father lying on the bed, bragging profanely of the fight; his mother ministering to the cuts on his arms and the gash on his back, deploring his behavior and the possible consequences. Julio's older brothers and several neighbors from the nearby cabins were still singing under the tin roof.

The large pot of chili his mother had made was half gone. The singers and their audience had plates or cups full of it, and Julio helped himself. He could never have done this on any other day but the festive Sunday. He would have had to wait until supper time no matter how hungry he was. He finished eating and sat on a stump, joining in the singing. A teen-age girl one of his brothers was interested in came out of a house in what were obviously her best clothes. Julio's brother had been watching her cabin, and now he handed the guitar to Julio and started toward the girl. Without the slightest hesitation Julio took up the accompaniment to the singing, playing strong forceful chords, keeping a steady, intricate rhythm.

No one heard the big sedan until it pulled to a stop in front of the Salazar cabin. In it was the ranchowner, a tall, lanky, and muscular man in his mid-forties, clean-shaven, sandy-haired, dressed in pressed trousers and sport shirt. The group ceased singing and waited respectfully as he got out and approached them. Julio's brother stepped forward and addressed him pleasantly in English.

"How are you, Mr. Thompson?"

Mr. Thompson smiled benignly. "Fine, Salazar. Having a little music, eh?"

"Yes. We like to keep in practice."

The ranchowner's eyes lighted on Julio, standing with the guitar hanging by the cord around his neck. "We're having a little party for the youngsters at the house," he said. "Wonder if we might borrow the kid here to give us a little music."

Julio's brother was puzzled, but he said to his young brother in Spanish, "Want to go to the ranch house to play for a gringo party?"

"Yes," Julio said with a little excitement showing. He had never been to the ranch house, but he had lain in the shrubs around it and watched the activity of a boy and girl about his age. Now he was being invited, although he knew it was only because of his musical ability. He started forward to get into the sedan.

"You can put on some clothes, can't you?" the ranchowner said, as close to politely as he could manage. Julio looked at his brother, who motioned him inside the house with a flick of the head.

Julio heard Mr. Thompson talking with some of the others who spoke English, about crops, water problems, market value, next year's possibilities; in a few minutes Julio stepped out in dress pants and a white shirt buttoned at the collar. He also wore a sash his mother had hurriedly tied around his waist when she heard, to her great relief, what Thompson wanted, and his hair was slicked down with oil. He wore no shoes. He had outgrown his last pair months earlier.

Mr. Thompson held the front door of the car open for Julio, who climbed in quickly. On the ride to the ranch house Julio was inclined to be shy, but he was learning the lessons of life well. He sensed that his appearance, his straightforward, naïve attitude and his handsome brown face and quick smile were things all people liked.

They drove into the yard through large pipe-framed gates with chain link. Here was a green oasis in the middle of the watered desert, where all else that was not irrigated was dusty and brown. Here were lush shrubs and a rose garden, a large green lawn and shade trees. The house was vaguely colonial, with a large porch across the front. Julio saw many children, dressed for a party, he guessed, playing about the yard. It was his first close look at a home with play equipment for children—a slide, swings, monkey bars—and his heart leaped as he saw the shiny bicycles. He wanted to run and touch them, to turn on the lights on the handlebars, to ride around the yard.

On the porch were several adults, men and women. Thompson led Julio to the porch and then went into the house and returned with a guitar.

"I want you to listen to this here kid play and sing," Mr.

Thompson said to the others. They all stopped talking, drinks in hands, and turned their attention to Julio. He took the guitar and strummed it a few times, quickly and expertly tuned it, and looked around questioningly. One woman, pleasant-looking, asked of Thompson, "Does he speak English?" Thompson was about to answer but Julio cut in, "Yes, ma'am, I do." The others showed a rather amused interest.

"Hey, kids," Thompson shouted to the children playing in the yard, "come over here. We got some special entertainment." He turned to one of his guests. "I was walking by the camp the other day and I saw him singing and playing. Never heard anything like it for his age. How old are you, kid?"

"I'm thirteen," Julio said brightly. "What do you want me to sing?"

"Do you know 'Rancho Grande'?" asked a guest. They were seated around him, looking at him expectantly. The children had approached the porch and stood with some boredom watching Julio, their eyes, he could feel, traveling up and down him, lingering a bit perhaps on his bare feet. Julio thought he should have been nervous, but he wasn't. Smiling at all of them, without looking at the guitar, he pressed down on the frets for the proper chord and began singing. "Do it with the hi-yi, yi," a thick voice called out. Julio obliged. As he finished the song he saw the children moving away, back to their play, but the adults were now captured, he thought. Someone else asked for a well known Mexican song, and then another. Finally a red-faced man said, "Play everything you know," and Julio did. As he sang he heard them talking, sometimes about himself, "He's great, isn't he?" ". . . try to get him on radio . . ." ". . . country fair amateur program."

Long before he had exhausted his repertoire, Julio found he

was singing to himself. But he was occupied watching the children, taking in the way they were dressed, seeing the games they played. He wanted to run and join them and hoped Mr. Thompson would let him.

Thompson's wife came out of the house. "I heard you singing," she said enthusiastically. "You have quite a nice voice. You'll have to sing more for us some time." Then she looked out at the children. "Hi, kids!" she hollered. "Come on, cake's ready. Ice cream's melting!"

The children left their game and came running, thundering onto the porch, past Julio and into the house. As the door opened Julio caught a glimpse of a large cake with candles on it. His eyes went wide. He had never seen such icing or such a big cake. Then the door closed and he was standing on the porch with the adults who were lost in conversation. He looked uncomfortable a moment, and then Mr. Thompson noticed him. He rose, saying to the others, "I gotta run the kid back to the camp. Back in a sec," and he led Julio to the car.

As they turned onto the dirt road Mr. Thompson pulled a half-dollar from his pocket and handed it to Julio. "Thanks, kid" he said, and Julio could clearly smell the breath laden with liquor, "you play that guitar good. Keep practicing." He let Julio off in front of his cabin and drove off.

His father was sleeping in the cabin, the sun was relenting in the western sky, his older brothers and mother were questioning him about the afternoon at the ranch house, and the younger children were playing in the dirt road. A neighbor hurried down the road. He raced into the cabin and began to wake Leonardo Salazar, shaking him, hollering at him. The others crowded around. "What happened? What happened?" Mrs. Salazar demanded. When Leonardo was awake, the neighbor blurted, "The man he fought with this morning. He's dead. The police are coming soon!" Mrs. Salazar went into panic. "Ay! Dios mio! Ay! Dios mio! I knew it would happen. I knew it." Leonardo looked frightened. He grabbed his trousers and hurriedly pulled them on, while his wife continued to wail. "Give me the money," he said with desperation.

His wife took some crumpled dollar bills from a hiding place. Leonardo rummaged through a wooden box and found some extra clothes. He counted the money she had given him, plus what he had in his pocket.

"Where are you going?" his older son asked.

"I don't know. I don't know." He wrapped a shirt around his extra clothes, pulled on his work shoes. Julio, standing by the door, looked down the dirt road. "Papa," he said. "A cloud of dust down the road." His father froze a moment, then dashed through the door. "Papa!" Julio called, reaching into his pocket, where he had nearly a dollar and a half. His father stopped, terrible fear on his face. "Don't worry, son," he called, "I'll be back for all of you." Julio almost, but not quite, took the money out of his pocket to hand to his father. Instead, he kept his hand clenched tightly around it and looked down the street. "Run, Papa, run!" And his father ran around the cabin and headed across the rows of grapevines. Within seconds, bent low, he had completely disappeared from view.

L ife began for the Salazar family without a father. At first the police came every day or so to see if he had returned. Then the visits became less frequent. Within two months they stopped. This was not the first crop picker to commit a crime and vanish into the world of shifting migrants who roamed the thousand-mile length of the state of California.

Mrs. Salazar tried frantically to locate her husband. All people coming near the ranch were questioned, but no one knew his whereabouts. She regretfully relinquished her position as lady-housekeeper and went to work in the rows of grapevines. Few were those women whose husbands were workers enough and who had sons old enough to permit them to remain home during the day and tend to the clothes and food of the family. Her older sons now increased their effort, and to the surprise of all, they found that by the time the crop was giving out and it was time to move on, there was more money in the family savings than they'd ever had. The older boys argued about who would drive the car when they departed, deciding to share the privilege, and so one day the family packed all its belongings, not much more than a mattress or two, cooking utensils, lanterns and clothes, and left during the evening, to avoid crossing the steep desert mountains in the heat of the day.

J ulio dozed as the car droned along. He pulled a blanket up around him because of the chill, more from the rushing wind than from the temperature of the air. The car coming to a stop awakened him, and he saw they were at a service station far from any other lights except those of the cars on the highway. Gas, oil and water, and they were on the way north again, this time with Carlos driving, while his older brother Ernesto rode in the back to sleep as well as possible.

Soon after dawn Ernesto turned off on a smaller road and drove until the highway was out of sight. He pulled into a little clearing in a grove of trees and stopped. The family alighted. Julio knew his job: he quickly gathered firewood. Carlos placed large stones together and laid an iron grill across, and the family had breakfast of warmed-over chili, fried salt pork and reheated tortillas, using tin pie pans for plates. Among the important items in the car were several two-gallon cans of fresh water, and Mrs. Salazar heated water in a metal basin, washed the utensils and then bathed the smaller children. Then the older boys heated more water and shaved, trimmed their mustaches with great care.

"Julio," his mother called, "take the little ones to go to the toilet." He obeyed, herding them behind the trees, explaining patiently they might not come upon a place to go again for hours. Well he remembered one time, in almost an emergency, his father had stopped to use a restroom at a filling station. His father had gone into the men's room before the attendant knew what was going on. He remembered the latter's extremely annoyed look when he saw the vehicle parked at the side with the Salazar family. The attendant had waited, arms crossed, at the restroom door until Leonardo came out. Then a look was enough. Young as he was, Julio saw what it meant and what it implied. He had been somewhat puzzled at his father's reluctance to drive into the station. Surely no one would mind his using the restroom. But that look, under which his father had wilted—a look that said, "The law is on my side if I want to make trouble. Don't ever use this rest room again. It's not for people like you. My white American customers will think less of me if they see you." It said all that, and more. It showed the unbridgeable gap between a dirty Anglo service station mechanic who was "American" and a well-read literate crop picker who was something else. What was that something else? Julio had wondered many times. "It's because the American guys don't like the Mexicans," his father had explained one day in the fields. But Julio saw that was not altogether true. He had seen Mexicans go into American restaurants and stores. And he had studied the ones who did. He saw that they dressed in pressed pants, spoke English well, used American slang, and above all, he noticed, they looked at the dirty ragged little children, the young adults with defeat and humiliation written on their faces, with the same look the attendant had given his father for sneaking in the restroom.

When the car was loaded up again, the family got in and Carlos drove back to the highway and headed north. Julio was in the rear, but on his knees watching the country unfold in front of them, when he saw a man standing beside an ancient car on the shoulder of the road. As they drew closer, Julio could see the man was a crop picker. He was giving no indication that he needed help, but merely looked at each passing motorist, knowing that inevitably a peer would happen by. Carlos pulled off the highway, stopped, and walked over to the man. Julio and Ernesto followed, and Julio saw the man's wife and many children jammed into the car.

"Qué pasó?" Carlos asked. What happened?

The man was smiles and earnestness. "The clamp holding the hose to the radiator fell off, I guess." The hood of the car was folded up on both sides of the engine and smoke and steam rose. "You happen to have an extra clamp?"

Carlos and Ernesto examined the radiator and hose.

"Momentito," Carlos said. He went to the Salazar car and returned with a small box containing an adjustable wrench, a pair of pliers, a screwdriver and nuts and bolts and bailing wire. Without a word spoken, Ernesto held the hose in place while

Carlos wrapped the wire around it, twisting with the pliers until the wire cinched up tight.

"There," Carlos said, still speaking Spanish. "That should hold longer than a clamp. Julio! Trae el agua." Julio dashed to the car and brought a can of water. "Start the engine and let it run while I add water slowly," Carlos instructed the man.

Within minutes the car was running smoothly and coolly.

"Mil gracias," the man said, offering his hand. He introduced himself as Macho and conspiratorially motioned Carlos and Ernesto to the rear of the car, where a large, hand-made wooden trunk rested on the bumper. He reached in and pulled out a gallon jug covered by a hand-stitched dampened burlap shroud. Julio watched as all three ceremoniously in turn hooked a forefinger into the loop grip and, letting the jug rest on the back of the forearm and crook of elbow, drank deeply. Each then suppressed a little belch, wiped his mouth with the back of the hand, and commented on how good it was.

By this time the two families were visiting by the side of the highway. The younger children were chasing one another a short distance from the road. Mrs. Salazar was asking if Macho's wife knew anything of the whereabouts of her husband. She went into great detail about his habits of drinking and fighting and the frightful consequences. Yes, Macho's wife knew of many such cases, drink was a terrible thing, the devil is in the bottle.

Macho had just finished a job near Bakersfield. A brother told him crops were ripening ahead of time near Olmo, and top dollar was being paid for harvesters. "Near Olmo, eh?" Carlos remarked, looking at Ernesto. "Let's go there."

"Fine with me," Ernesto said.

Soon brief good-byes were being said; Macho's wife gave Mrs. Salazar and the smaller children some tacos.

Just before starting the motor, Carlos said, "Maybe we'll see you in Olmo. Know any names?"

"My brother mentioned a Gibson ranch. Said five hundred acres of tomatoes were in danger," Macho replied.

"Gibson ranch, eh? We'll try to find it." And the two families parted, the Salazar car traveling ahead.

Several years had passed since that season when the fatherless Salazar family had arrived in Olmo. Work had been found immediately, and the family had lived in the abandoned ranch house complex on the Gibson ranch. The Gibsons had built new living quarters across the fields, and the old houses and cabins were far better living quarters than the Salazars had ever known. Leonardo Salazar had not been heard of since that day he scurried into the vineyards after learning he had killed a man and the police were looking for him.

The Salazars now made a point of coming back to Olmo every year to live in the rickety old ranch house. The second summer Ernesto had married a girl from the fields, and added her to the household. Then the next summer Carlos had done the same. The summer after that the babies started arriving, Julio stuck it out for two years, traveling with Ernesto and Carlos, their wives and their children, his mother, his younger brothers and sisters. Then desperation to get away forced him to think of long-range plans.

Among the old unused pieces of equipment at the abandoned part of the ranch where the laborers lived was an old truck. All it needed was a new engine, lights, a windshield, and tires. Mr. Gibson said Julio could have it for five dollars.

Julio had become acquainted in the barrio of Olmo, which was the largest Spanish-speaking settlement he had ever encountered, and he managed to locate a motor for the truck. From nearby wrecking yards he got the other parts. He worked evenings and Sundays, and when the time came for the family to move on to another area, Julio announced he was now on his own. His plans met with little opposition, in fact with enthusiasm: ten persons living in a room or two and traveling in the same auto was beginning to tell on the others.

So now he was saying good-bye to them. Carlos was behind the wheel of the family car, and the others and the family belongings were piled in. He embraced his mother, who cried and said, "Be careful, don't take up drinking. Look hard for your father. I know some day we'll find him. If you do, you know where we'll be; the Thompson ranch in May, the Gibson place in August, Selma in October . . ." And then they were gone. Julio stood looking after them. Yes, I love them, he said to himself, but they're stuck in a rut.

He stood looking around at the old ranch house, built some sixty years before. A shed for firewood was now a home for a crop-picking family—they had left today too. The old livery stable usually housed four families, and farther away the giant old barn stood, seemingly able to accommodate any number. Now they were all empty until the crops came again next year. Julio went into the house and put on new shoes, trousers and shirt and walked over to the old truck he'd rejuvenated. Climbing in, he stepped on the starter and it fired up.

He didn't have his personal belongings, as he intended to

stay a day or two in the empty house. He drove out the long drive that wound through the groves, then out onto the road and to the barrio of Olmo.

He had skimped for the clothes and shoes. He wanted to enjoy them. He felt a sudden exhilaration at being alone, having his family gone. He was alone, free, he felt, for the first time in his life. Now for those plans he had.

The city of Olmo lies spread in the midst of a vast flat farm land, technically part of a valley system, but with no characteristic limiting barriers visible. It appears to be, and is, irrigated desert. The profusion of sunlight teamed with the abundance of water to cause all forms of vegetation to grow frantically, which in turn caused human beings who worked in the area to work frantically, clearing the land, planting the crops, harvesting the fruits of sunlight, water and labor.

The town begins by promising cold beer, lodging, clothing, appliances and farm equipment outlets to the highway traveler. These promises are fulfilled within a few blocks upon entering the city limits. The nicely paved streets proceed farther to be lined by the establishments of those who have to do with land division, wholesale produce, livestock, fertilizers, and pest control. The men who work here wear light cotton suits and broad-brimmed straw hats. They greet heartily and slap the backs of men who drive up in expensive pickup trucks wearing spotless coveralls and denim shirts, or pressed khaki trousers with shirts to match. The paved roads run to the honkytonk area, where a few cheap hotels and movie houses advertise AIR COOLED! Then the paved roads stop abruptly at the beginning of the barrio. The barrio is on the edge of town. Until two generations before it had been the town. Some of the buildings were original, having been built when the handmade, rough red bricks showing through the peeling plaster were the principal material for walls and steps. Occasionally a smooth-worn brick or cobblestone sidewalk graced the sides of the unpaved streets, politely bypassing a huge dead tree stump or an ancient olive tree which refused to die. Driving into the center of the dozen square-block area that was the barrio, Julio sometimes had to swing into the oncoming traffic lane to avoid large hogbacks and swales in the road. There were few cars to be encountered in the area. The crooked walls and irregular tiles on the roofs of buildings vouched for authenticity, put there in a vanished era by a people who no longer existed. One large building with a sign saying it was a bakery was made of lumps of granite, hauled in generations past from some quarry by oxen dragging a sled in the dust. The polygonal stones were closely fitted, making a complete jigsaw puzzle, where no puzzle had been before, forming perfectly square doorways and windows which attested to the patience of the builder in sorting his material as well as his natural eye for what looked good. Tall, broad walls faced the street, with small windows, placed high, all painted either recently or in years past, advertising the wares or services available within. PANADERÍA, the lettering across the bakery read. LICORES on the wall of the liquor store; ZAPATERO where the cobbler stitched leatherware on a treadle-powered ancient stitching machine, and CAFÉ over the restaurant. LA POSADA, the inn, the tavern, was the unpretentious name of the large stone and plaster building which Julio parked next to and entered. The letters of the name had been kept vivid, unnecessarily perhaps, as the establishment had been standing at that corner of two dirt roads for the better part of a century. The rest of its vast wall at first seemed blank, but dimly could be seen the characteristic green and red on white, advertising the once well-known name of a now forgotten product, or perhaps a product remembered only by the great-mustachioed, white-haired men who strolled by during the working day, sometimes pointing out a rectangle of mortared stone here or there which once had supported a water trough, or arguing over the exact location of a long-rotted-away tie rail. The west wall of the tavern was a yard thick, evidenced from the inside by the relatively small windows recessed an arm's length. The recessed windows gave the only testimony of the wall's fortress-like dimensions, the heat of the sun being the only enemy it was designed to repel. Bulky, hand-sawed wooden beams, stained brown, a generation old but not the originals, supported the roof, the lightweight girding quality of the wood having been considered fair exchange for its ephemerality. Inside, a factory-lettered enamel sign, on slick sheet metal, coaxed the patrons in Spanish to take of a drink the brand name of which blazed ridiculously in English. The dirt floor was hard, packed hard enough to sweep without raising dust, by uncountable footsteps, innumerable ounces of spilled liquor and beer, and blood too. The familiar smells that smote Julio's nostrils as he entered were sweat, drink and chili. And a little perfume. The back wall of the establishment was open almost the complete width of the room from waist-high up, allowing a gradual but perpetual air transfusion to take place. Against this giant window were the stoves with the cooking food, the ice box with its handles and hinges nearly worn through by incessant use, and the sinks, copper lined, with linoleum work space. In front of all this ran the bar, wall to wall, with a small section which swung upward to permit passage from behind. A single electric light bulb hanging from a beam in the center of the room competed feebly with the roaring light from the opening at the rear, but held its own against the deep, recessed windows. There were no bar stools, but a half dozen tables were scattered randomly around the room, with loose-jointed, handmade wooden benches. Behind the bar stood several guitars, and on the walls hung artistically hand-lettered signs, someone's attempt to display his literacy. One read: "Mientras se duermen, todos son iguales—" While asleep, all men are equal. And written in feminine character but in heavy pencil beneath, "Perhaps, but not before they go to sleep—Rosa," and beneath this, "Who should know better than Rosa?" in a man's writing. On one wall, where light could strike it well, was a large mural, showing a handsome young caballero, dressed in tight colorful vest and flowing pantalones, a sash about his waist and silver-plated pistols at his hips, strumming a guitar to an enraptured señorita on a low balcony, with long black braids and wearing a mantilla and a nineteenth-century European dress. The mural traveled on, to tell of endless pastures dotted with splendidly dressed vaqueros on horseback, carefree, as they tended grazing cattle, and a wide blue river lined by laden orchards—but nobody believed all this anymore.

Julio's casual entrance went unnoticed. Walking slowly toward the bar at the rear, he heard a half dozen old-timers exaggerating about wages they'd earned in the past. A couple with a tiny baby and two bottles of wine sat at another table asking about work and three men were giving them information on the local situation. The woman was pretty but plump, with large hands and muscular arms, dressed in a faded blouse and a skirt pinned to fit her. The man wore Mexican sandals, which Julio hadn't often seen, but other than that he looked much like any other crop picker. Leaning on the bar were two men, very drunk, one barely able to hold his head up while saliva dripped from his face. The proprietor, sallow-complexioned from lack of sun, paunchy, well dressed, stood with his arms folded by a cashbox behind the bar. A thin woman at the stove, whose ill-fitting clothes searched in vain for a waist at her middle, stirred chili, seasoned a huge pot of boiling beans, and patted balls of dough into tortillas.

Julio's eyes were still adjusting from the bright light outside as he took a place at the bar. A man in an apron who had been sweeping came and looked questioningly at him.

"Cerveza," Julio said, putting fifteen cents on the counter. As he lifted the beer, an aroma of common perfume told him that whom he sought was nearby. Glancing behind and to the right he saw her, Rosa, the girl he'd seen the previous time he'd come here. She was sitting with a man who was laughing. Julio listened to them.

The girl spoke English without much of an accent. "Keep your hands off me. I'm not in the mood. Particularly for a drunk cholo who's broke."

The man laughed and continued trying to paw her. She raised a beer bottle. "I mean it. I'm going to let you have it with this. Now get out of here."

"Rosa, I bought you that beer. Now is that any way to show gratitude, by hitting me with it?"

Julio saw the girl's eyes travel to his own. Then she was pushing the man away from the table. "Now go. Beat it. I have business to attend to."

The man laughed. " 'Business'! You sure picked the right word." He shrugged and left. The girl moved over a little on the bench she sat on and looked invitingly at Julio. Carrying his bottle of beer, he went to her and sat down. Almost immediately the man with the apron set a fresh bottle of beer in front of the girl and looked at Julio.

"Quince centavos, señor," he said quietly to Julio. A little irritation showing, Julio gave him fifteen cents and turned to the girl. They spoke English; for those who spoke it well, it was an elite thing to do. "My name's Julio Salazar," he said to her, looking her over. She was twenty, a couple of years one way or the other, Julio thought. She wore a black and orange dress, knee-length, high-heeled pumps. The dress fit tight at the hips and bust, and was pulled tighter by a wide belt at the waist. Her buttocks were full, but not out of proportion, her mid-section muscular, but not fat, and it flowed upward into firm, aggressive breasts below a strong throat and well-built shoulders.

The pleasant fullness of her mouth could not be disguised by the flaming arches of lipstick above it, like a child's attempt to draw a bird in flight. Meaningful black eyes moved swiftly beneath plucked eyebrows with heavy mascara piled on to make her look as though she was astounded in an oriental way. She had shiny black hair, held in place by hairpins, each with a large red glass bead at the eye. Dime-store jewelry abounded at her wrists, ears, and throat.

"Hi," she said, "I'm Rosa. I saw you in here before. Thanks for the beer. Got a cigarette?" From his shirt pocket Julio pulled a sack of Bull Durham and his eyes questioned her. She nodded approval and he built her a cigarette.

"I been wanting to talk to you," he said as he held a match for her, "ever since I saw you the other night."

"Talk," she said. She was looking at him with admiration.

He started to say something, took a sip of his beer, and stammered. She laughed. "Speak up, Julie. You act tongue-tied." It was the first time he'd heard his name familiarly Anglicized.

"You called me 'Julie.' That's a girl's name."

"Honey, you don't need to worry about being mistaken for a girl."

"Okay. Anyway, this is what I wanted to talk to you about. I been doing a lot of thinking since I saw you. I . . ."

"You been with the crops all your life, right?"

"Uh . . . yeah. Why?"

" 'Cause. It shows. Damn few ever get away. But you might be the type. Like me. You know I'm a prostitute, don't you?"

Julio was somewhat taken aback. "Why, uh . . ."

"Don't be shy about it. Everybody else around here knows it. I don't try to pretend to be anything else."

He sat silently a moment. "But, why . . ."

"Why? Because. I got god-damned sick and tired of grapes and oranges and asparagus, and lettuce and tomatoes. I saw my old man kill himself. Poor old bastard. I was just fifteen. He was trying to save enough money to settle somewhere. He'd spent his life in the fields. Suddenly he decided it wasn't for him. He started working from dawn 'til dark, Sundays and holidays, picking, cutting, work, work, work. To save money. He was skinny as a broom. One day he just keeled over dead. We found him in the field, cutting knife still in his hand, he was reaching for a bunch of grapes. The son-of-a-bitch boss, the guy that owned the place, told us he'd just paid him his wages the day before. We knew damn well he hadn't drawn a dime in two months. There's my mom with nine kids and another coming." She paused and looked a little self-conscious at talking so freely. Julio was touched.

"Where's your family now?"

She looked defiantly at him. "You won't believe it. You got a car, ain't you? Let's go. I been in this joint for three days. I got to get out of here. I'll show you where they are."

He followed her out to the accompaniment of snickers and whistles of congratulation.

She looked approvingly at the battered old truck, and as they jostled and bounced out of the barrio, she listened with admiration and a trace of amusement as he told the story of the truck's rebirth. When they were motoring down the highway under her direction, she tilted her head back and let the wind take her hair.

"Now, tell me your plans. First, you must need me, for some reason. Second, it must be illegal. People always bring illegal plans to a prostitute."

He laughed, wondering why he felt so at ease, this being one of the few times he'd been alone with a girl, and the first time there was a good chance of something developing sexually. He wished she'd look off to the fields on the right more, as her dress was above her knees and he could steal quick glances when she was looking the other way.

"Well, I been thinking. And planning. You know how the picking business is. Well, every so often, a grower will see his crops are a little behind. He didn't hire quite enough help. Some will spoil. So he looks all over for a couple dozen hands for a few weeks' work. Pays 'em a little higher, if he can find 'em. Sometimes he can't. Then he plows the over-ripe crop in for fertilizer. His problem is finding idle workers when everybody's employed. Well, I got an idea. About how many wetbacks are in the barrio, you think? I mean, guys here illegally, with no papers, dodging la migra." La migra was the slang expression for immigration officials.

She pursed her lips. "Oh, I don't know—fifty, maybe. Those guys are usually without families, so I see a lot of them. They live in back rooms in the barrio usually . . ."

"I know. They wait for news of a chance to work back in the hills some place, hoping they can make a couple months' wages before la migra catches them and ships 'em to Tijuana. Then they have to get a stake and try to make it back here for a couple more months' work. Well, this is my idea. I got this here truck. It's transportation. I'm gonna drive around a couple days and find out who needs extra help. And here's where I need you. I need to find these wetbacks. I'll offer them a ride to and from the job I find for them. Every day. And a lunch. I need you to contact these guys and also to wrap some slop in some tortillas. That's the package. A job, transportation to and from, and a lunch. Good deal, huh?"

She was looking at him with interest. "Yeah. Sounds great. But you're going to have to be careful. A wetback stands out like a sore thumb, for some reason. First time a gringo in town sees them with you he'll call the cops."

"Right. So I gotta do it underground, kind of. That's why I need help. You're in good with the owner of La Posada. If we could get word for them to meet there, we could fix the lunches there and everything. How's it sound?"

She thought a minute. "How much you going to charge for this package?"

He shrugged. "I was thinking of a buck and a half a day."

She thought. "And how many can you handle? Get jobs for and deliver?"

"I figure I can get twenty into this truck without breaking a spring. I can leave with one load about daybreak, from the barrio, and be back for another load in two hours. That's forty a day. Dollar and a half each, that's sixty dollars. A *day*. Not pesos."

He drove on, watching her digest this. She gave a low whistle.

"Course, that's not all profit," he continued. "I need someone like you, who I have to pay. Then there's the tortillas and stuff. And gas."

She moved over close to him and took his hand, smiling broadly. "I knew you were interesting the first time I laid eyes on you."

"Then you're with me? You'll work for me on this?"

She seemed to grow a little younger and prettier as she glowed with enthusiasm, the first he'd seen in her. "Yes. Oh, Julio, I want to give it a try. This is the first deal I've ever been offered that wasn't either picking vegetables or jumping in bed. Let's do it! And don't worry about my wages," she gave a dimpled smile, "we'll share. Everything. I'll find the wetbacks. Don't worry about La Posada. With what I got on the boss, that place is like our own." He slid his arm behind her and she raised her arm so that his could more completely encircle her. "There. Turn off on this road here. Mama and the kids live in that little swamp over there."

Julio drove to the swamp, which was in an isolated area, and from a shack came Señora Grijalva, Rosa's mother. A dozen or so small children came running up, swarming over Rosa as she introduced Julio to her mother. Julio exchanged pleasantries with the older woman, who then took a stick and drove the children away from Rosa.

"Get away! Rosa has no pennies for filthy brats. Now leave her alone. She came to visit me." One small boy picked up a little rock and challenged her, but fled when Mrs. Grijalva charged him, brandishing the switch.

Then, to Julio's slight amusement, Rosa's mother began a tirade.

"Your older brothers, they never bring me a cent. Oh, once in a while, when they come home from whoring around the camps, they give me a dollar. Now I don't even have the money I earn from taking care of all these brats. We were so poor I had to borrow advance from the other children's parents. And you know when you ask for advance money, instead of twenty-five cents for watching their broods all day, they cut you down to fifteen cents. Your brother Juan now thinks he's old enough to pick fruit, so that means I'll have to buy him shoes as soon as I find someone who's going to a city where they have a good secondhand store . . ."

Long before she wound up Julio saw Rosa take some crumpled bills from a little purse she carried and give them to her mother. The older woman's eyes went wet as she kissed her daughter. "Surely goodness and mercy will follow you all the days of your life and you shall dwell in the house of the Lord forever," she said with intense sincerity.

When Julio and Rosa were ready to leave, Mrs. Grijalva called to the children, "Come say good-bye to Rosa. She's going now." And from the tules they heard:

"We can't. We found a funny looking animal in the water."

"Don't touch him. He might bite."

"We won't, we're poking him with a stick. He can't run very fast."

Julio drove back to the deserted shack at the Gibson ranch.

He parked in front of the house and turned off the motor. They sat and listened to the quiet as Rosa looked around.

"It's nice here," she said; "is everybody gone?"

"Yeah. My family left this morning."

She got out and he joined her as she walked around. He thought he was concealing his excitement.

"Your family live in the main house there?"

"Yeah. It's the nicest place we stay. We come here every year. It's sort of reserved for us."

Directly in front of the house the Salazars called their own was a watering trough for horses, dry, but with a hand-operated water pump at one end. Rosa pulled on the handle a few times and clear water came gushing into the trough.

"It works," she said. She looked at him a moment. "Do me a favor."

"Sure," he answered.

"Fill it up for me. I love to bathe."

He began pumping. She looked around at the barn, the wood shack and stables. "There's no one around?"

"Not a soul. 'Til spring."

As the water in the trough reached halfway, she began taking her clothes off. Soon she stood completely naked in the growing dusk. "That's enough," she said, and, her back to him, she placed a well-shaped buttock on the edge of the trough and lifted a leg into the water.

"Cold?" Julio asked, and was surprised at the sound of his voice.

"Yes, but it feels so good." She turned to him. "Soap?" He stepped into the house and returned with a slender piece of soap. She hunched her shoulders and presented her back to him. Both could feel the passion in his hands as he soaped and washed the brown, smooth back. Suddenly she pinched her nostrils with her thumb and forefinger and lay back, letting the water cover her, then she sat up, wiping the water from her eyes. "Soap me all over," she whispered.

He brought her a towel made from a cloth flour sack, and she followed him into the house. The only piece of furniture now was a bed made of a set of springs on blocks and a thin mattress. Julio realized he knew nothing of how to approach the situation. He frantically thought that unless he made his feelings known, she would dress, thinking he wasn't particularly interested in having her. But the training of the better part of two decades inhibited him so that he gawked and stammered. He had deduced from his experience that girls who screwed, prostitutes or not, would screw anybody, any time, and all you had to do was ask them in the vilest of language. And he knew that prostitutes were all business, and personal love or affection never occurred to them. And here he was confronted with evidence that perhaps all he knew of women was not true. But he did not know how to make an advance and broach the subject of desire. She somehow knew something about him, he guessed, as she solved his dilemma. She dried herself and lay down, supine, on the bed.

"Come on," she said with soft urgency, reaching a hand toward him. He obliged. "No, no. Take it easy, take it easy." But it was too late. Half amused, she slid out from under him and rested on an elbow, facing him. "You first timers," she said, faintly shaking her head in wisdom. "Talk to me a while. You'll be all right again in five or ten minutes."

He was still breathing deeply, as he pulled her to him.

"I'm all right again right now," he said. She laughed a little.

The enterprise began. Within two days Julio had made contact with a number of ranchers in the outlying areas. He kept notes on who was picking what, when a crop was likely to get behind schedule and what the farmer would pay for extra help at the crisis. Rosa rounded up the wetbacks in the barrio. Julio got permission from the Gibsons to stay on at the abandoned ranch house while he "looked around for something else."

On the third day Julio and Rosa were at La Posada at dawn, and found more than a dozen eager workers waiting. Some had the money to pay him for the job, transportation and lunch. He kept accounts on those who didn't. He and Rosa went broke the day before the men had their first payday, but when they settled up he had more than forty dollars.

One morning he found himself driving happily along, after just having dropped off fifteen workers, with little to do until time to pick them up in the evening. Now he would go back to Rosa at the ranch house. He just had to make one more stop to see if old Mr. Bivins was going to need extra help.

Mr. Bivins met him in the barnyard. "Hi, Salazar, I'm sure glad to see you. I'm going to be in a little trouble come two weeks 'less I can get two dozen good hands. Fix me up?"

"Sure," Julio said, not knowing where he could get them, as he had all those available now working.

"Good. Otherwise I'da had to haul 'em out from Fresno County and pay their way. I'll pay 'em top wages. Three cents over normal. Also, Jack Hibbs 'cross the hogback there, you know his place? He said to stop see him if you come by. I think he's in the same boat."

By the time he got back to Olmo after seeing both ranch owners he was thinking furiously. How could he supply the help? If he went to get workers from other areas, it would not only be risky, but the barrio couldn't accommodate them. Living quarters, such as they were, for the migrants were filled up during the regular season.

He had an idea. Driving through town he had seen a large farm equipment company unpacking new machines. He remembered that at the time he'd thought the large wooden crates were better than many homes crop pickers lived in. He drove to the company.

Walking into the yard, he was told to see Johnny Rojas in the office. "He's our bookkeeper."

When Julio stepped into the sales office he felt uncomfortable. The place smelled of new machines, had large windows and a huge air cooler poured a cool draft over everything. There were some salesmen standing around and Julio was aware that, while he thought he looked fairly well dressed in the barrio, he must look very out of place here. His dress trousers were rather bulky, he wore a long-sleeved sport shirt with a wide collar and a necktie. His shoes were run down.

He was sent to the rear of the large room, behind large, shiny pieces of new farm equipment on the floor. He found two girls working behind desks. They were Anglo, and looked at him with polite tolerance.

"Hi," he said, "I was looking for Johnny Rojas."

"Are you a friend of his?" one girl asked.

"No, I wanted to buy some things maybe, and they said to see him."

"One moment, I'll see if he's in." The girl went through a door behind her desk. She returned shortly. "Come this way, Mr. . . ." *She knew he was in all the time,* Julio thought, puzzled.

"Julio Salazar," Julio walked through the door ahead of her.

"Mr. Salazar here to see you," the girl said and left.

Johnny Rojas was standing at a file cabinet, looking through a folder. He wore a white shirt with a starched collar and a gray checked business suit. His shoes were shiny black and white. A fancy tie clasp held his neat tie in place. His hair was short and businesslike, and he wore no mustache. From across the room Julio could spot the gray eyes that sometimes occurred among his people and always caused comment. The man was darker than an Anglo, but not too dark. He glanced casually at Julio, and then his glance lingered a little before returning to the business papers he was studying.

"Be with you in a minute," he said to Julio. His English was perfect to the point of an American slang inflection.

It occurred to Julio that he had never heard one of his people use that phrase. He stood awkwardly. Looking around, he saw that the man had a picture of himself and a woman and children, obviously his family, on his desk. Just like the Anglos, he thought. A framed document on the wall caught his eye. He tried to read the large, unfamiliar print but could only make out:

"To Juan Rojas, who has successfully completed the
OLMO BUSINESS SCHOOL
Accounting and Bookkeeping Course . . ."

Julio saw Rojas regarding him.

"That's a college diploma," Rojas smiled. Julio examined it more closely.

"I've never seen one," he said.

"They come in handy," Rojas said in a routine voice. "Now, what can I do for you?" He sat down in his swivel chair, making a little tent of his fingers.

"I want to buy those big crates your machines come in."

"Those out by the fence? Just a minute." Rojas walked to a shelf and looked through some papers, finally finding what he wanted. "Let's see. Yep. Those boxes the Y-fifteens come in. 'Bout every two months a man comes and picks them up. Pays us two and a half for them."

Julio's face fell. "Well, would you sell some to me?"

Rojas' smile condescended. "We're in business . . . what did you say your name was?"

"Salazar. Julio Salazar."

"Oh, yes. If you want to pay us more, we'd do business with you. Can you use them all? We have about a dozen a month."

"No . . . I just need about five or six. Would you sell that many?"

Rojas pursed his lips. "I guess we can," he said slowly, "but you understand we don't like to. This other guy takes them all off our hands like clockwork. We like to do things in a businesslike way."

Julio felt himself caught between resenting Rojas for the subtle "we," with which he alienated himself deliberately, and admiring this obvious Mexican who had defected.

"Would you sell me six for three dollars each?"

Rojas debated with himself a moment. "I guess so, Salazar. Can you pick them up?"

"Yes, I have a truck of my own." Quickly he took a roll of bills and counted off eighteen dollars. He held the money out for Rojas, but Rojas made no attempt to take it.

"Pay the girl at the outside desk," he said. Again, Julio was undecided whether to take this as a slam at his own background or to admire this man who did things the gringo way. He decided to admire him. He said thanks and turned to go, giving a last look at the business diploma on the wall. He made a mental note of the name, Olmo Business School. *I've got to look into that school, if it'll do this for you,* he thought, knowing he probably never would.

He transacted the brief business with the girls at the desk as he looked them over. Quite good looking. Both single, if no ring meant anything. Smart, sharply dressed, hair styled. He realized more than ever that to girls like this he did not exist. They looked at him and didn't see him, and didn't care. Why? Rojas came out and their attitude became that of girls flirting with their boss. Julio felt as though even his discomfort was wasted: as a Mexican hand worker he was too insignificant to these girls to make an impression one way or the other. The girl took his money, gave him a purchase receipt, directed him to his merchandise and turned her back on him.

The image of Johnny Rojas in Julio's memory continued to haunt him. As he became more acquainted with the city of Olmo he kept an eye out for the Anglicized Mexicans. They were few, but he noticed they dressed a little differently. As soon as he could afford it, when his services to the crop people brought a steady income, he went shopping and bought a suit. He was thrifty and choosy, but he soon realized the kind of suit the likes of Rojas wore were different from the kind he could get in the store where he shopped. And he realized that it took more than just a suit to make you appear as Rojas did. He investigated the possibility of going to a business college, where, he was sure, he would learn a great deal more than the subjects they taught. He started saving money. His plan was to save enough to live on while he enrolled in a college. But that took lots of money. He'd already learned there were no high school requirements for this type of college and he read and wrote quite well.

But money was hard to save. Particularly with Rosa, who now felt completely relieved of any earning responsibilities. They now lived in a little rented house. Julio grew selfconscious of the truck he drove, but if he bought a car now he'd never save enough to go to business college. Thank God, he thought, Rosa was not the type to be wanting new clothes and a new car. She was pretty well satisfied with everything they had and did. She still helped him prepare the lunches and make the contacts of newly arriving workers in the area. And every night she was his alone.

Then one day a gentleman farmer called Julio into his house for a drink. This rarely happened, and Julio strove to play the part of an equal in business.

"Julio," Old Man Smith began, "I'm in bad shape. Financially. I need help."

Julio sipped the alien whiskey and waited for him to go on.

"I'm not going to be able to make my payroll," Smith said at length. The two sat saying nothing for a few minutes.

"I wish I could help you," Julio offered, "but I'm just making it myself."

"Maybe you can," Smith said. In the long pause that followed, Julio and Old Man Smith finished their drinks and Smith poured another. "You see, I got about twenty hands in the field right now. Your men. Wetbacks to a man. They got about two grand in wages coming. I asked them to work by the month. Anyway, I ain't got the money. To pay 'em.'"

Julio nodded and sipped. This was indeed a serious thing.

"I'd hate to have twenty wetbacks mad at me 'cause I couldn't pay 'em," he said.

"Exactly my point," Smith said. "So, I'll make a long story short. If the immigration boys were to make a raid on my fields come this Friday, and haul 'em off on the spot, it would save me a lot of grief. And I could pay 'em whenever they got back here. You know well as I do these wetbacks get deported to the border and they're back here in a few days, sometimes."

Julio nodded. "Now *I'll* make a long story short. What's it worth to you?"

Smith stroked his chin. "Four hundred."

"Make it five."

"It's a deal."

J ulio was watching from within a grove on top of a hill when they came, three cars full of agents and a U.S. Immigration bus. They rounded them up, showed their identification, and there was no resistance. In the clear still air he saw Smith come out and demand in a loud voice to know what was going on.

Another man, a legitimate worker, had also witnessed the raid, and when Julio and Rosa walked into La Posada that night the raid was on everybody's lips. It was the first Rosa had heard of it. "Twenty of our workers!" she exclaimed. "I wonder what SOB turned them in."

"I don't know," a man volunteered. "But I'd hate to be him when they get back here."

"*If* they get back here," Julio said confidently.

But he worried, and he stayed away from town several nights, and when he heard nothing he and Rosa began frequenting the inn again.

It was about a month later, as he and Rosa sat drinking at the inn, making plans for more placements, that Julio heard someone behind him say, "Oye, cabrón!" Hey, bastard!

He turned and at first didn't recognize the man as one for whom he had once found work and lodging. The man was in rags, dirt from head to foot, shoes scarcely more than patches of frayed leather, but the knife he held in his hand was shiny as though it were brand new.

The man said loudly, for everyone to hear, "This dog of a traitor, he informed on us so that the gringo boss would have to pay us nothing. I know. One of the agents was not a gringo, and he told us when we got to the border. Now he must pay."

Julio was at the bar, and without taking his eyes from the man he reached for the beer bottle he knew was at his side. He felt surprise when it refused to budge, and turning he saw the innkeeper hold it down firmly, shaking his head at the same time. The man with the knife now backed to the door and shouted over his shoulder, "He is here!" And three others, looking equally disheveled, entered. The four advanced on Julio. Rosa started to intervene and the man with the knife made a slash at her, deliberately missing her only by inches, and she retreated.

When finally the kicking and beating had stopped, Julio was only vaguely aware that Rosa was helping him into the truck. She drove to their house and took off his ripped and bloody suit and shirt. She bathed his wounds and put hot compresses on his bruises.

"You dumb son-of-a-bitch," she said with disgust. "What ever made you turn them in?"

"Five hundred dollars," Julio said through swollen lips, and it hurt like fury to talk.

"Well, you really fixed our little game here. Did you hear what he said? The guy with the knife?"

"No."

"He said the others are on the way too. They were all having a race to see who got you first. The others are liable to be here any time. We got to get out of here. You dumb son-of-a-bitch. Come on now, let's get packed. Got any idea where we can go? Where they won't find you, I mean?"

Julio was sitting on the bed dabbing at his face with a wet rag. "Yeah," he said after a while. "Los Angeles. We can start over again there. And they'll never find us. Besides, I was going there anyway. I hear they got some good business colleges there and also . . . I think that's where my old man is . . ."

The first thing Julio did when they got to East Los Angeles was start looking for his father in every bar. They got a small apartment and within a few weeks all marks of Julio's beating were gone. He left Rosa every morning and returned every night while he was "getting the feel" of the place. He had expected East Los Angeles to be a place where he would fit in easily, but he found he was just a country boy and that it showed in everything he did, said and in the way he dressed.

Their several hundred dollars dwindled rapidly to next to nothing. And one evening Julio got into a fight in a bar with a man over who the change on the counter belonged to. The police came and Julio and the man went to jail.

"Drunk in a public place, twenty-five dollars or twelve days."

Rosa was among the spectators in the court. She had no money, but tried to make encouraging signs to Julio. He sweated in jail two days, and then the turnkey opened the tank door and called his name, saying somebody had paid his fine.

"Where the hell did you get twenty-five bucks?" he demanded when they got to their little room, but he had already seen the full ashtrays and empty bottles. "Where's the rest of it?" he roared, and took the fifteen dollars she had left. He went looking for a job, but was unable to find anything. Two days later he returned home and found a drunken man, fairly well dressed, about to knock on his door.

"This is where that babe works, isn't it?" the man asked.

Julio went inside and talked to Rosa. They were down to nothing, he pointed out, and this once would see them through. She agreed, and Julio went into the hall and took the man's money and told him the babe was waiting.

"Well, I'm a pimp now," he said with resignation as he sat down at the nearest bar and ordered a drink.

He talked Rosa into being a whore for just another week or so, and the week stretched into a month—and the month into two years.

Meanwhile, Julio investigated the business colleges and the job opportunities in the area. It wouldn't be long, he told her, before he made his move.

Then one day he met a well-dressed man, who had a nice hairline mustache, and who spoke English and Spanish very well. The man and Julio quickly became friends. This man needed a girl bad, he told Julio. And he had money. Julio took him to the apartment and introduced him to Rosa, who still looked like a woman should, and just as Julio took the money from the man and was pocketing it, the man pulled out a set of handcuffs and arrested Julio and Rosa and took them to jail for pandering and prostitution.

"Sixty dollars or thirty days," the judge said.

Julio had—and Rosa knew he had—over a hundred dollars. They were both in the same courtroom, and Rosa's eyes looked like hell's fury as Julio paid his own fine and left without so much as a backward glance at Rosa.

He walked down the street, looking for something to do. He had forty-some dollars, good-looks, nice clothes—why couldn't he make it here where a half million other chicanos did? He wandered aimlessly down one street and then another. As he was passing a little stand of some sort he heard something inside. Looking in the open window, he saw a rather attractive girl trying to install a small gas range. She was using a wrench three sizes too small and the wrong kind to boot. He watched her, amused, while she was unaware of his presence. *This girl needs me,* he said to himself.

4

A ngelina Sandoval arrived in East Los Angeles and stayed with the family of her childhood friend, Olivia Ornelas. Olivia was a dark, lively girl who worked in a milling plant that cut wood into various sizes and shapes and shipped it to different companies which assembled the blocks and pieces into cabinets, boxes and frames of all kinds. She got Angelina a job at the plant, and the two girls stood side by side regulating the flow of precisely cut blocks and dowels coming out of the machines, and stacking and sorting them. Angelina's background of stoop labor in the fields made her extremely appreciative of the opportunities of city life, and she worked hard, putting in overtime, and made more than twice what her father had. Having had practically no experience with men outside her family, she found herself avoiding situations where courtship might develop. Her inability to respond to or recognize subtle forms of flirtation resulted in her being regarded as aloof and unavailable by men at the plant. She shrugged it off.

After several months she found work at the plant boring,

and discovered the quarter-mile walk to work every morning was the high point of the day. Each day she passed a little shoeshine stand where the shine man sold newspapers and magazines. It would be a good spot for a taco stand, she mused.

After work she would stop in to buy a paper (any girl in East Los Angeles who considered herself smart read one of the big English-language dailies) and she would chat with the proprietor, an old man who spoke no English but boasted he could shine shoes better than any Negro. One day the old man said to her, "Business is bad. I'm closing up when the rent's due next month."

That night Angelina tossed and turned in bed, thinking about the little taco stand she could run at that location. The next morning on the way to work she inquired about the lease. Yes, she could lease it by the year, with option to renew.

During her morning coffee break she made a few quick phone calls to see what city permits were needed to open a food stand.

She was excited as she pondered the prospects of working for herself. She was more than willing to put in long hours to catch some breakfast trade, the noon gang and late afternoon snackers. There was no such stand for blocks in any direction.

She quit her job and began to convert the shoeshine stand to a taco stand. She bought a little counter gas range and was trying to install it, and it was at this time Julio Salazar walked into her so-far-tranquil life. To her Julio was big, handsome in a suave way, articulate, good-natured and charming.

With extreme masculine chivalry, Julio had pointed out that she was using the wrong kind of wrench for installing pipes, and he offered to help her. One thing led to another, and before nightfall Angie was delighted with her new partner, who had

CHICANO

agreed to work for nothing except food and cigarette money "and a few things like that."

With his help the stand was ready for business weeks ahead of schedule, and both showed up at six one morning and put up a sign that read ABIERTO. Open.

And the customers came. By night time, Angie's supplies were almost depleted. Stores were closed.

"Oye," she said to Julio, "tomorrow, when the morning rush is over, you take charge while I go buy more meat, eggs and chili."

She was almost broke, but the day's receipts would buy enough supplies for two or three more days. And so it went. Each night Angie gave Julio a dollar or two until the place was making a steady income, then he got a considerable raise. He was still making far less than he could have at any man's job, but that didn't bother him.

What did bother him, though, was the way his long working hours cut into his sex activities. He tried in vain to see some sign of affection for him in Angie. He walked her home a few times, and each time she said, "See you in the morning," and left him standing on the sidewalk.

But Julio realized he had a good thing going. He was a sort of partner in a business (in fact, he told the people he met in bars after hours, "I got my own business") and he had a very energetic partner. Now, if he could only marry Angie, he would own both her and the stand.

One day, between rush hours, Julio broke down and tearfully confessed his love for Angie. He'd *never* loved like this before, he said. It was torture for him to go on, being so close to her, yet not having her as a wife. If only she would have him, he would work the stand night and day, give her a real house, treat her as such a beautiful woman should be treated. He could not go on without her as his wife.

Angie was bewildered. She had never given Julio much thought, but now he convinced her how inadvertently cruel she had been. Neither had she given much thought to romance, and while she was only fond of Julio, she reasoned one man was as good as another. Julio had no bad habits that she knew of and she wasn't unreceptive to the idea of marriage.

Julio talked her into saying "yes," then talked the Ornelas family into lending him their family car, and he drove out into the desert across the state line where a justice of the peace in five minutes united them until death did them part.

Julio's concept of marriage was not a new one. He believed every attention should be showered on a potential mistress or a fiancee. But once married, that was all over. The complete patriarchy had existed among his—and her—people for many generations, and Julio saw nothing wrong with it.

"When a man says 'Jump!' to his wife," he often told his bar friends, "she should say 'How high?' and when he says 'Three feet' she should say, 'How many times?' and he should say, 'Never mind that, just keep jumping till I say quit!' " This of course was a variation of an American maxim he'd once heard from a boss of his. He had simply adapted it from its original employer-employee premise to a husband-wife analogy.

Angie would be at the stand at 6 A.M. to get things started. They served burritos de huevos, chorizo, frijoles, tamales, tortillas, both the flour and corn types, and a few other things, such as hot dogs and hamburgers.

Julio would show up at the stand in time for the rush, and handle the cash register and perhaps shout a few orders to her. When breakfast was over, he'd take off on business—to see about getting cheaper supplies, perhaps—and come back in time to handle the cash register at noon. Afternoons were basically the same. All was well at the taco stand. It was making money. Julio rented a small house for the two of them. He had little trouble dominating the taco stand.

He did, however, have a little trouble dominating Angie in some areas. Angie did not want to start having children.

"Look, baby, we're married now. It's any time I want it . . ."

"I'm sorry, I'm not going to start getting pregnant when we're just getting started at the stand. If you want to screw, you'll have to get something to protect me," she said flatly.

"That's against the Church," Julio reminded.

"Well, it's not against the Church to remain unpregnant," she told him. "If you're so religious, you'll have to abstain, I believe it is called."

Grumbling, Julio went down to a local pharmacy where he could charge things. Confiding in the pharmacist, he had to listen to a long dissertation on how he should either go to bed with women who want babies, or Protestant women, or Catholic women who'd had hysterectomies, which, the pharmacist, had to admit, narrowed the field down somewhat. But Julio bought condoms and was once again the complete master of his house.

As time progressed, the shop did better and better. Julio resisted all Angie's advice to renovate or expand. He thought they were doing fine and his adamant position led to more and more arguments until knock-down, drag-out fights became common. Actually, there was little dragging out, but lots of knocking down—all on the part of Julio.

Julio had refused to give up completely several of his female friends, and refused to give up any of his drinking, and Angie was naïve—or perhaps Americanized—enough to believe that, by God, if she could work and earn equally as well as (indeed, better than) Julio, she should enjoy equal rights so far as wanting to know where he spent his evenings and their money.

It was during one of these fracases, a few years after their marriage, that two Anglo policemen happened to be driving down the street in front of Angie's and Julio's home. It was a warm evening, the windows of the prowl car were rolled down, and both policemen clearly heard the unmistakable sound of shattering glass and screaming voices. They stopped. Shaking his head, one officer radioed in the address and said they were going in to investigate what seemed like a Code 415 Family Disturbance.

Thus it was that as Julio was slapping Angie around because she was bitchy enough to demand to know his whereabouts earlier, there was a loud knock on the door. Still seething over the insult, Julio jerked open the door and saw the two young policemen standing on his porch, looking very businesslike.

"What do you want?" Julio snarled.

"We thought we heard fighting and wondered if someone might be in trouble," one of the officers said.

"There's no trouble here, now get the hell out of here and don't come back, or I'll run you out of my house with a shotgun."

Unperturbed, the officers looked into the front room and saw Angie, looking exactly as though someone had been roughing her up. One eye was swollen and her lower lip protruded almost an inch beyond the upper.

"You all right, ma'am?" an officer asked. Angie was catching her breath.

"Mind your own goddamn business. This is private property. Now get out of here and let us alone," Julio thundered.

One policeman looked at Julio. "Sorry, sir, but if the lady's in trouble, we'll have to help her. If she wants help."

"She don't want no help from you or anybody else," Julio shouted. "No one called you here. Now get out!"

The officer ignored Julio. "You okay, ma'am?" one asked.

Angie came to the door. "There's nothing you can do," she said, still out of breath. "Please go. It'll be all right."

"There's plenty we can do, ma'am, if you think you need help. Just tell us."

Julio was livid, mostly at being ignored. He screamed, "Will you goddamn bastards get the hell out of here before I bash you . . ."

One officer cut in, opening the screen door. "Now you *are* breaking the law," he said evenly, with quiet authority. "You better either shut up while we investigate this, or we'll take you downtown. Now, ma'am, is there any way we can help you?"

Angie had caught her breath. "Would you . . . really arrest him?" she asked.

"Ma'am, all you have to do is tell us that he did that to your face—put those bruises there—and we'll take him."

Angie stood looking at them, then at Julio. Julio was still furious, but not reckless enough to jeopardize his chances of remaining free. Now another police car arrived, it being generally customary on quiet evenings for one unit to back up another car making an investigation. Within seconds yet another police car came slowly down the street and stopped, motor running.

Angie looked scornfully at Julio, then at the two officers in front of her, then at the three police cars in front of the house. She saw Julio's attitude change from one of fury to one of apathy to one of pleading.

He said, "Baby, you know I didn't do nothing to you, did I?" She debated. Another policeman from one of the prowl cars got out and approached. As he came in the circle of light on the porch, it was apparent he was a chicano.

"Need me here, Walt?" he called to one of the officers on the porch. They turned to him.

"Hi, Raul. No. Everybody here speaks English. Routine four-fifteen, we can handle it. Thanks anyway." Raul waved and got into his car and left.

Angie was still thinking.

"Then," she said, still looking disdainfully at Julio, "if you take him, it'll be worse for me when he gets out."

"Oh, no it won't, ma'am. We can assure you of that. But I'll tell you this. We handle this sort of thing every night. And this'll keep happening to you, till you have him put in front of a judge."

"And all I have to do is say he did this to me?" she asked, suddenly liking the feeling of power.

"That's all," the officer said simply.

Bitterly, Angie spat the words out. "Take him. The no-good son-of-a-bitch. This isn't the first time, or the second or third or fourth. He comes in smelling like a French perfume factory every night, spending money, slaps me around. Yes, he did this to me. And I hope the judge locks him up for a year!"

Both officers stood a little straighter, a little more alertly.

"What's your name, fella?"

"Julio Salazar," Julio replied, defeated.

"Step out here, please, Mr. Salazar," one officer said politely, holding the screen door open for Julio. One officer quickly searched Julio while the other put the handcuffs on him. Julio looked wretched. He glanced about the neighborhood and saw heads at every window. Two of the police cars remained on the street, both had their red lights blinking. One officer firmly led Julio out to a patrol car, while the other made out a form on a clip board.

"Now, Mrs. Salazar, if you'd sign this please," he said quietly. "It's just a complaint, saying what you already told us."

Angie hesitated. "What if I don't sign it?" she asked.

"Then we'll just leave him with you and go away." Angie grabbed the pencil and scribbled her name on the form.

As Julio was shoved roughly into the car, he well understood his position. He didn't have one. The officer proceeded the few blocks to First Street and turned west and drove directly to the Hollenbeck Station jail. Julio was led through a door to the booking room.

"I know my way here," he said sullenly, as one shoved him.

"Then you'd better behave, Pancho. We fight back," one told him warningly.

Julio bristled inwardly at being called Pancho. He wanted to say, "My name's not Pancho," but he knew better. In this jail, you took whatever the Anglo cops gave you, and kept your mouth shut. Otherwise, when they took you in front of the judge looking like raw hamburger, they had written on the report, "Suspect required necessary force to subdue," and that was that. There was no way in the world to prove they had worked you over until they tired.

Julio was shoved into jail with two dozen other men, all Mexican-American. He looked them over and finally saw two familiar faces.

"Julio!" they cried, coming forward to embrace him. "How are you, you old son-of-a-gun." Julio smiled.

"Fine, fine. Working regularly now. Got my own business."

"Yeah, so I heard," one of his friends said. They sat down on a bunk and lighted cigarettes.

"So how you been, Charlie?" he asked.

"Fine," Charlie answered. "My oldest is graduating from high school. He's really quite a kid. Strong and smart."

Julio asked, "Say, whatever happened to the little cocktail waitress you had an eye on over on Brooklyn Street?"

Charlie laughed. "Turned out she was a lesbian. 'Magine that? I didn't know it. That joint she worked in was a dyke hangout. She was knocking down on the bulldykes that came around. I thought it was all tips."

They talked far into the night. Finally Charlie asked, "By the way, what'd they bust you on?"

Julio shrugged. "I was having a little argument with the wife. Two cop paddy mothers happened to drive by just as she threw a big vase at me. They heard the racket, come busting in and she told them I clobbered her."

"Did you?"

"A little. Hardly enough to notice. She signed a complaint."

"You've had it, Julio."

"What d'ya mean?"

"I mean when you get in front of that judge, you just better be so full of promises to be a good boy when you get out it shows in your face."

"When I get out of here, I'll kick that bitch's fanny so hard she'll think a freight train hit her."

Charlie smiled. "This is your first rap on wife beating, isn't it?"

"Yeah."

"Ten bucks says you'll sing a different tune when you get home tomorrow."

"Don't bother me now," Julio said, stretching out on the floor. All the bunks were taken. "I'll talk to you in the morning."

"Good night."

Breakfast! Breakfast, you lucky dogs!" It was the turnkey pushing a wheelcart loaded with hot oatmeal and coffee just outside the bars of the tank.

The prisoners awoke stiffly, yawning, swearing casually. Julio got to his feet and went to the bars, looking at the pushcart. He could almost go for some oatmeal and coffee, if there had been any sugar and cream. He looked at the turnkey.

"I know you'll forgive me if I pass it up this time," he said. "It might spoil my dinner."

The turnkey smiled broadly. "Think of all the starving Chinese. And here you are turning down this delicious repast."

About half the prisoners refused the oatmeal, nearly all took coffee. In a little cubicle, under supervision, the men were allowed to shave with a safety razor. "The better you look, the better Judge Morganthau will like you," the turnkey warned. Julio well knew this was a peculiarity among judges. He spent considerable time cleaning himself and combing his hair. He trimmed his hairline mustache perfectly. Soon the door was unlocked and those who were to appear for pleading were taken by bus, chained together, to the courthouse in the Los Angeles civic center.

The prisoners were led to the empty jury box to await the arrival of Judge Morganthau. Julio took a seat and looked about. The spectator gallery was almost full. Seated there in the second row, wearing dark glasses to cover her bruises, was Angie. Julio gave her no sign of recognition.

Soon a tall Anglo bailiff, in uniform, spoke to the courtroom.

"Everybody rise and remain standing while His Honor enters and takes the bench." Judge Morganthau came in briskly.

"Hear ye, this court, in the city of Los Angeles, in and for the County of Los Angeles, in and for the State of California is now in session, Judge Richard Morganthau presiding," the bailiff droned.

When everyone was seated again, the judge addressed the prisoners: "You are here to enter a plea, not to have your case tried. When you stand before the bench, you will have the charges against you read to you. At that time you will indicate whether you are guilty or not guilty. No more. If you are guilty, I will pass sentence on you. If you believe you are not guilty, you are entitled to legal counsel. In the event you cannot afford an attorney, the court will appoint one to represent you. If you plead guilty, only under rare circumstances will I listen to any explanations. In the eyes of the law, you cannot be just a little bit guilty any more than you can be a little bit pregnant."

Judge Morganthau picked up some papers and read a few minutes.

"Ruben Santos," he said, looking toward the prisoners. One of the prisoners rose and walked out of the jury box to stand before the bench. Judge Morganthau continued reading the police report a few minutes. Then he looked up at the city attorney's table.

"Counselor," he said, "this man is charged with selling liquor to minors. Where are the minors? I don't see any indication here they were arrested."

The deputy city attorney made an effort not to stammer.

"As I understand it, Your Honor, the minors fled the scene. The arresting officers saw them purchase liquor and went in the store to make the arrests, but the kids—they were teen-agers—ran out the back door."

"I see. And where are they now?"

The deputy city attorney gestured helplessly. "They got away . . . they . . ."

Judge Morganthau cut in: "Then how do you know they were teen-agers?"

"It . . . was obvious. The arresting officers saw . . ."

"I don't care what they saw. You should know better than to bring a case like this in here. This sounds like harassment to me."

"Your Honor, I don't believe they intended to harass . . ."

Ruben Santos cut in politely. "Your Honor, may I say something?" He spoke with a thick Spanish accent.

"Yes?"

"These policemen. They always try to harass me. They wait in front . . ."

"Much as I'd like to, Mr. Santos, it is not my duty to hear complaints against the police department. There's a proper place for that. It is my duty, however, to dismiss a case which is improperly prepared. Counselor, did you really think you could convict on this kind of evidence?"

The city attorney saw the trap. "I think the arresting officers thought there might be a chance . . ."

"If the arresting officers thought they could get a conviction on this case, I suggest you need some new officers. If they knew the case was too weak, then this does constitute harassment. This man was arrested, taken from his place of business and kept in jail overnight, and there's no case against him. What do you intend to do about that, counselor?"

The counselor knew the answer Judge Morganthau wanted.

"I'll talk to the officers and make sure this doesn't happen again."

"You'd better. Or I will," the judge said. Then to Ruben Santos: "You're free to go, Mr. Santos. No charges against you." Judge Morganthau picked up another report and read. "Next case is the City versus Julio Salazar." He pronounced the first name HOO-leo, correctly.

Julio rose and approached the bench. Judge Morganthau silently read the report before him. Then he looked up.

"Do you speak English?" he asked Julio.

"Yes, Your Honor."

"You're charged with physically assaulting Mrs. Salazar. Are you guilty or not guilty?"

Julio looked down. "I guess I'm guilty, Your Honor. It was just a little argument . . ."

"Mr. Salazar," the judge cut in, "do you know how many 'little arguments' such as this were reported in East Los Angeles the past year?"

"No, sir."

"There were hundreds. Four of these so-called little arguments ended in death." He paused to let that sink in. "What do you think of that?"

Julio tried to think of something to say. "I guess . . . that's pretty bad," he said finally.

"Three women received injuries from their husbands that proved fatal. Another woman shot and killed her husband in self-defense. That's what these little arguments can lead to. I personally believe there is no excuse for a man striking a woman. No excuse whatsoever. Do you have anything to say for yourself before I pass sentence?"

"No, Your Honor."

Judge Morganthau thought a moment. "Are you ready for sentencing?"

"Yes, Your Honor."

"Is Mrs. Salazar in the courtroom?" the judge asked, looking at the spectators. Hesitantly, Angie rose. "Would you come forward, please, Mrs. Salazar?" Judge Morganthau asked.

Angie came forward. A bailiff opened the swinging gate separating the spectators from the court area. She stood beside Julio, who wouldn't look at her.

"Would you take off your dark glasses, please?" asked Judge Morganthau. Angie removed them. The judge regarded her black eye a few moments. Julio stared at the floor. He knew how to act before a judge.

"Mr. Salazar," Judge Morganthau said as he wrote on a paper, "one of the things you must learn if you're to get along in this society is that you do not strike a woman. Our laws will not tolerate it. In other countries, in other societies, what happens between a man and his wife seems to be nobody else's business. That is not the case here. Do you understand that?"

"Yes, Your Honor, I've learned that," replied Julio meekly.

"Well, it seems it's taken you a long time to find that out. According to the arresting officer's report, Mrs. Salazar said this has happened many times before. Is that right, Mrs. Salazar?"

Come on, dammit, Julio thought to himself. Give me my five days in jail and quit treating me like a ten-year-old.

Angie nodded. The judge scribbled more and said, "Tell you what I'm going to do. I'm sentencing you to one year in jail . . ." Julio looked up, stricken. ". . . and I'll suspend that sentence on the condition you report to a probation officer every week for two years. Liquor seems to be part of your problem also. Another condition of suspension is that you refrain from drinking alcohol during your probation. Does that sound fair to you? Or would you rather serve your sentence?"

Julio was at a loss for words. "It's . . . fair," he managed to say.

Judge Morganthau went on. "I understand you two run a business together. During your probation you will remain gainfully employed at all times. And you will refrain from touching your wife in anger. Any violation of these terms will result in your serving your one-year sentence. Is that clear?"

You no good Anglo bastard, Julio thought. "Yes, Your Honor. I think you've been more than fair with me."

"So do I, Mr. Salazar. Now, Mrs. Salazar, your husband may go home with you. If he violates the terms I have set down for his probation, it is your duty to report it either to the probation department or to the nearest police officer. Don't worry. If he strikes you, or threatens to strike you, you only have to pick up the phone, and he'll be serving his sentence." Judge Morganthau smiled benevolently, "You're free to go now, Mr. Salazar. And I hope I never see you again. For your sake."

You dirty white son-of-a-bitch, Julio thought. "Don't worry, Your Honor, you won't. I've learned my lesson. Thank you for your kindness."

Julio's attitude seemed to have undergone a change by the time they arrived home from the courthouse. Angie realized the power the law had given her, regretted not knowing she had these rights all along. Well, by God she had them now, and she was going to take advantage of it.

"Okay, lover boy," she said, taking off her dark glasses. Julio winced at the sight of the black eye. "You knocked me around for the last time. Got that straight? This brings us to number two. You toe the mark at the taco stand, or it's out on your fat ear. And I'll make sure the gringo judge knows you're not gainfully employed. Entiendes tu?"

Julio looked sullen. "Yo entiendo." I understand.

"All right. I'm running things around here from now on. And the first thing we do is start expanding the taco stand. I'm buying out the store next door. We—you and I—will start re-modeling it into a full-size cafe. With a kitchen. Guess who's going to do most of the remodeling? Take a wild guess."

"Okay, okay," Julio said. "What are we going to use for money?"

"We're going to use the salary I was paying you. As of now, your wages have been drastically reduced. To zero. And you'd better stay off the laughing sauce, or I make a phone call to your probation officer."

Julio exploded. "Listen, bitch," he said. "I don't have to take this crap from you . . ."

"Then don't. Beat it. Get out. Go get yourself a job some-place else. I don't need you."

Julio was hurt. Partly at the thought of finding a job. Partly because she'd hit the soft spot when she said she didn't need him. At first she had needed him. He'd been useful. Then he started goofing off, taking money, shoving the work onto her. Now he heard those words, "I don't need you." And he knew it was true. He saw her face soften and he knew the hurt showed on his face.

He began ad libbing. "Okay, okay. Now let me tell you something. You think I was just goofing off, boozing it up and all that just for no reason, without any plan or anything, don't you?"

"That's exactly what I think."

"Okay. You don't need me, huh? Let me tell you what I had in mind. I didn't want to discourage you or kill your spirit, 'cause you've done such a great job with the stand. I didn't want to tell you this, 'cause I know you never finished high school. But you need me, bitch. You need me bad. All those times when you thought I was out blowing our money, I was saving most of it. I was notified some time back that I was qualified to enroll in a class in restaurant accounting and management. I just about saved enough to pay for the course, but now I think I'll go ahead and take it and open a place of my own."

He paused and watched Angie's face light up.

"Julio. You mean . . . you're planning to go to college?"

"Right. And if you think you can start expanding and run a big place without someone who knows what he's doing, sweetie, are *you* in for a surprise."

She tried desperately to believe him, and succeeded. "But . . . why didn't you tell me?"

"Because, God dammit. A man doesn't have to check with his wife every time he thinks of an idea. I realized long ago that somebody's got to know how to keep accounts, figure out tax deductions and all like that if you're going to run a big operation."

She looked at him with affection. "I . . . I'm sorry I said I didn't need you. It was just . . . I didn't need you the way you were. But I really desperately need somebody who can keep track of everything."

Julio became haughty. "Ha! Now the shoe's on the other

foot. Suddenly you're crying for me to help you, now that you know you can't do it without me."

"Of course I need you. Really, Julio, you've been planning this all along? Going to college to study how to run a big place? And you saved enough money for it?"

His mind raced. "Of course I did. The course costs $140, and I just about saved that much. The new semester starts in September, and I'm all set to join the class."

Perhaps subconsciously, Angie refused to press him for specific details of his plans. She stepped close to him and put her arms around his neck. He took a step back.

"That paddy judge said I'm not supposed to touch you."

"He said in anger."

He embraced her briefly, and then led her toward the bedroom. In one part of his mind he was anticipating her body. In the other he was figuring out how the hell many friends he'd have to hit up to raise that $140, and was hoping to hell the nearby business college had a course in restaurant management and accounting.

An hour later they were lying close together, breathing deeply and slowly, near sleep, when the doorbell rang. Julio sat up, blinking. It was not yet late afternoon. Who the hell could that be? The bell rang again.

"All right, all right," he hollered, and rose to pull on his trousers. Angie opened her eyes and looked at him with love. Julio stopped in front of the dresser to make sure his slick black hair was in place, and went to open the front room door. He saw a man in his twenties, but looking older because he was nearly bald. Large teeth were capped here and there with gold, Julio saw as the man grinned a little. He was short, not much over five feet tall, and wore an Army uniform. His stature combined with the huge bulge-toed combat boots to give him the appearance of a bantam rooster.

"Hi, is this where Angie lives?" the man asked in fairly good English.

Julio eyed him, suspicious. "Yeah. What can I do for you?"

"Are you her husband?"

Julio was ever wary of saying anything that might somehow be used against him. "Why?"

"I'm her brother Pete," Pedro answered. "You must be Julio."

At once, both men grinned broadly, threw their arms wide and embraced.

"Cuñado!" they said simultaneously. Brother-in-law! Julio pulled Pete into the room. At the first sound of Pete's voice Angie had leaped up and put on a slip. Now she raced into the room and threw herself at Pete.

"Pedrito! Pedrito! Pedrito!" she said, kissing him on the lips, the ear, the nose, the cheek. Pete just squeezed hard on her body, his eyes closed, tears streaming. He tried to speak and croaked, "Angie!" Angie started sobbing. Julio began weeping openly, and all three took seats and sobbed aloud for several minutes.

Then the talking between brother and sister started. Had he seen mama and papa? Yes, he'd gone there for a week. He gave them half his $600, which was what he'd been mustered out of the Army with, which was also more money than he'd ever had in his life. Julio's ears pricked up.

Yes, it was terrible about Gregorio. The mention of the dead brother brought another interval of weeping. Pete asked about her black eye.

"Julio and I had a little argument," Angie explained. Pete accepted this with a nod. How's the restaurant doing? Fine. We're about to expand. Julio's going to take a college course in restaurant management.

"How about a drink, Pete?" Julio asked, going to a shelf where a whiskey bottle stood. "We quit drinking, but this is a special occasion."

"Choor," Pete said, meaning sure. Julio looked at Angie, who nodded her approval through her happy smile.

About the time the bottle was empty Julio asked Pete if he was hungry.

"Starving," Pete said. When he wasn't laughing, he always looked a little alarmed. Angie knew this was her cue to go into the kitchen and get busy.

"While you're fixing it, Pete and I will walk down and get a beer," Julio said, knowing that her rapture at Pete's presence would preclude any immediate enforcement of the terms of his suspended sentence. Angie embraced Pete once more, starting to cry a little.

"Please come back soon," she said. "I'll have tortillas, the homemade kind, and frijoles ready when you get back."

At the corner tavern, on First Street, Julio and Pete took a booth and talked, nearly shouting to be heard above the roar of a juke box. They ordered Mexican beer and chicharrones— fried porkskin—which they dipped in a bowl of tongue-stinging salsa.

"What do you plan to do, Pete?" Julio asked, after he had volunteered a fairly accurate account of his recent encounter with the law and his subsequent probation.

"Well, when I was in the Pacific, they had me helping to build barracks and buildings. I learned a little about the construction business. I still have more than $300, and I'm going to buy a secondhand pickup truck and get a job with a construction company. A guy told me they pay sometimes $100 a week just for labor."

"That's right," Julio verified. "At the taco stand at quitting time we always get a gang of construction men. I know some of them pretty well, and I'll bet I can get you fixed up with a job."

Pete was delighted.

"You can stay with us. I'll take you down tomorrow and introduce you to some of the hard-hat crews at the stand," Julio said. He found he genuinely liked Pete, and sensed Pete was fond of him.

As they drank beer and ate chicharrones, Julio continued the story of his troubles with Angie. "You see, she really needs me, but she can't realize that. So I got to make her aware of how important it is to have a competent man around." Pete was in full agreement. He could see nothing wrong with a man like Julio, and was a little disappointed in his sister to hear how she treated him. "So anyway," Julio finally got around to saying, "this course here costs about $140. I told her I'd been saving it and I had that much. But I don't."

"What'd you do with the money?" Pete asked sincerely.

"I boozed it up. For Christ's sake, it was only a dollar or two a day. The rest of my labor I didn't get anything for."

Pete saw the injustice of this. "So now she thinks you have the $140."

"Right," Julio said, "which brings me to a good idea. I've been thinking, ever since you said you were going to buy a pickup truck with that money you got. Tell you what I'll do. You loan me that $140 and buy a pickup on time."

"I can't. I got no credit. I'm just discharged from the Army."

Julio was ready. "I was thinking of that. You can't buy much of a truck with that kind of money. So how's about, if I get Angie to co-sign for a good truck, you loan me that money— this is just between us, understand—and you got your truck, a better one than you would have, and I got the money for the college."

"I'll drink to that," Pete said, using one of the many American phrases he'd picked up in the Army.

Julio continued confidentially. "And Angie doesn't need to know a thing about the money."

Pete looked a little indignant. "It's none of her business," he said emphatically.

"And I'll pay you back the dough soon as I can."

"Don't worry about it," Pete said with a wave of his hand. He pulled out his wallet and peeled off $140 and handed it to Julio. Instantly Julio regretted he hadn't asked for more.

The two men were wobbly but hungry when they got back to the house two hours later.

"Pete's going into construction work, honey," Julio said as they ate. "I told him there was a lot of hard-hat guys drop in at the stand, and I could probably fix him up with a job."

Angie was pleased. "I'm sure one of them can get you on. They better. Some of them run a tab at the stand, and I've been pretty lenient about it."

Julio made a mental note: *Check drawers to see where she keeps records of tabs.*

After dinner Pete and Julio sat talking in the front room as

Angie made up a couch for Pete to sleep on. He watched her as she moved in her soft sweater and knit skirt. Now and then tears would come to her eyes and she would come and kiss his bald head murmuring, "Pelón." Baldy. He stood up.

"Julio's going to show me a little bit of the town," he said putting on his Army jacket. Julio got his coat. "We won't be late," Pete promised. She kissed him and then went to her purse, took some money out and pressed it into Julio's hand. Julio showed his appreciation by rubbing her buttocks and then he followed Pete out.

· 5 ·

The few days Pete had spent with his parents in Irwindale thoroughly convinced him it was no place for him. He had visited his father at the orange packing plant where he worked, and watched as the old man took pride in his job, which was to sort out the most magnificent specimens from high grade orchards and wrap each one separately in a piece of purple tissue paper. He took great care to wrap it properly and place it gently in a special box. The oranges were huge, rich orange and pungent.

"Why do you wrap them so well?" Pete asked.

The old man glanced up at the house foreman and didn't break his pace at wrapping. "Because the best ones go other places. There are lots of places in the United States where they don't grow oranges. These go to those places."

Pete was a little puzzled at the logic. "If they don't grow oranges there, why not send them our worst ones? They'd be glad to get them."

Neftali shook his head superiorly. "You don't understand.

In places where they are rare, people buy them one or two at a time. For special occasions, or for gifts. They must be really special. They pay a high price."

"Well, if you sent them the ordinary oranges, then they wouldn't have to pay such a high price, and they wouldn't be so rare, and they would buy more. I've never seen oranges like that for sale in Irwindale."

Pete stood around until the noon break, watching the workers in the giant factory. Although he'd grown up just a few miles away, he'd never been inside this packing plant.

He watched as the trucks laden with oranges pulled up at the huge sliding panels in the walls. He saw the fruit come onto a conveyor apparatus which spread them evenly for a stamping machine to put the citrus organization's name on each orange. Women—all Mexican—stood and packed them in various types of boxes after another machine had sorted them according to size. Conveyor belts carried the packed boxes to the far side of the factory and up and into waiting railroad boxcars, where men—all Mexican—lifted each box off the conveyor and stacked them at one end of the car. As soon as a car had a load, it was moved up and an empty car took its place. Pete understood that different types of oranges ripened at different times of the year, and knew many workers probably worked year round.

At noon Pete's father proudly took him to the foreman.

"Tell him you're my son," the old man said. Pete looked at the red-faced, sandy-haired foreman.

"I'm his son," Pete said in English.

The foreman looked at him. "Just out of the Army, eh?" he said, eying the discharge emblem on Pete's uniform and shaking hands hurriedly. "Looking for a job?"

Pete looked around. "Doing what?"

"If you're as good a grade sorter as your old man here, we can put you on right away. Takes a knack to work fast and get the specials. Looks easy, but after a few hours they all get to look the same, 'less you know what you're doing."

Pete pretended to consider. "How much does it pay?"

"We pay sixty cents to veterans. Fifty to others. Your old man gets fifty-five 'cause he's fast."

Pete thanked him and the foreman went on his way. Neftali wanted to know what the conversation had been, and Pete evasively told him a little different version, not wanting his father to start badgering him into taking a job.

The noon hour ended, the workers started returning to their all-day positions, the motors which drove the belts and apparatus started a low whine, and quickly climbed to a tireless, relentless pitch. Pete said "Hasta la vista" to his father and walked away from the clanging, banging, and humming of the orange plant.

Tearfully his mother, still wearing a tattered old dress, still making the same delicious tortillas and fried potatoes and rabbit, still smelling of chili, a little more gray in her hair, tried to talk him into staying in Irwindale. "We need you. Papa makes little money. Rabbit and potatoes are expensive now."

"I will send you money. I promised Angie I'd live by her."

On the morning of his departure he cut short the crying scene, and, with a little exasperation, reminded them he was only going twenty miles away. He hugged and kissed mama and his little sister Dolores, who worked in another factory nearby. He walked with his father to his job and then, still wearing his Army uniform, hitchhiked down Irwindale Avenue to Valley Boulevard and then caught a bus into Los Angeles.

After his arrival at his sister's home Pete walked the streets of the city for a week or so. While in the Army small bits of the vast world had unfolded for him. Vividly he remembered his basic training in a state bordering on Mexico, how he'd taken for granted the fact that his weekend passes in town were spent in the "Latin section," the MPs pointing to WHITE ONLY signs when he'd entered a bar or restaurant. He was a little surprised to find that in East Los Angeles the Anglos, or Gringos, or Americanos—he'd always used one or the other of the terms—were called whites, as they were in other big cities.

He had explained to Angie and Julio he wanted to look around before going to work. After his experiences in the barrios in other Southwestern states, he expected East Los Angeles to be a huge Irwindale. He was surprised to find little similarity.

He turned onto a street teeming with people, little businesses, restaurants, bars, and open markets. He walked through a dirty market place, noticing many types of food, parts of animals and vegetables, which he knew the names of but had never seen in Irwindale. Those with whom he talked made him realize the Spanish language was different here from where he'd learned to talk. He heard the word "chicano" for the first time.

He saw two Anglo policemen drag a man unconscious from a bar, and he wondered if the man were drunk or had been knocked out, and if so by whom. He noticed the passers-by refused to look directly at the belligerent officers, and he got the distinct impression nobody dared question their rough handling of the victim.

Walking through a residential section he saw houses on what had recently been vacant lots. They were combinations of discarded billboards, sheet metal, rough boards and bottles stacked together. Electricity was brought into these homes by a series of short extension cords running from a nearby permanent house. He passed the garage of a home and saw, as the doors were open, that it was the complete living quarters of a ragged family.

As he passed a bar and grill he smelled a delicious aroma of frying pork and chili, and abruptly swung in. Seated at the counter, he noticed a homely woman cooking, watching a game of pool at the rear. There were only women here. He ordered pork and chili and asked the woman about the job situation in the area.

"Try the 'waiting place,'" the woman answered impatiently, turning her attention to an argument between two hefty women arguing over the pool table.

"Waiting place?"

The fry-cook looked at him. She pointed. "Down the street and to the left at the next corner. You'll see."

Pete finished his meal as the argument at the rear drew closer to violence, the massive lesbians screaming the most profane Spanish he'd ever heard at one another.

He walked out, down the street, past a band of ragged children each with a homemade shoeshine kit. They spotted him as one with money and followed, pestering to shine his shoes, but he knew enough to ignore them completely and soon he was abandoned in favor of some men in uniform.

He came to the street and looked both ways, still wondering what the "waiting place" meant. He saw nothing unusual, dirty buildings, dirtier homes, ragged children, dogs eating from overturned garbage cans in the gutter, and down the street to the left he saw a crowd of men.

Pete walked toward the waiting place.

As Pete approached he saw that the group he'd seen from the corner was only a small part of the greater group gathered in a vacant space between two buildings. More than a hundred men milled, argued, talked, shouted, passed bottles. Some were literally in rags, some in fairly decent work clothes, some had not shaved in weeks, some were ancient, some were hardly more than teen-agers.

Pete experienced fear and curiosity as he neared the mob. "What the hell," he thought as he walked into them (there was nothing else he could do, except retreat). "After what I been through in the Pacific, there's nothing could scare me right here in my own back yard." But they did scare him. And it was not his back yard.

Against one wall two dozen men were propped or lying. Vomit was common on the ground. Pete was aware he caused a ripple of turning heads as he walked through, being by far the best dressed, cleanest shaven of the lot. He heard no English. Before he was halfway through them, he noticed nearly a dozen following him. He turned.

"Looking for help?" one tattered man asked in Spanish.

Pete tried to look confident. "No," he answered, then stood his ground.

"You are looking for work, too," one man remarked.

"Yes, I am."

The man eyed Pete's suit. "You must be down to your last best suit. Right?"

Pete blurted, "I just got out of . . ." he saw it was too late, ". . . the Army . . ."

The men shrugged with understanding, tried to appear casual and came closer.

One man in particular approached Pete. He was of medium height, dark, would have been nice looking with a shave and haircut, Pete thought. He wore filthy, wrinkled trousers that had once been part of a good suit, rundown shoes that had once been stylish and a torn old sport coat over a T-shirt.

"I call myself Canto," the man said. "What's your name?"

"Me llamo Pete."

"What kind of work you looking for?" the man asked. Pete noticed he gave severe stares to some others nearby, and they turned their backs, as though relinquishing this prize grudgingly to Canto. Pete appeared casual.

"Oh, I don't know. What kinds are available here?"

"Come on, man," Canto said, urging Pete along. "You can buy me a beer, I know that. I'll tell you about it. You're new in town, eh?"

It was a game, Pete saw. He regarded the man with indifference. Canto's slightly belligerent attitude was assumed with the knowledge of Pete's fear and uncertainty in this situation, but Pete knew that as long as he had the money, he was in command.

"All right," Pete agreed, and they started for a tavern across the street.

Just then the entire crowd, like a liquid creature, surged toward the road. Pete saw a stake truck coming to a stop. Before its wheels stopped rolling, the truck was engulfed in men, shouting and pushing. The truck driver opened the door and stood on the running board, shouting in Spanish, holding up four fingers: "I need four strong ones. To stack sacks of cement. Four hours of work. Two dollars!"

About half the group—the lame, the emaciated drunks, the old men—walked away from the truck on hearing this. The others crowded around, shouting, waving. The driver was selective. He leaned down and slapped one husky man on the shoulder and the man scrambled up onto the bed of the truck.

With care the driver selected three more the same way, and as soon as they were on the truck, seated backs to the cab, the driver lurched the truck ahead, through the crowd, by some miracle running over no one.

Pete saw a man coming down the sidewalk wearing a sombrero. He had an ill-concealed bottle of wine under his flimsy shirt. He joined the crowd and fiercely scolded most of those who crowded around begging a drink. He handed his bottle to one friend and let him take a sip. Then he handed it to another, who immediately tried to drink as much and as fast as he could. With an oath, the man in the sombrero grabbed the bottle away and smashed a heavy fist into the offender's nose. Blood spurted and he went down on his face and lay still. Before Pete could think, a wraith-like creature who had feigned sleep against the wall drifted like a puff of smoke to the fallen man and went through all pockets in an instant, finding only a long cigarette butt, which he kept. The wraith fled.

The fallen man lifted his head, rose to his hands and knees, whereupon the sombrero man placed a foot against his buttocks and shoved, sending the man tumbling again. The man regained his feet and fled like a chicken in a crowded coop, trying to get lost amongst the others.

Seated at the bar in the beer joint across from the waiting place, Pete and Canto talked. Pete gave up any pretense that all this was not new to him.

"This is the bottom of the road," Canto explained, taking delight in being the tourists' guide. "When you get thrown in jail for drunk, and you go back to find you're locked out of your room until you pay up, and you've bummed all your friends for the last two-bits, you come down here to the waiting place and wait."

"But why?" Pete asked. "Why don't they go get jobs some place? There's lots of work."

"Not lots, but there are some jobs," Canto agreed. "Most of these guys are dodging something or somebody—police, draft boards, immigration people—or they have problems and work only when they have to. None of them wants to work steady. Look, here comes 'Geev-eet-to-heem.' Years back he was a fighter. Now all anyone calls him is 'Old Geev-eet-to-heem.' No last name 'cause he's on the dodge from something or other. Watch this."

Pete watched the dreary old man enter and approach the bar. He recoiled inwardly at the sight of the man's face. It was scarred, battered, the nose obviously broken several times, and the mouth was half toothless. But the real damage to the face had been done by liquor, as the drooping folds above the eyes and the sagging baggy cheeks testified.

The man reached across the bar and snapped on a peculiar looking lamp. Then he put his hand under it and examined it at some length, although there was no visible light emanating from the lamp. Finally the man cursed in dejection and sat down on a bar stool. The bartender approached.

"Hello, Geev-eet-to-heem. Does it still show?" the bartender asked.

Geev-eet-to-heem looked desperate. "A tiny bit, that's all. It'll be gone in a few days. Trust me? Please?"

The bartender shook his head. "In a few days you might be dead. No credit." And he turned away. The former prizefighter seemed to muster his entire strength as he rose and walked away, his worn-out shoes scraping the floor with each step as he dragged his feet.

Canto laughed. "That's the old 'muscatel shuffle.' You can

always tell a wino nearing the end of the trail by the way his feet drag."

Pete was puzzled. "But . . . the light, what was he looking at?"

"Wow, you are new around here, aren't you?" Canto said, again assuming the role of the lecturer. "That lamp, it's ultraviolet. One way to raise a few bucks here is selling blood to the blood bank down on Fourth Street. But you can't sell your blood any more than once in six weeks. So when they take it from your arm, they dab a little invisible dye on your little finger nail. The dye lasts about a month and a half. When you go to sell your blood, they put your hand under a lamp just like this one. They can tell when you last had some taken. Watch this."

Canto placed his left hand under the lamp and the nail of the little finger glowed brightly, fluorescent. "Three days ago. I got a long wait," he said stolidly.

Pete was intrigued. "How much do they give you for blood?"

"Two and a half dollars. There's a place across town where they give three, but it's a long way."

"Do they mark the fingernail over there too?"

Canto shook his head sadly. "Exactly the same. You can't beat 'em. There's supposed to be some guy down on skidrow—around Main Street downtown—who, if you split with him, will put something on your fingernail so the dye won't show. I've never been able to find him, though."

"But, why do they have a lamp like that in here?"

"So the bartender and the customers can tell when they're ready to sell. If that guy'd had a clean nail, the bartender would have given him a drink or two on credit."

They talked on, Canto telling Pete in shocking terms the life of the people "down an' out." Pete ordered another round for both—it was understood Canto had no money—and soon Canto was ordering rounds for both.

Toward evening Pete was standing in the vacant place between two buildings surrounded by a crowd of admirers and telling them how his training in the Army was helping him to land a hundred-dollar-a-week job. He was not yet too drunk, and they were pointing out how with such a job, which he would undoubtedly get and could handle, within a short time he would have a good car and really be living high. Yes, he said modestly, he guessed that would be the case. He wanted a Cadillac. He didn't hesitate when someone suggested he spring with a dollar for a gallon of Dago red, and the wine was brought and gone within minutes. After all, a dollar is nothing, he said as he handed out another bill for another jug.

Night was drawing near. Pete realized he was reeling, and someone offered him a wooden box next to the wall to rest on. And before long he knew he had to just close his eyes for a few minutes. He leaned against the wall, his last bit of awareness causing him to fold his arms to protect his wallet in his inside coat pocket, where rested the remainder of his mustering-out pay.

He awoke with a start, chilled. He looked about for a minute, remembering where he was and why. Then he clutched for his wallet. He realized his coat was gone. His shoes also, and his wrist watch. By the clock in the tavern window he saw it was nearly four in the morning. Perhaps two dozen men were huddled in groups in the vacant lot, some talking, some dozing. He got up and walked around, looking for his coat or shoes. He tried to find Canto or any of the others he'd been drinking with. He recognized no one.

He waited around, his mind still not clear enough to realize exactly what had happened to him.

He stood around, cold and shivering, for an hour. A stake truck pulled up and the men made a rush for it. Pete was puzzled and walked toward the truck. Listening, he heard the driver say ten men were needed to distribute shopping circulars in the residential areas across town. Dollar and a half, and you'll be having your vino by noon. The truck pulled away with its human cargo.

Suddenly Pete realized he was not going to see Canto, or his drinking friends, or his wallet, watch, or coat or shoes. As his mind cleared the nightmare of it all struck him, and he started hurrying away. It was still dark, and if he walked fast, he might get to Angie and Julio's before daylight.

Dawn was breaking as he slipped quietly in the back door. He went to the bathroom and took a hot shower, shaved and changed into clean shorts and T-shirt and was just settling in the crisp white sheets his sister had put on the couch when he heard the alarm clock in Julio and Angie's room go off. Julio tiptoed in. It was almost daylight.

"Ho, you're awake," he said to Pete. "Good. Some construction guys said to be at the stand in work clothes this morning. You can start on a job today. Union scale. Better hurry. They'll be at the stand ready to leave in about an hour."

Angie came in and sat beside him on the couch. She smiled radiantly, pleased, and squeezed Pete's hand. "You look like you had a rough night," she said knowingly. Julio grinned down at him.

Pete thought that he had never seen such good, honest, clean, decent, worthwhile people in his life.

P ete's social circle began forming when he met the gang of a
half dozen steel-helmeted construction laborers having
coffee and doughnuts at Angie's that morning. They all lived
within a few blocks of the stand and rode together in a pickup
truck, taking turns at riding in the cab.

They were cordial, informal, friendly to the point of inti-
macy from the first, and none of them, Pete could tell, held
much hope for his lasting long as a construction laborer.

"You gotta be on your toes," they told him in English.

But Pete fooled them, and he fooled the boss.

The men took Pete to the boss in the construction site office
just before 8 A.M., introduced him cursorily as "that new man
you needed" and abandoned him. The boss, a gringo, signed
Pete up, asked him briefly about his experiences in the Army,
and then said, "Follow me."

He led Pete to a point near a bridge the company was building. "We mostly build bridges," he told Pete in a friendly manner. "That means we pour concrete walls, abutments, piers, do
paving, put in sidewalk, curb and gutter, lay pipes and about a
half god-damn million other things. Right now we gotta put
some heavy pipe underground right here." He pointed to two
stakes driven into the ground. "Dig a ditch four feet deep here
between those wooden stakes. You'll find equipment over in
that tool shack."

The boss stood and watched as Pete broke into a trot toward
the tool shack and returned in a moment with the proper type of
shovel. The boss grunted. God-damn few of these new men
knew what kind of a shovel to use for a particular type of work.

The boss stood and watched as Pete started digging. He saw Pete knew how to dig a little, and then move into the hole so it wasn't necessary to stoop quite so low, dig a little deeper and then move into that spot. Pete was pleased the boss was watching. Digging a ditch the proper, easy and efficient way was a thing few men knew how to do. An inexperienced man soon would wear himself out and move little dirt. The boss left but returned soon. "Better take those carpenters up there a keg of sixteen commons," he told Pete. Pete dropped his shovel and trotted easily to the tool shack, where he quickly found the right keg of nails, hoisted it expertly to his shoulder, walked to the ladder at the bottom of the bridge and climbed easily to the top hanging on with but one hand. The boss walked away.

By the end of the day Pete was tired but happy. And he was delighted to learn his companions were in the habit of stopping at a particular bar and grill every day after work.

That evening as they walked into the barroom Pete suddenly felt at last as though he'd found a place where he belonged. He was wearing khaki shirt and trousers, high shoes and a steel helmet issued to him that very day. When his companions entered all were immediately hailed by other men similarly attired. Pete was introduced around as all took seats at the bar or in booths and began shop talk. Pete found his training in the Army enabled him to stay with and even join the conversation about joists, four-bys, vibrators and slabs.

When a feminine voice asked for his order, Pete looked up and saw a girl in her twenties, eyebrows arched high with mascara, heavy rouge, ruby lipstick, wearing a skirt and blouse a little too small. A heavy odor of sweet perfume hung about her and her black hair hung to her shoulders.

She smiled shyly as she took his order and Pete nudged the man seated next to him.

"Who's the babe?" he asked, not taking his eyes from her.

"Oh, that's Minerva. Not bad, eh? But nobody stands a chance. She won't give you a tumble."

When they left Pete left her a half dollar tip.

Within a week, Pete had his own pickup truck and was driving to work. At quitting time he went straight home to Angie and Julio's house, changed into sport clothes and went to the bar and grill where Minerva worked. Each evening he would sit alone at the bar, only occasionally joining in the shop talk with his fellow workers. Soon it was understood he was courting Minerva, although he never asked her out or did anything but sit at the bar and quietly converse with her in between her taking orders. Soon he noticed when he entered every evening she would smile warmly at him—and only him—and he would take a seat at the end of the bar where she could stand and watch the customers. Pete showed a great deal more affection for his colleagues than he did for Minerva, but it was understood a relationship was evolving that would end in marriage. He became more possessive as the weeks went by, and soon he was telling her not to wait on a certain customer because he didn't like the way he looked at her. They talked at length about their brothers, sisters, parents, nephews and nieces, and one day Pete said, "I think we should get married." She agreed.

Few things interrupted the routine of Don Neftali and Doña Alicia Sandoval. For many years now the packing plant had been on a five-day week, after lingering on a five-and-a-half-day week during the depression, and now he worked Saturdays and Sundays only when he wanted to or when a big citrus rush was on for one or more of various reasons.

Irwindale had grown little in population, but the cheap, rocky land had been ideal for rock and gravel quarries, and there were many rock crushers in the area. Also, brick and concrete block and pipe companies had made headquarters there, making the once-desertlike community a center of heavy industrial activity.

Neftali and Alicia had the house to themselves now. They slept in a bedroom that had once been alive with children every night. Alicia slept in an ankle-length flannel nightgown, while Neftali slept in only BVDs and an undershirt. She shook him awake.

"It's Saturday," he said grumpily. "I'm not going to work today."

"You must have forgotten. Victorio is coming to take us to buy some clothes for Pedro and Minerva's wedding tomorrow."

Neftali rose and donned his khaki trousers and shirt and put on his high-top shoes. He went into the kitchen while Alicia dressed. There was a small chill in the air and so he lit all four burners of the ancient gas range a daughter had given them when her husband bought a new model. Soon Alicia appeared and fixed a breakfast of eggs scrambled with chorizo.

"How come," Neftali asked, "for this wedding we have to have brand new clothes?"

Alicia, with a fork in her right hand, was carefully putting egg and chorizo on a piece of tortilla held in her left hand. "This is in the city," she explained, "and there will be lots of people we don't know."

He was treating his eggs and chorizo the same. "It seems if we went to our other children's marriages in our own clothes, this should be no different."

"Times are changing, I guess. Besides, I'm glad to be getting a new dress. We might be going more places."

"Our regular clothes are good enough for any place we might go in Irwindale," Neftali said.

Victorio swung his near-new Buick into his parents' driveway and tooted. He shook his head a little as he saw his father in wrinkled khakis and cotton jacket, hair over his ears, and his mother in an ancient dress and twenty-year-old dress pumps come out to his car. His father, who really wasn't too old, moved slow and was stooped a little. His mother, he realized, reminded him of the Anglo woman in one of the several recent movies which made great fun of rural Anglo Americans. *She is the counterpart,* Victorio said to himself with a smile.

"You see," his father began as they drove, "it's not too good when poor people want too much. Then you have to work hard and get a better job. Then you feel you have to have better things, and so on. People should stay near where they're raised and be content."

Victorio had heard it many times. He knew his father resented his getting away from farm work and moving from Irwindale. It was useless to argue.

Victorio took his mother and father to a large secondhand clothing store in East Los Angeles, where his father promptly picked out a little-worn suit which was very stylish two decades before, and his mother picked out a dress as close to the lavish styles of her girlhood as she could find, and then they both managed to find and insist upon shoes to match. They were waited on by an immaculately dressed man with a neat hairline mustache who spoke in very crisp and proper Spanish and acted as though he had dealt with this situation many times. As the clerk handed an exasperated Victorio Alicia's and Neftali's packaged old clothes (they insisted on wearing the new things home) he spoke quietly in English for the first time: "It's useless to argue."

P eople began arriving in the back yard of Angie and Julio's house in the morning of the wedding day, although the service was not to be until the afternoon.

Pete's brothers and sisters came with their children. Minerva's brothers and sisters came with their children. Angie and Julio's neighbors came with their children. Minnie's friends came with their children and Pete's fellow construction workers came with their children.

Angie appointed herself Minnie's overseer, and kept her in the house out of sight, while the rest of the women went to work preparing mounds of food in the kitchen.

Pete nervously swaggered among the menfolk, talking of work, wages, cars, trucks, everything except the wedding. A highpoint was the arrival of the bride's and bridegroom's parents, who were formally and stiffly introduced. The old folks fell into a pained, polite conversation, while the other menfolk surreptitiously drank whiskey. The smaller children wandered among the throng searching for their respective parents to take them to el escusado while those a little older scattered throughout the neighborhood to make friends or enemies, as fate decreed.

By noon almost a hundred persons had gathered, and still they came. They milled, breaking into indistinct groups of young women, middle-aged women, young men, middle-aged men, and old folks. A priest from a nearby church whom Julio had engaged came and searched in vain for a familiar face. He tried to get a rehearsal of the ceremony started, but when he got Pete and the best man Julio to stand still, the bride's father had wandered off, and when he got the bride's father the others were off. He finally settled for telling Pete when and where to make his entrance and then he found Minerva hiding in a room in the house and instructed her on the procedure.

Steam and the aroma of cooking billowed from the kitchen as mountains of food piled up to be taken out to the many patio and card tables in the back yard following the ceremony. A ripple of interest went through the crowd as the mariachis arrived, in tight trousers and ornamented ranch-style shirts and large sombreros. There were six of them, and the priest called them to him. As he instructed the leader, another member of the ensemble struck a few chords of an old familiar favorite, and the other musicians jumped into it, as the falsetto yipes began ringing from the crowd and those who were singers began edging forward. The priest gave up and went looking for a drink.

The bottles became overt, and Pete found drink after drink forced upon him as he circulated through the singing, shouting and conversation. He heard his father talking to Minerva's parents as they all sat off to one side: ". . . I was only thirteen, but large and strong, and I knew how to handle a rifle well. So when the outlaw Guzmán saw we were ready to defend our village to a man, he sent a henchman with a white flag to us. My father was the village spokesman, and he walked out, with me right behind him for protection, to talk truce with the bandidos . . ." Pete had heard it many times, differently each time, and knew his father was relaxing and finding friends. An occasional Anglo face appeared, uncertain, hesitant, and Angie, or Angie's brothers, or Julio, or Pete would rush to him and take him to a group and say in English, "He's my friend, I work with him, take good care of him," and the newcomer would be left to fend for himself.

Empty stomachs more than anything started the throng calling for the ceremony, and Pete was pushed, staggering a little, to the center of the patio with the priest and Minerva's father. The mariachis finally quit playing as Minnie, striking in her white wedding gown and severely painted face and shiny black hair, came from the house. The priest tried to drag it out, but saw that the audience was very impatient and rather drunk, and he no sooner pronounced them man and wife than a shout went up: "The food!" And the food came, tray after tray, first to the table with the old folks, then to the others. Steaming platters of chili, enchiladas, tripe cooked in red sauce, and a half-hundred other items in abundance. No places were provided for the children, and they ganged around, little brown hands darting in to snatch plump morsels, and Pete, still staggering, pretended rage as he drove off children who obviously by their attire were wandering strays from the neighboring homes. All his guests had dressed their offspring in Sunday finery.

Hardly a head turned as Pete announced he and Minerva were leaving. The mariachis had started again and he had to shout. He and Minnie went to his old pickup truck, parked in the driveway headed toward the street. He was staggering, and his brother Victorio pleaded, "Pete, don't drive, please."

"I'm fine. Let me alone."

Minnie put her hand on his shoulders and looked into his face. "Pete, let me drive. Please."

Reluctantly, he handed her the keys, not wanting an argument to mar his wedding night. He climbed in on the passenger side and Minnie got behind the wheel. The truck had JUST MARRIED and WOW! written on the sides and tin cans tied to the rear bumper. Minnie started the engine, slipped it into gear, and the pickup lurched out into the street. Minnie weaved through the heavy traffic of East Los Angeles toward an open highway, blushing when other motorists saw the pretty bride behind the wheel and the slack-jawed, glassy-eyed Pete grinning blankly out the window.

"I haven't been to Ensenada in a long time, let's go there," Pete said just before he laid his head on her lap and began snoring.

Pete had rented the house next door to Angie and Julio, and they returned Sunday night. Pete had furnished the house with secondhand items, and Minnie was delighted with it. She would not work at the bar anymore.

No sooner had they arrived home Sunday night than Julio and Angie came over. It was Pete and Minnie's first evening as host in their own household, and Pete was more content than he ever had been. About midnight, Pete yawned and stretched hugely, announcing it was bedtime. Angie and Julio lingered only a half hour more before leaving.

As they were beginning to doze off, Minnie with her back to him snuggling deliciously close, Pete murmured, "Maybe I'll take the day off tomorrow. The boss might be mad, but there's lots of jobs." But he dreamed he saw himself at the waiting place, living through the horrors he'd seen, and he was up at six ready to leave for the job.

As month after month went by Pete became a "regular" with the construction company. When the job ended and the company began a new one they kept Pete, along with a select few, on the steady payroll. He was making more money than he ever had and was very content with his work, until one day the boss called the cement masons' union for skilled help to finish concrete.

Pete was quickly aware of the air of superiority the skilled men sported when they arrived on the job, giving orders with quiet confidence to the laborers like Pete who shoveled the concrete. All six of the masons were Chicanos, and each had a box of trowels, floats and specialists' tools with which they went to work after the concrete was in place, without a word from the boss. At the noon break Pete found himself eating by one of the skilled men named Old Antonio. He had seen this man among those who frequented Angie and Julio's.

He questioned the old-timer about wages, and learned that masons, with overtime, made twice what he did. "How can I get into your union?" he asked.

The old man shook his head. "Muy difícil," he said. Very difficult. "Only a man with experience can get in. The best way is to volunteer to do little cement finishing jobs on your job. Then when you know something about it, go down to the union hall and pay them a hundred dollars."

Pete bought a trowel and edger and began learning. He even poured a little patio slab in his back yard, and then a little sidewalk running to the clothesline, just for practice.

Whenever a small troweling job came up, and Pete's boss

would have had to hire a skilled man and pay him all day for a few hours' work, he was only too happy to let Pete handle it. Pete still spent most of his time doing pick and shovel work, or carrying lumber and nails for the carpenters, but he became the unofficial mason on the job. He was now obsessed with the idea of being a skilled worker, and his opportunity was slow in coming.

The success of Angie and Julio when they expanded their taco stand into a restaurant and obtained a liquor license seemed to point up Pete's static position. He kept watching the progress of the construction job and one day he took a deep breath, lit a cigarette, put his hands in his pockets to conceal his nervousness, and approached the boss.

"Say, I was thinking," he said casually. "Pretty soon you're going to need a cement finisher full time, right?"

The boss, a gruff, old-time construction foreman, liked Pete. He liked ambition, and he had been around Mexican-Americans a long time and was fond of them.

"Yeah, and you want the job, eh?" he replied.

Pete was a little chagrined at being so transparent. Before he could answer, the boss went on. "Tell you what, Sandoval. You get a clearance from the union hall, and I'll put you on the payroll as our full-time concrete man. Within a couple of weeks we'll be pouring every day, almost, for the next four or five months. If you can handle the job, it's yours."

Pete reeled with elation, and self-doubt.

Pete Sandoval parked his battered old pickup truck carefully next to the curb on San Pedro Street in downtown Los Angeles and got out. He stood on the sidewalk a moment, looking up a little apprehensively at the large brick building with a sign reading, CONSTRUCTION TRADES UNION—American Federation of Labor. He seemed to brace himself as he pushed the door open and entered.

He walked uncertainly down the hall, reading the signs on the doors until he came to: "International Brotherhood of Cement Masons—AF of L." He stood looking at it a while, his hand stroking his clean-shaven chin in what he hoped appeared a casual manner. He pushed the door open and walked to a waist-high counter in front of several desks. A half dozen men and two women were working. One man looked up and came toward Pete.

"Can I help you?" the man asked. Pete did not allow himself to become rattled.

"Is this where you join the union?" he asked in his broken English.

"You want to be a cement finisher?" the man asked. Pete nodded. "Yes, this is it," the man continued. "You had any experience?"

Pete knew the answer could be incriminating. It was expected that any good union man would never dream of scabbing, yet it was impossible to become a union member without experience. "Only when I had to," he answered, actually believing this to be an original and believable excuse. "I been doing some labor for some companies, and sometimes when they pour cement somebody gets sick or something and then I pick up a trowel and get a little experience."

The man eyed him severely, yet Pete sensed friendliness.

"Been doing quite a lot of cement finishing, eh?"

"No," Pete explained, "I don't believe anybody should do certain work unless they belong to that union."

"Well then what makes you think you're qualified to be a finisher? We don't want men in here who will go out and mess up a sidewalk job and get the contractor down on us. We have enough trouble with them."

"Well," Pete swallowed, but he knew he was good at making logical excuses, "I didn't do very much—like I say, only when it was to save the concrete from drying too rough—but what little I did, I learned very fast."

The man eyed Pete with a trace of amusement. Pete continued.

"I thought that before I do very much more, I should come in and get a union card, so I won't be breaking the rules anymore. So here I am."

The man forced himself to remain serious. Pete's naïve sincerity, his simple logic built on simple lies, plus his appearance, would cause anyone at least to smile.

He eyed Pete's five feet, three inches, his bald head, the beautiful set of large teeth in a big mouth set in a prematurely wrinkled face, and knew the Los Angeles local cement finishers' union had another brother.

He sighed, guessing accurately what was coming next.

"Okay. You got a job to go to? As a finisher?"

Pete pondered a moment. "No. How can I? Nobody will hire a cement finisher who doesn't belong to the union." He got a little indignant. "That's why I came here. To join. So I can go . . ."

"Okay, okay," the man said hurriedly. He extended his hand to Pete. "My name's Harrington. I'm one of the business agents. What's your name?"

"Pete," Pete answered. "Pete Sandoval."

"You know it costs a hundred bucks to join the union, don't you?" Harrington again guessed what was coming.

Pete reached his hand into his pocket and felt the five twenty-dollar bills nestled there. His face showed a little dismay. "A hundred dollars? I don't think I can pay that much 'til I'm working. Another cement finisher said you would let me bring you twenty dollars each time I get paid until I pay it."

Harrington gave a disgusted grunt and started writing on a form.

"Okay, Sandoval," he said as he wrote, "we'll let you in. You bring me in twenty bucks every time you get paid, understand? And you got to have three of your amigos who are members come in and sign that you're qualified to do the work. Can you do that?"

Pete grinned broadly. "Sure," he said. The sh being an alien sound combination to his native tongue, the word came out "Choor."

Harrington helped him fill out the necessary forms and gave him a book of union rules and a badge which read "I.B.C.M., A.F. of L., Local 627, L.A."

By the time Pete had walked back to the tired old pickup truck his usual swagger had returned. In fact it was a little more pronounced. He coaxed the engine to life, smiling with satisfaction that, after many generations, a Sandoval in the family was finally a highly skilled, highly paid worker. He was so pleased with the events of the past half hour, so pleased he had saved himself a hundred dollars—at least for the time being—that he failed to see a car coming as he pulled out from the curb. The car slammed on its brakes, wheels locking as the driver blasted the horn and barely avoided a collision. Pete got a glimpse of the freckle-faced man glaring at him as he swerved out and passed the old pickup. Pete glared back at him accusingly.

"Look where you're going, you Goddamn dumb Oakie son-of-a-bitch," Pete muttered as he coaxed a little speed from the reluctant motor. And his last word came out "beach."

Pete headed down San Pedro Street to Fourth Street and turned toward East Los Angeles. He smiled again over his good fortune.

To him, he had just made one hundred dollars. And he wanted to share it with Minnie. True, it was she who had saved and skimped for months to save up that money they knew the Union would demand as an initiation fee. But it was still just like finding a hundred dollars not to have to pay it. The fact that he would have to pay twenty dollars each payday until it was paid off was canceled out by the fact that he would be earning at least that much more than he would have as a common unskilled construction laborer. And when it was eventually paid, it would be like getting a twenty-dollar-a-week raise. This also pleased him. Yes, he wanted to share his good fortune with Minnie.

He frowned now as he thought of something. He wanted to give her $50 and tell her Harrington had insisted on half payment. But he had only five twenty-dollar bills, and you couldn't divide that in half. He thought about giving her two twenties and saying Harrington had taken $60. But $60 was too much to hold out on a good wife like Minnie. After all, she had saved it. Giving her only $40 would hurt his conscience. She was too good a woman for that kind of treatment. But on the other hand, $60 was too much to give her unexpectedly—and that would leave him only $40. Well, only one thing to do. Stop and change one bill. Then he could split with her. And he might as well stop at a bar and have a drink while he was changing it. That way he could hit two birds with one rock.

The next day Pete approached the gringo boss and showed his union card and work permit, which entitled him to do work as a qualified concrete mason. He reminded the boss he'd been promised the job.

"I can handle it," Pete said, with what he hoped appeared to be typical Yankee confidence. But inside he was in doubt.

"Good," the boss said. "It's settled, then. Come with me and I'll show you what our pour schedule is."

For the first time in his life, Pete felt important. As the dozens of other workmen sawed and hammered and chiseled and welded and operated the huge machines, Pete accompanied the boss around the job.

"Tomorrow," the boss explained as they stood near one bank of the approach, "we pour this little bit of the deck. Only a small pour compared to what's coming up. How many men do you think can handle it?"

Pete's mind raced, but he appeared calm. "Give me two laborers to shovel, and one more cement finisher," he said casually.

"You get your own finisher. Either call the Union Hall or bring a skilled man. But I want a top-notch job here. I'm having enough trouble with the state inspectors. Just make sure it's done right. Now come over here and I'll show you what we got lined up for Friday, Monday, and Wednesday . . ."

That evening after work Pete again drove straight to Angie's Bar and Grill. It never occurred to him to call Minnie to say he'd be late.

He ate dinner and then had a few drinks. Before long the men with hard hats began arriving. They traipsed in in steel helmets, dirty khakis, huge heavy shoes, sweaty, grimy-faced, but somehow laughing and not tired.

They ate and drank, shouted and quarreled, half in English, half in Spanish. Another day was over for them, and a night was beginning. None thought of the wife and children waiting at home. None brooded over the day's drudgery. All took pride in telling how hard they had worked, yet how much strength and energy they had left. Many would drink until the small hours of the morning, then stagger home to say "shut up" to the wife and sleep until dawn, at which time they would get up and do it all over again.

Angie's waitress circulated among them, taking orders, swearing loudly and slapping at gnarled, black hands that tried to feel the ample buttocks. The juke box roared the latest hit tune from Mexico, and everyone in the place outroared it.

Truculently, Pete wandered among the groups at the tables, casually—or so he thought—bringing out his new union card. He pinned his I.B.C.M. AFL badge to his baseball cap which he always wore to cover his baldness when he wasn't wearing his steel helmet.

Presently Pete saw the man he wanted to talk to enter. It was Antonio.

Old Antonio was the resident and reigning old-timer at concrete work. Many years before, he'd been one of the first to join the concrete finishers' union. He was an old man now, and he spoke practically no English, but many were the gringo bosses who breathed a sigh of relief and relaxed when they saw the union hall had sent out Old Tony. He knew everything there was to know about his trade, and when he told a boss a certain job was worth more than the usual wage scale, there was no argument.

Old Tony, Pete knew, made a great deal of money and was revered among his peers, although all generally agreed he worried too much.

Pete sat Antonio down and showed him his new union card and badge.

"Qué bueno!" the old man said. "You have graduated."

Then Pete told him what was on his mind. He was very worried about the pour the next morning. He knew it was completely unlike troweling sidewalks, floors or finishing curbs; in fact, Pete knew, no trowels were used on a deck pour. He described what was to be done in detail and asked Antonio to tell him how to do it. Antonio shook his head.

"No," he said, "it cannot be told. I will go to your job in the morning and help you. The bosses are Americanos?"

"Sí."

"Bueno. They will not understand as I show you what is to be done. Believe me, I know how to handle this so they will know they have made a wise choice in promoting you. Do not worry about my job. We are doing nothing important and I will call and say I am sick."

Pete gave Old Tony instructions as to how to get to his job and soon the old man, after a serious good-bye to many friends, left to go home.

"Hasta mañana," he said to Pete as he left, waving a gnarled hand.

Pete suddenly didn't feel like drinking and being carefree anymore. A vague uneasiness gnawed at him, and he kept thinking of the pour coming in the morning. He grew quiet and suddenly decided to go home.

At home he was unusually noncommunicative with Minnie. He was a little irritable and when in bed he lay thinking to himself a long time, worrying. What if his truck didn't start in the morning? He sat up, wanting to go out to make sure it was reliable. What if he overslept? Maybe he'd better not sleep. He got up and tested the electric alarm clock. He adjusted it to go off at four-thirty instead of five-thirty. Twice during the night he decided he couldn't hear the clock motor humming, and he got up to check it.

He was awake at four o'clock, getting dressed. Minnie got up and made his breakfast, but before he was half through eating he found himself looking at the clock. Maybe Old Tony would oversleep. Maybe he wouldn't be able to find the job.

He said good-bye and told Minnie he might work late and went out to his pickup truck.

Dawn was breaking as he parked beside the project and climbed up the approach to the waiting bridge-to-be. He looked around. The 600-foot-wide strip of fresh dirt splitting the city looked raw and primitive to him. The freeway bed stretched out to the horizon, gently winding among the factories and buildings, disappearing somewhere near the mass of structures that was the Los Angeles civic center. From the bridge's height he was about even with the tops of most of the packing plants, storage silos, assembly plants, steel mills and industrial complexes which stretched out before him, behind him and on either side as far as the eye could see. In the brightening morning light he could see the huge earth-moving machine abandoned at quitting time the previous day lined up on the dirt right-of-way. A few men were appearing here and there, starting the little auxiliary engines which, when warmed up, would turn over the main engine in each machine. He heard one start, blatting like an outboard motor. In the relative quiet the engine's raucous sound sputtered and coughed, then steadied to a high-pitched whine, then the pitch suddenly dipped as the clutch was thrown to engage the main engine, and in a few moments the boom . . . boom . . . boom, boom of the diesel engine's thunder drowned out the outboard sound. The operator moved the earth-mover along to scoop up dirt where the freeway would dip below street level and deposit it on the approach where the freeway would rise to the height of the overhead bridge. As he watched, another earth-mover began moving, and then another and another. A bulldozer began spreading the earth evenly, a huge water truck saturated it and a compacting machine followed, packing the freshly deposited dirt to granite hardness.

A grader put the finishing touches on a temporary approach from the nearby street, and any minute the great transit-mix trucks, with black spirals painted on a gray drum to give the illusion of motion, like a barber pole on its side, would be turning in, anxious to disgorge their semi-liquid cargo and then, empty of the awful weight, go bouncing ridiculously over the rough dirt, to bring back another load as quickly as the driver could maneuver through the traffic-congested streets.

The men concerned with the deck pour began arriving. The boss, looking worried and then relief obvious in his face at seeing Pete waiting atop the bridge, waved from the little house trailer that served as an office near the end of the bridge. The state inspectors, breast pockets bursting with notebooks and pencils of various colors, their belts laden with plumb-bobs, hand-levels, slide-rules and measuring tapes, began a systematic check of reinforcing steel and metal plates to be left in the concrete. Pete pretended to understand as they set up telescope transits and checked the positions of everything to be covered by the concrete, including the forms and false work.

The boss came running to Pete from the trailer.

"Concrete company on the phone," he said seriously. "They're ready to send the first loads. Be here in twenty minutes if they leave now. Shall I tell them okay?"

"I'm ready," Pete said, and his heart leaped as he saw Old

Tony climbing up on the deck, ready for work. The boss ran back to the office. He returned soon, and stood with the state men, who had finished checking positions. Pete knew the boss was uneasy, and he made a show of casual talk with Old Tony. This pour was to be part of the decking over which traffic would move at high speed. Pete understood it had to be level, even. The state allowed only a sixteenth of an inch irregularity in ten feet. It took experts in the field to finish concrete according to highway specifications. Finishing machines, which would be used to pave the freeway over the dirt bed, could not be used here because of their weight. This part of a bridge had to be done by hand and had to be perfectly smooth, Old Tony explained, because if there were any bumps, causing traffic to bounce when the bridge was eventually opened, it could conceivably endanger the structure. An uneven concrete deck would have to be torn out, at prohibitive cost to the contractor.

The giant trucks full of freshly mixed concrete began arriving. The company supplying the concrete allowed each truck only so many minutes standing time after arrival on the job. After that the contractor was charged standing time for both the truck and the driver.

The first truck made a wide arc on the dirt approach and then started backing up, the engine thundering as the huge drum revolved slowly, churning the twelve tons of concrete inside. The driver expertly stopped inches from the one-and-a-half-yard bucket attached by a steel cable to a tall crane. The state inspectors made a final quick check of the wooden forms. The project boss ordered a check of all equipment; compressors, vibrators, and machines. Nothing must go wrong. Once started, under no circumstances could the pour be stopped for any length of time.

Pete was standing next to Old Tony, watching the activity. He suddenly realized everything had come to a stop and all eyes were on him, expectantly. The boss cupped his hands to his mouth and shouted mightily above the rattle and roar of equipment and machines: "Whenever you say, Pete!" Old Tony, without looking at him, said: "Tell him to begin."

Only vaguely was Pete aware this was the high point in his life. Heart pounding, he cupped his hands and shouted, "Let 'er rip!" in what he thought was good gringo English, but the last word came out "reep."

The boss signaled the truck driver, who threw levers this way and that and wet concrete began pouring from the rear of the truck. Within seconds, there were two tons of concrete in the bucket, and the crane operator threw the throttle forward and the shiny steel reel started winding up the slack in the steel cables, lifting the bucket up and over the heads of the workers, then gently down to within a few feet of the wooden forms at the far end of the pour where Pete and Old Tony stood. A worker tripped the handle on the bucket and the first two tons of concrete emptied out onto the forms, its thick, jamlike consistency causing it to form a knee-deep puddle. The common laborers wearing high rubber boots waded into it, bent almost double, grunting loudly as they plunged their short-handled shovels into it and began spreading the concrete around to the approximate depth required. Old Tony stood beside Pete and the two watched.

"We do nothing until they pour the entire width of the deck and move up out of our way," he advised Pete in Spanish quietly.

The pour was underway.

Back and forth across the width of the deck the bucket unloaded its heavy contents, and the laborers evened out the puddles, until the concrete was placed fairly evenly more than a dozen feet from the beginning of the pour. Then Old Tony quietly told Pete how to move out the low scaffolding over the wet concrete which would allow them to work with their finishing tools without walking on the fresh surface. The workers involved in placing the concrete all moved up another dozen or so feet to repeat the whole process while Old Tony and Pete smoothed the deck to paved finish.

As the pour progressed the length of the deck, Antonio kept up a steady stream of quiet instructions to Pete. Pete relayed this to the workmen, the man operating the crane with the huge bucket, the laborers placing the concrete. Ostensibly, Pete was running the pour as a good cement foreman should. The other workers, Spanish-speaking almost to a man, quickly saw what was happening, and all on the job except the gringo boss and the state inspector, joined in the silent conspiracy to put Pete across as the hero of the day.

By noon the pour had reached the halfway point. Stopping for lunch was inconceivable. The boss and the state inspectors stood watching the work proceed, the worried lines lessening in their faces as they saw the smooth, even pavement Pete and Old Tony left behind each time they moved the low work scaffolding ahead to keep up with the pouring. Then near-disaster struck.

While they were waiting for the pour to progress enough for another "bite," Pete saw Old Tony squatting beside the section just finished. Almost imperceptibly, Antonio moved his head, beckoning Pete. Pete approached him and knelt, looking out on the newly finished still wet deck.

"See the spot near the center where moisture is standing?"

Tony asked without pointing. Pete strained to see. The wet concrete glistened all over, but in one area a puddle of water perhaps a quarter of an inch stood. Only an extremely practiced eye could have noticed. Pete nodded.

Old Tony explained quietly, "When we finished it, it was perfectly even. But the forms beneath have given under the weight and vibration. That little puddle indicates a depression."

They both squatted silently, Pete waiting for him to continue.

Antonio said, "The inspectors will not check it with a straight edge until it becomes hard. Then it is too late to do anything about it. They will blame you."

Pete panicked a little. "Can we fix it?"

"Do just as I say," Tony said, still speaking softly, not looking at Pete. "I will return to the pour. Stay here a while, then call the gringos here and show them the little puddle. Tell them what I told you. They will check and find you're right, and they will get very excited. Then you call for me. I can fix it."

Pete was a good actor. He remained kneeling, squinting at the finished deck. Soon he caught the eye of the state inspector and the boss, and beckoned them. They hurried toward him, worry on their faces.

"Something wrong, Pete?" the boss asked apprehensively.

Pete pointed to the wet spot. "See that water standing there? I think the forms gave way underneath a little bit. We better check it now."

Quickly, the boss produced a straight-edge ten feet long, and they placed it across the deck, spanning the little puddle of water. Where the moisture stood, the deck was nearly an inch lower than the surrounding areas. The inspectors looked accusingly at the boss. Their reputations were at stake and they would hold him responsible for a poor job.

The boss was near panic himself. It was one thing to be able to spot a bad place, quite another to be mechanic enough to know what to do about it.

"Should we stop the pour, Pete? Can you fix it?"

"Yes," Pete said wisely, "it's still fresh enough to be fixed. Lucky we caught it in time, though. I'll call Old Tony back here and tell him what to do."

Pete summoned Old Tony. The boss and the inspectors stood watching as the two jabbered at length in Spanish, and then Antonio shouted for two shovelers to bring shovels full of fresh concrete. He took one shovelful and with the expertness of a basketball player threw the concrete out onto the wet spot. He then quickly nailed a long handle to a flat board and, standing at the edge of the deck, he gripped the handle and expertly guided the flat board over the area where he'd thrown the concrete until suddenly as if by magic the wet spot was gone. The inspectors checked the deck again and found it perfectly level. They broke into big grins. The boss beamed at Pete. But Pete didn't have time for compliments.

"Come on, Tony," he said impatiently, "they're ready for us to move up again." By quitting time the last great transit-mix truck had roared away. The deck was poured out, smooth, perfectly even. The boss was delighted. Not a single delay had cost truck-and-driver standing time. The highly paid equipment operators did not go on overtime. Pete's handling of the pour had been a model of efficiency, and saving of time and money.

The boss' praise for Pete was brief but sincere. The next day another pour was scheduled. And again Old Tony saw Pete through. And again on the next pour.

Time flew. After a month, Old Tony left Pete on his own, to hire his own skilled men and make his own decisions. The state engineers assigned to the job, whose reputations were at stake in seeing that the contractor did quality work, were delighted with Pete's work. The contractor was delighted that the state's men were delighted.

Pete wallowed in the glory of his newfound skills, his newfound importance and his newfound wealth. His reputation for his special skill spread, and he found his earnings increased in proportion to the demand for his work. And when Minnie told him the doctor said she was going to have twins, Pete nodded casually. After all, what would you expect from such a man?

· *6* ·

Although Neftali Sandoval was in his late fifties, he looked more than a decade older. Doña Alicia had almost aged comparably and the two still lived alone in the family house of stone and mortar on the main street in Irwindale.

On weekdays hundreds of giant trucks pulling great trailers roared out of the town laden with sand and gravel, and returned for another load in a few hours. The rocky, cactus-covered five-mile-wide strip of river bottom had become the rock, sand, and gravel capital of Southern California, and the huge quarry holes, some a half mile wide and hundreds of feet deep, crowded the residents into narrow dwelling strips. The massive corporations which had erected the rock crushers had leased the land from the owners, and none of the original Spanish-speaking residents of Irwindale shared in the $100 million-a-year plus business of quarrying.

But this day was Sunday, and the quiet was conspicuous, as was the absence of the constant dust cloud that weekdays accompanied the hiss of air brakes and rumble of trucks. It would be Neftali's birthday in a few days, and his sons and daughters would begin arriving shortly today, their cars laden with children. If only Gregorio had lived, he mused, Gregorio would have talked the neighbors into leasing this property to the rock crusher people and he might be independent now. Instead he still had to get up early every morning and go to the packing-house and sort oranges. But maybe not so much longer.

He was sitting in his big chair in the kitchen-front room, wearing his cleaned and pressed khaki trousers and shirt, ankle-high shoes, and a wide tie. On impulse he went to the hiding place where he kept his valuables. It was a loose stone at the bottom of the window. Removing the stone, he reached into the cavity below and took out a wooden box he'd made to fit there. He carried it back to the chair and went through it. Birthdays were a time for reminiscing.

He still had a brass-encased compass, a jeweled belt buckle and some coins, all of which he'd taken from the burned and looted ranch in Mexico so long ago. He let the memory of that day come forward, the outlaws with their guns, the villagers picking over the spoils, and then he saw the soldiers, remembered the terror of his conscription and the subsequent escape. The long journey with his fat father and pretty mother. He set the compass, buckle and coins on the table and delved further. Three stubs of tickets. He remembered the fight his sisters had taken him to so long ago right after his father had died. What was the fighter's name? A common name. Oh yes, Salazar, the same as his son-in-law Julio. He'd forgotten about seeing that fight. He'd have to tell Julio about it.

Next, from the box he took a handmade knife. He remembered the village smith making it for him, from a piece of metal that had been part of the train that had brought his father to the tiny village of Trainwreck before he or his sisters were even born, the village his mother had returned to, with what he regarded as her lover, after his father had died. Undoubtedly, his mother was now dead. He had last heard of her twenty years before, when he journeyed to San Bernardino to see a man whom he heard had come from Trainwreck. The man had verified that his mother was then alive and still with Eduardo, who was working for the Church in rebuilding the ancient mission the Jesuits had built at Agua Clara in the sixteenth century.

Yes, here were the two things he was looking for. One was the legal deed to the tiny bit of property on which the family house was situated. His heart ached as he thought how glad Gregorio would have been to inherit this deed when he and Alicia died. Since the rightful heir was gone, he had really never given much thought to how he should distribute his possessions among his sons and daughters. It wouldn't matter, as it wasn't intended to go to them anyway. He didn't know what the deed said exactly, as he couldn't read, but he knew it was legal and registered with the proper authorities.

Then there was his birth certificate. It had been given to him by Hortensia and Jilda when he was leaving the barrio bajo to come to Irwindale. They had explained the Americanos were getting strict about citizens from other countries coming in, and someday they might decide to take all his property away from him and ship him back to Mexico if he couldn't prove he was an American citizen.

Accepting that birth certificate was one of the few dishonest acts he had ever committed. His sisters told him it was a genuine birth certificate, from a doctor who died and whose personal records were destroyed in a fire. There was a man who for $100 would give you a birth certificate signed by the doctor. This man had somehow come into possession of a batch of certificates the doctor had signed in anticipation of use among the many patients he had in San Diego County. Neftali had gone along with it and accepted the false document only for the protection of his future family. But now it served another purpose. At the age of sixty-five he would get a pension, free, the rest of his life. It wouldn't be much, but enough, and he could then just enjoy his grandchildren and sons and daughters to the end of his days.

But all this brought him to his great problem area. Always, he had taught his children to be honest in every respect. He had also passed on to them his moral code, the code of the village people, which his father had pretended to believe in but in actuality had not. Neftali was sure none of his sons drank excessively, philandered, beat their wives or were otherwise untrustworthy or dishonest. How then, when the time came for his pension, would he explain it? He saw how true was the old adage that one lie must lead to another. Through the years he had been afraid to apply for citizenship papers, lest he be unable to learn to read or recite enough and thus be subject to deportation. But perhaps, when the pension came he could tell his children he had applied for and received citizenship papers long ago. The problem worried him frequently.

He sat back, smoking a tailor-made cigarette. He looked at the giant alarm clock on the mantel. The sound it made was in proportion to its size. It was many years old, but he still got the thrill of ownership every time he looked at it and remembered when a clock in a house was a luxury. His son, Orlando, had learned stone laying, and had come one day and removed a section of the wall and installed an open fireplace, complete with tall brick chimney and flue and mantel. Neftali immediately set about acquiring such items to go on a mantel. Yes, time had been good to him. The entire house had a solid concrete floor now. That was his son Pete's contribution. Pete was by far the most successful of his sons; his success was comparable to Angie's, who owned her own restaurant, although he was somewhat disturbed when he learned she now sold alcoholic beverages. That's bad business.

Pete had done a magnificent job in finishing the concrete floor. His sons had offered to have a flush toilet put in the home, but he had resisted, saying he never did like the idea of having the toilet in the house, and besides, those pipes were always clogging, weren't they? No, the old-fashioned outhouse was preferable, even though he knew there were few left in Irwin- dale now.

He had no transportation, but few were the days when he left for work on foot that a driver of one of the giant gravel rigs didn't recognize Old Man Sandoval and slow down to give him a lift, against all company and teamster rules.

He would hop on the running board, in that way somehow lessening the gratuity of the ride and at the same time denying his physical waning, and ride until they came to the cross street on which the orange-packing plant was situated. The truck would slow, and he would jump off, the less to inconvenience the driver and again to reassert his physical competence, and he would start walking. Again, few were the times he walked more than a hundred feet before another employee of the plant would drive by and give him a lift.

At the plant the foreman sometimes became exasperated with Neftali's slowness and inability to change work habits, or adapt to new methods, but no one ever said anything to him.

Management liked him, as he had worked for the same wages for many years, had maintained the same output—almost, anyway—and never once complained of anything or asked for a raise. He had never shirked, never been late, and never missed a day. It didn't matter that he'd never learned English, Old Sandoval was an ideal employee. Maybe a little slow, but then, the company didn't pay him much, either.

The big hands of the clock moved sluggishly to ten o'clock, and Neftali heard a car enter his gravel drive. The first of his offspring was arriving. He went outside to greet Pete and Minnie and their three-year-old twins, arriving in a shiny big pickup truck. He embraced Pete and Minnie warmly, but had his eyes on the wide-eyed children, dressed in spotless, pressed baby clothes. He picked up the boy, Sammy, and held him high.

"Hey, little one! How big you're getting, eh? You'll grow up to be a fine man and take over your father's business, no?" He turned to Pete. "I hope you appreciate him. No matter how many you have, you'll never have another first-born son, you know. He'll someday fill your shoes well."

Pete glanced at Minnie with a little meaning, then dismissed the remarks. "Papa, we have some presents for you."

He reached into the cab and pulled out a wrapped gift and handed it to his father, who saw it was obviously a carton of cigarettes. "From Minnie," Pete explained. Then he reached in and took a large ceramic black panther lamp. "For your mantel, so you can look at your magazines better."

Minnie spoke up. "Also, I brought you some magazines." She gave him a half dozen slick magazines. The old man saw Sammy's twin sister, Mariana, standing near him, looking hurt at being ignored.

"Ho, pretty one! You have a kiss for your grandfather, too?"

He picked her up and kissed her and put her down. Taking his gifts, he led them into the house. He set the lamp on the mantel. Pete had also brought an extension cord. His father produced a hammer and some nails and Pete, standing on the table, drove the nails into the ceiling rafter, ran the cord alongside them and bent the nails over to hold it against the ceiling. "There," he said with finality when he climbed down and plugged in the lamp. "Now, papa, you have a real lamp." The old man looked approvingly at it.

"Es un tigre, verdad?" he asked.

"Sí, papa," Pete answered.

"Qué bonito!"

A horn honked from the drive, and they saw it was Angie and Julio in a huge new car. Both came in dressed in their finest, as Pete and Minnie were, and each had a gift for Neftali.

The three men sat around the room and talked, while the women automatically began making piles of tortillas and a giant pot of beans. Both couples had brought groceries, and as others were expected to be arriving throughout the day, a fiesta was in the making.

Before long Victorio arrived with his wife and children, and then Rosita with her family, and then Orlando, and Roberto and Dolores, and the house and yard were a mass of running, screaming children from a few months to several years in age, and the men were jammed together on benches or chairs, and the women stood around the stove stirring beans or turning tortillas.

Pete saw Julio stroll outside toward his car a little too casually, and he strolled after him and took a drink from Julio's bottle. Then they returned.

"Oye, Julio," the old man addressed his son-in-law. "I was

sitting here remembering things in the past today. And I thought back to a prize fight I went to when I was first in this country. I remember because the fighter's name was Salazar also." The others were listening, and now they saw Julio's reaction.

"Do you remember what else they called him? A first name or something?"

"No, I don't. They called him something in English. I forget now. I think I called him that first. I had to ask my sister how to say it in English, because I wanted the gringos to understand."

"Was it Geev-eet-to-heem?"

"Sí, sí. That was it. He was a relative of yours?"

Julio smiled. "Sí. He was my father."

They all exclaimed at the coincidence. Then the old man continued. "What ever happened to him. Is he still living?"

Julio shrugged. "I don't know. He . . . had to leave us up near Fresno when I was a boy. We were supposed to meet him again, but he never showed up. I've been looking for him ever since."

Pete was thinking hard. He started talking. "Geev-eet-to-heem . . . I heard that somewhere, not too long ago. I met him, too. Where was it . . ." He concentrated. Julio's face tightened.

"You met him? Recently? Where? Where?"

"I'm trying to think. It was . . . I can't remember now. But I'm sure. Somebody said, 'That's a fighter who used to be called Geev-eet-to-heem.' They didn't say his last name."

Now Julio was quite excited. "Think hard, hombre. Remember! I've looked high and low for nearly fifteen years."

All looked at Pete expectantly. He thought hard, and then seemed to give up. Julio's face fell, and he seemed worked up.

"I'll think of it after a while," Pete said. The general conversation resumed, but Julio went outside to his car once more. Pete watched him and soon got up and followed.

"I remember now, Julio," he said when they were alone outside. "When I was first staying with you when I got out of the Army, I happened to go by that slave market place, you know what I mean?"

"Sí. The waiting place."

"Right. And it was there I met a guy named Canto. And he pointed this other guy out to me. He said that was his name, but he was dodging somebody or something. I remember now that I didn't really meet him. He looked real old. Face all broken up."

"What was he doing down there?"

"I guess he was looking for work like everybody else. Yeah, I remember now. He was selling his blood. They all do down there. At least that's what Canto told me."

Julio seemed to be holding back more questions. He puffed a few minutes impatiently on a cigarette and then without a word returned to the house.

Guitars had been brought, and the music was pouring out. It was not just song sung in the sense folk songs are sung, but entire emotional frames of reference, translated into tangible words and harmony. The old man listened attentively to the vows of faithful love, the legend of great fighters and stories of magnificent horses and pastures and cornfields.

By midnight there were children asleep on the chairs, the bed, the floor and in all the cars parked outside the house.

Minnie laid one child down between herself and Pete as he drove home, and held the other.

"Where did Julio and Angie go so early?"

Pete told her about the mention of Julio's father and his excitement. "I guess he couldn't wait to get back and find him."

They drove in silence a while. "By the way, I don't want to raise our kids to think the oldest son is a favorite. It's a bad custom," Pete said.

"Yes. I didn't like the way mama and papa served all the oldest sons first on their own plates, and then let all the other kids just help themselves to what was left."

"It's a custom I don't agree with." He looked at his sleeping daughter. "I want her to feel just as important as if she was the oldest son. To do that we've got to show her a lot of extra attention."

"I'll see that she gets it. Paying more attention to sons is old-fashioned. Us girls are just as important."

Pete nodded agreement.

The next day when Pete got home from his job Julio was waiting for him. "Let's go down to the waiting place and show me where you saw him," Julio said.

Pete changed into his best, so that he would be as well dressed as Julio in his suit, and they drove down to the waiting place. Nearly five years had passed, but the waiting place had not changed. The men hanging around misinterpreted the good clothes and businesslike manner and refused to cooperate. Finally Pete mentioned Canto. No, nobody had seen him for a long time. He didn't hang out here anymore. Julio and Pete walked to the beer joint, and had no better success. Julio was dejected as they walked back to their car, parked half a block from the waiting place. They were about to drive off when a man approached. Pete recognized Canto, and realized that someone at the waiting place had gotten a message to him.

"You asking for somebody?" Canto said.

"This guy," Pete said to Julio. "He's the one I met. He knows Geev-eet-to-heem."

"You know him?" Julio snapped.

Canto became evasive. "I might. I know lots of guys around here."

"Can you find him?"

"I don't know. What do you want him for? I'm not going to rat on a buddy."

Julio looked him up and down. Canto wore a ragged pair of wool trousers, a sweat shirt and shoes without socks.

"Hop in the back," Julio said knowingly.

"What for?"

"Would you like some better clothes, a full stomach, some good whiskey and a couple of dollars?"

Canto got in.

tarting school already? It seems like only a little while ago they were babies."

"They start all kids at five years now. Tomorrow I'm going shopping for clothes. Mariana and Sammy will be the best dressed kids in school," Minnie assured Pete.

"When you take them the first time, make sure you tell the teacher how smart Mariana is and not to expect too much from Sammy. She should know those things."

"Sí, I'll tell her."

And when Minnie told the teacher she saw Sammy drop his eyes and Mariana move a little closer to him protectively.

The teacher had given a little inward sigh and said, "Well, maybe we can do something to change that."

And Minnie had said without thinking, "If you could, I don't think his father would like it."

On the first day of the new semester Mrs. Eva Weimer sat at her desk in the elementary school in East Los Angeles and waited for the classroom to fill. She was heavy, with a sagging, bulgy face, and wisps of red hair testified that she had not always been gray. She looked out through thick spectacles as one little dark head after another protruded into the room from the hall, looking this way and that.

"Come in, find a seat," she would call out pleasantly in Spanish. Her grammar and syntax were perfect, but in the dozens of years she had spoken Spanish she had found it impossible to master the flat *e*, the lightning trill of the double *r*, or even the flick of the single *r*. She had given up on accent, but found solace in the ability to carry on a conversation in Spanish at any pace, and say anything in that language as well as it could be said.

Soon all the seats were taken and Mrs. Weimar stood up and confronted the class.

"Buenos días, niños. Me llamo Señora Weimer." Good morning, children. My name is Mrs. Weimer.

From the class came a half-hearted attempt at coordinating the sentence, "Buenos días, señora."

The children were seven years old, and even at this age they understood that the gringos who spoke Spanish fluently but with a poor accent were usually the kinds of persons who went out of their way to be helpful.

"This is our first day in second grade," Mrs. Weimer told them in Spanish. "And this year we are *all* going to learn to work in English. Can anyone here tell us why we must learn to work in English?" She looked out over the dark eager faces and felt the children's trust in her. One large, homely boy raised his hand and she nodded to him.

"Because we live in the United States," he said matter-of-factly in Spanish, and quickly sat down. She noticed he glanced around for signs of approval or disapproval among his peers.

"Yes," Mrs. Weimer continued. "We all live in a country called the United States, or America. And in the United States most people speak English. But there are many other languages spoken here, too. Here in Los Angeles many of us speak Spanish. Can someone tell us what other language is spoken here?"

A girl's hand went up and Mrs. Weimer gave consent. The girl stood up.

"Japanese," she said and quickly sat down. Another hand went up and Mrs. Weimer nodded. The boy stood up and announced:

"They had to lock all the Japanese up because they were spies, but they're out now."

Mrs. Weimer listened with warmhearted amusement as the children named the various languages they'd heard spoken. One boy rose and said, "My father says we aren't Spanish, we're Mexican, so why do we speak Spanish?"

"We do speak Mexican," another volunteered.

Mrs. Weimer sighed a little. It was too early in their lives to go into the differentiation between Spanish, Mexican, English, Mexican-American, and American. They were not ready for any attempt to crystallize the opaque walls of their little world. She knew her job this semester was to get these youngsters communicating in English as well as possible. She opposed this rule—at least so far as youngsters this age were concerned—but she had no choice but to comply. The board had run into too much criticism by graduating teen-agers unable to speak or read English.

"All right, now," she still spoke in Spanish. "We live in America, which is an English-speaking nation. Some of us speak Spanish. Now, tell the truth. Everyone who can speak English raise your hand." She raised hers to start them off.

A few hands shot up quickly, others slowly, and then more slowly yet the remaining hands went up. There was no child present who did not hold up his hand. Mrs. Weimer smiled and slightly shook her head.

"All right," she said warmly. "Hands down. Now, we'll start in this row here, and I want each one in turn to rise and say something in English." It was the only way she could think of to find out for sure. "Please rise, say your name, and say something in English." She didn't want them to feel pressure. "Say anything you want."

The first boy stood up. "My name ees Jorge Alesandro," he said fairly clearly in English. He paused, and Mrs. Weimer could hardly refrain from laughing as she saw him wrinkle his brow, racking his mind for something to say. "I have two dogs at home with fleas," he finally said, then sat down and twisted so that he might watch the child behind perform.

"My name is John Garza. John is the English word for Juan."

Next a little girl stood up. "My name is Alicia Herrera. I live with my mother and father in East Los Angeles and have three sisters and five brothers." Mrs. Weimer nodded approval.

The next boy hesitated. He looked around the room in embarrassment. Mrs. Weimer said comfortably in Spanish: "Do you care to tell us your name and say something in English? We're all going to learn English here."

The boy stood, looking down. After a pause he said, "Raul Gomez. Got dam son-off-a-beech," and sat down. It was obvious he had no idea what it meant. Some of the students giggled a little and Mrs. Weimer forced herself to remain straightfaced. They always learn the swear words first, she remembered.

The next child rose and said, "Maria Torrez. Ice cream, candy, doughnuts." It was obviously the extent of her English vocabulary.

The next girl caught the eye of Mrs. Weimer. What would some day be breathtaking beauty, she thought, was already firmly started. She must not favor this child, for already, because of her childish beauty, she received special attention wherever she went. Already, this child had an image of herself as something special. It could be damaging. The girl stood up.

"My name is Mariana Sandoval," she said in a clear and exuberant voice. "I live with my mother and father and my brother. He's right here. His name's Sammy." Mariana turned to Sammy, seated directly behind her.

Sammy rose. "I'm Sammy Sandoval," he mumbled awkwardly. "She's my sister." Mrs. Weimer sensed Sammy was aware how Mariana outshone him. Although they were obviously twins, the girl was much more advanced. Mrs. Weimer knew how shattering it could be for one sibling to be overshadowed completely, at this age. This is where the tendencies began. She guessed his poor English, as compared to hers, was the result of lack of confidence in himself, a lack caused by her irresistible dainty charm and bright manner.

By the time each child in the class had given his name and talked, Mrs. Weimer knew that less than half could converse in English, a dozen or so could recognize many words, and a half dozen knew either no words or a little profanity. Among the first things she did was have Mariana and Sammy sit as far apart as possible to eliminate sibling comparison, if not rivalry, in the classroom.

By the time for the first recess she had them seated the way she wanted. She carefully explained how long the recess would be and that they should be back in their seats promptly at the end of recess.

She watched as they got up when the bell rang. She saw those who were advanced seeking one another out cautiously, while those who spoke no English quickly formed a league and felt much more at ease together. She sighed.

When they were all seated again she took a deep breath and approached the blackboard.

"Now, everybody together, say 'I want to learn English.'"

The class repeated the sentence and she wrote it on the board and started to translate. "Now 'I' means me in Spanish," she still spoke Spanish. A hand went up. "Yes?"

"It also means 'there is,'" a student said.

" . . . Yes. In Spanish it means 'there is.' But that's a different word. It sounds just like it but it's spelled H-A-Y. 'H' is silent in Spanish, and 'A' is pronounced 'ah,' so it sounds like the English word for 'me,' which is I."

She saw Mariana Sandoval's hand go up. "Yes, Mariana?"

" 'Hay' also means 'is there?' in Spanish."

So sharp, some of them. So confusing to some. Maybe it was better when they put all the non-Englishers in one class and the bilinguals in another. But that had resulted in one group being miles ahead of the other, and one whole group quickly became hopelessly behind.

She gave another big sigh. "Yes, you're so right, Mariana.

Now, let's skip this and come back to it later. Clase, por favor, repited éste ..."

In the third grade Mariana met Elizabeth Jameson, and a friendship developed. The third grade teacher, Mrs. Flanner, believed the purpose of school was to educate children as much as possible. She was another kind of teacher and was well aware that the children in this school had problems uncommon to most children this age, but did not believe her primary job was to orient them to the world outside.

Without regard to feelings, she determined the level of each student and put them in groups. The slow children worked at their level, the medium at theirs, and so forth. Thus Sammy and Mariana found themselves at opposite ends in the class. He was well aware much less was expected of him than of Mariana, and was self-conscious and somewhat troubled by it. He found himself thrown with a group of boys and a few girls most of whom spoke hardly any English, and the boys formed a sort of clique, sticking together at recess time and during lunch hour. Their image of themselves was poor, and worsened as they began to take a defensive pride in being intellectual failures and outcasts. "We are the worst of the lot," they unconsciously thought, and when any one of them showed himself to be inferior or lacking intellectually or, more important, morally, the others rushed to his defense, eager to lower themselves to that level and thus assure the individual he was not abandoned. A pattern was forming.

Mariana found herself "in" with a group of advanced

youngsters, mostly girls, who took pride in being bilingual, good at math, and in reading well. Mrs. Flanner believed that refraining from complimenting the advanced group was sufficient assurance to the others that they were not unequal. But each student in the upper group knew well the lack of interruption and correction on the part of the teacher was praise of the highest degree, and they each strove to improve.

Mariana and Elizabeth Jameson were the stars of the third grade class. Elizabeth was the only Anglo—"American girl," Mrs. Flanner and the others considered her—in the class. She was aware of it, but it did not bother her.

It was natural that Elizabeth and Mariana have a lot in common, and they should become good friends. They discovered they lived not far apart. Not long after they became acquainted they were having lunch together and walking home together.

On the way home one day Elizabeth asked, "Can you come to my house to play a while?"

"I'll ask my mother. She usually lets me," Mariana replied.

Minnie's natural maternal instinct made her like all children. She noticed when the little gringa girl came in she did not stare around the house, examining—comparing. Elizabeth was well-dressed, clean and well-mannered. Mariana introduced Elizabeth in a formal manner, and Minnie was aware this was not a natural custom for Mariana. But it pleased her.

"All right," she said to Mariana in English, "but come back before it gets dark."

The first thing Mariana noticed in Elizabeth's home was that everything appeared planned. The color of the walls, she noticed, agreed with the furniture. The furniture agreed with the floor. Paintings on the walls were in frames not contrasting with anything in the room, and the paintings were obviously done by the same artist in the same mood.

In her own home, and that of every friend's she'd been in, there was little scheme. When her parents needed a chair, or a table, they went out and bought the nicest one they could afford. They chose it according to how pretty and stylish it was, with no thought of how it would relate to anything else in the room into which it was going. She remembered her mother taking her to buy material for drapes. Minnie had shopped until she found the most attractive cloth she could afford. She took it home and made drapes, never once considering the color of the furniture in the room.

In Elizabeth's bedroom Mariana noticed the drapes were the same material as the bedspread, and the rug matched.

"Hi, Liz," Mariana heard a woman's voice call from another room.

"Come on," Elizabeth said, "I want you to meet Mom."

Mrs. Jameson had set her magazine down and was giving all her attention to the two girls, Mariana felt. Why?

"I am *very* pleased to meet you, Mariana," Mrs. Jameson said. "Elizabeth has talked a lot about you. She says you're her best friend at school."

Mariana's smile was genuine as she looked gratefully at Elizabeth. "I guess we go well together," she said, and saw Mrs. Jameson's quick smile of approval.

"Do you live near here?" the woman asked.

"I live on Second Street, Near Soto."

"That's not far. I hope we'll be seeing a lot of you."

Elizabeth chimed in: "You will, don't worry, Mom."

Mrs. Jameson sat forward earnestly. "What would you girls like to do? Play in the back yard? Listen to records? Sew?"

Elizabeth looked at Mariana, who was somewhat taken by the attention. She smiled self-consciously.

"Do you like to cook?" Elizabeth asked.

"I . . . I've never done much cooking—except toast and eggs . . ."

Elizabeth looked at her mother. "Could we bake a cake, Mom?" she asked.

Mrs. Jameson thought a moment. Mariana thought she was deciding whether to give permission. "We don't have any baking powder. But you girls start, and I'll run and get some." She got up and went looking for her purse while Elizabeth led Mariana into the kitchen.

"Let's see, we'll need eggs, flour, sugar, vanilla . . ." She went on listing the ingredients and utensils needed.

Mariana was thoughtful. "Is your mom going to the store just to get us some baking powder?" she asked.

"Uh huh. She'll be back in a few minutes."

Mariana was still thinking. "Why don't you use a cake mix? It's not expensive and very easy . . ."

"Aw, that's no fun. The fun is doing everything just right. Haven't you ever made a cake?"

"No."

"Well, the main thing is to do everything exactly right. First, we have to have aprons." Elizabeth went to a cabinet and found two small aprons, children's size. Mariana was again impressed. An apron was a thing her mother would never have bought for her own use, let alone Mariana's. Minnie always tied a dish towel around her waist.

Soon Mrs. Jameson returned with the baking powder, and Elizabeth set about mixing, sifting and preparing. She instructed Mariana and before long a large cake was baking in the oven.

When it was done, Mariana and Elizabeth applied the frosting and then summoned Mrs. Jameson.

"Mom, you get the first piece," Elizabeth said, beaming. Mrs. Jameson's eyes went wide with wonder at the taste of the cake.

"It's absolutely the best cake I've ever eaten," she exclaimed. "It's delicious. Save Dad a piece."

When it was time for Mariana to go, Elizabeth cut the remainder of the cake in half and placed it in a cake pan with a cover. Mariana again noticed that in the Jameson home, although obviously they were not well off, everything had a use and was in good condition and attractive. Somebody plans a lot, she thought.

She carried her part of the cake home and ran into the kitchen.

"Mother, look what I made over at Elizabeth's," she said excitedly, setting the pan on the kitchen table. Minnie sampled the cake, but was much more impressed with the cake pan and cover.

"That's a handy thing to have," she commented. "Keeps the flies off it, too."

"We made it ourselves," Mariana told her. "Without a mix. We mixed the eggs, the flour and everything. The frosting, too."

"Cake mixes from the store are the best," Minnie said sincerely. "They have a frosting too. It takes much less time, and it only costs a few cents more. Next time you want to bake one, invite her here and I'll buy it for you."

Every day Mariana and Elizabeth played together. Once in a while they spent time at Mariana's house, but almost invariably they ended up at the Jameson home. To herself, Mariana wondered why, and tried to analyze it. Part of the reason, she saw, was that Elizabeth had more things to play with, but that wasn't all. It was because there were more things to do there. Why weren't there more things to do in her home? It wasn't because the Jamesons could afford more; in fact, she'd learned, Pete made a good deal more money than Mr. Jameson. But why wasn't her own home as nice as theirs? Was it because Pete and Minnie didn't spend as much on it? No. The TV set in the Sandoval home was twice the size as that in the Jameson home. The stove in the Sandoval home was the biggest, most modern one available. On the rickety screen porch were a matched, gleaming white automatic washer and dryer, far more luxurious and expensive than the apartment-size washer and dryer in the Jameson home.

Mariana mentally listed the things in the Jameson home lacking in her own, and came to a startling discovery. Elizabeth had a little camera of her own. Mariana didn't, but Pete had an expensive, complicated camera—she remembered him saying it cost several hundred dollars—which he kept locked away and brought out only on special occasions, and guests would crowd around while Pete showed off the automatic adjustments and gauges. The Sandovals had a large, expensive hi-fi set, far superior to the record player in the Jameson front room—but Elizabeth had a little cheap phonograph all her own, with a rack for records. Whenever Mariana wanted to play records in her home, Pete always said, "I'll put it on for you. The needle alone cost $40."

One Saturday Mariana was leaving the Jameson home when Mrs. Jameson said, "I'm going that way right now. Let me drop you off."

Mariana accepted, and when the car pulled up in front of her home, Mrs. Jameson said, "I'd love to meet your mother. Is she home?"

Mariana showed her into the living room and called Minnie. Minnie came in, wearing capri pants a size too small and a blouse a size too big. Mariana noticed Mrs. Jameson paid no attention to the house or furniture.

"Hello. I'm Lyn Jameson. I've heard so much about you. Hope you don't mind me dropping in like this."

"No," Minnie said, holding out her hand. "Pleased to meet you myself. We enjoy Elizabeth playing with Mariana. You know they're the smartest ones in the class at school." It was more of a statement than a question.

"Mariana is a darling girl. We just can't get enough of her. She and Liz play by the hour together. Honestly, when they're together we never hear a peep out of them. I'm so glad we're close enough so they can be good friends."

Mariana stood watching the two women as they talked, comparing. There was something about Mrs. Jameson she didn't quite understand.

"By the way," Mrs. Jameson said, "I'm on my way to shop for groceries. And I've found a place where you can get fantastic meats and produce. Come along, I'll show you."

Mariana sensed that this was the real reason Mrs. Jameson had come—to take Minnie some place. Minnie was undecided.

"It's really only a few minutes drive. And the bargains you get, it's worth it. I go every week," Mrs. Jameson coaxed.

"I usually send Sammy or Mariana to the store every day," Minnie said. She was uncertain. She thought perhaps the proper thing to do would be accept Mrs. Jameson's invitation, and she wanted to be proper.

"The girls would enjoy going along, I'm sure," Mrs. Jameson added.

"Okay," Minnie said, looking at Mrs. Jameson's attire, which was casual and neat. "Wait till I get changed."

Minnie disappeared and returned in a few minutes looking as though she was going out to dinner. Mrs. Jameson appeared not to notice.

The girls rode in the back seat as Mrs. Jameson drove. She headed straight for the freeway and drove fast.

"Actually," she explained to Minnie, "this market isn't any cheaper than stores in our neighborhood. But the quality!"

Within minutes she got off the freeway and they were in an upper-middle-class residential section. Mrs. Jameson pulled into the huge parking lot of a modern shopping center and parked near a large supermarket.

Mariana had never been to such a market. She noticed lots of new cars and many small foreign cars. The parking lot was landscaped and clean.

Inside, Mariana and Elizabeth followed the two women as they pushed their shopping carts around. Minnie was impressed with the spacious, immaculate store. Mrs. Jameson stopped her cart in front of the produce displays and examined the vegetables. Minnie was truly impressed, Mariana noted. The tomatoes were firm, ripe, picked at just the right time. The lettuce was fresh, with no limp outer leaves sagging. Mariana had never seen such celery.

"Where do they get vegetables like this?" Minnie asked. She saw other women feeling the tomatoes, sampling the lush bunches of grapes. "The prices are the same as we pay, but what a difference."

Mrs. Jameson laughed a little. "It's worth driving over here, isn't it?" she said. "We used to live not far from here. That's how I happen to know about it." But Mariana suspected this store was not unique, that in the gringo neighborhoods everything was a little better.

At the meat counter, Minnie was even more impressed. She examined carefully all the meat behind glass, and then asked the butcher on duty to cut some filet mignon. Mariana couldn't ever recall hearing her mother order that, and she noticed it was the most expensive meat. She thought she understood why her mother had ordered it.

On the way back to East Los Angeles, Mariana sensed her mother felt defensive and perhaps a little offended because the gringa had shown her a better way to do something, had shown that shopping near home was not good enough for someone with taste.

She heard her mother say, "Next week Pete's buying me a new Cadillac. Then I'll take you shopping with me," and Mariana had never seen such a forced smile on her mother's face.

"Oh, that'll be nice," Mrs. Jameson said.

Mariana knew that perhaps once in a while her mother would shop at the big supermarket, but the Cadillac would be used to drive to the old market three blocks from home, where the vegetables looked as though they'd been in a warm oven all night and the meat was brown.

When Sammy began bringing home poor reports through first and second grade, Pete consoled him: "Don't worry. I got bad marks too. When you're old enough so you don't have to go to school, you have a good job with me. You'll make more money than most gringos, watch and see."

When the third grade teacher sent a note home with Sammy requesting a conference, Minnie went alone. After a brief talk with her, she said, "Perhaps it would be better if I could talk to Mr. Sandoval."

That night Pete agreed. "Okay. I'll take a couple hours off in the morning tomorrow and see what she wants."

Mrs. Flanner eyed Pete curiously when he came in to see her. He was wearing heavy shoes and khaki trousers and shirt.

He introduced himself and shook hands with her.

"I'll be quite frank with you, Mr. Sandoval," she said. "I think Sammy is headed for trouble at this school."

"Trouble? He's too young for trouble."

"He's not too young to form the patterns," Mrs. Flanner said seriously. "I don't have to tell you there are a lot of delin-quents in this part of town. Sammy's in with a group which . . . well, they don't have the best background in the world. Some of his close friends come from families where, for one reason or another, there is no father in the home. These boys are simply a bad influence on him. Already, I've discovered they're starting to ditch school. I've taught a long time in this part of town, and I know what I'm talking about. Sammy is very fortunate to have a father so successful. I think you should do everything you can to help him."

Pete was puzzled. "What can I do? I'll do anything."

"You're in a position to take him away from here. Out of East Los Angeles."

"Move away from East L.A.?" Pete narrowed his eyes.

"Yes. Most children here never have the opportunity to get away from here. But you do. You could buy a nice home in a suburban area where Sammy and Mariana could have all the advantages you can afford to give them. They'll never have those advantages while they live here."

Pete talked to her at some length. She again pointed out the high rate of delinquency in the area, the high rate of crime. This was a slum area, she told Pete, and a parent owed it to his children to do everything possible to get them away from the influence of East Los Angeles.

Pete came away thinking about it. He'd known other chicanos who had moved away and did all right. Guero, one of his deck finishers, had bought a high-class home and was living there with his Anglo wife.

Pete had never before considered moving into an Anglo neighborhood. The more he thought about it, the better he liked the idea. He got along fine with Anglos, he knew, and there was no reason why he couldn't go buy a nice home. He made a lot more money than most of the gringos who worked in factories and offices.

He could just see himself in a new home with a nice back yard, nice trees and lawn, a patio with a barbecue—these things he'd never had, never missed. But why not? A nice garage with a little workshop, like the gringo magazines show all the time. It would be fun.

The more he thought about it, the more he liked the idea. What he enjoyed the most was the ability he now had—the freedom due to his financial success—that allowed him to make a decision to move where he wanted. This was a luxury little known in his environment. And on the way home from his various out-of-town jobs he began dropping in to look at houses in new tract developments.

It was an old story, but new to Pete. The ghetto protects as

well as imprisons. As Pete drove along in the burgeoning suburbs, he saw tract after tract, with signs advertising the homes
for miles in all directions.

TWO MINUTES TO PLAZA DEL RIO—NOTHING DOWN TO VETS.
live luxuriously—pay modestly

TURN RIGHT FOR SUNSET ACRES—$200 MOVES YOU IN
fireplaces, patios, two-car garages

LAKETREE HIGHLANDS—HOMES TO SUIT YOUR PERSONALITY
air conditioning, kitchen built-ins, tile roofs

Pete almost believed it when the salesman at the first office
where he stopped told him there were no homes available. He
didn't want to argue. But a few days later, when he'd stopped at
the fifth or sixth tract office, he was a little better prepared. Not
much, but a little.

"No, I'm sorry, Mr. Sandoval. The houses are all taken."

"Well, that one on the corner, it has a for sale sign on it. I
want that one."

"It's taken. We haven't had a chance to take the sign down
yet."

"I don't believe you. Show me the name of the guy that
bought it."

"Just a minute," and the salesman went to consult a more experienced man. The other man came back to Pete.

"All our homes are taken," he said simply.

"Then why . . ."

"Make what you want out of it, sir, but we have none to
sell you."

Pete got in his shiny new pickup and drove away. He drove several miles to a new-looking development and drove in a new driveway. He sat a moment thinking, then he honked loud and long. After a moment a man came out and approached him.

"Hi, Pete. What you doing out here?"

Pete looked serious. "I want to buy a house like yours, Guero, and I can't seem to find one."

Pete saw the sympathy spring on Guero's face for an instant, then disappear. He hadn't underestimated Guero. Guero understood perfectly.

"I'll find you a house, Pete," he said. He didn't ask why Pete wanted to move, or anything else personal. "When do you want it?"

"Can you find me one tomorrow?"

"Sure, Pete. I'm sure I can."

Pete casually reached into his pocket and brought out a roll of about $2000. He tossed it to Guero. "Use what you need and give the rest back."

Mariana and Sammy were starting fourth grade by the time Pete obtained a house in what he considered a middle-class suburban area and moved his family away from East Los Angeles. He considered the advantages his children would have in a nice neighborhood. It would be as different for them as moving away from Irwindale had been for him, he thought.

He realized such a move should be a family decision, and his idea of this was to mention it to Minnie as he left for work one morning, and then, after Guero had secured a home, he announced it one night when he came home.

Minnie was surprised and delighted. "What's it like?" she asked with enthusiasm.

"You'll see," Pete said absently as he opened the paper and began reading laboriously. She stood waiting, wanting to pursue the subject further, until he glanced inquiringly toward the kitchen. Then she hastened to prepare dinner.

The following Saturday a group of Pete's friends in the construction trades industry arrived early with their pickup trucks. Dark, brawny men with loud voices and heavy shoes laced with thongs. Minnie courteously offered them food, which they courteously refused, and then she brought out whiskey, which they courteously accepted. The men and the pickups were loaded before noon.

The parting of Mariana and Elizabeth was sincere and sad. "Walk home with me," Mariana requested, knowing it would be the last time the two of them took such a walk.

"But why are you moving?"

"Oh, I don't know. Daddy seems to think it will be good for Sammy. He's running around with the wrong kind of friends, I guess."

There were tears in Elizabeth's eyes when she waved goodbye to Mariana as the Cadillac pulled away from the Sandoval home, household items protruding from the windows.

"I'll write real often," she called.

"Me too!" Mariana answered.

· 7 ·

All the residents along Corson Street in the Dow Knolls Prestige Homes tract (A New Concept in Split-Level Living) had heard that the Sandovals were moving in. Although there was no collective agreement, all residents on the block remained inside that Saturday. More than one house-wife said, "Here they come," to her husband as she peered out the window and saw the four pickup trucks careen around the corner, piled high with ancient beds, tables, rugs, and modern new appliances.

The trucks parked in front of Pete's new home and two to four men got out of each cab, some with bottles in hand.

All talked in loud voices, commenting on the house, as Pete proudly unlocked the front door and took them through. The thick carpets extending from wall to wall brought exclamations of approval. They all eyed the split-level living room.

"Man, I wouldn't want stairs like that across my front room," one man said. "Somebody's going to fall down when they're drunk and sue you."

Pete was indignant. "That's the latest fashion," he said. "It's called spleet level. All the rich guys have it in their houses."

His friend never even paused. "That's 'cause they can afford to be sued. Man, I wouldn't want to be you with that death trap in your house."

Pete guessed the reason behind the criticism.

"Just because you're jealous because I have a fine home and all you'll ever have is a junk house because you spend all your money on wine is no reason for you to make fun, hombre," Pete scolded. He led them into the spacious bedroom. They admired the plush wall-to-wall carpeting, commenting on how a bed was unnecessary with such carpeting, some bragging that they'd had intercourse on bare floors, even.

After the tour, the unloading of the trucks began. Minnie arrived in the Cadillac, with Sammy and Mariana and the wives of the other men with her. In a few hours, during which the men drank only sparingly, and the women began making pots of chili and beans, most of the furniture and appliances were in place. An impromptu party began. Pete had had a phone installed prior to moving in, and he called a few more friends and relatives and invited them over. It was not yet late afternoon when carloads of people began arriving. One of the feature attractions of the home was a small fish pond on the front lawn, with a fountain powered by a small electric motor. Pete proudly flipped the switch and all exclaimed with wonder as the fountain spouted. The smaller children squealed and began taking off clothes to play in the water. Soon a half dozen naked children, ages two to ten, were splashing and frolicking in the pond, screaming at the top of their voices. Surely Corson Street never saw the like.

"Papa! Pablito's going to the bathroom in the water," a dark-faced little tattletale screamed.

"Pablito!" the child's father scolded. "Stop it." Then the father returned to his conversation with the other adults.

Pete gave one man some money and directions for finding the nearest liquor store. The man drove off, steering erratically, but returned with the prize.

A tiny little girl playing in the pond suddenly shrieked with pain and came running to Pete, showing him a bleeding scrape on the knee. Pete picked his niece up and comforted her, then tickled her and tossed her into the air, catching her gently, until the tears turned to laughter. He carried her back to the pond, hoisted her high once more, kissed her naked bottom, and put her back in the water. Then dinner was ready.

When darkness came, after all present had eaten their fill, the children were dressed and put down to rest in beds and on the carpets, to talk, play and fight until fatigue overcame them and they dropped off into sleep. The women stayed in the kitchen to talk and clean up, while the men went to the front porch to drink wine from gallon jugs. The hour grew late and their voices grew louder. The men argued, gossiped and urinated on the front lawn. Pete challenged a brother to an Indian wrestling match, which he lost, and then demanded a rematch, which developed into a wrestling match, which he won, and another man challenged him and soon there were several wrestling matches going on by the light of the front porch. When they were exhausted, they all lay down on the lawn, gallon jugs by their sides, and discussed inconsequential events in loud voices until the womenfolk came out, sleeping children in arms, and forced the visitors to leave. Pete said an affectionate good-bye to all, embraced each man, kissed each woman, waved at the disappearing trucks and cars, urinated one final time on a rose bush, and went inside. As he did, he thought he saw a face at the darkened window of the house next door, and wondered why in the world anybody would be looking out the window of a darkened room at three in the morning.

"Must be some odd people live there," he said to Minnie just before he fell across their bed and began snoring. She began routinely undressing him.

D on Cameron realized his nerves were a little frayed as he walked from his home to the house down the block and across the street. *Neighborhood meeting, for chrissake, that's what I get for letting Beth talk me into moving out here in the middle of Oakieville.* He walked casually, taking in the small, well-kept but flimsy tract homes. There were three basic designs here, but by the setting of the houses at different angles and alternation of design a casual observer might be fooled into thinking there were perhaps a dozen different models. That is, if you drove through at sixty miles an hour, he mused. And most of the inhabitants were as much alike as the houses. The fellow in this house here, Cameron reflected, spent his time building a hotrod that stood in the driveway under a plastic cover during the working day. The fellow next to him has a Master Shop power set, which was a table saw that could be converted into a drill press, which could be turned into a lathe, which could also function as a jointer, which was also a sander, ad infinitum. He spent his time making hideous blond furniture, mainly low, modern coffee tables, sofas, bedtables and telephone stands.

Odd, he thought, how this tract seemed to attract people with an incredible amount in common. Each home owner seemed to have achieved his uppermost rung and was arrested there in his capacity as machinist, accountant, county inspector, electrician, auto mechanic, or telephone lineman. Not a doctor, architect or professor in a carload. Beth accused him of being a snob because he was disappointed in the class of neighbors, and perhaps he was. He was just bored to death with the people who talked only of converting the garage into a rumpus room, enclosing the patio or covering the front of their house with flagstone. Now here, in this house he was now passing, was a fellow who for a small fee would make an exact miniature of your house to be placed by your driveway entrance as a mailbox. *God!*

He walked up to the Nueman home and rang. Mrs. Nueman answered, she was glad he could make it, and invited him in. She asked him what he'd like to drink, a scotch and soda or gin and seven. He said gin and seven and then waited while she mixed it in the kitchen and brought it to him.

"The others will be arriving soon," she said pleasantly as she took a seat on a couch across from him. Bill Nueman came into the room.

"Hi, Cameron," Bill Nueman said. "Be with yuh in a sec." He went into the kitchen and Don Cameron could hear him mixing a drink.

"Beth couldn't get here?" Mrs. Nueman asked.

"She had a splitting headache," Cameron answered. Bill Nueman came into the room, drink in hand. He shook hands with Cameron.

"Glad you could make it," he said.

Nueman took a seat beside his wife and was about to start talking when the clock-type chimes sounded, indicating someone at the door. Mrs. Nueman rose. "Here they are now," she said. She ushered in a couple, and while Bill Nueman made sure everybody knew one another and took orders for drinks from the newcomers, another four couples arrived. When all were seated as comfortably as space permitted, Bill Nueman began.

"None of us here know each other too good," he said, sounding vaguely like a union organizer addressing the rank and file. "And I think that's kind of a good thing. It's sort of the way us Americans choose to be: independent. If I got problems, like I do, I usually keep 'em to myself. If you, any of you, got problems, I guess you do the same, 'cause I haven't heard nothing about them." His wife poked him gently with her elbow.

"Bill. No speeches. Get to the point."

"Okay, honey, you tell 'em. I never was any good at talking in public anyway." Mrs. Nueman took over.

"All right. There's no use beating around the bush. It's about our neighbors next door here, which I'm sure you're all very aware of." She paused and looked around, waiting for a reaction.

Cameron suddenly was enlightened. "I don't understand," he said, sitting forward, straightening his horn-rim glasses. "You mean, you called us all here to talk about some neighbors?"

"Not just any neighbors, Cameron," Bill Nueman said, jerking his head in the direction of the Sandoval house next door. "It's about them Sandovals. That Spanish family next door. You met 'em?"

"You mean that Mexican family," Cameron corrected. "No, I haven't. I've seen them often though. I'm half a block up, you know."

"Half a block, next door, or five blocks," Nueman said pontifically, "it's all the same. So far as what it's going to do to the neighborhood, anyway."

"And believe me," Mrs. Nueman put in, "it's not all the same when you live right next door. You've no idea what we've been through."

Another man whom Cameron recognized as living across the street and down a house or two from him spoke up.

"I was wondering about that myself," he said trying to sound emphatic. "It was my understanding when we bought here there wouldn't be anything but whites in the tract. How'd they get in, anyway?"

Cameron sat back to watch what he knew would happen. Bill Nueman spoke up.

"Way I get it, he had a light-skinned Mex with a good credit buy the place, then he took over."

Mrs. Nueman waved her hand as though to quiet an uneasy flock. "Now wait a minute. Let's don't get side-tracked. How they got the place is in the past. We already investigated and found there's nothing we can do about that. What we—Bill and me—called you all here for is to make sure everybody knows just what they're like, and then we can decide on a proper course of action. Within any laws."

Another man spoke up. Cameron recognized him as the one who spent his weekends picking minute particles of something or other out of a dichondra lawn.

"Frankly, I was aware of it when the Sandovals moved in. I saw them in their old trucks. But I figured, in all fairness, we should give them a chance to prove themselves one way or another before we draw any conclusions."

Mrs. Nueman spoke. "Well, they've proved themselves.

And not in one way, but the other." All except Cameron thought this a fairly funny joke.

Another previously unheard-from resident joined in.

"I'm almost all the way down to the corner. But just what, exactly, is it like living next to them?"

Bill Nueman grinned broadly. "I'll put it this way. Wanna trade houses?" They all—again except Cameron—laughed hilariously and on this note many finished their drinks and indicated they wanted more. Bill Nueman went to make refills.

Mrs. Nueman carried on. "Well, there's nothing wrong with living next to them. That is, if you don't mind seeing people run around the yard in the raw. Or go to the john on the front lawn, or even in the street in front of God and everybody."

There was a general reaction of exclamations, during which Bill Nueman roared from the kitchen, "Tell 'em where we seen him kiss that little kid that day. Go ahead, tell 'em."

Mrs. Nueman came as close to blushing as she could. "Bill! That's one thing I *couldn't* tell. And I wish you wouldn't, either. Some things I just can't . . . I don't know." She shrugged.

Bill Nueman returned with a tray of drinks. He passed them around while everybody waited to be told where Pete Sandoval had kissed that little kid, and all were equally curious as to whether the kid he kissed, wherever it was, was a boy or a girl. All except Cameron, who analyzed his feelings and found his desire to get up and walk out was just about equally balanced by a morbid curiosity to stay and see to what hideous length this was going to be carried out. Mrs. Nueman chose to continue. As she did she closed and opened her eyes several times, sure that she was lending emphasis to her words, Cameron thought. "I am *not* joking when I say they go to the john on the front lawn or in the street. I am *not* joking when I say they run around in the raw," she gathered momentum, "or when I say they carry on wild orgies parked in front of their house at two ay em." She held her eyes open. "And I'm telling you, the *people* who come and go into that house night and *day,* those women look *exactly* like the prostitutes you see all over in Tijuana."

Cameron looked annoyed. "Mr. Nueman, just what was the purpose of inviting us here?"

A note of hostility appeared in Bill Nueman's voice.

"The purpose, Don, was to tell you and all the rest of us here exactly what we got to contend with."

"Well, exactly what *do* we have to contend with here?" Cameron asked. "So far, all I've heard is some gossip, most of which I don't believe, and the rest of which is probably your misinterpretation of events . . ."

Nueman cut in: "Misinterpretation!" He looked at another man who had so far remained silent. "Max, you live on the other side of the Sandovals. Now I ask you. Is what I said fact or is it fancy?"

The group looked at Max. He cleared his throat. "Well, I have to admit, although I live alone now and I'm not home very much, I can verify a good deal of what you say. The Sandovals are not the most savory people one could live next to . . ."

Cameron started to speak, knowing it would be useless.

"Now wait a minute. I'm sure if you leave them alone, they'll . . ."

"We *tried* leaving them alone," Bill Nueman cut in. "But they won't leave us alone. That little kid of theirs, Sammy, he was over here every day 'til I put my foot down. We got a daughter about his age, you know. She's the cleanest, nicest kid you could hope for. And by God, I want to keep her that way."

"What do you mean, 'put your foot down'?" Cameron asked, his voice taking on a cold edge.

"I'll tell you what I mean. I mean I caught him and my kid in the garage together, and I sent him home in no uncertain terms."

"Just what were they doing?" Cameron asked.

Bill Nueman glared a moment at him. "What were they doing? Huh. What *won't* kids do when they get in a garage together?"

"You mean," Cameron persisted, "you caught the Sandoval kid and your daughter doing something immoral?"

Nueman looked around and saw he had the others on his side.

"Look, Cameron. When you see something's about to happen, you don't go ahead and let it happen. A parent's duty is to try to keep his kid wholesome. What do you think I shoulda done? Sit by and wait 'til he undressed her? I nipped that business in the bud."

Cameron rose to go, setting his glass down. "Well, if you've said all you're going to . . ."

Bill Nueman stood up. "Now wait a minute, Cameron. You're in this as much as we are, whether you like it or not. The worst course of action when something like this arises is to sit back and do nothing. We all got a stake in this. This house here, it's a damn nice house. Everything I saved for for years is tied up here. What's going to happen here is going to cost me—and probably everybody in this room—a couple of thousand bucks."

The conversation ceased while Bill Nueman talked. Cameron took the challenge.

"And just how, precisely, will it cost us all a couple of thousand bucks?"

"When they start moving in, that's how. Now, everybody that's ever had anything to do with real estate, like we all here have, will tell you that when Mexicans and colored move in prices drop."

Another man spoke. "I didn't know they let colored in this tract."

"They haven't, yet," Nueman answered. "But what's going to stop Sandoval from selling to Negroes? I mean, what's the difference? Max here, he don't like living next to this kind of people. Same as we don't. Now, just suppose I was going to move. Don't panic, now, I'm just saying just suppose I decided to move. Who'm I gonna sell to with them next door? Not people the caliber of us here, I'll tell you that. Not one single person here woulda bought his house if he saw this Mex family next door. So what happens? If I wanna sell, I gotta drop my price. Or else I can't sell. And the minute I drop my price, who buys?"

"Negroes," someone put in simply. "They can't afford high class prices like we can."

"Right. And it's a vicious cycle. One house goes to a Negro, the others just have to. There's no way in God's earth to stop it. Same as with what we got on our hands here."

The man who picked things out of dichondra spoke. "The Sandovals have already cost us all a pretty piece of cash. You don't believe me, just try to sell your house to somebody and tell 'em the neighborhood's not all white."

Bill Nueman again. "And, by God, if Mexicans are considered white, then I been misinformed all my life."

A woman in her late twenties, rather pretty, dressed in a neat suit arose and introduced herself to those whom she did not know as Miss Ann Clark. She spoke as though she were addressing a PTA meeting.

"I teach fourth grade at the local school," she said, "and I've had considerable experience with these people." She paused and it was evident she wanted to be asked how she came by this experience.

"How's that?" Cameron obliged.

"I taught school in East Los Angeles prior to coming to this school district. And I think that all present can rest assured that these people will come to the conclusion all by themselves that they're out of their element. It just won't work, they're trying to become something they're not. They'll find that out soon enough for themselves. Leopards can't change their spots. Water eventually, if given enough time, seeks its own level." She paused and her eyes traveled around the room. "It's a shame that so much damage must be done—to everyone—before the Sandovals realize what a mistake this . . . blockbusting is, but we all must learn through trial and error, through making mistakes for ourselves."

"I don't follow you," Cameron put in. "Just what do you mean?"

"I mean, like where the children are concerned. Last week those kids, Sammy and Mariana, their names are, enrolled in school. The boy is in my class and I'm getting to know him. The girl, she was put in an advanced class for some reason. But I can tell you right now these kids will find out they can't compete with American kids. They don't have the intellectual background our kids do. Putting them in one of our schools will just give them deeper feelings of inferiority."

"You've already decided that? And the boy's been in your class only a week?" Cameron asked.

Miss Clark looked indignant. "As I said, I've had experience with these people. In East Los Angeles that's all I had in my classes. I'm a trained, professional teacher and I know what I'm talking about."

"Tell me, Miss Clark," Cameron said, ignoring the antipathy he was arousing, "you don't like teaching these kids, do you?"

She paused before answering. "I'd rather teach more receptive kids. It's a little discouraging to teach youngsters who don't absorb. Yes, I like the feeling of fulfillment I get when I see children absorbing knowledge like a sponge. Any teacher will tell you there's nothing like the feeling of reward you get when you impart knowledge."

Cameron pressed on. "You say the girl's in an advanced class. I take it then you teach the slower ones here."

". . . I don't teach the advanced class, no . . ."

"Why not?"

"Because. Perhaps the administration feels I'm more effective in the harder-to-reach . . ." She trailed off.

"But you didn't like that sort of thing in East Los Angeles."

"No. I told you. I wanted the reward of . . ."

"Then, not liking teaching this kind of student, you weren't assigned to East Los Angeles because you wanted to work there. Right?"

"I don't see where that's any of your business. I'm a highly trained, professional . . ."

"I know, I know. But I also happen to know that it's the policy of the Los Angeles school district to assign a teacher to work in the minority communities as a disciplinary measure. Except when a teacher volunteers to work there, and you obviously didn't, in view of your feelings."

She looked at him coolly, a forced smile on her lips. "I don't have to take this from you. Are you insinuating I may be incompetent?"

"I'm not insinuating anything. I'm just saying what I know the L.A. school policy to be."

"That's not necessarily true! *Somebody* has to teach in those areas . . ."

"Right. And since nobody wants to, any teacher who gets in bad for some reason, who can't get along, usually winds up in East L.A. or in Watts."

Bill Nueman stood up, pointing a finger at Cameron. "Look, Cameron. I don't know why you feel you have to buck public opinion. We're just having an intelligent conversation and you think we're . . ."

"Good God! Here you're letting this woman say how she's going to make life miserable for a kid because of the way she feels . . . you're going to condone her taking out her personal feelings on this boy in the name of teaching them their place . . ."

"Mr. Cameron," it was Miss Clark, "I'll tell you what I'm *not* going to do. I'm *not* going to lower my classroom standards for one individual. Is that what you mean?"

"In other words, you're going to flunk him."

"If he can't stay with my class, he doesn't belong there. Every parent in this room would be furious at me if I didn't adhere strictly to a uniform demand of performance."

The others agreed. After all, they paid the taxes that paid

the teacher's salary, that built the buildings, the least they had a right to expect was a measure of standards second to none.

Cameron started for the door, just as the chimes sounded. Mrs. Nueman quickly got up and went to the door. She peeped through the little lens that allowed a full view of the doorstep outside. She turned back to the others and said almost in a whisper, "It's the Sandovals."

L ooks like they're having a neighborhood get-together or something over there," Pete remarked. Although it was evening, the long afternoon of September retained daylight.

"Yeah," Minnie replied, "I've already seen three couples from this side of the street and one from the other go in there."

"Maybe we ought to go over and get acquainted, introduce ourselves."

" . . . but . . . I think around here you should be invited before you drop in."

"Naw, neighbors are just like neighbors everywhere. If we waited to be invited we'd never see any of our friends. Like if our friends waited for us to invite them, we'd never see any of them either."

"Okay, Pete. Wait'll I put on something a little nicer. We can leave the twins watching television, verdad?"

"Sí. Hey, you kids. Your mama and I are going next door for a little bit. If anybody calls or comes, come to get me, huh?"

They walked to the Nueman house next door. As they approached they heard voices.

"Sounds like they're arguing about something," Pete said.

"Yeah, about school or something."

"We won't stay long," Pete said as he rang the bell. "They have a bell just like ours."

They waited a few moments. "Funny. Now I don't hear anything."

"Ring again, Pete." He rang again. Another long silence.

"Maybe they went out to the back or something."

"But they still should hear the bell."

"Ring it some more."

A long silence. "I was positive I heard people in there."

"Maybe it was the television, or something."

"Maybe, but maybe something's wrong. Can you see in the window?"

Minnie stepped to a window. "No, the curtains are too thick. I can't see anything. Go around the side, see if they went to the patio."

Pete walked to the side of the house and returned.

"Nobody there. Both their cars are in the driveway, too."

They started slowly walking home, looking back.

"Do you think something's wrong in there?" Minnie asked.

"I don't know, it sure is strange." But by now both their voices lacked conviction.

Dear Mr. Sandoval:

It has been several weeks now that Sammy has been in this class and he has shown no inclination to overcome his weaknesses. He is weak in Spelling, Arithmetic and Reading in particular. You must at once help him to catch up to the other students in the class if he is to remain with us.

Miss A. Clark

Minnie read the note and handed it to Pete. They had just finished dinner and Mariana and Sammy were in the living room watching television. Pete called Sammy in.

"Hijo! How come we got a note saying you don't do your school work?"

Sammy shrugged. "It's too hard."

"Too hard? The other kids are doing it, aren't they?"

"Yeah, but . . . I just don't understand it."

"Why not?"

"I just don't know how."

"Okay. Bring me your arithmetic. I'll show you."

Sammy brought his work and laid it on the table. Pete looked it over. "What's this little thing here mean?"

Sammy smiled a little. "That means to divide this number by that number there."

Pete studied the page more. "And this, that little 'X' means that number has to be *times* that one, right?"

"Sí."

"Okay, so what's so hard about that? Let's see you do that now."

"But, papa. I just don't know the times table and the division things. I can't."

"Okay, then, call Mariana. Mariana!"

"Manda, papa," she called.

"Come here to help Sammy with his arithmetic. You can do this stuff easy, can't you?"

Mariana came in. "Sí, papa. But he won't let me help him."

Pete looked at Sammy. "What's this you won't let her help you?"

He was sullen. "I don't want her to teach me."

"That's silly. I never heard of anything like that. Now you let her help you or you'll be sorry. Ándale. Now beat it."

The next day the teacher called to him from her desk.

"You turned in a very nice paper, Sammy. You learned quickly, didn't you?"

Sammy nodded.

"Look, class," Miss Clark said, holding the paper aloft. "Sammy did all his work correctly. I'm very impressed. Now Sammy, go to the blackboard and take the chalk."

Sammy was looking directly at her. He didn't move at first. "Come on, Sammy. Go to the board. I'll give you a problem to work."

Sammy went to the board and took the chalk. "Now write these numbers . . ."

He wrote the problem and then stood, back to the class, hands at his sides. And as first the coaxing came, then the demanding, then the ridicule, he stood still, unflinching, until finally he heard, ". . . now take your seat and don't ever try cheating again. It doesn't pay. In this school we don't cheat. You've got to learn to own up to it."

He took his seat near the rear of the class and kept his eyes on the desk.

At recess time he waited to be chosen on one side for a game. When all were chosen but him he quickly set about doing something else. He felt before that he was being left out, now he was sure of it. When school first started he was chosen as much as anybody else, but now it was changing. He decided one of the big differences between this school and the one in Los Angeles was that over there when the teacher got after you, you had buddies. All the other guys she got after met with you at recess and made you feel better. But here it wasn't the case. In Los Angeles the guys who wanted to do everything the teacher said were considered sissies, goody-goody boys. The guy who got left out and bullied the most by the other guys was the best student, always.

He liked the other school better.

A week later his class was reading aloud in turn. He had only been called upon to read once or twice before, and he had stumbled through, self-consciously, knowing he was the only one who talked with an accent. But he tried to read along when others read aloud and was learning to recognize more and more words. This story was about some children watching a repair crew working on the street. "All right, Sammy, your turn," Miss Clark called out.

"The foreman walked to the . . ." he fumbled.

"Excavation," the teacher put in. Sammy skipped it.

" . . . and took a . . ." he knew the word wouldn't fit his tongue, "cha-bull." A titter went through the class.

"That word is 'shovel,' Sammy," the teacher said with an air of tolerance. Sammy started on.

"He looked at the . . ." But the teacher cut in.

"Say 'shovel.' I want you to pronounce it."

Sammy hesitated and a little silence developed. "Go on, say it," the teacher coaxed. Sammy twisted his tongue, but the vowels and consonants were too alien to him.

"Chabull," he said again. This time the class, thinking the teacher critical of Sammy, snickered louder.

"Sammy," the teacher said in a tone implying extreme patience, "you must learn to say these words if you want to stay in this grade level. Now say 'sh-sho-vel'." Sammy retreated. His face went expressionless and he dropped his eyes, aware that every eye in the class was on him. What had she meant by saying if he wanted to stay in this grade level? Was she considering setting him back? With that thought drenching his consciousness he tried to read aloud with a corner of his awareness. Desperately, he tried to put his tongue and lip muscles into the attitude which allowed those words to come out sounding like the white guys' talk. He saw the word "pick" rushing toward him in the sentence he was reading. He knew words containing the vowel as in "pick" were the ones most often seized upon by those who lampooned the Mexican. "Pee-eek," they always said, making their voices drop a little for the last half of the word. Sammy read the word, straining to avoid his natural pronunciation. It came out "peck." Again the teacher stopped him.

"Say 'pick,' Sammy." Sammy was silent, eyes on the book.

"You've got to at least try," the teacher said in a demanding tone. Sammy remained silent. "Now listen," she said, "one of the things you've got to learn is that when we say something, we mean it."

Sammy raised his eyes to her. He understood what she said, although she herself didn't. He knew when she said "we" she meant all the others, the Anglos, the "Americans," and when she said "you" she meant "you people." This was as far as he could reason it out. He could never have put it in words, English or Spanish. He remained silent and the teacher allowed a long silence to develop. "Say the word 'pick,' Sammy," she said sternly. Sammy glanced at the nearby door to the hall. That was the only escape. To run. Solve the problem immediately, for now. Never mind that tomorrow must be dealt with. The teacher, seeing that Sammy might bolt, quickly moved so that she was between him and the door. Feeling trapped, Sammy made a rush to get by her. Miss Clark seized him by the arms and they struggled, Sammy breaking into great uncontrollable sobs. The class was fascinated, motionless.

"Sammy, stop it! Sit down," Miss Clark demanded. By her superior physical strength she managed to force him back into his seat. Still holding his hands, she turned to the boy behind. "Go get Mr. Scott," she ordered. The boy scurried out to the principal's office. In a few moments he returned with the worried-looking principal. Miss Clark was still holding Sammy.

"What's the trouble?" he asked, laying a hand heavily on Sammy's shoulder. In the presence of his greater strength Sammy quit struggling, gave up, sat shuddering, eyes down.

"He refuses to read," Miss Clark reported. "He tried to run away. I don't know what to do with him." The principal looked around at the other children, most of whom sat, mouths agape, watching.

"All right," he said soothingly, "I'll talk to him in my office." He took Sammy firmly by the arm and led him to the door. "Come to my office as soon as the bell rings," he said to Miss Clark.

Walking down the hall, Sammy could feel Mr. Scott's fingers dig into his arm. "You're hurting me," he said in a tiny voice.

"Will you not try to run away if I let you go?" Mr. Scott asked. Sammy nodded. Deep within his chest was a terrible spasmodic jerking. He proceeded down the hall one step in front of Mr. Scott, half-expecting at any moment to be cuffed. But the blow never fell. Mr. Scott's long arm reached in front and took the door knob as they reached the office. Sammy felt he was being herded.

"Sit down, Sammy," Mr. Scott ordered. Sammy took a seat

on a couch across from Mr. Scott's desk. His breath was still jerking. Mr. Scott sat down at his desk and looked severely at Sammy. "Now," he said, "tell me what the trouble is." Sammy sat, hands in his lap, eyes down. He shrugged. "Are you unhappy in Miss Clark's class?" Sammy shrugged again, remaining silent. "Very well, then we'll wait 'til Miss Clark gets here."

The boy sat still, listening, while Mr. Scott started going through some papers and books. Sammy could hear the great clock on the wall click twice every minute or so. The school seemed strangely silent. He kept his eyes down. Presently the bell sounded announcing the end of class. For perhaps a half minute the school remained silent, and then sounds began. Just far away noises at first, doors opening, feet scuffing. Then the sounds of children's voices began rising, a high-pitched chorus of unintelligible syllables. As the halls filled the sound grew, louder yet muffled. Sammy imagined all the students were discussing his plight. The door opened and Miss Clark entered.

"He just refused to cooperate," she said to Mr. Scott. "It was reading time and he just took it upon himself to be above the others, I guess." She looked at Sammy accusingly. Mr. Scott was also looking at him. Sammy sensed Miss Clark's defensiveness. It puzzled him a little. He had always regarded the school staff as being in unison, collectively united. Now Miss Clark was afraid of Mr. Scott.

"How long has he been acting up?" Mr. Scott asked.

Miss Clark hesitated before answering. "Actually, today was the first time I became aware he was a problem reader. But he's completely unwilling to try. I tried to get him to make an attempt, but he just wanted to walk out of class." They were both looking at him. For a moment Sammy looked up at them, a pleading expression on his face. He wanted desperately to say something, but he knew the words would have a thick accent. He remained silent.

"What do you suggest?" Mr. Scott asked.

"I think, for his own benefit as well as that of the rest of the students, he should go back to third grade and learn the fundamentals of reading a little better."

Mr. Scott regarded Sammy a few moments. "You hear that, Sammy? Miss Clark thinks you ought to be set back a grade. What do you think?"

Sammy thought. Above all, he didn't want to go back into her class again. He nodded.

"All right, Sammy," Mr. Scott said with finality. "But I do want to talk to your parents about it first. I'll give you a note to take home." He wrote a note to Pete and Minnie, and although it was only afternoon recess, he allowed Sammy to go home, knowing it would quite possibly save him embarrassment and perhaps ridicule from the other boys in his class.

That night, after Minnie had read the letter to Pete as he sat soaking up the remaining chili on his plate with a piece of tortilla, Pete grunted.

"Why does he want to see us?"

"I guess like the letter says, to talk about Sammy."

"Doesn't Meester Scott know it's a working day? I can't take off. We got a big pour coming."

"Okay, Pete, okay," Minnie said before he could work himself into a pretended small rage. "I'll go see him. I can handle it."

Pete raised his voice so that Sammy could hear in the next room. "Oye, mijito! Ven aquí." Sammy came in. "Why are you giving trouble to your teacher? Don't you know no better?"

Sammy knew his father's gruffness, when he was stern, was

all put on. It was an effort for Pete not to sound like the loving father all the time. Sammy smiled. He had no fear of his father.

"She wanted me to say some words I couldn't."

"What words?"

" . . . Pala. Pico. In English."

"Those are easy words. Chawbool and peek. Why didn't you say them?" Sammy shrugged. Pete went on: "Now your mother has to go to school to talk to the principal. Please don't make any more trouble." And he turned to the TV set.

Mr. Scott and Miss Clark appraised Minnie severely when she entered the principal's office the next day leading Sammy. She wore a black taffeta dress with frills and lace, a black bead hat with a heavy veil over her face and white gloves with glass beads. Scott and Miss Clark noticed she was a remarkably attractive woman in spite of the heavy lipstick and volumes of eyeshade and rouge she wore.

"Mrs. Sandoval. Glad you could come. Have you met Miss Clark?" Scott eyed her as he talked. Minnie stepped to Miss Clark and boldly held out her hand, smiling. The scent of her perfume quickly filled the entire room.

"Pleased to meet you," Miss Clark smiled sweetly.

"The same here," Minnie said. She sat down, Sammy beside her.

"Mr. Sandoval was unable to come, I suppose," Mr. Scott said.

"Yes," Minnie answered, "he has to work every day. But he takes his truck. I have the Cadillac." Sammy glanced up and saw Mr. Scott and Miss Clark exchange glances. It troubled him a little that instead of a swell of pride at his mother's mention of the Cadillac, he felt a little ashamed.

"I see," Mr. Scott went on. "As the note said, Sammy seems to be having a little trouble reading at fourth-grade level. Did he tell you about it?"

"No," Minnie said. "I just got the note. But he's always been a fair reader before. We all are. He got some A's in the school in East Los Angeles. His sister—do you know Mariana?—she reads real good."

"You see, Mrs. Sandoval," Miss Clark put in, "we want Sammy to . . ." she chose her words carefully, as though she were trying hard to say it as simply as possible, "be as good a reader as possible. It seems he doesn't grasp the fundamentals . . . the first things he should know about reading. We think perhaps if he continues at this level it would hurt his chances of developing into a fine reader. Perhaps he should go back to some easier reading for a while."

"Okay," Minnie said agreeably. "You want him to start reading easier books?"

Mr. Scott spoke up. "Yes . . . that's it in a way. Miss Clark feels that if we put Sammy back into third grade he would quickly grasp what he lacks."

Minnie looked a little shocked. But she knew she was helpless. She looked down tenderly at her son. Sammy sat still, eyes still down. Once he looked up at her, pleading. She said to him gently, "Entiendes tu?"

"Yes, I understand," he answered her in Spanish. "But she just wanted me to say words I couldn't pronounce." They talked at some length in Spanish, much to the annoyance of Mr. Scott and Miss Clark, who were quite sure Sammy was berating them in their presence. Mr. Scott wanted to say, "What are you saying?" But he didn't have the courage. Soon the conversation between Minnie and Sammy ended and Minnie turned to the teacher and the principal.

"He says he will do what you tell him and he will try harder to please you," she said.

Sammy was set back from fourth to third grade. His new teacher was Mrs. Sanford. She listened with practiced patience as Miss Clark explained Sammy's problem and the subsequent official action.

"Take a seat, Sammy," she said in her gentle voice. "As soon as I give the class some assignment I'll have someone show you to the school library. There you can pick out any special books you want to take home overnight."

Sammy felt all eyes on him as he took an empty desk. Mrs. Sanford passed out material and gave instructions to the others.

"Now. Who will show Sammy to the library?" she asked. The children looked a little puzzled. "Who's Sammy?" someone asked. Mrs. Sanford pointed. "The . . . Spanish boy," she said with some difficulty. Sammy felt his face flush. One youngster held up his hand.

"All right, Charles," Mrs. Sanford said. "Take him to the library. Then come right back. Understand?"

Charles took Sammy to the librarian. "This is Sammy, he's supposed to pick some special books to read," Charles recited. Then he added, "He's a Spanish boy." Sammy looked at him, then up at the librarian.

"I am not," he said.

The librarian dismissed Charles with a wave of the hand.

"Oh? You're not? I know your sister. I thought you children came from a fine Spanish family."

"We're Mexican," Sammy said almost belligerently.

The librarian winced a little at the word. She groped for the right thing to say. "Well, around here we'll just use the word 'Spanish.' It sounds . . ." she fumbled, trapped, "more . . . accurate."

She showed Sammy where the simpler books were, encouraging him to choose whichever he wanted, yet selecting some which she thought he should read.

Sammy looked over the books. It showed children, about his age, but they didn't look anything like him. They were all light-complexioned. He thumbed through a particular book, noticing all parents represented were nearly identical. They had typical Anglo features. The fathers all wore suits to work and the mothers all were slim and beautiful. He didn't recall seeing any books like these in East Los Angeles. He read carefully, but spent equal time studying the pictures of the family in the book. He saw them getting into their car for an outing. He saw and read how they sat at the dinner table, how they reacted to the visit of the grandparents. It made him somewhat uneasy that he could find nothing to indicate everything wasn't perfect for the family in the book.

"Find something you like?" The librarian surprised him. He nodded. "That's a good series," she told him. "Why don't you take a few of those with you? It's a whole series of books about a lovely family. You have very good taste, to pick out that book, Sammy."

She gave him three books on the family and he returned to his class. Mrs. Sanford smiled when he showed her the books. She explained to him that he didn't have to join in any of the class activities until he felt comfortable. She didn't want him to feel any pressure whatever. "Just spend your time improving yourself until you feel just like you're one of us," she told him.

Within a week Sammy had read the series on the Carter family. He found the world in the book completely foreign to him, and he wondered if the Anglos all secretly tried to be just like the family in the book. He tried other books, but found nothing he could get interested in. The books on adventure, the books on life in general all required a field of common understanding he did not have. Something, he knew, was amiss.

Mariana, in her advanced fourth-grade class, got out of school a half hour later than he did, and that half hour of waiting each day became an ordeal, as his former classmates began tormenting him. He didn't realize that what brought on the teasing and harassing was mostly his timidity and shyness. Soon it became a game for the other boys to trap him, corner him, jerk his books away. "Aw, we read those years ago," they would scoff, throwing the books on the ground. And Mariana would rescue him simply by her presence. They always quit teasing when she came. It really wasn't that important. To them.

One day during one of his free periods in the library at school he happened to pick up a first reader about a Utopian society comprised of small, benevolent, talking animals.

He read about Brer Rabbit living in the briar patch. Brer Rabbit wore only coveralls, no shoes, went fishing when he felt like it, associated with other small, carefree animals such as Bobby Coon, Unc' Billy Possum, Chatterer the Red Squirrel. True, there was an element of danger in the society, primarily from Reddy Fox and the crafty Old Man Coyote, but the more helpless members of the group could invariably forestall per-

sonal disaster by telling some outlandish lie to either Reddy Fox
or Old Man Coyote, setting the would-be predators on some
harmless but effective wild goose chase. The smaller characters
had a dauntless if unwitting champion of the oppressed in
Bowser the Hound, whose only duty was to chase Old Man
Coyote or Brother Fox whenever he saw them. Bowser the
Hound belonged to Farmer Brown, a rather obscure human-
type, who only infrequently wandered through the plots.

Life among Thornton W. Burgess' little animals of the
woods was truly paradise. There was no parental authority, yet
there was never the need for parental love. Indeed, there was no
moral behavioral problems at all among the little creatures.
Each was obviously different from the other, yet all were equal
in reasoning power—except, of course, the fox and the coyote.
These two could easily be outwitted.

Life in the woods was no struggle. Food grew for the picking. There was no school, no schedule, nothing was expected of
anyone except that he be a good friend.

Sammy read the first book with great interest. He was en-
tranced by the simplicity of life in the woods. He grew to know
the characters. He was delighted to find the Burgess animal series was almost endless. He began reading more of them.
Within a month he had finished all the books on the little animals in the school library. Then he started all over and reread
them.

Somehow, when the other boys picked on him now, he
didn't seem to mind. He would endure their tormenting until
they tired or help came, then he would go home to his room and
read about the little animals.

He began daydreaming, interjecting himself into the world
of little animals, longing to be able to touch them, talk to them,

be a friend among them. He pictured himself seated against a tree in the woods, the little animals in their coveralls gathered about him, looking to him as a friend, knowing Old Man Coyote and Reddy Fox would give them a wide berth with Sammy in their midst.

He lost interest in trying to catch up in his school work and read and reread animal books, then searched for similar books.

"Sammy, this is the third time today I've caught you reading that book. You have to pay attention to what the class is doing," his teacher warned. He tried, but felt he was hopelessly outdistanced by the others. He just wanted to get back to the woods.

"What's the matter with you?" Pete scolded each time Sammy brought a note telling of his unsatisfactory performance at school. "Your sister gets the top grades all the time. You make me ashamed. The neighbors don't want you at their houses anymore. I don't blame them." When Pete said this Sammy noticed his father and mother exchanged glances. *They don't want you either,* he said silently to himself, *you think I don't know about those telephone calls and the flat tires when you go out some mornings?*

Since the house had been vandalized that weekend they were away, the family had never gone away overnight. Sammy knew that the worry every time they all left for the store was telling on his parents. One night in bed he heard:

"That damn Nueman. I know it was his boy who put the tacks under the tires this time. He was the only one in the yard. When I told Nueman he got mad and said we should get out."

"That's what Miss Clark said. She called again and said we should take the twins back to Los Angeles to school, or they'll both be flunk-outs." "We've got to go back home." "Yes. Soon."

Good, Sammy thought as he lay back to try to sleep through this night as his sister was doing so easily across the room.

It was only a few months later when the Jameson doorbell rang and Elizabeth shrieked with delight to find Mariana there. "And we're back for good this time," Mariana said.

All the old friendships were renewed. Sammy was placed back in the fourth grade with his old friends and took up where he left off. When his gang invited him to ditch school and go to a boy's house whose parents worked all day, he went. When he worried about school work, they reassured him: "Ah, don't worry. They got to pass you in this school. Even if you don't know nothing. They can't flunk us all," they laughed.

"Just stick it out 'til you're sixteen. Then you can quit and go to continuation school. That's only half a day a week."

Through grade school he was placed in different classes from Mariana, and this made it easy to cut school, as he wouldn't have to get her to lie to Pete and Minnie for him.

He learned that the farther he stayed from Mariana and her circle of friends, the more freedom he had.

"How come you're coming home so late?" his mother asked one evening when he'd spent the day with four boys and two girls from the sixth grade in an empty apartment.

"I played baseball," and that was the end of that.

In first year high school it was easier; the teachers seemed to care less, and there were many more youths his age who cared about nothing except getting out of classes and getting their kicks. Marijuana was common; some actually smoked the weed walking down the hall between classes, the cigarette concealed in a cupped hand. An unspoken truce existed between the "squares," those who went to school to learn and take part, and the others who were there only because the law demanded it.

The uncaring crowd left the squares alone, generally, and the squares closed their eyes to the drugs in the rest rooms, the burglarizing of a supply room, the gangster-like vendettas, feuds, and beatings.

One day the principal called him in. "Sammy, you're going on sixteen now. I advise you to get a job and go to continuation school. You're not learning anything here, and you're not doing the school any good either. I've no doubt you can get your parents to sign the necessary form. You have a job to go to?"

"Yeah. I do work now and then for a guy that owns a little car lot. I think he'll put me on full time."

"Good," the principal said, writing on a slip of paper. "Take this to the main office and they'll process you. I do just want to say a few things. I just don't understand how this happens. I've met your parents. Nice people. I know your sister Mariana. An honor student. Some day we'll learn how to prevent this gang sort of thing that seems to seize you boys and dictate your behavior and social laws and removes you from anything that's good and desirable. I know just where you're headed, Sammy. Exactly. I only wish someone knew how to do something about it. That's all. Good-bye."

After school as soon as he met his gang he grinned broadly and said, "I got the speech today, man." The others envied and congratulated him and accompanied him down to the used car lot to get a note of verification of employment.

Mr. Hitchcock ran his fingers through his thinning hair and stood at the front of the classroom, arms folded, glaring, or at least he hoped he was glaring, at the boys as they

filed insolently into the room. He remained that way until five
minutes after the bell had rung, waiting for the boys to quiet.
Several talked in normal conversational tones until they were
ready to quit talking. All slouched down in their seats and returned his glare. *Let's see, there's a new boy today. That must be
him there.*

"Are you Samuel Sandoval?"

"Yeah."

"You're required to be here four hours every week. In the
event you refuse to attend this class, the authorities will be notified and you'll be put in a corrective school. You understand
that, don't you?"

"Yeah."

"All right. Vargas? You weren't here last week. How
come?"

"I was sick, man."

"What was wrong with you?"

"I don't know, man. I'm not a doctor." Laughter. Mr. Hitchcock glared around the room.

"Do you have a statement from your parents?"

"They can't write, man." Again laughter.

"You'll have to furnish some evidence that you were home
ill or it'll go on your record as unexcused absence."

"Nobody's home all day at my house. So you just gotta take
my word I'm not a liar." There was loud laughter at this.

Mr. Hitchcock decided not to pursue it.

"Sam Sandoval, in this continuation course everyone must
show proof he has a job."

Sammy stood and approached him, taking a crumpled piece
of paper from his pocket. He handed it to Mr. Hitchcock and returned to his seat. Hitchcock read it.

"You're working as a used-car salesman at Timmy's Car Lot?"

"Yeah."

"I see. You seem rather young for that, but if it's legitimate work, that's all that's required. Now, let's see, where were we . . ."

Mr. Hitchcock began the lecture. He talked and talked, hardly aware of what he was saying. Occasionally two or more boys would commence a conversation and he would walk toward them, raising his voice as he talked on U.S. History, and they would sullenly quiet down. At one point, when he came to a pause in his words, someone near the rear of the class loudly broke wind, and the others rocked with laughter. Mr. Hitchcock continued. He found his eyes wandering to the clock, waiting for this four hours of torture to himself and the others to end.

When finally it did, and a bell rang, he stopped talking in the middle of a sentence, just as the boys walked out.

As he arranged his desk, he murmured to himself, "I never would have believed I'd come to this. I never would have believed it's absolutely hopeless."

When Sammy left the school he walked down Fourth Street to Timmy's Car Lot. Timmy, the tall, skinny Anglo who ran the lot, always had work for Sammy. He had about a hundred junk heaps for sale and maybe a half dozen decent cars. Sammy found him in the repair shop at the rear of the lot. Timmy quickly described Sammy's work for the evening. Another boy Sammy's age had just phoned to say he had a car spotted. The owners had just gone into a movie and wouldn't be out for nearly four hours. By that time Timmy wanted the car brought here, stripped of the plush seats and big carburetor, the air conditioning, radio and heater, any good tires and wheels, and the car had to be abandoned across town before the owners came out of the theater and reported it missing.

It was routine and Sammy performed admirably. He was paid by Timmy with a can of marijuana. He ditched the can in a nearby vacant lot, kicking it carefully under some tall weeds and went to find a buyer. Within an hour he found a man who would give him twenty dollars for it. He walked with the man to the vacant lot and, taking the money, told him where the pot was.

Twenty bucks. He smiled to himself. Not bad for a dumb chicano who can't hardly read. He walked back to Fourth Street and turned down. He was within sight of his own house now. But he wasn't going home. He saw his father's pickup truck parked in front. He saw his sister Mariana walking the other way with that Anglo babe Elizabeth.

He was in front of a house which was typical of the area. It was an old frame house, yellow paint peeling, trim around the windows rotting and cracking. A narrow paved driveway ran at the edge of the property line, a foot from the house next door. The driveway was too narrow for a present-day car, and was grown over with shrubs and plants. He walked down the drive to the house in the rear. This house, not visible from the street, was worse than the front house. He entered without knocking and saw Celia lying on the couch watching television.

Celia was a dark girl, fourteen years old, homely of face but with a precocious body. She was lying on her back, head propped up on a pillow against the arm of the old overstuffed sofa. She said "Hi" to Sammy with neither enthusiasm nor disappointment, and scooted closer to the back of the sofa so that he might sit next to her. Her eyes were already back on the TV screen. He sat beside her and placed his hand under her skirt on the inside of her thigh and moved it up. She moved so that his hand had easier access.

"What's happening?" he asked, indicating the TV screen. She filled him in on the plot. Then she suddenly pushed his hand away.

"Don't. I got a special kick for you today."

"What?"

"Wait 'til the program's over. It's something special."

They watched in silence until the episode ended. Then she went to a vase of artificial flowers and took two hand-rolled cigarettes. They lit up, inhaling deeply, exhaling slowly. "So what's the new bag?" he asked.

She went to a telephone on a table. "Wait 'til I check to see if mama and papa are working as usual."

He heard her dial a number, ask for her mother.

"Mom? I was going to make something nice for dinner. Shall I save you and Dad some? What time will you be home?"

She listened a while, then said, "All right, good-bye," and hung up. She turned to Sammy. "Same as usual. They'll be home when the bar closes, after two. They haven't missed a night tending bar for months, but it's best to check anyway."

She led him into a bedroom where a painted wooden three-quarter bed stood, gray sheets thrown back and wrinkled, covers half on the floor. She was wearing a sweatshirt and skirt, and she removed them as Sammy also undressed. They had brought their marijuana cigarettes, and now she took his and put it out in an ashtray. They both stood naked in the half dark room. There were no curtains to draw, but the windows were small and dirty, and the screen was rusty so that little light filtered through the branches of a shade tree outside. From a handbag she took a

CHICANO

small container and opened it. She showed Sammy two small gelatin capsules.

"These," she said, "are the new kick. I got them from the girls at school."

"What are they?"

"They give you about a five-minute kick like you never had before. They're for sick people when their hearts almost stop beating. You take one and, brrrr . . ." she whirled her hand rapidly, "your heart takes off." She lay down on the bed.

Under the influence of the marijuana he watched her body become exaggerated in its femininity. She too felt the heady exaggeration and expertly worked him to a pitch of high excitement. "Now," she said, and they sat up long enough to take the capsules and wash them down with water from a glass on a stand beside the bed. "Now start."

Under her direction and the influence of the pot he was able to synchronize his climax with the climax of the pill.

It seemed consciousness left him briefly and when he again became aware, he heard his heart pounding frantically and his breathing was as though he'd run a race. He was still on top of her and he rolled over and lay back, head on the pillow. He looked at her and she was sweat-streaked and also breathing heavily.

"Man oh man, what a kick!" he managed to say.

"That's what I told you," she gasped.

He reached over and took the remains of his cigarette from the ashtray and relit it. Still breathing deeply, he let his inhalation carry the marijuana smoke deep into his lungs, and he felt himself go into another phase of intoxication. He was sure his mind was brighter, sharper, although his voice had a faraway, detached sound to it. "Now, where'd you get those caps? How much can I buy them for? And how many can I get?"

"Hi, Mom."

"Sammy. You don't look well. Your eyes look funny. Anything the matter?"

"Naw, I just need to lie down, is all."

"I think maybe you're working too hard at that Timmy's Car Lot. A sixteen-year-old boy shouldn't have to put in such long hours as you do. You always look nearly dead."

"I'm fine. I like it, and I make pretty good money. He paid me twenty dollars today."

"Yes, but look what time you're getting home. Did you go to the continuation school today?"

"Sí. I wish I was eighteen so I could quit altogether."

"Well, I wish you'd go to work with your father."

"Maybe I will in a few months."

"Going to bed now? See you in the morning . . . why do you pull away from me? Don't you like your mother to kiss you?"

" . . . I'm tired, Mom. See you in the morning."

"Your papa and Mariana ought to be home any minute. Why don't you wait up to see them? You never see anybody hardly anymore."

"What for?"

The next morning Sammy walked to Timmy's Car Lot. He walked into the shop at the rear before he saw Timmy standing there in handcuffs and Big Ed of the Narco squad searching the place. They had uncovered Timmy's cache of grass and were searching for more.

"Hold it there, kid," Big Ed ordered as Sammy hesitated at the entrance. He quickly searched Sammy. He looked at Sammy's school identification card.

"Okay, Sammy. You in on this with Timmy?"

"I don't know what you mean, man."

Timmy spoke up. "Let him alone. He ain't got nothing to do with it."

Big Ed searched Sammy once more, thoroughly, then shoved him roughly toward the street.

"You're clean this time, kid. But I betcha you won't be next time I see you. I can tell a hophead a mile off. Now beat it."

Sammy left. *Well now, that's over. I better find a gig quick, or the old man will make me go to work with him. Long as he thinks I'm making it, he'll leave me alone.*

He remembered the name of the girl Celia had got the heart pills from. It was Saturday. She'd be at home, maybe.

Roberta was another homely, well-developed girl less than sixteen years old.

"I get them from a doctor," she told Sammy. "He's a real doctor. From Mexico."

"Tell me how I can get hold of him."

"No, I can't do that. But I could take you to him. If I say you're okay, he'll do business with you."

She took Sammy across the east side, down an old street with dilapidated buildings on it. "He's in here," she said, and led him around to the alley. The building seemed deserted. The windows were boarded up. She tried a back door but it was locked. Then she led Sammy to a window. The nails in some of the boards pulled out easily and they climbed through after she made sure no one was watching. Inside, she led him up to the third floor and into an office. The doctor looked surprised and a little annoyed. He spoke Spanish.

"Roberta, what are you doing here? I told you not to come . . ."

"This is my friend Sammy. He wants to know about those heart pills."

The doctor looked at Sammy carefully. He questioned him at some length, then turned to Roberta. "Please leave. And don't come back again unless you're with our friend who first brought you here. I want to talk to Sammy a while."

When the girl left, the doctor paced as he talked to Sammy. "I got a good deal here for the right guy with the right contacts. I run an abortion business. I'm the best. But I charge a lot. Here's the deal. You set up some transportation for girls who want to get rid of a kid. You find them, bring them in an enclosed panel truck or something. Make sure they got three hundred bucks. I'll give them the operation and give you a hundred. It beats pushing pills all to hell."

Sammy felt a flare of importance as he and the doctor made plans.

Julio and Angie's restaurant had been doing a substantial business consistently. It had been many years since Julio had parted with Rosa and found Angie, and steadily they had expanded, first to a counter-and-booths cafe, then to an informal family-type restaurant, then to an Anglo-catering dinner place and now finally to the huge dining room-cocktail lounge and gift shop combination place. For the final alterations and additions Julio had to use all his training in making his pitch to the bank for finances. He'd learned the way of finance in business college, and his framed diploma was the possession he was most proud of.

The big fly in the ointment, he realized, was Angie's frugality, her tendency to watch where the money went. How that dumb broad could claim to love him so much and at the same time insist on keeping an eye on the books was more than he could understand. She acts like a gringa broad sometimes, when it comes to money, he thought. But now he had a side income, thanks to Canto.

That had come about when he'd first installed a gift counter a few years before. Canto had never been able to find Julio's father, but periodically showed up for a grubstake to continue the search, and Julio financed him to pursue the leads the stumble-bum grapevine system of the waiting places supplied.

One day Canto had come to him and said, "Listen, Julio. How'd you like to pick up an extra hundred bucks, for doing practically nothing, every time you run down to Tijuana to buy that crap for your gift counter?" The "gift counter crap" consisted of little ceramic bulls, ashtrays carved of rough stone, turquoise and silver work and the like.

"What do I got to do and how dangerous is it?"

"All you gotta do is drive to a certain gas station in Tea Town and leave your car there for a lube job or something."

Julio waited and when no more information was forthcoming, he asked, "That's all?"

"That's all you need to know. In fact, that's all I want you to know. And I'll give you a hundred bucks when you get back."

At first Julio liked the idea of knowing nothing about what was going on. Every week he did as Canto said, and when he arrived back at his restaurant Canto showed up later and gave him one hundred dollars. He knew that something was placed on his car, and that Canto made money on it too, because now Canto was dressing fairly well and always had cash. Little by little Julio got more information on the operation. He demanded more money from Canto, who told him the size of the narcotics hauls would have to be increased. Julio was thus enabled to keep an apartment that Angie knew nothing of, which he told himself he kept for the day he found his father. He also used it whenever an adventurous Anglo woman called him up and said, "Mr. Salazar, could you *possibly* give me the recipe for that sauce you serve . . ." And Julio would say with a little put-on Spanish accent, "No, but I could show you how to make it. I have a little place where I cook myself now and then. If you care to come by . . ."

Julio sat behind his oak desk and worked on his figures. From a wire basket he occasionally took a receipt or statement or invoice and studied it in conjunction with a finely lined chart with numbers and headings, then punched rapidly on a small electrically operated adding machine, ripped off the answer sheet and made entries. The door suddenly burst open and Angie came in, exuberant and lively.

"Julio!" she exclaimed, "it's finished! I can't believe it! Our grand opening. Tonight. I finally got the carpet layers to finish the last of the carpet. Come on, let's take a final look before we open."

Julio rose and walked around his desk to her. He smiled as he tilted her chin up and kissed her. "Happy, baby?" he asked.

"I've never been so happy in my life. This is it, Julio. Our final expansion. We're big time now. The best place in the east side. And I owe it all to you."

He laughed his charming little laugh. "I owe it all to you, sweetheart. Without you I'd probably be still bumming around, doing odd jobs."

"No. But I'm glad we did this together. It was you who went to business college nights to learn how to really run a business. I never in a million years could have floated the loan to do all this, figure how many cooks we'd need and know how much it costs to stock a full cocktail bar. *You're* really the one who's responsible for this. Now come on. Let's look the place over. We open in a couple of minutes. Our big neon sign is just magnificent."

He smiled condescendingly. Then looked serious.

"One thing, Angie. I know you think I spent a lot on this office . . ." indicating the plush drapes and paneled walls, the high-backed leather executive chair and elaborate chandelier.

"I don't think any such thing! I know a man who runs a business like this has to have a nice office. That's one of the things you said they taught you at business college." She looked proudly at his business course diploma hanging in an expensive frame on the wall.

"Well, there's one other thing a businessman should have. And that's privacy. I wish you'd knock, or anyone else, who wants to come in to see me. I'm going to be doing business with some big shot suppliers, and you can't interrupt business transactions, okay?"

She looked more puzzled than offended. Then pride showed on her face. "Of course. That's only right. I'll tell every member of the staff that they knock before coming in here." She giggled in ecstasy. "We have *fifteen* people working for us now, Julio. Not counting part time help like dishwashers and car parkers. Just think! We finally made it. You and me. I can't believe it."

He walked to a coattree and took his suit coat. "We haven't made it until the people start coming in." He donned his coat, buttoned the proper button, straightened his tie and clasp, took her arm and stepped out into the thick-carpeted hallway that led to the dining room.

They walked outside to look at the big neon sign that was about to light up. A crowd was waiting. Julio smiled at those who called his name, shook hands with many, and had a slap on the back for friends. His parking lot was already full. He stood watching the sign, and on the hour one of his employees threw the switch and it blazed up: *ANGIE'S*—Fine Mexican Food—Cocktails—Gift Shoppe—

The doors opened and the customers poured in. Julio and Angie were following them when his eye caught one man in the crowd. Canto didn't stand out too much now that he had half decent clothes and kept his hair cut. But he still somehow looked grubby, and Julio didn't want him hanging around the place.

"Go on in, honey, I'll be there in a minute," he said to Angie. She obeyed. He walked over to Canto.

"What are you doing here?" he demanded.

"Got a kid here needs a pop bad," Canto said. Infuriated, Julio looked around to see if anyone was within hearing distance.

"God damn. I told you never to come here, and now you bring a junkie . . ."

"This one's different. He says he's your nephew, and he wants some junk on credit. Says you'll stand good for it."

Disbelief showed on Julio's face as he followed Canto to his car. Sammy sat in the front seat looking as though he had an acute hangover. "Sammy! What's the matter, kid? What's this all about . . ."

"You gotta help me, Julio," Sammy said, shuddering. "I been a regular with Canto. But now he says he can't trust me, and I gotta have a fix quick."

Canto cut in. "But he ain't got no bread. He says . . ."

Julio waved Canto still. "You hooked bad, kid?"

Sammy nodded. "But I usually have bread. I got a deal going with a doctor, and I make a good killing now and then. It's just I'm tap city now."

Julio had been leaning inside the car. Now he straightened

and looked at Canto. "Take him out of here and give him a fix." He looked at Sammy. "Come back and see me when you're straight, kid. Try kicking it and when you gotta have it come and see me. We'll work something out." And Julio went inside.

Julio nervously paced the thick carpet in his office. He smoked heavily, glancing at the large brass pendulum clock as it softly struck the hour of nine. Listening closely he could just hear the soft Spanish music mingled with the soft talk of a half-hundred diners in the restaurant beyond the door.

The soft knock came at the rear door leading to the alley. Quickly he walked to the door and opened it, admitting Sammy.

"For Crissake, I thought you'd never come," Julio said a little irritably.

"I'm right on time," Sammy replied.

Julio went to the combination wall safe behind the picture on the wall and opened it, then after some elaborate manipulations opened a false rear end in the safe, revealing another small compartment. He removed a small plastic sack containing white powder and handed it to Sammy.

"Here you are, kid," he said. Sammy tucked the sack under his belt. He looked at his uncle warily.

"Something gone wrong?"

Julio drew heavily on his cigarette and paced a little, then settled in his chair behind his desk, indicating a seat across, which Sammy reluctantly took. Julio took Sammy's nervous hesitation about everything for granted.

"Not really," he said, letting out a cloud of smoke while

mashing the cigarette into a large brass ashtray. "But I got a funny feeling. You know what 'intuition' means?"

Sammy shrugged. "Ain't that something you pay to colleges?"

Julio smiled benevolently. "God damn, you're stupid," he said. "No. It means, like I got a hunch this deal's going to blow soon. The man's bound to wise up. Canto's been sneaking around like a ghost, he's so hot."

"The man knows he's pushing, but they're saving him. They want his supply man."

Julio looked sharply at his nephew. "You positive about that?"

Sammy shrugged again. "Where the man's concerned you can't be sure of nothing. They can bust him holding just anytime. It's not like grass. On pot, you try to never carry more than you can swallow in a hurry. Smack's a little different."

"Okay, okay," Julio said impatiently. "The reason I wanted to talk to you is this. I figure you owe me some favors." Sammy nodded in insipid assent. Julio continued. "I been supporting your monkey for quite a while. Just cause you're my wife's brother's kid, and I don't want to see your ass in the joint because you have to go out pushing like Canto and his flunkies. You understand that?"

Sammy nodded. He was only concerned about the continuation of his free supply of heroin.

"All right," Julio said pontifically, swinging around a little in his chair. "I'm going to let you in on the ground floor. Let you handle certain things I'm getting too busy for."

Sammy looked doubtful. "Honest, Julio, I like things the way they are. I don't mind . . ."

"Course you like things the way they are!" Julio exploded

mildly. "For two years now you had nothing in the world to do but come knock on my back door here every few days and I give you junk free. What junkie wouldn't like that? If you added up the going price for all the H that I gave you, you couldn't pay me back in ten years. So you just listen."

Sammy was silent, waiting.

Julio continued. "Like I say, I'm going to let you in on the ground floor. If you can handle it. You know how to cut pure junk?"

Sammy looked up. "Sure. Nothing to it."

"You know how to portion it, how much to put in a sack for two, three pops, maybe burn some dude once in a while to make a little extra?"

"Sure. Simple. Ain't much about smack I don't know."

"Good. Then I need you." Julio paused to let it sink in.

"How?"

"I want to cut Canto out of this deal. I don't know what he makes on it, but I know I'm taking the risk, he's getting the profit. On top of that, like you say, he's hot. We keep trading with him, we'll all get busted."

Sammy was thoughtful a moment. "You're right. He's overdue."

"Okay. Now. You know how we operate this thing?"

Sammy showed interest. "No."

Julio rose and began pacing as he talked. "Well, I never see nothing. I usually keep my car parked here in my parking spot. When I'm ready to leave for Tea Town I make a call. About ten minutes later somebody, Canto or one of his stooges, puts some money in my hubcap. I never see it. I drive to Tea Town. I pull into a certain gas station and tell a certain guy I want a tire worked on. Then I go for a walk and tend to some business.

When I come back I pick up my car and go buy the crap for our curio counter out front here. When I come back here I park my car in my spot. Somebody, I never see who, and I don't want to, takes the junk out of my hubcap. Then Canto, in person, comes in here to this office and hands me an envelope with three C's in it. That's all I know. That's all I ever wanted to know. Up 'til now."

Sammy let out a little whistle.

"What's the matter?" Julio asked nervously.

"Man, are you a patsy."

"Why? 'Cause I might get busted?"

"Naw, not that so much. You got a clean record. If the man found a stash in your hubcap, you'd probably get off. That's an old trick. Pushers go to Tea Town and make a buy, then look around till they find a tourist's car with a registration that shows they live around L.A. Then they plant the junk in the hubcap, or maybe a better place. Lots of squares have been caught with the stuff on their car, and they didn't know about it. You got a clean record, you could operate that way until they caught you once. But you're a patsy 'cause I know what Canto makes on it. If he's paying you three hundred just for that, he's making a grand or two each time you make the trip."

Julio looked disgruntled. "That's what I figured. But the reason I want to include him out is he's too hot. We got a good thing going here, and he's going to lead the man straight to this place. I can't afford that. But I've got to have someone who knows the ropes. Someone who can handle the stuff, cut it with powdered sugar just right, package it, and get rid of it safely. You're my nephew. I figured I could cut you in on it and trust you."

Sammy looked troubled. "But, like I said man, I like things the way they are. I . . ."

Julio became stern. "Look, kid. You want to keep popping steady? You got a King Kong and you know it. You either do it my way, or I cut you off. That stuff I give you. I know it's pure. I don't know how you cut it, but I'll bet you got enough left over to push a little. Right?"

Sammy just looked down.

"Right?" Julio asked louder, raising his voice.

". . . Right," Sammy stammered. "On what you give me, I keep myself going and make spending money on the side. Mom and Dad think I still got a job selling cars."

"Okay. You play this my way, you'll have all you can use, and I'll cut you in on the big end."

Sammy regarded his uncle inscrutably. "What all you want me to do, man?"

Julio began pacing again. "I've already set it up with the gas station attendant in Tijuana. You can borrow your old man's pickup weekends, can't you? I told the contact starting next week to expect you to pick up the stuff instead of me. I already told him what you look like and what you'll be driving. I told him you'd be making the run regularly within a month or so. Meantime, we're setting up a retail operation here."

Sammy looked puzzled. *"Here?"*

Julio smiled and walked to a large cardboard box. He opened the flap and removed a small Mexican ceramic figurine.

"See this?" he said. "There's a little hole in the back. I want you to start cutting the stuff. A single pop. In a little plastic bag. I have them here in my desk." He went to his desk and took some small plastic bags out of a drawer. "Now." He walked to the wall safe and took out another sack of white powder just like the one he'd given Sammy earlier. "I made Canto agree to give me some H each time. For you, kid. That's how I happen to have it on hand here. I never touched the junk, myself." He looked at Sammy, whose nose was running. "You're shaking, kid. Need a fix?"

"Yeah," Sammy admitted. "I gotta get somewhere pretty soon."

"Here," Julio said, walking to a paneled door. "Use my private bathroom." Sammy hesitated, looking at the door to the restaurant. "Don't worry, no one can come in here without knocking. I keep it locked from the inside. Go ahead."

Sammy reached into the pocket of his jacket and took out a little case the size of a pack of cigarettes.

"I don't usually carry an outfit with me, but I needed a pop quick tonight."

He went into the bathroom. Julio followed, watching in fascination, as Sammy took out a little spoon with the handle cut off. He prepared the heroin in a precise amount. Then, taking a small disposable syringe, he opened his mouth, held back his tongue with one hand and injected the narcotic with the other. Julio looked incredulous.

"Why in the mouth?"

Sammy barely winced as he made the injection, then replaced his paraphernalia. He smiled. "Pops in the arm leave tracks. See?" He pulled up his sleeve and tiny specks of scar tissue, barely visible, could be seen. "Popping under the tongue don't leave tracks. Makes your mouth sore, if you go too heavy, but no fresh tracks show."

Julio was momentarily horrified, but quickly became his suave self again. "Okay, kid. Let's see you cut some of this stuff, put the right amount into a bag and put it in one of the little Aztec god statues or whatever the hell they are. What do you need? Scales or anything?"

Sammy smiled. He now seemed confident and proud that he had useful knowledge. "All I need is some powdered sugar. Got some here?"

"Just a minute," Julio said, walking to his desk. He held a button down a moment and the unmistakable sounds of kitchen activity could be heard on the intercom.

"Chepita?" he barked into the apparatus.

In a moment a woman's voice answered him, "Mande, jefe." Order, boss.

"Por favor trae a mi officina una cajita de azucar en polvo." Please bring to my office a little box of powdered sugar.

"Ahorita," came the reply. Right now.

In a moment Julio answered a soft knock at the door and took the powdered sugar from the woman. He handed it to Sammy in the bathroom, who had poured out the powdered narcotic on a paper towel. Sammy measured by eye, mixing a pile of dope and powdered sugar, then looked at his uncle. His eyes had life, an alert smile was now on his lips, and his apathetic attitude had disappeared.

"Okay, man. One dose to a bag. You want it a soft dose or a tough one?"

Julio considered. "Might as well make it a weak dose. No use playing Santa Claus to hopheads."

Sammy expertly poured a precise amount of the mixture into a little bag, then quickly crossed the room to Julio's desk and helped himself to some rubber bands. He then secured the bag with the rubber band and held the packaged product up.

"There you are. Let's see if it fits into the little statue."

He easily pushed the bag through the hole in the back.

"By the way, how much you gonna ask for this?" he said, holding the figurine.

"I pay two-bits for the statues. I tell people they were made by a fierce tribe of former head hunters in Oaxaca. I get five bucks for it. I think packaged like this, we can ask $20."

Sammy was quick to think. "But you can't sell these to everybody who comes along. You gotta keep 'em separate . . ."

"I got all that figured out. Come on. I'll take you up front."

As Sammy followed Julio out of the office and down the hall into the dining room his step was quick, sure, his talk alive and animated.

"You got a neat setup here, Julio. How about Angie? Is she in on it?"

"No. She don't know nothing. And I want to keep her that way. I'm telling her I'm letting you help out with the importing and selling of the curios. Don't tell her nothing. She knows I know what I'm doing, far as business goes, and she don't ask too many questions. Except about the money we take in."

They walked to the front, near the entrance. Two dozen or more couples sat eating at the tables and booths. A cashier stood behind the register on top of a glass showcase with china bulls, little piñatas, small stone mortar and pestles, Mexican matches and finely spun silver pins and earrings. Behind and against the wall was another showcase, up higher, with sliding glass panels and a lock. Julio produced some keys.

"This, up here, is where we'll keep the loaded Aztec gods," Julio said as he waved the cashier away. "Only you and me will have a key to this showcase. At twenty bucks apiece, we got an excuse to keep this stuff locked up. They're the most expensive items for sale. Your old Uncle Julio has thought of everything, huh?"

"Yeah, man," Sammy said smiling.

"Now," Julio went on, lighting a cigar, more to play the part of the successful restaurant owner than anything else, "we'll keep a few Aztec gods—empty ones—in this display case under the cash register. Just in case some gringo wants to fork out a fin for it. The loaded ones will be behind in this locked glass case at all times. You bring the buyers here. We're in the retail business now. And I want high class customers. Understand?"

Sammy nodded. "I got 'em. I been doing a little business with some high-class Anglo swingers. That's why I been dressing nice like this. I go into their neighborhood looking like class. It's safe over there, and these kids pay twice what I can get for smack around the East Side here."

"Good. That's the kind of clients I want you to develop. I don't have to tell you to be careful who you send down. You go get in good with these Anglo hopheads. Make more contacts. But you send 'em here to make the buy. I figure I'm doing you a favor, cause you don't have to carry the stuff all over town and risk getting busted for holding."

Sammy was excited, but a little hesitant. "You sure it's safe here, Julio?"

"It'll be as safe as you make it. You make sure you know who you're sending down here. Tell 'em if they show up with somebody you don't know, there's no deal. But they can buy all the loaded Aztec gods they want, if they got the bread and you *know* them personally."

Sammy smiled. "Don't tell me my business, Julio. I try never to take on a new customer 'til I've watched him take the junk from somebody else and pop. Then I figure he's safe."

"Good. I'll show you how to work the safe in my office. Whenever you cut a batch and sack it, I want the joint cleaned up so there's not a trace of H around. If something goes wrong with the operation, I got a clean record. I can always say I didn't know nothing about it. I was a patsy. I even got a fall guy picked out," he smiled. "But nothing's going to go wrong, as long as you send in the right guys. You can quit pushing on the side to the bums around East L.A. I figure I'll cut you in for five on every Aztec god you sell at $20. How many you think you can move?"

Sammy looked thoughtful. "With a good supply, like you got, if I work to develop the right trade—not the kind of bums the man's following to bed every night—I could send in . . . five, maybe ten buyers a day."

Julio's pleasure was evident as he calculated mentally.

He saw Angie approaching dressed in a Spanish costume that could have come from the wardrobe room of a second-rate movie company. She smiled fondly at Sammy.

"Sobrino!" Nephew! she greeted him. "You're looking good. Nice clothes too. You must be doing well selling cars."

"It's . . . a living, anyway," Sammy said modestly.

"Yeah, but he's not going to sell cars anymore. Like I told you, Angie sweet, I'm putting him in charge of the curio department. You never can tell, it might go great guns and be a good source of income for the place. He'll be hanging around here. I want him particularly to handle the little Aztec god things behind the locked glass. They're . . ."

"They're not Aztec gods," Angie smiled. "They're just plain machine-molded, Baja California . . ."

"As far as the customers are concerned, they're little Aztec gods made by a fierce tribe of head hunters from the jungles around Oaxaca. Unless you can come up with a better gimmick."

Angie smiled apologetically for intruding into her husband's business and left to mingle with the diners, stopping at a table of Anglos to explain the significance of the painting of the two mountains of Mexico City, the warrior and the sleeping woman, laughing when they couldn't get the pronunciation of the Spanish names of the volcanoes, asking if the service was satisfactory, then drifting to a table of well-dressed middle-class Mexicans to see if everything was well.

Julio led Sammy back to his office, locking the door.

Julio looked at Sammy. "Everything okay with you?"

"Aces, man. When we start operating?"

"I'll show you how to open the safe now. The back compartment, too. I'll give you a key to the glass case and to this door to the alley. You cut and package as much stuff as we got on hand now. Starting tomorrow you come here and handle the Aztec gods. Let your contacts know of the change in operations, that they have to come here and do it this way now. And you be here every day to handle the gods. We'll be in business."

"Gotcha," Sammy said with enthusiasm. He looked solemn a moment. "Mom and Dad will be glad when they see I'm holding down a job at your place. Dad will be glad when he sees I'm making good money." He was pensive. "I think," he added.

"Lock the door behind me," Julio ordered as he left to mingle with the guests and look over the feminine prospects.

S unday morning Sammy awoke feeling good. He needed a little pop, but he'd make it a small one, as he was trying to cut back. Julio wanted him at the curio counter by noon, so he'd better get moving soon. He heard Mariana in her room next to his. He heard her go quietly to the living room and dial a telephone number. She listened a long time and then hung up and returned to her room. He got up, shaved in the bathroom and while he was there with the door locked he took a shot of heroin. He dressed in a fine tan jacket and narrow trousers, shiny shoes, combed his hair and went into the kitchen where his mother and father were reading the paper and finishing breakfast. He began warming some of the chili on the stove and fried two eggs. He could easily go without eating when he popped, but he couldn't afford to lose the weight. It wasn't hard to eat when he wasn't hungry.

He was about to say something to his father when Pete said, "What's the matter with Mariana? She's so quiet lately."

Minnie answered, "I think she broke up with that gringo college student. Remember last week or so when she called us together to tell us something and then changed her mind? All she said was she didn't think she'd be going with him much longer. I think she wanted to tell us she's now going with a chicano boy, but she was too bashful."

Pete shrugged, looking over the sports section. "Too bad. He was a nice kid. Rich, too."

Minnie looked at Sammy, who was starting to eat. "You have to work today?"

"Yeah. Sunday's a good day for curios."

He had one stop to make before going to the restaurant. The old whore's place. He'd met her when she needed an abortion. Sammy had fixed her up and then got acquainted with her. She was old, maybe forty, but she still looked good, and Sammy kept her in junk. She just popped now and then, nothing heavy, but he spent many hours talking to her, and she was one of the few people who he thought liked him. Sometimes when he was there a visitor would come, and Sammy would go in the little kitchen of her apartment for twenty minutes or so. She was very interested in him, and also in Uncle Julio, for some reason. Now he wanted to give her some junk and tell her about working in the curio gift shop at Julio's.

When she let him in she was wearing only a slip as usual. She asked him if he needed to go to bed with her, but he didn't; he'd been shooting a little too heavy lately. That junk cut your sex down to nothing.

He told her all about the new operation, the Aztec gods and how he was indispensable to Julio now.

"Real interesting," she said with a funny little smile, "so now Julio has the stuff right there, on the premises?"

"Yeah, but we're going to be careful."

"You haven't ever mentioned my name to him, have you?"

"No. Of course not, Rosa. You said not to. Ever."

She fixed a mild shot for each of them and gave him a motherly kiss as he left to go to the curio counter.

As he stood behind the counter he had a vague uneasiness. He had seriously doubted the wisdom of this curio counter front. No place to go to stash the junk if you see the man coming. But maybe Julio was right; it was just as safe to push it from a respectable place as in back alleys, bars or hype pads.

A few customers were in the dining room, more in the bar, but the main body would be coming in toward the middle of the afternoon.

A waiter came from the kitchen area. "Sammy. Telephone. Pick it up there."

He picked up the phone and heard the voice of Nano, a hop-head flunkie who hung out in a cheap bar nearby.

"Sammy?"

"Yeah."

"Can you talk?"

"Shoot, man."

"Listen, there's a gringo dude here looking for a doctor. You still got your contact?"

"Yeah."

"Okay, he's waiting. Here in the Tortuga. Can you come over?"

"Yeah, right away."

"I get my cut?"

"If it comes off I'll give you ten." He hung up.

He walked back to Julio's office and knocked and heard Julio say come in. "I gotta leave a while, Julio. Be back soon."

"Okay. Be back in time for the heavy trade. I'll watch the counter."

Sammy's friend Nano was waiting in front of the Tortuga. He pointed in the window. "That's him. Sitting at the bar there." Sammy looked.

"I know him."

"You know him? Is it a set-up?"

"Naw. He's just a rich student out at the university. He goes with my sister. He used to, anyway. Must be trying to fix up some knocked-up college babe."

Sammy entered and spoke briefly to the student, then came out again. Nano was waiting. "Give me my cut, man."

"When I get mine. I got to line up the panel truck, get hold of the doctor, and like I say, if it comes off, you'll get yours."

Sammy went to a pay phone and made several calls. Then

he walked back to Angie's. Just as he turned in from the sidewalk he saw Big Ed the narc coming out. Then he saw that Ed was leading Julio, who was in handcuffs. Another plainclothesman followed. Sammy stopped. Big Ed grinned as he recognized him.

"Well, well. Sammy. If I'd known you were coming I'd have waited another ten minutes. Had a real party. You're overdue, you know, Sam."

Sammy put his hands above his head and leaned against the wall, spread-eagled. "I'm clean, man." Big Ed searched him thoroughly.

"Yep, you are this time, Sam. Like I said, I guess I was a little early." He shoved Julio roughly ahead of him. All of the employees were coming out to watch Julio being taken away. The headwaiter came to Sammy. "Better call Angie, kid. It's going to be a shock to her. She's still at home."

PART TWO

On one of the two giant university campuses which punctuate the sprawling city of Los Angeles a class in sociology was being conducted by Professor William Rowland.

"You will be graded," Professor Rowland was saying, "on your performance in this project. That means the amount of imagination you show, the effort, the time and the quality of your work. But grades aren't necessarily what we're after here. In this experiment we're attempting to accomplish two things, actually: Find a way to motivate the minority member high school dropout to continue his education at least up to the college level, and two, find out for ourselves just why we have a 60 or 70 percent high school dropout rate in certain areas. There's been a great deal of work done on this problem already by social workers, probation departments and various research groups, and while seemingly they've come up with a lot of answers, nobody seems to be able to do anything about it. Maybe we can.

"This isn't the first time this has been tried. College students have been used before to try to reach the hard-core dropouts. But I'm giving you carte blanche; throwing you on your own devices, so to speak. I'm assigning some of you hard cases: dropouts who never cared and couldn't wait for the day they could quit school completely. Some of you will have border-line cases: kids who just lost interest and didn't care or see any advantage in education.

"Maybe some of you will find you can strike dialogue by having a beer—or worse—with your assignment. Maybe by demonstrating to your dropout what's to be gained by going to school. I don't know. You all use your imaginations and maybe someone will come up with something exciting.

"The dropout problem of course is encountered in every area of economic deprivation, but inasmuch as the statistical curve gives a big hop among certain ethnic groups, we're start-ing in the Mexican-American section here in our own back yard, in East Los Angeles. If any of you reports back here that you've discovered the dropout problem is caused by the cul-tural barriers I'll personally brain you. We know all that. We want to know *what* in the cultural barrier is so insurmountable to the individual and *why*. It's complex. Okay, who's first? Stiver. David Stiver. I told you you should have played basket-ball. With your height my eyes always alight on you first." He handed the student a sheet of paper. "Here's your assignment. His name's Samuel Sandoval. About all we know about him is his name and address and that he quit school. Get going. Good-bye and good luck."

In spite of Professor Rowland's instructions to get going Stiver hung around and compared his assignment with those of the other students. He waited by the door for Martha Coulter, but saw her deliberately leave by the other exit. Hell with her.

David Stiver went to his bachelor's apartment, opened a bottle of beer and fixed a sandwich. He sat alone, enjoying the silence while he ate and drank. Idly, he took out the slip of paper Dr. Rowland had given him with Sandoval's name, address, and telephone number on it. He wondered about the correct pronunciation of the name, wishing he'd taken a little Spanish instead of lots of French and Latin. Suddenly he reached for the phone and dialed a girls' dormitory on campus. When Martha Coulter came to the phone she said, "David, we really don't have anything to talk about," and hung up.

"Goddam her," he muttered, then he dialed the Sandoval number. A mature woman's voice answered.

" 'allo?" That would be Sammy's mother.

"Hello. Are you Mrs. Sandoval?"

"Yes, that's me."

"Uh . . . My name's David Stiver, and . . ."

"What?"

"I said my name's David Stiver."

"Okay," politely. "What do you want?"

"I'm a student"—he gave the name of the university—"and if possible I'd like to come over and talk to Sammy tonight."

"You want to talk to Sammy?"

"Yes. If it doesn't interfere with any plans for this evening."

"What?"

"I said, if it's all right, I'd like to come over tonight and talk to Sammy."

"He's not here right now, but he's coming back soon. What did you want to talk to him for, so I can tell him?"

RICHARD VASQUEZ

"Well...uh, it's about school. He did quit school, didn't he?"

"Yes, but that's not against the law. He's old enough . . ."

"I know it's not against the law, Mrs. Sandoval. But, well I'm a college student and we have a project to . . ."

"You go to college?"

"Yes, and part of our . . . well, would it be all right if I came over to see Sammy? Just for a few minutes."

"Sure. I guess so. He'll be here soon. What time will you come here?"

"I'll be there in an hour or so. Is that all right?"

"I guess so."

"Thank you very much. I'll see you in a little while then."

"Okay. Good-bye."

He sat back, wondering just what Sammy and his family would be like. He'd had relatively little contact with Spanish-speaking people, although he'd done a term paper on the plight of 750,000 Mexican-Americans in Texas.

Stiver remembered a near-disastrous evening a few months back when he'd gone to a little beer tavern and struck up an acquaintance with a Mexican-American. The man had been very articulate and perceptive. When Stiver had drunk several beers he asked if the man knew any little Spanish girls around the area. The man had shaken his head and shrugged, "Nope. No Spanish girls. Don't know any." Oh, surely you know a few. "Nope. Most Spanish people are over in Spain." Oh, you know what I mean . . . and the man had trapped Stiver into saying all sorts of things he didn't intend to. But the episode had taught Stiver some things. Mainly, that he had some distinct preconceptions about Mexican people. Among them was the assumption that the attentions of someone with his obvious assets of

290

social and cultural background would be more than welcome by a Mexican girl.

He had taken a survey of his feelings and found that he had some prejudices he had never been aware of, and had gone to work to erase them.

As Stiver drove toward East Los Angeles he wondered more than idly what the Sandoval family would be like. Although he'd been attending the university for more than three years, he'd never been in this part of town, other than when he'd passed through on the landscaped sunken freeway.

He pictured himself giving fatherly advice to Sammy, helping him, determining his weak spots scholastically.

"You don't understand the Newtonian gravitational theory? It's quite simple. You see, Sammy, every object in God's universe, whether it's a grain of sand on the beach at Acapulco or a distant sun in the Milky Way, has a relationship with any other object. They're all attracted to one another with a force proportionate to the product of the body—I'll explain product later—and the inversed square of the distance between the two centers. Thanks, Mrs. Sandoval, I will have another cup of coffee." And as he would work with the boy into the night, he would be rewarded by a look of comprehension. Yes, that would be his reward, seeing understanding dawn on this boy's face, as he began to understand things for the first time.

Perhaps he would take Sammy to one of the nicer restaurants where students hang out near the campus. Maybe introduce him to some of the varsity football players. Let him meet some of the higher type co-eds. That would impress him, open his eyes to a world other than this sordid environment Stiver was driving through now.

He continued, half consciously, with his fantasy of the Sandovals. Papa Sandoval would be dark, bushy mustache and thick hair, feeling humbly proud in his work clothes as he greeted Stiver.

"Enter, señor, and make my house yours," he'd probably say with a sweeping gesture of the arm. "You do not know how grateful we are that you take your valuable time to try to help our son. He is a good boy. He would make a fine doctor or perhaps an engineer, if he could but be convinced he needs education."

Mama Sandoval would be fat, bosomy, with the natural charming smile of friendliness that so characterized these people—at least the older generation only recently removed from the villages of Mexico.

And, oh yes, Sammy had a twin sister, according to his information, a shy girl, awed that a tall gringo, handsome and worldly, would come into their home and admire her. "You're very pretty," he'd say to her, and she'd blush and tell her girl friends the next time she saw them.

Mama Sandoval: "We have little, but let me bring you hot chocolate and tortillas."

"Well, Sammy, tell me just what the trouble is with school. Many times I was discouraged myself when I went to high school. I'm here to help you take advantage of an opportunity your mother and father never had. Isn't that right, Mr. Sandoval?"

"Heed him, Sammy. Had I but had the chance you have, today I would not be a . . ." Wonder what he does do, thought Stiver.

He found the address near the heart of East Los Angeles on

Second Street. It was an old two-story duplex, separated from the street by a small lawn. Better than he'd expected, he thought as he walked up and rang the ancient doorbell. Pete opened the door.

"Yeah?" he said.

"Hello. I'm Dave Stiver. From the university. You're Mr. Sandoval?"

"Oh, *you're* the guy. Yeah, come on in," Pete said, leading him to a chair. "Sammy!" Pete shouted toward the rear of the house, "that guy's here."

Stiver sat down, looking about the room. Most of the furniture was old. Two brilliantly colored table lamps, with giant, gaudy shades, lighted the room. An expensive TV set with the largest screen on the market stood out.

Pete sat down across the room. He wore loose slacks, a nylon shirt and a casual sweater. His bald head glistened.

"You want Sammy to go back to school?" Pete asked.

"Yes," Stiver said sincerely. "We're trying to encourage dropouts to continue through high school . . ."

"What for?" Pete asked sincerely.

"Well, because a high school diploma helps immeasurably . . . very much, to get a job and . . ."

"How much money can he get with a high school diploma?"

"Well, statistics . . . records show the average income of a high school diploma holder is about $425 to nearly $500 a month, as compared to . . ."

"That's nothing, $500," Pete said. "I'm offering him $650 to start with me, but he won't take it."

Stiver was surprised. "That's quite a bit for a youngster. But a good salary isn't the main thing to work for. It's a great advantage to have a high school education."

"I never finished high school," Pete said, still being sincere.

"That's too ... well, we've found those who do usually have higher paying jobs than ..."

"I make a thousand dollars a month. Sometimes more," Pete said simply.

Stiver was at a loss for a moment. "You're very fortunate. What do you do?"

"I'm the foreman for a cement crew. Sammy's going to work with me, I hope."

"It's nice you have a trade, Mr. Sandoval. Sammy's lucky to have a father in your position. Otherwise he might have to take a job as a common laborer."

"That's what I'm starting him out as. He has to belong to the Common Laborer's Union. Union scale is more than $150 a week."

Sammy came in and Stiver stood up. "Hello, Sammy. How are you?"

"Fine," Sammy said, taking a seat. He sat there expectantly, as though to say, "Let's get this over with."

Stiver took in Sammy's pretty but weak face, the small, light build, a sort of emaciated look about the eyes, his nervousness, which he seemed to be trying to hide.

"Your father tells me you're going to take a job with him," Stiver said. Sammy shrugged. "Do you have any desire to continue on in school?" Stiver asked.

Sammy shrugged again and mumbled, "No."

"Was school difficult for you?"

Sammy thought a moment. "Yeah, I just wasn't interested, I guess."

Minnie Sandoval came in then with a tray of coffee and cream puffs and éclairs. She offered the tray to Stiver. No one made any attempt to introduce her. "You're Mrs. Sandoval," Stiver said.

"Pleased to meet you. I talked to you on the phone," Minnie said pleasantly. She set the tray down and then sat silently.

Sammy stood up, looking at his watch. "I'm going to have to go now," he said. "I got to meet some guys. It's important."

Stiver stammered. This had been a total loss so far. "I was hoping we could have a little talk," he said.

"What about?" Sammy asked sincerely.

"About maybe returning to school. I'm sure if you could just be aware of the advantages . . ." but he could see Sammy was completely disinterested, and at that moment Mariana came into the room.

She stood there looking at Stiver, her simple cotton dress clinging to her curves, dark hair nuzzling her creamy neck.

Although Sammy looked younger than his age, Mariana, because of her unchildlike figure, could pass for twenty or so. Also her poised attitude contradicted teen-age immaturity. She smiled a little as Stiver looked at her. It was Minnie who broke the silence.

"This is our daughter, Mariana. She's Sammy's twin. But they're not much alike."

Stiver rose. "How are you?" he asked courteously.

"I'm fine, thanks," she said, and he noticed her English had just a hint of accent.

"Well, I've got to go," Sammy said.

"Can I come again when you've got a little time to talk this over?" Stiver asked. Sammy shrugged and walked out. He had not been impolite.

Stiver looked at Mariana, and an idea came to him. "You're still in school?" he asked of Mariana.

She nodded. "I graduated last year. I was a year ahead of Sammy. I'm going to stenography school now."

"This is very interesting," Stiver said mysteriously.

During the pause, Pete took the bait. "What's interesting?"

"That you have twins. Apparently of equal ability," he was looking at her, "of identical background, yet one drops out of school, the other goes on after graduation. I'll tell you what, Mr. Sandoval. Let me explain this project to you. With your permission, I'd like to study Sammy and Mariana, learn a little more about them. It might help a great deal in our research on school dropouts. You see, our sociology department is quite concerned . . ."

With his glibness David Stiver had little trouble convincing Pete and Minnie he was studying the twins as a class project to determine why students of identical background react differently. He talked himself, as well as the parents, into believing his reasons for the study—and his methods—had validity.

By his third visit to the Sandoval home he still had only briefly consulted with Sammy, but had become completely taken by Mariana's shy charm and beauty. He suggested rather casually that she accompany him to a campus function. "She'll be in good hands, I promise," he said to Pete with what he hoped was an indifferent smile. Pete and Minnie had no objections. They had overcome much of the natural distrust they had of the class of people Stiver represented.

Mariana smiled a little shyly. David was aware she knew exactly how she looked, that many people must tell her often how beautiful she was.

"What should I wear?" she asked.

Stiver shrugged. "Nothing fancy. It's just an informal get together." There was a social thing near campus, but he had no intention of taking her there.

She made an attempt to mimic a typical American girl type. "I'll just throw on any old rag," she said with humor.

David realized a rapport had been established, and he saw the lampoon went completely over her parents' heads.

Mariana sat with her legs tucked under, knees pointed toward Stiver, as they drove. She watched him and the road ahead, noticing his nervousness while fighting the heavy traffic in East Los Angeles. She knew the Anglos unfamiliar with this section were always ill at ease here. Stiver seemed to relax as he took the freeway on-ramp and let the powerful auto surge ahead.

She liked him, she decided, but she was honest, and would not allow herself to think of him as a ticket to the other world so soon.

"Do you date much?" he asked.

"If you call going to a dance or a movie dating, I guess I do." He drove silently a while. "No steady boyfriends, huh?"

"They're all steady," she replied a little disgustedly. It was the first time in their conversation she had allowed her voice to communicate her feelings. Then she smiled at his look of surprise.

She looked at him earnestly for a full minute, deciding something. "Tell me the truth," she said. "Are you really interested in finding out about us? The Mexicans in East L.A.?"

"Why, of course," he said with too much sincerity. "And . . . I'd also like to get to know you better. You're a very attractive woman."

"Take me where they'll serve us drinks," she said suddenly. He slowed and took an off-ramp, turned onto a boulevard and soon pulled into the parking lot of a cocktail lounge.

Dave knew many places where they served college students on the legal age borderline. They were usually nice, quiet places where there was never trouble, and it was usually dark inside.

When they were seated at a booth, drinks in front of them, she looked at him evenly. "Well, ask away. What do you want to know about us?"

"I sense that you're very upset for some reason. You want to blow off steam."

"Not upset, no more than usual. It's just that . . . do you know you're the first Anglo that's ever taken me outside East L.A.?"

"You've gone with . . . Anglos . . . before?" He was surprised.

"They come to our parties and dances. They use our slang and mingle, but they have just one thing on their minds. Why is that, I wonder—why the white guys always think darker people's women are easier to get into bed with. Can you tell me?"

She could tell he was surprised by her conversation, and perhaps a little embarrassed. She knew her conservative, demure exterior was deceptive, and everyone to whom she spoke naturally was surprised not to find a naïve prudish maiden inside.

"Well . . . no . . . I guess it's true, what you say. Maybe it's because throughout history, primarily by coincidence, lighter-skinned people have generally been in a position to take advantage of others." He was ad libbing to the best of his ability.

"No," she said thoughtfully, "I don't think that has much to do with it." He blinked at the contradiction. She went on: "Look, why does a guy like you come over to East L.A. and think he can make out with a girl he hardly knows?"

Stiver thought a moment. He almost said something he didn't want to.

"Put it this way, then. Why don't you go to some white girl you hardly know and proposition her? Aren't there plenty of girls at college?"

"Well, yes, but . . . Look here, Mariana. I haven't made any advances, have I? And why do you insist on saying 'you white guys'? Don't you consider yourself white, too . . . ? "

She looked at him coolly. "The way you say that, you think it's a privilege to call yourself white."

"No, I don't mean that at all, it's just . . . well, you see, there are really only three races. White or Caucasian, Negro, and Oriental. Now, where do you fit in? Are you colored? No. Are you Mongolian? No. So why don't you call yourself white?"

"Because I'm not. But you never answered my question. Why will a . . . an Anglo, then, like you, try to make a Mexican girl he hardly knows, but not another Anglo girl? Aren't you attracted to other girls like yourself, sexually?"

David was a little irritated, but then he forced himself to think about the question. He started to answer without thinking, to see what kind of explanation would come out.

"I would never go up to a girl I hardly knew and proposition her. Because, I'm not that kind of . . . I mean, a decent guy doesn't . . ."

"A decent guy doesn't try," she cut in.

"No! I mean, you don't walk up to a decent girl and . . ."

"Aha! And you reached the answer all by yourself, didn't you? I don't know what kind of grades you're getting in sociology, David, but I give you an 'A' tonight."

Stiver's first reaction at being graded by Mariana was anger. Then he forced himself to examine what she said.

"I know what you say is true, so far as some guys are concerned," he said thoughtfully. "It's kind of like, like some Jewish guys at school. Four or five of them hang around in a little clique, sort of. They're hell-raisers, like anybody else, but one thing about them really teed me off. When they go out chasing girls, they wouldn't think of trying to make out with a Jewish girl. When I asked them about it, they said, 'Nice Jewish girls are for marriage.' I felt like saying, 'What the hell do you think nice gentile girls are for?' But I knew what their answer would be."

"Kind of hurts when the shoe's on the other foot, doesn't it?" She laughed softly. They sat saying nothing, listening to the music coming from the dining room.

He was watching her in the dim light, very aware of her rare, unspoiled beauty. Her bold talk, her direct manner when she spoke of things important, had somewhat surprised him at first, but he was beginning to see she was a direct person, direct without being forward.

She suddenly looked at him. "Sometime I'd like to take you out to see my grandparents."

He was a little surprised. "Why?"

"Oh, just because. If you knew something about them, I think you'd know a lot more about my family. But I don't know whether that would be good or bad."

"They live around close?"

"Out in a little place called Irwindale."

"Irwindale?"

"Few people have ever heard of it. All there is there is some Mexican people and great big holes in the ground where they get gravel. But you'd like Grandfather. He doesn't speak English, but he's just the gentlest and kindest man I've ever known."

"Is he from Mexico?"

"I think he came here when he was a little boy. He won't talk about all that much, for some reason. But he's always terribly interested in what his grandchildren do. He can tell you every single grandchild's birthday."

"Why is that remarkable?"

"Because there's about forty-five of us."

"Forty-five? That's incredible!"

"No. My father has seven brothers and sisters. Each has about six kids, except our family. Figure it out."

Driving back Stiver asked her if she could name all her cousins. She promptly started with Pete's older brother's brood and continued saying names without a pause until she'd named all. "Then, there's my mother's family," she said.

"Some day it would be interesting to trace back your family tree. Ever thought of it?"

"No, but I'll bet you've thought of tracing yours back."

He felt the sting. "Do you know anything about where your family came from?"

"On Dad's side, they come from a little village in Mexico called Trainwreck, for some reason. Mom doesn't know anything except that her folks and their parents were born in Los Angeles."

"Then, you wouldn't say you were from . . . an Early California Spanish family?"

She looked at him evenly. "I'm a Mexican, David. It's not a dirty word. Let me hear you say it." He hesitated. "Go on. Say, 'You're a Mexican.' I want to hear you say it."

He took her hand and looked into her eyes. "You're a very beautiful Mexican girl."

She smiled and relaxed. "Thank you," she said. "I know it's hard for you to say that word, but please don't shy away from it. That hurts most of all."

When he pulled up in front of her home she started to open the car door, but he pushed her hand away and quickly went around to open it for her. "That's nice," she said almost inaudibly. He walked her to the house and she started to open the front door, paused, and said, "I like you very much, David," and she was gone.

Pete and Minnie actually weren't much concerned when it became evident David Stiver's interest in Mariana was more than academic. They accepted it as parents do when a daughter begins dating an unusual type of man. Stiver for a while maintained the thin pretext that he was interested in studying Mariana and Sammy as a case history, but Sammy was rarely home when he called.

The freedom Pete and Minnie allowed Mariana was definitely a cultural concession, but they knew a girl of eighteen had to be more or less recognized as an adult, although Minnie could well remember that when she was age eighteen a man had to ask her father's permission to take her out, and then a younger brother or sister had to be with them at all times. But they knew that times change.

Mariana told Stiver what it had been like to live in the middle-class suburb, the family's subsequent return to East Los Angeles, the lack of job opportunity for those branded with names like Sandoval, García, Montez, or Rodríguez.

"Actually," he told her one night as he was taking her for a drive, "I've never encountered the discrimination toward your people. But I know it exists. This hatred."

"It's not just hatred," she tried to explain. "It's . . . an image. An image you know the Anglos have every time they look at you."

"Really, Mariana, do you find people have an image preconceived every time they look at you? Lots of people don't."

"Maybe not me, so much. I'm accepted because I'm considered beautiful. That makes up for a lot, in your society. But take someone like my father. You don't know how it hurts him when an Anglo calls him 'Pancho.'"

"I don't see anything so vicious in calling someone Pancho."

"No, I guess you wouldn't. But it just shows how they've already decided you're like Gordo in the comics. You're lazy, your eyes bug out whenever a young girl walks by . . . it's like seeing a Negro and saying, 'Hey, Rastus!' Or calling a very Jewish-looking person 'Abie.' Does that make it clearer?"

"It does, but . . . not everybody who says something like that intends an insult . . ."

"That doesn't matter. It doesn't matter. What counts is it hurts."

"I guess you're right. But these problems, Mariana, they only come up where there's a large minority. In other places, where people hardly know what a Mexican-American is, there's none of this—pre-judging. That's what it is. It's . . ."

"I don't understand what you mean."

"I mean, take places like . . . like Montana, or where I come from in Illinois, there's nothing like what you've gone through."

"You mean, where there aren't a lot of people of a minority, there's no discrimination?"

"Usually that's the case. Where there's a small minority, the community attitude is different."

"Why?"

"For lots of reasons. We studied this in sociology. Throughout some states there's just a smattering of Orientals and Latins. They seem to be much more accepted in those places."

She was thoughtful a while. "Just where do you live, David?"

"In a little . . . well, it's not little . . . town outside Chicago. It's small compared to Chicago."

"And you have no minority groups there?"

"We have a lot of Negroes around there."

"But no Mexicans?"

"None to speak of."

"What about your Negroes there? How are they treated?"

Stiver sighed a little. "About the same as they're treated in other parts of the country. Not very good."

"How would I be treated where you live?"

"Believe me, you'd be a sensation."

"Why?"

"Because. You're something to look at."

"There're lots of beautiful girls everywhere."

"Yeah, but there's none like you where I come from."

"How am I different?"

"Well, you're ... your eyes, almost coal black. Your skin color, so even and ... yellow-tan ... you look ... exotic. That's it, exotic."

She thought a moment. "Exotic means alien, doesn't it? It means different from yourself. Like you were from some place far off."

He was watching her. "I suppose. I always thought it meant that you looked like you came from some island near the Orient or in the South Pacific."

"Yes. That's what I said."

They rode in silence for a while.

"David?"

"Yes?"

"Answer me something truthfully."

"Sure. What?"

"You'd never take me to your home town, would you." It was a statement. "I mean, even if you were in love with me."

He groped for words. No, he told himself, it had nothing to do with what she was, or what her parents were like. It was, how could he tell her? He couldn't. It was because she had no sophistication. She would never be able to recognize a symphony from an overture, or discuss Maria Montessori and progressive education, or baroque and renaissance art. He thought about Martha Coulter. She was his kind of woman, he thought. Smart-looking, socially aware, snobbishly down-to-earth. He could picture her doing things Mariana could never hope to do, such as decorating a home in French Colonial or contemporary Mexican ... Mexican ...

He realized something with a start. That Mariana was no more Mexican than Martha was European. Actually, he saw, she had no culture. Her home, her parents, were barren of culture in the national sense. The family pattern of tradition, the language, everything about her was composite.

If there was a culture here, it was the culture of being a subculture. Hers was not the culture of poverty as he had studied poverty. No Aztec art adorned her house, no Moorish European influence.

He realized she was still waiting for an answer to her question. What was it? Oh, yes.

"Would you take *me* to meet *your* people? I mean, like your grandparents you told me about?"

She smiled as though accepting a small challenge.

"Sure. Get off at that ramp there."

As they alighted in the gravel driveway at the old Sandoval home, David was impressed by the yard. She explained: "The walks and the curbs by the drive, my father put them in. And the cement porch, too. The benches and table were made by my uncle Poca Luz. He . . ."

"Your Uncle who?"

"Poca Luz. That means little light."

"Why do you call him little light?"

"Because . . . here comes Grandfather now."

As they stepped onto the porch the door opened and Neftali Sandoval greeted them. His face was wrinkled, dark, his hair gray with streaks of black still running through, matching his great mustache. He was stooped and moved slowly, his eyes seemed receded. He wore an old wide-lapeled sportcoat and a flannel shirt, baggy cotton trousers and ankle-high shoes. It seemed that his world came alive when he saw his granddaughter. He embraced her, his voice cracking a little as he said something in Spanish. David distinctly got the impression Mariana was a favorite grandchild.

Then she turned to introduce him. Stiver stood a little uncomfortably until he heard Mariana say his name, and then he shook hands with the old man. He noted that her grandfather made no move to extend his hand until he did. He saw the puzzled look on the old man's face as he asked Mariana a question. She nodded and made a reply.

Inside Mariana's grandmother seemed struck dumb by David. He suddenly became aware of how ridiculously helpless he was if someone didn't speak English. Mariana talked to her grandmother and then said to David, "She wants to know if she can get you something."

" . . . Tell her no . . . not right now, thanks."

"She'd feel more comfortable if she could."

" . . . All right. Tell her yes."

Mariana talked with her grandmother briefly and then again turned to David. "She wants to know what you eat." David laughed a little, and Mariana did too, but she said, "It's not funny. She has no idea what you might like. I'll just tell her to fix you some chocolate and tortillas, all right?"

"Fine. That'll be swell."

David saw the house was obviously furnished by cast-offs from the old couple's offspring. A painted wooden table and chairs, an old gas range, several pieces of dated overstuffed furniture and well-worn rugs. A shiny black panther lamp and a great alarm clock were on the mantel. The walls were painted white, but he could see the house was almost entirely of mortared rough stone.

He took a seat on the long, overstuffed couch and Mariana sat beside him, still talking to her grandparents. Alicia was making hot chocolate and warming tortillas as she talked. The kitchen was part of the same living room. Neftali Sandoval went into the next room and returned with a *National Geographic* magazine. He sat on the couch on the other side of Mariana. The girl put her arm around the stooped shoulders, and David suddenly and fleetingly felt the great love the old man and Mariana had for each other; as they looked at each other it seemed to be as much respect and admiration as love they shared. She talked with him a while, then turned to David.

"David, however rude it seems, I'm going to have to read for him. He waits for me. I'm the only one who does this for him. The others won't . . . for one reason or another. Please don't feel neglected or uncomfortable."

The old man turned to a page in the magazine. Holding one finger on a picture, he asked her questions and held it for her to read. She read silently for a minute, then began telling him about it. David could see it was a section about South America. He watched with interest as the singsong language flowed with animation. She turned to him.

"Do you know why the Argentine gauchos wear baggy pants?"

He thought a moment. "No, I don't," he said and felt a little inadequate as she translated his lack of knowledge.

The old man turned the page and David saw a photo of some pretty girls petting a llama. After a conversation Mariana again turned to him. "What do they use llamas for mainly?"

He thought a moment. "I suppose for transportation. Milk too, I guess. And I think they use the hides for leather."

He realized it was apparent he was guessing, but it was the best he could do.

Doña Alicia brought him his chocolate and tortillas. She nodded with a toothy smile in lieu of conversation and David felt himself foolishly doing the same thing. He knew his composure was gone and he felt very defensive and uncomfortable. The old woman took a seat opposite the couch and remained silent. When David looked at her she smiled and nodded. He realized the only thing he could do other than ignore her was the same thing. He looked about the room. On one wall hung an ancient cowhide. The fur was almost gone and it was cracked and wrinkled. He tried to compose a likely history for the hide, but could not. In the corner was a large mortar and pestle. He knew in past centuries natives had used such things to grind corn, and idly wondered when it had last been used. A guitar stood nearby and he wondered if it was ever played.

An hour went by and Mariana still read and explained the magazine to the old man, who listened intently. Finally she stood up as though to leave.

"He says he's enjoyed having you in his house and hopes you will come again," she said to David. Stiver went through the ritual of saying how nice it had been, how much he'd enjoyed the tortillas and what a pleasant house it was. Her grandfather said something to her and she translated. "He says he would appreciate if you had old magazines with pictures you're through with to give to him."

David said eagerly, "I can do better than that. I know a magazine store that has Spanish magazines in L.A. Tell him I'll be glad to get some for him."

But she didn't speak to the old man. "No, David, Spanish or

English, it wouldn't matter to him, he can't read either language."

Stiver looked very embarrassed. "I . . . I'm sorry . . . I didn't realize . . . I've never known anybody completely . . . I mean . . ."

"Don't be embarrassed. He can't understand what we're saying. I'll just say you have some for him."

Driving back, she said, "You've really never known anybody who couldn't read?"

"No, I haven't. At least if they couldn't, I didn't know it. God he must be completely isolated . . ."

"No, he has the radio. There're several Spanish language stations. And he has a TV. He can get the Mexican station."

"I didn't know there was a Mexican station. It broadcasts from Mexico?"

"No. From L.A. You don't know very much about . . . us . . . do you?"

"No. I thought I did. I thought I'd learned the problem areas of Mexican-Americans, but I see now . . . I see I, or any professor, for that matter, will never be able to identify problem areas until they get to know . . . and see things . . . like I'm doing."

She sat quietly, watching the road, debating to herself.

She cleared her throat. "David, I want you to come to a party with me tomorrow night."

"Sure. Whose party?"

"Some friends. I think it will be good for you."

"Where?"

"In Boyle Heights. Not far from where we live."

"I'd love it. Who'll be there? Your granddad?"

"No. The old stuffy folks don't get invited to parties where they drink. I was going by myself, but I want you to go with me. Will you?"

"Sure."

"Okay. Pick me up at the business college after school."

When David saw Mariana waiting at the corner near her trade school he realized with a start that his heart gave an involuntary little extra jump, and he felt it down to his palms. It had been a long time since anything like that had happened within him, he reflected. That girl, back in the private school in Illinois, she had done this to him. Just the sight of her. That was a long time ago, and he thought he was beyond that now. But maybe he wasn't. Then she was getting in the car beside him, smiling as she unloaded an armful of books in the back seat and relaxed and sat back, allowing her skirt to come up over her knees a little.

Then suddenly she sat forward, looking at him. He began weaving through the heavy traffic.

"David. Why aren't you dressed? For the party?" She looked at his sweatshirt and jeans.

"Oh, I got tied up, and there wasn't time. You said things wouldn't start happening 'til eight or so, so I figured we'd have time to run over to my place while I changed." This last he said a little hurriedly, he knew, and he saw quick understanding on her face and then acceptance. She sat back again and stretched a little. He knew that somehow, he was more sensitive to her attitudes and expressions than he ever imagined he could be. They rode silently a while, then, "Wow, that course in steno is murder. You have to memorize, memorize . . . you know, I've never been in a man's apartment before." She looked directly at him in that way that was typical of her. There was a trace of mirth on her face, as though they were children and she had just accepted a challenge to cross a log over a stream. Yes, that was it. My God! he thought, feeling a little giddy, I'm reacting like a school kid.

He tried to shrug. "It's not much of an apartment."

"I'll bet it's a mess," she said.

"Why do you say that?"

"Because. I don't think you've had many girl friends around since you've been seeing me."

"You think girls keep my place clean?"

"No. I think you keep it clean for girls. But maybe it'll be neat because you thought I'd be coming. Besides, I shouldn't worry about the other girls."

"You don't care about the other girls?"

She sat up, a little fire in her attitude. "Sure I care. What do you think I am, anyway?"

They drove in silence, onto the freeway, out near the university, onto a side street, where David wheeled the car into a narrow drive between two apartment buildings. He parked behind in a carport and switched off the ignition, turning to her. She looked directly at him and he knew she was being deliberately inscrutable. "Want to come in?" he asked, leaning toward her a little. He wasn't sure how she would answer, but he found himself a little disappointed as she opened the car door and moved out, away from him.

"Sure," she said simply.

She followed him down the hall toward his room, and a man came out of a door and pretended to look for a newspaper that wasn't there. As David inserted the key in his door he started to say something about nosy neighbors, but saw by her expression nothing had escaped her. She followed him into the apartment and stood in the center of the room, looking around. He stood watching her. She couldn't move, he suddenly realized, without suggesting sex. It was there, built into her, in the way she turned her head, showing a soft neck, the shape of her calves—and he'd seen little more—suggesting the rest of her legs were equally inviting. She looked at a sketch hanging on the wall, and the way she placed a fist on her hip and tilted her head back seemed to taunt his desire, like some subtle charade game. He remembered with a little start what she looked like and how she acted the first time he saw her. She not only looked completely different now that he knew her, she was completely different. She turned to him abruptly.

"I'll bet you were going to offer me a drink."

"Uh . . . I was," he headed toward the kitchen.

"Anything will do. I don't like the taste of it anyway."

He mixed two drinks, watching her from the tiny kitchen as he did so. She went to a shelf and stood very still as she looked at a picture of him and his mother and father together. She was looking at the titles of his books when he brought her the drink.

"Recognize any of them?" he asked, then instantly regretted the question.

"Only this one," she placed her forefinger on one. He glanced at it casually, then realized it was a play by Shaw.

"Pygmalion?" He tried to assemble some significance.

"Uh huh."

"You read that?"

"Yes, David, I read books. Extraordinary?"

"No. Of course not. It's just that . . ." He was at a loss.

She laughed. "You don't have to worry though. I'm not a challenge to you, or competition for your gringa bookworm girl friends."

He smiled, not knowing exactly who was being cruel. "But . . . why did you read *that* one?"

"You don't know how to be honest, David. But I do. To tell the truth, I saw it at the library when I was little and I thought it might be about a little lion." She looked at him with simple sincerity. He started to laugh, but checked it.

"Go ahead and laugh. You must learn to be honest."

He broke out in genuine laughter. "That *is* funny."

"Then when I read it and saw what it was all about, it made me think a lot. It's really impossible, isn't it? What that man tried to do with that girl."

"Books are written to make you think a lot. But, I'm curious, why did you want to read about lions?"

He led her to the couch and they sat, completely involved in talking to each other.

"I guess I was twelve or so. I'd read a little about the family life of lions. I was fascinated. You know, that great big beautiful male, with a head this huge," she made as big a half circle as she could with her arms. David didn't look up. "About all he does is sit around and pose, breed, of course, and occasionally fight for a female. He's really something to look at, but he doesn't take any responsibility. He makes a lot of noise, but the females raise the cubs, organize the hunting and do all the killing. The females keep on the alert for danger."

"Why does all that hold such a fascination?"

"I don't know. I guess because, I know some day I'll marry some guy and . . . like the rest of us, never have anything to say about where we live, what we do, or anything. You know, that's one thing about you Anglos, you give women a voice in things. That's something a girl like me can never look forward to."

"Unless you marry an Anglo."

She laughed a little. "I guess there's always that possibility. But I won't hold my breath. Besides, I'm not sure I'd want to."

"Oh? What's wrong with people like me?"

She looked thoughtful. "Well, first, you're all so dishonest."

"Me? I'm not dishonest."

"I don't mean that you do things that are dishonest, illegal. You just . . . don't face things. Like you being afraid to ask me if I know what a certain big word means. Or if I read a certain book."

"I just don't want to insult somebody."

"No, it's not that. You think. 'Well, she may be dishonest enough to pretend she knows something when she doesn't, so I'll go along with the lie.' You people form opinions of people in advance, and then try to cover it up. It's dishonest."

"Look," he said, taking her hand, "it's not being dishonest trying to save someone from embarrassment . . ."

"But it *is*. I've noticed one other thing about Anglos. If a person has a defect of any kind, it's never mentioned. Just like when you talk to somebody you really believe comes from inferior people, you pretend there's no problem there. You won't mention it."

"Yes, but this is out of consideration for the person. I was really shocked when I learned what your father's brother's name meant."

"You mean Poca Luz?"

"Yes. Why on earth call him that? You said it means . . ."

"It means 'little light.' You know, it's dark up there," she pointed to her temple. "Not much light gets through."

"But you call him that to his *face?*"

"You think he's unaware of it? That he's not very bright?"

"No, it's probably quite obvious he's retarded. But why be so cruel . . . ? "

"So we call him 'little light' to his face. And you'd call him 'dim wit' behind his back. Who's being dishonest, David?"

"It's not a matter of honesty. You just can't call somebody a half wit just because he's not too bright."

"What *do* you call him? To his face."

"You call him . . . whatever his name is."

"His name's Poca Luz. That's all anyone ever called him."

"It can't be. What did his mother call him?"

"She called him Poca Luz too. Ever since he was old enough to tell he wasn't quite all there."

"But . . . it's inhuman. I've never heard of anything so cruel."

"I'm glad you're going to this party with me tonight. You'll meet a cousin named 'Cojo,' that means someone who limps. He has a club foot. And another uncle named 'Cacarizo.' That means scar face. He had smallpox when he was little. His face is a mess."

"And you call them these names to their faces?"

"Why not? They're very aware of it. Much more so than anybody else, in fact. I think if you call them that, then pretty soon it really doesn't matter any more. It's much less cruel than pretending somebody who's different is really the same. Like you people do."

He laughed a little, feeling futile. "Maybe you're right. I better start getting ready if we're going. By the way, what would you call me? Do you have a nickname for me? Other than gringo?"

She smiled. "Yes we do. My mother calls you 'guapo' when you're not around."

He stopped walking toward the bedroom. "Wah . . . what was that?"

"Let's see," she thought a moment, "in English you'd spell it W-A-H-P-O. Guapo."

"And just what does that mean?" He was a little indignant.

"It means handsome." He smiled and walked toward her. She stood straight as he took her face in his hands.

"You know, you're incredibly beautiful." She almost giggled.

"Tell me, if you had to choose a nickname for me, what would it be?"

He looked at her at length, his eyes going over her features.

"Well, you have a little, kind of upturned nose. I guess I'd call you pug-nose." She laughed aloud.

"You're right! That's just what they call me. 'Chata.' Because my nose is so little."

"I better change," he said, going to the bedroom. He left the door open and she went to it and closed it firmly, and then hollered through it, "Hurry, we'll be late."

2

David Stiver and Mariana Sandoval found all parking places taken for a block on each side of the house where the party was to take place. It was a warm evening and as they walked back toward the house, Stiver examined the neighborhood. He tried to analyze how his feelings had changed about the community since he had become somewhat familiar with it.

"How do you feel about East Los Angeles now?" she asked, guessing his thoughts. He reflected a moment.

"You're trying to teach me to be honest," he said, "so I'll try to tell you. One thing, I feel as though you're protecting me. Just being with me. You're kind of my passport."

"Do you feel uncomfortable still?"

" . . . Yes, I certainly don't feel like I belong here."

She walked in silence for a moment. "I think everybody belongs anywhere. Or at least they should. But of course that's not the way it is."

They passed a house with several persons sitting on the front porch. One man strummed a guitar, while the others sang.

"Would I be safe, really, walking down this street alone?"

"You'd be safe from all these people. It's the young punks, the rowdies, who might give you a bad time. You'd be pretty safe in a neighborhood like this with just homes."

David looked at the homes. All seemed at least thirty years old. Many had small lawns in front, some had old jalopies in the front yard.

"Look at that place. Five cars, all heaps of junk, in the front yard and in the driveway. Why do they keep them there?"

She laughed. "That's called 'chicano landscaping.' I don't know why there's so many here. There's some joke, I don't know how it goes, about a guy who got so drunk he couldn't find his way back to Boyle Heights, but he knew he was getting closer by the number of junked cars on the front lawns. You're the sociologist. Why do you think there's so many heaps around? Nobody really needs them. If a car's worth a hundred dollars, and it costs a hundred and fifty to get it fixed, an American will throw it away. A chicano will give you ten dollars for it."

"That reminds me of a Greek or maybe it was an Egyptian fable. A man loved diamonds terribly, so somehow he got a magician to turn all pebbles and stones into diamonds. Of course they immediately lost all value, but he still thought they were as beautiful as ever. The funny part was, certain people, even though diamonds were worthless, couldn't help collecting them and hoarding them. They were still obsessed with diamonds. The pattern was too strong to break."

They came to the house. The party was well under way. They stopped in front, to finish their talk in private on the sidewalk.

"And you think somehow that's similar to all these cars?" she asked with interest.

"Yes. I think until so recently was a car, any car, a luxury item to some classes that just the ownership, even if it's a financial liability, is really an obsession for status."

She looked at him admiringly, and he realized he always inwardly warmed when she did. "I think you're right about that, David."

"You see," he explained, "a car is something more than just a mechanical possession. It must be registered in your name, you must get the pink slip, and most important of all, to some, the great big state must make a record of little ol' *you* as the owner and no one else can claim it without your written consent in the form of your signature. When it comes to owning a car, the richest man with the biggest Cadillac is registered in the same way, by the same government agency, must submit the same material and papers and receives the identical ownership certificate as the poorest dishwasher with his jalopy. He pays more for his license, the rich man, but this is really equal treatment. Real equality."

"I see," she agreed. "You're saying it isn't the value of a car that's so important, it's owning it."

"Yes. The mechanics of ownership. I think all this registration, sending to Sacramento, your address, all this, is really as satisfying to your people, if not more so, than calling a pile of junk your own. By the way, just what kind of a thing is this we're going to here?" he indicated the house.

She pulled his arm, starting toward the front door. "Come on," she said.

The main body of persons was in the back yard. David estimated sixty or seventy people seated, standing, or wandering around. In one corner there was lively music. It seemed everybody was singing, laughing, shouting or drinking. Mariana tugged his arm and he bent to hear her.

"This isn't what us kids would call a young folks' party. No swingers here. The few younger ones our age you see here are either square or going along with it for the old folks. There's Mom and Dad over there. See?"

Stiver looked and saw a group of a dozen or so standing around a small goat. The animal was about half grown, and looked alarmed and confused by the noise and activity.

"What's the goat for?" David asked.

"To eat," she said.

"But he's *alive*," David said uneasily.

"Yes, right now, anyway."

Stiver watched. Pete was feeling the goat's head, talking, arguing loudly, a little drunkenly, with another man, in Spanish. The other man said something, and the group roared with laughter, except Pete. He shook his head and argued some more, gesturing emphatically. The other man shook his head in disagreement. The two were fairly shouting at each other.

"What are they saying?" Stiver asked.

Mariana laughed, squeezing his arm. "My father is saying that the color of the goat's little horns indicates the meat will be very tough. He says a purple color means it hasn't eaten the right vitamins. The other man says no, the goat has eaten mainly leftover beans and watermelon rinds, and that makes the most tender, delicious meat of all."

"Does your dad really know about goats?"

She chuckled, turning away. "No. He doesn't know a thing about them. I really think he's making that up, about purple horns."

"Then why the argument?"

"Because. Dad's barely over five feet tall. He's funny look-ing. He's successful, and he knows he can make people laugh all night with his ridiculous statements. He's aware everybody knows he's lying. Didn't you have psychology in college?"

David smiled. "You mean he's a ham."

She looked at him with affectionate appreciation. "That's exactly what I mean. Come on. Let's see the mariachis."

"Mariachis. Those are musicians. Right?"

"Right."

As they made their way across the wide concrete slab which took up half the entire back yard, Stiver looked for traces of Spanish or Mexican dress or décor. Subconsciously, he realized, he'd pictured piñatas, gay yellow and red pinks and bullfight posters. A string of bare bulbs lighted the area. A dilapidated garage was at one side, its doors open to show a jalopy standing on concrete blocks, the wheels long since borrowed for another vehicle. He noticed that in general the older folks wore old sweaters, shawls and baggy dresses or trousers, while the mid-dle-aged generation wore outmoded suits with no necktie, and the younger ones near his age dressed fairly nicely, with an in-evitable anachronism such as highly pointed shoes or string ties.

A girl with yellow hair and freckles stood out among the crowd. She and Mariana saw each other at the same time. The girl was with a dark youth in tight trousers and suede jacket. As the couples came together the yellow-haired girl was looking at David.

"Betty!" Mariana said, genuine pleasure showing. "Hello, Rudy. Betty, you've never met Dave. Dave, this is Betty."

Stiver nodded to her and shook hands with Rudy. He smiled. "So you're the one," he said lightly to Elizabeth.

"She's my white liberal friend I was telling you about," Mariana laughed.

Elizabeth smiled plainly. "And it's not always easy," she said. Stiver noticed she was appraising him from head to toe.

David tried not to react as he saw Rudy crudely and obviously jerk his head, indicating he wanted to talk with Mariana alone. He saw a look of helpless annoyance cross Elizabeth's face, and saw quick anger in Mariana as she glanced at him. David nodded and Mariana stepped away a few paces with Rudy. Elizabeth stood close to David, talking quietly.

"You get used to it after a while. At first it seems these people have no manners or consideration. But actually it's just a way of thinking. Or not thinking."

Stiver looked at her. "Maybe he has something important to say to her."

"Even if it was important, which it's not, it's the sort of thing you never get used to around here. It's very typical, this business of having something secret to discuss. Interrupting others to go off and whisper. It stems from deep-rooted feelings of inferiority."

"You sound like a psych major."

"I am. Cal State, L.A."

"You've lived in this part of town all your life?"

"Just about. Mariana and I grew up together."

"I'd give anything if I could say her name the way you do."

"It's a beautiful name, isn't it? When it's said right. But I hate to hear 'Merry-anna.' Makes me want to puke."

Stiver laughed. "I'll do my best to say it right. The broad 'A' isn't so hard, it's the 'R'."

They were both watching Mariana as she talked with Rudy. Elizabeth said, "She's something awfully special to us, that girl. We've been best friends since about the third grade, but she's more than that. She's sort of my special project."

Stiver was puzzled. "How's that?"

"My dad is one of the world-changers. We moved down here because he thought we could do some good for the cause. Everybody in East L.A. falls into the culturally deprived category. We've tried like hell to give Mariana some realistic values. I couldn't talk her into going on to school after we graduated from high school. But I did talk her into the business school she attends. After seeing her develop into such an utterly sweet, unpretentious, proud girl—her looks haven't spoiled her—it would have killed us to see her marry some factory worker at eighteen and start having babies every year. A girl like Mariana belongs to the world. If someone could only get her out of East L.A."

Stiver was still watching Mariana. "Wonder what they're talking about," he mused.

"Rudy's pestering her for a date."

Stiver showed surprise.

"That's right," she went on. "He's with me, she's with you, but that doesn't stop him from calling her aside and pestering her. Stick around. You'll get used to it."

David saw Mariana shake her head, turning away from Rudy. She raised her voice so the others could hear. "I said *no!* Please leave me alone." Rudy's face darkened with embarrassment as he realized the others heard. Then he wheeled and walked quickly away.

Mariana joined David and Elizabeth. "I'm sorry I had to do that. Say it out loud, to embarrass him. But these things have to be dealt with."

"So he just leaves Betty standing here," Stiver mused.

"Don't worry," Elizabeth said. "He'll be back. He's lost face, but he'll get over it."

A man at a table nearby was serving punch in little paper cups. Mariana addressed him: "Pablo!"

The man turned his attention to her, frank admiration on his face.

"Mande?"

"Give us two, please," she said. He handed her two cups.

Stiver took one. "I'm learning a little," he said, "but what was that he said to you? Sounded like 'mande.'"

"Yes, 'mande'," Mariana nodded. "It means, let's see, actually it means 'command me.' Kind of gallant, isn't it?"

Stiver mulled it over a little. They drank their punch and talked with Elizabeth a while. Although not interested in her personally, David made a mental note to sometime talk to Elizabeth more about these people. He had a lot of questions to ask, and the more he was around Mariana, the more questions he wanted answered.

In a few minutes Mariana said, "David?"

He snapped erect and looked into her face. "Command me," he said.

She laughed. "Let's go see the musicians."

The music became louder as they walked toward a group of perhaps thirty people surrounding a dozen musicians.

David looked at her, puzzled. "How come the trumpets?"

She stopped, pulling him to a halt as she did so. "This is Mexican music. Not what you call Spanish. You think of Spanish music as soft guitars, fancy rhythms, castanets. I know. But listen to this." She pulled him through the crowd, up to the musicians.

There were a pair of guitars, three violins, two huge bass

guitars, three singers, and two trumpeters. As David watched, he heard the trumpets playing a soft accompaniment. Then as the verse ended, for a few brief measures the trumpets went into a wild loud duet, zigzagging, triple-tonguing and flutter-tonguing. Then, as the next verse started and the singers began again, the trumpets returned to the soft accompaniment. By the time this was repeated two or three times, David began to like it. He noticed most attention was given to the trumpeters during those brief two or three measure fillers, during which they displayed their maximum talent, volume and dexterity. Evidently, there were innumerable stanzas to this particular song, and about the fourth time through, two men from the crowd stepped forth and almost by force took the trumpets away and took over the soft accompaniment. However, at the end of the verse, these two outdid the former trumpet players for the two brief measures, and applause broke out among the spectators as the singers began the next verse. Near the end, a near drunk man grabbed the trumpet from one player and delivered dazzling ornaments and embellishments when the singers finished and were catching their breaths for the next stanza. David saw it was a show-off contest, and evidently everybody knew how to "fill in."

"Come, I'll show you something else," Mariana said, pulling him toward the crowd around the goat. For the first time, David noticed a large hole in the ground with a glowing bed of coals and hot stones nearby. He watched as one man held the goat's rear feet and another held its forelegs, while yet another held the frightened animal's head.

"Jorobado! Jorobado," they called. "Where's that damn Jorobado!"

Pete was standing close. All looked around for Jorobado.

"That damn guy," Pete said in English to no one. "He wanted to do the honors and now he's gone. I . . ."

"Here he comes now," a man holding the goat said. "Jorobado! Ándale! I can't hold this damn thing like this all night."

David recoiled inwardly as he looked at the man called Jorobado. His face was cruelly twisted out of shape and he had a huge hump on his spine, causing him to half drag his feet as he walked, waddling almost like a duck. Jorobado came forward, pulling from his belt a shiny hunting knife.

"Here I am, guys," he said, speaking English with a fairly thick accent. "All you lilies! Where would you be if it wasn't for your good bloodthirsty friend Jorobado?"

A woman seated nearby jumped to her feet. "Bloodthirsty! I'm glad you said that, Jorobado. Wait. Wait. I won't be a momento." She ran into the house. Jorobado stood looking down at the little goat. "She has all night, and then she forgets," he said, trying to look swaggeringly like a pirate, David thought. In a few seconds the woman returned from the house with a metal basin.

"Okay," she said, holding the basin under the goat's throat.

Although it was happening fast, David was aware he was about to see something he didn't particularly care to see. But he was fascinated. He glanced around to observe the general reaction. He saw some of the women averting their eyes, others walking away, smiling squeamishly in mild disgust. He looked at Mariana, and found her watching him, her face serious. He returned his attention to the goat. The animal was still being held. Jorobado placed the blade of the knife against the goat's neck and in one quick jerk, cut the neck half through. The creature jerked wildly as it tried to jump, but couldn't move its feet.

Its lungs still breathed, and little jets of bloody foam shot out of each side of the neck. Its eyes rolled upward, and the basin nearly filled as the heart sent its life blood gushing through the severed jugular veins. Then the goat collapsed.

A huge fat man wearing a white apron appeared, carrying a large butcher knife. "Help me. Don't make me do all the work," he said to the others. The carcass was laid on a canvas, and the butchering began. David watched as the belly was slit expertly, and the entrails removed. "Para los perros," someone said. David understood it meant "for the dogs." The man in the apron was obviously a professional butcher, David realized, as he saw him skin the goat, cut off the hoofs and tail. David was a little puzzled as he saw them leave the head attached and place the whole body in a large tub. A heavy burlap cloth was placed over the goat, and then the tub was lowered into the bed of glowing coals and hot stones. Then several men took shovels and covered coals, stones and goat with a foot or more of dirt. The fat man in the white apron wiped his bloody hands and said, "Now let's have that party!"

The crowd in the back yard had grown, and groups were collecting here and there to talk in loud voices. Bottles of wine were on tables everywhere, and all present seemed to be drinking heavily. Mariana and David walked slowly around the groups.

"That man, Horo . . . what's he called? The one who killed the goat."

"Jorobado?" she said.

"Yes, he sort of gave me a chill. He's so . . . deformed."

"That's why he's called Jorobado." David looked puzzled. She went on: "There's a famous French book. Haven't you read it? *El Jorobado de Notre Dame.* It's a classic."

David thought. "De Notre Dame. Of Notre Dame. Oh, the Hunchback . . . you mean, that's what you call him? Hunchback?"

She looked at him with sincerity. "I'm beginning to see how hard it is for you to understand, David. I only hope you'll . . ."

"No," he said. "I'm beginning to see a little, myself."

They came to an old woman seated alone on a bench. She had a shawl over her head and wore a dress that came to her ankles. She smiled at Mariana, showing toothless gums, and said something in Spanish. David heard Mariana say a sentence with "gracias" in it. Then she turned to him.

"She says you're a very handsome gringo, and she says you also look like you're very rich."

"What'd you tell her?"

"I told her thanks, and she's right, you're rich, handsome and 'muy simpatico.' A nice person."

The old woman grinned broadly, trying in vain to conceal her toothlessness with her hand. She took a drink of what looked like red wine in a glass and said something else to Mariana. Mariana conversed briefly with her and then translated.

"She asked if we two are in love."

David smiled. "What'd you tell her?"

"I told her I love you, but that's all I know."

Stiver looked sharply at Mariana. She returned his gaze serenely. The old woman spoke again, grinning broadly.

"She wants to know if you'll have a drink with her."

David saw there was a glass pitcher with a dark red fluid in it on the table in front of the old woman. "Tell her yes . . ."

"It's blood," Mariana cut in. David had started to reach for the empty glass the old woman held out, but he froze. He looked at Mariana, feeling his stomach muscles contract involuntarily. He started to stammer. Mariana said nothing, did nothing. There was a little smile on her face.

"Tell her . . . I . . ." To his great relief, the old woman burst into laughter, and David was able to graciously refuse. Mariana tugged him and they walked on.

"How come," he asked, "nobody introduces anybody else to anyone?"

"That's just one of the stupid ways of the chicanos," she answered philosophically. "This party isn't so bad, because almost everyone knows each other. But usually, half the people don't know anybody, and unlike the gringos, nobody has the courage or whatever it is to walk up and introduce himself, so everyone just stands around, hoping conversation will develop somehow."

"Tell me," he said as they strolled, "is this . . . drinking of blood, is it pretty common?"

She laughed a little. "No," she said emphatically, "it's not. Just the old-timers do it. And I think they do it mostly to get a reaction. I guess years ago it was the ordinary thing, when everybody slaughtered their own cattle. They still make sausages out of blood." She looked at him. "You can buy blood sausages in lots of Anglo stores, can't you?"

He thought a moment. "Yes, I guess so. I guess that's not much different from drinking it."

She snorted. "Oh, yes it is, David. It's lots different, and you know it. But I'll bet you like your steak rare. With blood running out."

He smiled reflectively. "Yes, I do."

"And I'll bet if no one's looking you sop up the blood with your bread."

"No, I mash my potato into it and get it that way."

They both laughed.

Two hours later about a third of the guests were in various stages of collapse or near collapse. David had refused most of the dozens of bottles or glasses of wine offered him and Mariana had sipped sparingly. David saw Pete walk unsteadily over to the side of the yard and begin vomiting. He nudged Mariana and directed her attention to him. Another man hurried over to Pete and steered him to the nearby fence. He pushed Pete's head over the fence. "If you have to throw up, don't do it in my yard," he said.

"I take it he's our host," David said quietly to Mariana. She nodded. Pete retched over the fence again and again.

"What about the neighbor that lives there?" David asked. "Maybe he doesn't want vomit in his yard either."

Mariana pointed to a man vomiting on the other side of the property. "You're right. That's him throwing up in the yard on the other side."

David saw the humor in the situation. "Why do they all drink so much they get sick?"

"Some of them want to. To make room for that. Look there."

David saw some men had uncovered the roasting goat and with pot holders were lifting out the huge tub. They carried it to one of the tables and lifted the carcass out onto a large wooden board. Many of the guests were beyond the hunger stage, but two dozen or so crowded around the table, sniffing and exclaiming. The man with the white apron stood by the goat, butcher knife in hand. Plates were passed around.

"Wait! Wait!" the man said, looking around. "Where's our gringo guest?" His eyes fell on David. "Come forward, please sir," he said to David. David hesitated, unsure, and Mariana pulled him along to the table.

"For you," the man said to David. "The special treat."

He took the knife and expertly cut out one eyeball of the goat and placed it on a plate. He held it out to David, and everyone stood watching. David regarded the steaming eyeball, not knowing just what to do. The eyeball stared up blankly at him. David took the plate and looked miserably around. All the faces were serious. Someone put a fork in his hand and he stared stupidly at the fork. He looked pleadingly at Mariana. *Save me, please,* he seemed to say. But she only smiled a little. David again looked at the two dozen dark faces watching him earnestly. Then he raised the fork and tried to cut the eye, which was nearly the size of a golf ball. He found it very tough and leathery. He pressed harder. Suddenly the huge man in the white apron threw back his head and rocked with laughter, clapping David so hard on the back he almost dropped the plate. Then the others began laughing. It was a joke, he saw. They hadn't really expected him to go through with it. The big man stopped laughing and took the plate from David's hand.

"Look," he said, popping the still steaming eyeball into his mouth. He chewed vigorously. "Eyes are good for the sight. You notice I don't wear glasses? That's because I eat eyes. It's the best thing in the world for the sight." David laughed.

Someone shouted, "You're eating the wrong part. You should be eating the brains." This brought a swell of mirth. A woman who David guessed was the man's wife pushed her way through to him.

"I think you must eat too much tongue. Always you talk."

The big man grinned. "Honey, tell 'em what other part I eat.

When it's a male goat like this." The woman blushed and looked away. "Go on. Tell 'em. Tell 'em how I am. And past fifty years, too."

"That goat meat was out of this world," David said to Mariana as they finished the meal. "If you could sell this at a restaurant you could . . ." He was interrupted by a crowd talking loudly. Looking, they saw Jorobado, the hunchback, pushing some other men out of his way.

"I know when I'm sober enough to drive," Jorobado was saying, struggling toward his car parked in the drive beside the house.

"Don't do it. You'll wreck," someone warned him.

"I only live two blocks," he said with determination, "I'm going home, and nobody better not stop me."

He was barely able to walk, but he staggered to his car. The others watched as he got in and started the engine. The tires squealed as he backed up suddenly. David could hear the engine roar. Then there was another screech of tires and a thud. David and Mariana joined the others hurrying to the front to see what had happened.

Jorobado had missed the driveway entrance by ten feet, and the rear wheels were suspended above the gutter, spinning uselessly, as the weight of the car rested on the frame, atop the curb. Jorobado raced the engine, but the wheels just spun in the air. Finally he got out, looking resentfully at the others gathering around.

"Now look what the hell you did," Jorobado accused. "I'm stuck." He surveyed the situation, started to fall over, and leaned against the car. He staggered to the front bumper and pushed it in vain. Then he turned to the others.

"Help me, god dammit! We can push this son-of-a-bitch into the street if we try."

The big butcher came forward. "I told you not to drive. You're too drunk to walk, even."

"Just shut up and help me push," Jorobado persisted, still pushing by himself. "If you don't wanna help me, then get the hell away. You god-damn meat cutter."

Although there were perhaps thirty people gathered around Jorobado's car, no one offered to help free it. David first noticed the police car driving slowly toward them. It pulled up directly in front of the other car. David saw one officer inside pick up the radio mike and speak briefly, then replace the mike. The group had grown quiet. Jorobado leaned against his car for support, looking at the prowl car. The two officers got out and approached them. They walked to Jorobado, who was standing beside the driver's seat. A bright street light illuminated the entire scene. The officers were Anglos.

"Having a little trouble here?" one asked.

"He struck his car," someone said from the group. David felt Mariana's hand grip his arm.

"This your car?" the officer asked Jorobado, looking him over.

"Yeah, it's mine," Jorobado said.

Both officers walked to the rear wheels and examined the situation. David noticed they glanced up and down the street, expectantly. Then they walked back to Jorobado. "Were you driving it when this happened?" one asked.

"Yeah, I only live two blocks . . ."

"How much you had to drink?" the other officer asked. David saw they were young, middle twenties perhaps.

"I'm not drunk, if that's what you mean," Jorobado said.

The officers surveyed the crowd, looking casual and confident. Then one said, "You'd better step over to the police car, fella," to Jorobado. The hunchback shuffled, staggered toward the patrol car parked in the center of the street. Its red light on top was blinking. The crowd surged forward as far as the curb to watch.

"Leave him alone," the white-aproned man hollered. "We'll take him home. He only lives two blocks."

One of the officers turned, pointing his night stick at the crowd. "You people better stay out of this," he warned. The other officer reached into his pocket and produced a coin. He placed it on the pavement in front of Jorobado. "Now. Let's see you pick it up," he ordered.

"He can't. Can you see he's crippled?" a voice from the crowd said. The officer paid no attention.

"Come on, Pancho. Pick it up," the officer commanded. Jorobado, misshapen as he was, had to brace himself against the patrol car to bend over. His grip on the car slipped and he started to fall. The officer caught him and whirled him around, taking out his handcuffs at the same time. He wrestled with Jorobado trying to force his hands behind him. Jorobado cried out.

"Don't! I can't put my hands behind my back. They don't bend that way because of my hunchback!" The officer continued to wrestle him into position. The other officer turned his attention to the crowd.

"Stand back, all of you," he said, a hand resting on his pistol. He glanced down the street. David followed his glance and saw another flashing red light coming. Within seconds the two patrol cars braked to a halt and two officers climbed out of each car, hurrying toward the scene of the struggle. Two turned their attention to the crowd while the other two grabbed Jorobado by the arms and bent them behind him. Jorobado yelled: "My arms! Stop it!" And then the handcuffs were on him.

Jorobado was kicking at his captors, swearing loudly. The three officers picked him up bodily and threw him into the rear seat of the patrol car. The crowd, led by the meat cutter, moved off the curb into the street. All the policemen turned to face them, their faces looking grave, ready to do battle in the line of duty.

"Now, all of you get back up on the curb!" one officer shouted. The crowd edged forward. "Leave him alone." "He's a cripple." "Untie his hands, it hurts him." "He's not drunk, he's lame." David, though apparently none of the others, noticed another police car arrive, and in a few seconds another, and then another. David looked the other way and saw more. A dozen squad cars were either there or arriving. Policemen leaped out with shotguns. The butcher, leading the others, started toward the two original arresting officers.

"Look, mister, that's no way to treat a guy when . . ."

A policeman ran to intercept him and the two collided. The officer went down, turning a somersault backward. As though it were a signal, another officer leaped forward, shouting, "Assaulting an officer. You're under arrest!" As the meat cutter turned to face him he was struck down by a night stick. He went to his knees, blood coming from his nose. Two policemen were on him instantly, bending his arms behind his back and in a second or two he was also handcuffed. The crowd surged forward, voices rising hysterically, and as though by magic, a solid line of fifteen policemen formed abreast, each leveling a shotgun on the group. "Raul!" a policeman with sergeant's stripes hollered. A Mexican-American officer came forward. He didn't need to be told what to do. He stood between the row of shotguns and the crowd.

It was the first time in his life David had ever faced a loaded shotgun. The many headlights of the patrol cars made the scene bright as day, and he could see each gun clearly, looking hard, cold and hideous.

"Go on home, all of you!" The Mexican-American officer ordered.

"Since when do you order us off the street?" came a voice.

Raul stood defiantly, glaring at them. "You can't do any good. The law has been broken, and it must be enforced. Somebody will get hurt if you come any closer."

David saw fear on Raul's face. A trapped fear, as though he had no side to go to. The crowd pressed closer, angry voices rose. Less than ten feet separated the line of policemen with shotguns and the group from the party. David noticed, though the others apparently did not, that the meat cutter had been placed in a car and whisked off. Now the car with Jorobado in the back seat started moving away slowly.

David looked at Mariana. Her face was white. "My God!" he said. "This is unbelievable!" As he looked at her he saw her face contort with terror. Looking back on the street he saw Pete forcing his way to the front of the group confronting Officer Raul, who stood his ground; the buffer between the Anglo police and his people. Pete began talking rapidly, but relatively quietly, in Spanish. The two cars with the prisoners had left the scene. David found his heart pounding. "What's he saying? Good God! Somebody's going to get killed."

Pete talked at length, shouting Raul down when the officer tried to speak. The police sergeant gave a signal and the shotgun line began falling back. "Okay, let's get out of here," the sergeant said. The officers began getting in their cars, leaving Raul and one patrol car with a frightened Anglo policeman waiting for him. Pete kept up his monologue, and Raul said nothing, looking indifferent. Then Raul turned his back and walked toward the remaining squad car. As he did so the crowd broke into angry curses, shouting threateningly. Raul climbed in and as he slammed the door the tires squealed and the street was empty except for the party-makers and the parked cars.

The group remained in the street, talking angrily, apparently having no plan to disperse. Mariana pulled David by the arm and they started walking down the sidewalk.

"What's going to happen? To those two they took?"

"They'll go to jail. Be tried for resisting arrest, being drunk, and maybe a half dozen other things."

"But the man, the butcher. He did nothing. That officer bumped him deliberately and then pretended to fall down."

Mariana smiled bitterly at him. "You want to really be the white liberal? Then go to the court trial and tell that to the judge. It won't do any good, but you'll be getting a real lesson in sociology."

"I still can't believe it happened. They . . . they were ready to start *shooting*."

"You're very right. You think everybody there didn't realize that? And in every bunch of Anglo cops, there's one who's itching to pull that trigger. You never know which one, but there's one there."

"If I hadn't seen that, I wouldn't believe it. Does this happen often? The shotguns and phony arrests, I mean?"

"Only in East Los Angeles. No, I take that back. It happens in Watts too. Maybe worse there."

"Your dad. What was he saying to that chicano cop?" He used the word without being aware of it at first.

She laughed. "David, you wouldn't believe what Dad was saying. He called him everything from the son of a two-peso whore to the father of perverted children, with lots more in between. Then he called him a Leo Carrillo."

"A Leo Carrillo? He was an actor."

"Yes, he was an actor. An actor who acted just like the white man told him to act, who acted out the white man's image of a Mexican exactly like the white man wanted to think about Mexicans. In Watts they call a guy like Leo Carrillo an Uncle Tom."

They were walking toward his car, and he stopped her and placed his hands on her shoulders. "Mariana—do I say it right yet? Your name?"

She smiled. "Pretty close. The single R is almost trilled."

"Mariana, I'm going to do something about this. What I saw tonight." She was silent, serious. "Don't you believe me?"

"I believe you may try. Dad tried to help some poor Negroes once. A contractor was cheating them. They started calling him 'Nigger-lover,' and he wound up getting fired."

"Mark my word, Mariana, I'll see that someone in a high position hears about what happened here tonight. If I have to I'll go to the president of the university to get pressure put on to bring all this to light."

She shook her head. "David, how can you tell them what East L.A. is like, when you don't even know yourself? Let's . . . let's go to your apartment. I know it's late, but I want to tell you lots of things you never dreamed of."

It was after two in the morning as they sat together on the couch in Stiver's apartment, Mariana talking on and on, for the first time in her life, he realized, expressing how she felt about the injustices she'd seen in the communities where she was raised. He watched her face as she talked softly, her voice becoming softer when she was angry, sometimes her eyes narrowing as she recalled frustration.

" . . . and then, Dad was nervous as he argued with the policeman, and he took out a package of cigarettes and opened them. You know how there's a little bit of cellophane paper that comes off the top? Well, he dropped it and it blew into the street. The policeman became furious. 'You trying to needle me?' he asked. 'You can get a $500 fine for throwing trash on the street. Now go pick it up. Pronto.' A little crowd had gathered, and the policeman stopped traffic while Dad got out on the street and found the little bit of cellophane. He made Dad put it in the car ashtray, and said Dad should be glad he wasn't writing him up on the anti-litter law instead of just an illegal turn. I've never forgotten that, even though I was little, nor how Dad just wouldn't talk the rest of the day. But instead of driving to the beach, where we were headed, he turned around and we went to see Grandma and Grandpa in Irwindale. Whenever Dad gets real upset and hurt, he always wants to go there."

He took her chin in his hand and tilted her head up.

"Tomorrow I'm going to do something about what happened at the party tonight."

"What are you going to do?"

He paused before answering. "I'm going to take a complaint

to the proper place, wherever that is. I'm going to tell someone, the chief of police, if I have to, what happened. I'm sure it's not generally known the police pull shotguns and provoke arrests. I'm going to bring it to light."

She smiled genuinely. "You're turning into a knight in shining armor, David." She sipped her coffee. "I believed you would all along. I think I worked at making you fall in love with me."

He blinked. Uneasily: "I wasn't aware I'd mentioned it."

She looked at him wide-eyed. "I guess that shows how positive I am of impressions I get from people. You do love me, don't you?"

He looked away, a little exasperated. "You've tried to teach me to be honest. It's hard. Yes, I do, Mariana. So much, I never would have believed it. At first it was . . ."

"At first it was just me. The way I looked. I know I look good to men." She smiled. "How I know! First I was different, exotic, to you. But I knew this would happen. It's not just me you love now. It's something more. Something very important."

He took both her hands, pulling her closer, looking into her eyes to see what it was that made him feel the way he did. With a start he realized she was a mature woman, ready to be a mother—more so than any girl he'd ever known, and yet she was softness and sex. It was this combination he found maddeningly desirable. He wondered idly if he suffered a little from Oedipus complex or if he had a little of that rare maturity that looked upon sex and pregnancy and parenthood as all part of the same emotional frame of reference.

"I want you, Mariana," he said simply.

She rose. "I know. I think it's the proper time."

He looked puzzled, then, "Oh, you mean, the right time of the . . ."

"No," a trace of a smile, "I mean it's all right for us. We're ready."

She walked surely into the bedroom. He felt hammers at his temples as he went in. She stood, by the tall dresser and bed. She only gave him a glance, and then took off her sweater. A little smile as she unbuttoned her blouse. He watched, sharpened to the marrow by the sight of her bare shoulders. He found himself holding his breath as she pulled back the covers of the bed, clad only in bra and half-slip, and leaned back against the bedstead waiting. She seemed incredibly calm. He sat on the bed and she ran her fingers through his hair.

Her voice sounded tiny and he could barely hear her say, "Come on." He fidgeted with his tie, then threw it down. He fumbled at his collar button. He gave it a little yank and the button popped off and landed on her bare midriff. He was aware he was surprised to see that her midsection and shoulders were even-colored, surprised that she was not white underneath her clothes like all the others were so bleach-white. He reached for the button, smiling a little foolishly, but she was quicker and snatched the button away. As she pressed against his back with her hands, her fist with the button was clenched tightly.

I t was two days and a dozen or so phone calls later when David Stiver pulled his car into a lot near the Civic Center and walked to the police building. As he passed a bronze sculpting of three figures near the entrance he recalled dully the work had been the subject of a theme paper by an art major he knew.

He knew he was not one of those people who could look at something arty and tell if it was good or not, and he dismissed it. Entering, he was directed to the office of the man with whom he had an appointment.

The office was paneled, quiet and plush for a police department, he thought as he waited. Presently the man came in. David wondered if he would have automatically disliked him before this whole business . . .

The man looked at David as though his name had just slipped his mind a moment before.

"You're . . ."

"David Stiver."

"Oh yes. I talked with you on the phone. And also your professor . . ."

"Right." David tried to fit him to a type and decided he could have been the youngest coach of the Big Ten Conference. He was blond, with hair perfectly combed, his physique was one that had once been very athletic and was still powerful and his nice-looking, young-success face seemed immobile, as though he was preoccupied with incorruptibility and efficiency.

He identified himself as a sergeant of the department's Internal Affairs Division and leaned forward over his desk so that Stiver had to leave his seat to shake the extended hand.

"I've looked into the incident you and Professor . . ." he looked up.

"Rowland."

"Yes. Rowland seemed to have a complaint about and found there seems to be no grounds for any action by the department." His face was bland, inoffensive.

David blinked. This was the fastest attempted brush-off he'd ever heard of.

"I don't understand. This was concerning the arrest the other night of two men in East Los Angeles . . ."

The sergeant picked up a folder. "Yes. I have all the facts here. You seemed to think there was some misconduct on the part of the officers . . ."

"I don't seem to think anything. I was there. I saw police in battle helmets with shotguns pointed at people, one of them deliberately bumped a man, then they beat him and . . ."

"Hold on a second," the sergeant said quietly, pressing a buzzer. In a moment a voice answered. "Ask Jack to come in, will you please?" He didn't wait for an answer. "Being quite truthful with you, I personally didn't interrogate the officers involved . . ."

"Why didn't you?"

"Because I have assistants who are quite able. I read all the reports concerning the matter, including the report by Jack Flowers, who will be here in a second. He talked to the officers involved."

The door at the rear, through which the sergeant had entered, opened and a well-shaped, handsome Negro of perhaps thirty entered. He wore a dark stylish suit and his hair was well cropped. He nodded to the sergeant and looked with friendly interest at Stiver.

"Jack," the sergeant said, "this is Mr. Stiver. Mr. Stiver, this is Officer Jack Flowers, also of the Internal Affairs Division. He questioned the officers involved."

Jack Flowers smiled broadly as he stepped to David and extended his hand.

"Glad to meet you, Mr. Stiver," he said. His face still held friendly interest.

"The same," Stiver said.

The sergeant continued. "Mr. Stiver had a complaint about the case. That's why we put you on it, Jack." To Stiver, "We look into every reported incident of misconduct that comes to our attention."

Jack Flowers: "Yes, a department can never be sure when it has a bad apple or two, so we check out every story." He smiled broadly. "It's a lot of leg work, but that's what we're here for."

Stiver realized that, except for a few traffic citations, he had never come in contact with a policeman. Well, by God, I'm not afraid to speak up, he told himself.

"The sergeant here just informed me that an investigation revealed no evidence of any misconduct by a policeman in that arrest on the east side the other night," Stiver said confidently.

The sergeant cut in quickly, "I never said we had an investigation. I said we looked into it."

"Well, whatever you call it, then. Anyway, I have here the newspaper clipping of the incident . . ." He pulled out the clipping and read, "'CROWD TRIES TO TAKE PRISONERS—A crowd of more than one hundred persons attempted to take two prisoners from police custody in East Los Angeles last night' . . ." He put down the clipping. "This report isn't true. This is your version of . . ."

The sergeant spoke: "We have no control—nor do we want any—over the free press. What the paper prints is none of our . . ."

"Then how did they get this information? There was no newspaperman present when this happened."

Flowers smiled. "How do you know there wasn't?"

"Because I was there, that's how." Flowers was only momentarily chagrined. "But I want to know, if this isn't your version, whose is it?"

"Our police blotter is open to representatives of the free press. We have no right, under ordinary conditions, to withhold information of public interest—nor do we want to." The sergeant had a particular manner he used when repeating this last phrase, David noted.

"Well, then, it *is* just your version."

"If you have differences with the reporting done by the newspaper, you should take it up with them," the sergeant said politely.

"Now wait a minute. Wait a minute. Let's don't get sidetracked by this newspaper business. The other night I saw the most flagrant example of atrocious behavior imaginable by police. I saw a mob of friendly people threatened with shotguns, a man tricked into seemingly knocking down an officer . . ."

Flowers cut in, "The officer said the man tried to knock him down. He arrested him for assaulting a police officer and interfering with an arrest."

"Assaulting a police officer my ass!" Stiver was becoming angry. He noted the policemen showed no sign of annoyance. "That's the phoniest thing I ever heard of!"

"That's not what the officer involved claims, or more than a dozen others who saw it, claim."

"Then they're lying!"

The sergeant spoke quietly: "Then you're suggesting that the officers who filed their reports of that incident were deliberately falsifying the evidence?"

"If that's what they all said, yes. They were lying through their teeth."

Officer Flowers looked serious. "If what you say is true, then this is corruption among the police of this department—this falsifying of evidence."

"All right, then. It's corruption. But I know what I saw."

"You know, I know Doc Howell out there at the university. He's head of Police Sciences."

"I know him too," Stiver snapped.

"Well," the sergeant's tone was a tiny bit menacing, "according to many surveys and many reports by independent, non-vested interest groups, the Los Angeles Police Department enjoys the most corruption-free personnel of any police department in the nation."

"That's a well-known fact," Officer Flowers put in. "Doc Howell out there could verify that."

"And here you are trying to tell us just the opposite is true. That a dozen policemen will conspire to falsify evidence—and that's a felony, by the way—and do it without any motive of personal gain. I don't see how you expect us to believe we have that kind of policemen, when even the *Reader's Digest* in at least two different articles has pointed out the non-corruptibility of our force," the sergeant said reasonably.

"Yes, I know all about that. But I'm beginning to see some things a little differently now. I'm telling you, charging that man with assaulting an officer is the most hideous thing . . ."

"Incidentally," the sergeant put in quietly, "although the charge could have been made to stick, it was dropped. Even though many police officers at the scene were ready to swear he assaulted the officer."

Flowers took over, "We have a policy of, when a suspect becomes unreasonable and infracts too many statutes, trying to drop as many of the more serious charges against him. We're not out to persecute anyone. That man was originally charged with assaulting an officer, resisting arrest, interfering with an arrest and drunk. All but the last charge was dropped."

Stiver was a little at a loss.

"I'd like to be able to say that was nice of you, but the thing was phony from the beginning. You police were out to get somebody. Just because of the area . . ."

In the presence of Officer Flowers, Stiver realized how weak an accusation of discrimination would sound. He was a little confused, unsure.

"If we want to 'get somebody,' as you put it, would we have dropped all the serious charges against this man?"

"You might have, knowing you couldn't make it stick . . ."

Flowers, smiling, "Believe me, Mr. Stiver. With more than a dozen witnesses, all completely incorruptible, all veteran officers with good records, those charges could be made to stick. I know. I don't know how much you've been around courtroom procedure, but . . ."

Stiver was aware his mounting anger put him at a disadvantage among cooler heads. "Wait 'til this comes to court. He'll have fifty witnesses that he wasn't even drunk. They'll all fight this frameup . . ." Too late, he saw a look of gratification, triumph, in their eyes.

The sergeant spoke as quietly as ever, "Evidently you didn't know the two men taken that night went to court this morning and pleaded guilty to drunk and disturbing the peace and drunk."

Stiver sat, silenced. "No. I didn't know that," he said finally.

"Well, you see, this is what happens when you don't understand these things. Now if either of those men had any complaints about an injustice being inflicted on them, they certainly wouldn't have pleaded guilty. To anything. I know *I* wouldn't. Would you, Officer Flowers?"

Flowers smiled genially. "I sure wouldn't. There's no

power in the world that can force you to make a confession against your will in *this* country. You think we used the 'third degree'?"

Stiver was exasperated. He sat back, pushing a hand through his hair, not knowing where to start again.

"All right, now listen. I'm getting nowhere. I'm a resident of this town. I want satisfaction. I think you've done a lousy job of looking into this thing. I think your eyes are closed to any misconduct."

The sergeant picked up a printed pamphlet.

"We make regular reports on this sort of thing. For the city. It's all a matter of public record, including the fact that fifty percent of all brutality charges investigated by the Police Department are confirmed, and action is taken. Do you believe that?"

Stiver hesitated. The sergeant held what he knew was proof of what he had just said in his hand, waiting.

Officer Flowers took it up. "And fifty percent confirmation by a department is probably the highest rate in the country. Does that sound like we're trying to conceal misconduct or brutality?"

"No . . . I guess it doesn't. But I'm not so sure you've really investigated this to the fullest extent . . ." He noticed the sergeant and Officer Flowers glance fleetingly at one another. He concentrated. "But wait . . . you say half of all cases investigated are confirmed and action taken?"

"That's right. No other department . . ."

Stiver cut in. "But when I first came in, you, sergeant, made it a point to point out you didn't say this incident was investigated, didn't you?"

The police officers looked at each other.

"Is that the catch? In that report to the citizens there?

'Fifty percent of all cases *investigated.*' That's what you mean, isn't it?"

Neither answered. Stiver continued. "All right, tell me this. Is this incident we're talking about here going into the record as one you've investigated?"

He waited. They looked at him. "I'm waiting for an answer, Sergeant."

Impatiently, "Look, Mr. Stiver. We're very busy. I told you we looked into this and found there's nothing to investigate."

"How do I know you looked into it?"

The sergeant smiled. "You'll just have to take my word for it. If you think we're going to pull fifteen men out of the field just to interrogate them in front of you, you're mistaken. This thing has been handled in the usual manner."

"Okay. Then tell me who decides whether a case warrants 'investigation' or not. Tell me who, and I'll go see him. I'm wasting my time here."

"You're also wasting our time, Mr. Stiver. If you don't like the way this police department is run, go see City Hall."

"I did. They sent me here saying you handle this sort of thing. Are you the one who decides whether an incident gets investigated or not?"

"Yes, I am." Angrily.

Stiver stood silent by his chair. "I see. A dead end, eh? And what about those people," he pointed, "out there? Who do they go to if they think they've been abused?"

The sergeant's composure had returned. "If they have a legitimate complaint it's handled through the proper channels."

"And what are the proper channels?"

Mildly, "Through this office. We'll hear any complaint and take some action."

"Even if that action is a decision to take no action or not investigate." It wasn't a question. The sergeant shrugged.

"Look, kid. Your old man may be a big shot back east, but don't think you can come in here and tell us . . ."

"What do you know about my old man?"

They looked at him, inscrutable. "Tell me," he continued, "what do you know about me? Good God! Since yesterday you've already had me checked out?" He looked at them, demanding. "Answer me! You've investigated me? Tell me, what'd you come up with? Did you find out I played hooky twice in the seventh grade?"

They just stared. "You didn't think the facts in this case warranted an investigation. But you had me checked out two thousand miles away."

His fury at being checked out was apparent, and as he turned to go neither policeman gave a parting word or gesture. At the door he turned back and looked at them. They remained motionless, awaiting his departure, faces blank. He looked hard at the sergeant first, then at Officer Flowers.

"Shit!" he said and walked out.

He dozed, awakening slowly. The afternoon sunlight streamed in between the nearly closed drapes of the window on the west wall of his bedroom. She was up and hadn't noticed he was awake, watching her. *Mariana, Mariana,* he said to himself as he watched her pull the simple cotton capris over her softly full hips and rump and then pull on her loose jersey. Her leather sandals seemed to put themselves on her feet and then she was in front of the mirror, stroking her shoulder-length black hair with the brush she now kept in his dresser drawer. Odd, he thought, how with other girls, afterward it was always an effort to keep from saying, "Okay, now get away from me and leave me alone." And now he wanted to get up and talk to her, listen to what she had to say, enjoy being the object of her attention. Now she was straightening things, putting books on the shelf, hanging a sweater or jacket in his closet. She suddenly saw something on the closet floor and stooped to pick it up. She looked at him and saw he was awake.

"David! Is that what you did with this cowhide I brought you? Just threw it on the closet floor?"

He sat up and stretched. "Honest, I haven't had time to find a place to hang it. I really like it, old as it is."

"That's the beauty of it. It looks like it came from another century, and it did."

"Is that the one I saw at your grandfather's?"

"Not the same one. He had two. There's evidently a real story behind them. He told me his father—my great-grandfather, had many when they decided to come here, and the family traded them off for food and shelter on the way. Only two were left and he gave me one. And I gave it to you and you threw it on the floor in your closet."

"I'm sorry," he said, sitting on the edge of the bed.

"It belongs on the couch in the living room," she said walking out of the bedroom. "Come on, get up. We've got to have this place ready for your mother and father. They'll be arriving in a few hours, you know."

When he walked into the living room, dressed, she was emptying ashtrays, stuffing old newspapers and magazines into a wastebasket. She held up a clipping that had been on a table. "You want to save the newspaper clipping about the arrests . . . that night?"

He suddenly seemed weary. "Yes, I suppose so. That seems to be the only thing to show for my efforts." He gave her a little despairing smile, "I'm sorry I failed you, Mariana. But I tried. For two months now. But the newspapers say it's dead copy, too old now. And nobody else will listen. Or else they send me back to that sergeant."

She came to him and put her hands on his face. He put his arms around her, his hands running up and far down her back. "You tried, David. As hard as you could. That's all anyone can do. And I love you more for it. And I intend to tell your mother and father about what a shining knight you've turned out to be."

He turned away. "Oh, I wouldn't do that just yet," he said, evasiveness creeping into his attitude. "Besides . . . I guess my mother's not . . . going to be on the plane."

She had turned back to her work but now she stopped.

"Your mother's not coming? How come?"

"Well, I guess she had . . . lots of things to do. She's awfully busy, you know, and after all, this was originally just a business trip for Dad. And I suggested they make it a visit. But Marge is coming. You'll love her, Mariana. She's really tops."

"Yes, you've told me all about her. But your mother. I'm really sorry she couldn't come. You did tell her about me when you went home last month, didn't you?"

"Yes, of course I did."

"Well, I'm disappointed she can't come. I . . ."

"Mariana," with a little irritation, "it's not like we were engaged . . . or something . . ."

She looked at him, then lowered her eyes to the floor, nodding slightly. "Yes, David, you're right. It's not like we were going to be married . . . or something."

He stepped to her and pulled her into his arms. "Now look here. There's no reason for you to feel . . . like you're feeling. It's not at all like you think . . ."

She gazed with wistful intensity into his face, and her voice was soft. "You really have a good thing going, don't you, David?" And she twisted away. He caught her.

"Mariana, we've never had a quarrel yet. Let's don't start. Dad and Marge will be here soon. Let's show them a good time."

As she looked up at him the serious lines left her face and a smile, only slightly forced, came. She hugged his chest suddenly. "Sure," she said cheerily, "come on, now. There's just time for me to pick up this place while you make us a snack, then you've got to run me home while I change and then we're off to the airport."

As he fixed sandwiches in the kitchen he called to her, "You're not nervous at all over meeting Dad and Marge, are you?"

She called back, "There's no reason I should be," and she waited just the right length of time, ". . . is there, David." It was not a question, and her tone made him feel miserable.

S tiver wondered how it looked to Mariana as he shook hands with his father and pecked his sister on the cheek at the airport. Here it is, he thought. Here what is? Had he really brought them together just for his own amusement? No, he hadn't, he reasoned. He was watching for their reaction when they realized the cream-colored girl was the one he was with. He noticed the eyes of both of them caught Mariana and held firmly as they turned to meet her. What were they expecting, anyway . . .

Keen interest, admiration, friendliness, he saw in his sister and father as he introduced each. Mariana stood tall, as she always did, her shyness scantily clad, her lips clipping her words to give them that trace of accent which conveyed the fact that she was crossing a gap to meet on their terms. Only when she smiled was it evident she was not yet out of her teens.

David's father, doing his best not to be a typical father, or a typical successful businessman, or a typical anything, was remarkably unobnoxious, David thought affectionately as Mr. Stiver mumbled something about being very pleased and charmed to meet Mariana. Marge was a good deal more original, genuine, with, "Honestly, how does a girl who looks like you, expect a woman my age to like you!" Then Marge laughed. Good girl, David thought, she could make even the most reluctant cynic like her almost immediately.

Mariana and Marge followed as the four rode the conveyor toward the street entrance to the building. David heard Marge rattling on, ". . . Closer to thirty than I am to twenty and don't give me that 'you don't look it' stuff."

His father, ". . . hope you're as hungry as I am, I can never eat much on a plane. Let's go to that hotel out on Sunset . . ."

They sat in the dark dining room, Mr. Stiver trying to crack the shell of his lobster quietly, Marge savoring her large salad, David and Mariana picked at their food.

"I'm glad you were able to come out here with your father," Mariana said to Marge. Marge finished a mouthful.

"Well, actually, Dad's afraid to leave me behind. He thinks I might get married again. He lives in dread of having an oft-married daughter on his hands."

"Marge!" Mr. Stiver said with polite annoyance. "You make it sound like you'd been married a half dozen times, instead of just once."

"Once and a half," she shot back. Then to Mariana: "I'm the family skeleton. An old divorcée at twenty-five. Dad drove my first husband away," she turned to him. "Thank you, Dad, by the way." She kissed two fingers and patted them on his lips.

"Marge, please don't say your 'first husband.' It sounds . . ."

"Well he was my first husband. That doesn't necessarily mean I've had others, just that he won't be my last. I hope. So do you."

"And as for my driving him away . . ."

Marge interrupted. "Yes, that is unfair of me. Dad really didn't. My husband became disenchanted when he found out he was expected to work at the sales management job Dad gave him."

Mariana laughed a little uncomfortably.

David spoke to her. "Mariana, one thing I must tell you. Marge thinks it's chic . . . or . . . sophisticated to speak openly about family affairs. I . . ."

"Oh, for Christ sake, David, quit apologizing for me. I don't think anything of the sort. If I hide something, then I'm an inhibited Puritan. If I don't, then I'm trying to be sophisticated. I just don't give a darn."

Mr. Stiver spoke next. "Mariana, you're a native of these parts?"

"Yes. I was born in . . . Los Angeles. My mother too. We're what you call natives, I guess."

"What is your father in?"

"He does construction work. I don't really know much about what he does."

Marge looked up from her salad. "By the way, Dad, what do you do?"

He looked a little annoyed. Marge laughed.

"Really, Mariana, I know what he does. But I don't know *how* he does it. He owns a company that sells class. For the mass. Company motto: Class delivered to your door."

Mariana smiled at Mr. Stiver. "Sounds interesting."

"Hell of it is, she's right. I have a door-to-door sales business. It's unique. At least I think it is, even though my son and daughter think it's funny . . ."

David cut in: "Dad! I don't think it's humorous. I never said . . ."

"I do," Marge said. "I think it's a riot. Dad has hundreds of salesmen going door to door, selling Rembrandt copies, prints of wall drawings of primitive man, lamps made out of Early American butter churns or spinning wheels, which he had made in Japan, incidentally. He even sells antique electric clocks, can you imagine."

Mr. Stiver was smiling. "And all this seems atrocious to my offspring, but not to me. When I started this business, a long time ago by the way, I felt I was filling a great need. I still feel that way. The people my men call on would ordinarily never buy anything like . . . like the things Marge just mentioned. No one ever before brought items of culture to the front door of Mr. and Mrs. John Q."

"With nothing down, ninety days to pay," Marge footnoted. "But Dad, please don't call them items of culture. This girl here probably has more artistic-ness in her little finger than we all have put together. She'd get a big laugh out of one of your

Aztec calendars which you have carved in Spain out of imitation Italian marble."

"That's not true," Mariana said earnestly. "I know nothing about art. I think if you can offer facsimiles of masterpieces you are filling a great need. Even if they are mass produced."

Mr. Stiver beamed. "Thank you, Miss Sando . . . I know you'll forgive me being unable to say your name."

"Sando-*val*," Mariana said. "Accent on the last syllable." She said the name with an explosive "ball" on the end.

Marge mused. "If I could develop an accent like you have I'd drive 'em crazy. You don't have a brother, do you?"

"Yes."

Marge brightened. "How old is he?"

David was only half listening to the patter. He thought of Sammy. And then of Sammy with Marge. And he saw, nothing to do with age difference, how ridiculous it was. Was he missing the ridiculousness of himself and Mariana somehow? As they talked he tried to picture her ten years hence in Illinois.

He couldn't make the picture come. She didn't fit. All right then, in East L.A. Yes, in a kitchen apron, dark children crawling on the floor, men like her father in steel helmets talking loudly as she served chili, warmed a bottle, poured wine, her jet hair perhaps in a kerchief, laughing and talking as shrilly as her gentle voice could to compete with the loud voices and the crying, tripping over a large dog lying in the middle of the kitchen floor, as oblivious to the goings-on as the other people. He imagined he could see the strength born in Mariana, a strength perhaps the result of a heritage of resignation, that could enable her to go through any amount of physical discomfort or hardship. He could see, comparing his sister to her, that it would kill

Marge to live in a two-room East L.A. shack for twenty years. And it would kill Mariana to find social rejection in Illinois, whereas Marge spat at the mention of rejection by his mother's social circle.

He was dragged back: ". . . Father hates sociology . . . don't butt in, Dad, you do too—I'm talking to her. You know, some kids, to spite their folks, turn hippie, or take dope. David takes sociology," she slowed to take a bite of food and added, "Some become divorcées . . ."

David saw the reason and logic for the seemingly senseless chatter Marge put out. The poor girl, he thought. Always desperately trying to help someone. She was trying to give Mariana a good family picture, let her really see the Stivers as they were, phony, yes, but real people too. Marge always tried to make things appear as they really were.

Mariana began making those almost imperceptible motions that mean a woman is ready to leave. "Really, I have things to do, David. I know you'd like to visit more with your sister right now, so why don't you let your father drop me off. I'd like a chance to talk to him." David agreed and gave the keys to his father.

"Nothing short of driving with a girl like you could make me face the Los Angeles freeways and smog," Mr. Stiver said sincerely.

She gave Mr. Stiver instructions and they drove silently for some minutes. She looked at him. "I guess it's an old, old story, isn't it?" and tears came as she suddenly bowed her head.

He nodded, eyes on the road, but his face suddenly showed lines that hadn't been there before. After a long pause, "I guess no father should ever be shocked. If he raises a son to manhood. Does David know?"

"No. And I won't let him, if it means he thinks it'll wreck his life." She looked up, blinking with determination.

"But he should. What about your parents?"

She thought a minute before answering. "I don't suppose you'd understand this, but they feel . . . it's kind of a custom to believe, that when a girl gets pregnant it's only her fault. Every man has the right to try to seduce every girl he can. And he should be responsible for a child only if it's his wife who has a baby."

Mr. Stiver nodded. "European style, sort of. But what are you going to do?"

She shrugged. "That's up to David. I'll find out how he feels, and if it will upset his life's plans, I'll just stay home with Mom and Dad and have the child. I won't be the first this has happened to. Or the ten-thousandth."

"But . . . you don't understand, Mariana. It's different, in a way. The law says that as long as David has a child anywhere he is responsible for that child . . ."

"Yes, I know. Among us . . . my people, an illegitimate child is another kid to have around. But in David's world it would make the difference in whether a certain family would allow him to marry a daughter, or whether he was socially acceptable or not, or whether Mr. Richpants would make him a superintendent of a factory. Mr. Stiver, as David's pregnant girlfriend, I represent a threat to him bigger than anything in the world. I don't think he wants to get married to anybody, maybe especially me. And when he knows I'm having his baby I'll be like a cannonball tied to his leg. He'll hate me. There's not the slightest doubt in my mind that I've lost him. Maybe I have a few more weeks, a month or two maybe, to be the girl in his life. That's all."

He looked at her and saw a pride and strength he'd never seen in anyone else.

"Then what will you do?"

She smiled, not a sad smile. "I'll stay home with Mom and Dad. Like I said, it isn't the first time this ever happened."

They rode silently again for a time. Then he said, "Mariana, I want you to know . . . that I'm positive . . . there's no doubt it could only be David's."

She put her hand on his on the steering wheel. "Thank you," she said softly with a soft smile.

He drove, looking straight ahead. Then, "I don't know where I failed . . ."

"You didn't! It's not your fault things are the way they are. You can't be blamed for anything."

"But . . . then, how, what can I do? How can I help . . . ? "

"There's no way you can help. There's nothing you can do. Except maybe learn that there are some things you can't do anything about. David wouldn't accept any help from you. Or advice. You getting involved in this would only make you two be farther apart."

He dropped her off, assuring her he knew how to get to David's apartment, making her promise she'd come see them off at the airport. He asked to come in to meet her parents and she looked at him, shaking her head, and said, "Why?"

David wanted to walk the ten blocks to his apartment, but Marge insisted on a cab. As he let her in and, without asking, began to make her a highball, she looked around.

"Not a half bad place. Dad keeps you in pretty good style, I'd say."

"You don't do bad by him yourself," David answered.

She took the drink and sat down. "She's a lovely person, David. You're in love with her, aren't you?"

He seemed to become irritable. "I think she's the greatest. Sweet girl, and all that."

Marge looked at him fondly. "Dearest brother. How do you get in these . . . ?"

"These what? For chrissake, I'm not in anything. I just have a beautiful Latin girlfriend."

"Fine. Okay. You're not in anything. Just in love with an adorable Mexican girl, that's all. Why don't you take her home to Mama, like you did that Coulter bitch last year? Mom thought she was the greatest."

He went to the kitchen and poured himself one, talking as he did. "Mom, you know her, doesn't understand everything. But if I felt like it, I would. If I wanted to marry this girl, nothing would stop me." He returned and took a seat.

"My ass, nothing would stop you."

Stiver laughed a little. "You know, you're the only attractive babe I ever knew who could say vulgar things and remain just as attractive. If Mariana ever said that . . ." His voice trailed off.

She sipped and looked knowingly at him. "That's how it is, huh? Mariana this, Mariana that. You know, David, I envy you tremendously, being able to fall in love. I can't. I go with or marry whatever man is the least repugnant."

He remained silent, thinking a moment. "Maybe you're right, Marge. But it doesn't matter. Mom and Dad have done too good a job on us. We have to fit in where our nests are made back home. Even you, who think you haven't fit in well, are acting out the part written for you. Things are the way they are and they won't change. You don't know about Mariana. It's an entirely different world. The fact that Mom would have a breakdown if I brought her home doesn't really make much difference. It's a million other things that would make life too complicated with her. And our life with our phony standards and values is complex enough without taking on a lifetime project of reshaping round holes to fit square pegs. I guess I love Mariana, but it will be over soon and that'll be the end of it. It can't be any other way."

"Attaboy, Davey. You always were made out of the stuff that knuckles under."

He looked at her sharply. "Don't get bitchy with me, Marge."

"I'll get bitchy with anybody I please. God! If I'd ever had something going with somebody outside our rat-race, how quick I would have chucked it all."

"That's easy to say, but nothing's ever stopped you. You love the way things are for us. You snub the tennis set and all that, but you really belong to the class Dad's money put us in."

"Tell me, David. When you started out as a sociology major, did you ever really plan to get your degree and then go out and become a five-hundred-dollar-a-month social worker? Or go with the Peace Corps?"

He was downcast. "No. I always knew I'd go to Dad and say, 'Okay, I'll take your area superintendent job.' I was just having a rebellious fling. But it's different now. I plan to go into Dad's business—some day I'll run it for him—and I'll implement a hundred ideas I have about equal opportunity employment, advancement. Really, I . . ."

"David, if bullshit was music you'd be a symphony orchestra. So this is how you rationalize not having the courage to marry the girl you love. You're trying to tell yourself you're making a great sacrifice so that later you can be in a position to make changes. Good Christ! I've really heard it all now. At least I hoped you would have some original excuse for being afraid to face up to Mother."

He felt his face grow red from the smart of truth. He remembered how it had been when he'd flown home for spring vacation. In grand style he'd broken the news he was going with "a fine Mexican girl," then realized such a statement conformed to the consensus that all Mexican girls weren't necessarily fine.

He recalled with a twinge of bitterness the conversation with his mother. She was about to leave the house to attend a meeting. As always, she was dressed rather conservatively but stylish, her clothes worn to emphasize subtly her still-in-the-thirties look, although she readily admitted to being several years older.

"David, I really would love to meet your little Spanish girl, in spite of the fact you think I'm . . ." She paused at his look of acute irritation, "What's the matter, dear? Now what'd I say?"

David thought a moment, then put his finger on it.

"She's not little. What makes you think she's little? She's five feet six. Taller than you."

"I . . . did I say she was little? I certainly didn't mean to. But now that you call me on *that*, I understand those people are smaller than . . . well, than the average. Aren't they?"

"Maybe yes, maybe no. Perhaps they were a generation ago. But she's not. No, Mother, funny I'd never heard the slur in such an innocent sounding thing as 'little Spanish girl,' but it's there."

Now his mother looked exasperated. "David! Good grief. There is no slur in what I said. 'Little Spanish girl' is just . . . an expression, that's all. Is that more of what sociology has taught you?"

"No, Mother. What you really meant is, let's see . . . insignificant. Yes. You had no reason to know or care how big she is. 'Little Spanish girl' is an expression of contempt, whether you realize it or not. It has nothing to do with how tall you think she is. And she's Mexican. Not Spanish." Mrs. Stiver thought a moment. "I was just being kind when I said 'Spanish,' David. I'm sure she's a lovely girl, and she wouldn't appreciate being called Mexican . . ." She stopped as she saw David's complete attitude of exasperation. "We can't even talk to each other hardly any more, can we, David?"

David looked straight at her. "Hardly."

"I guess we don't understand one another."

There was a little pause before he answered. "I understand you, Mother," and she had left to attend a meeting of the volunteer workers for her church group's Project Ghetto.

God! What a disaster that had been, his attempt to reach his mother. He now sat looking at Marge. She looked at him. And suddenly they both smiled.

"Look," she said with spirit. "Dad and I are on a visit here, and we're sitting here talking about miserable life. We only have tonight and tomorrow, so let's liven things up and quit commiserating."

A knock sounded at the door. David rose. "Ah, Dad's found his way back. He promised us a big night out on him. Let's get going."

They sat, the three of them, watching a floorshow after dinner. Marge danced and flirted. David watched and laughed. Mr.

Stiver studied his two children and said little. Toward the end of the evening Marge looked at him. "Dad! What's the matter? You look like you're almost crying."

He cleared his head, knowing he had drunk a little too much.

"I'm . . . so inadequate," he murmured, and then laughed at the floorshow. They didn't hear him.

3

Saturday. Pete and Minnie had gone visiting. Sammy was off somewhere. "I'll tell him today," she said as she dialed his number. But she wondered if she would.

His voice: "Hello?"

"Hi."

"Hi. It's a nice Saturday."

"Got your studying done?"

"Yeah. You?"

"Uh huh. How about a drive?"

"To where?"

"Oh, a place out in the country, kind of."

"Lonely there?"

"We can talk."

"Pick you up in an hour."

"I'm waiting."

I'll tell him out there in the country, tell him how much I want his baby. But she wondered if she would. Very shortly now, it would be graduation for him. He wouldn't be able to tell. She could let him go back to Illinois not knowing, completely free from any pressure to make his choice. And she knew what his choice would be. She knew that, when she said good-bye to him this summer, she would never see him again. No matter what he said. Yes, he would promise, and be sincere, that he would come back, but once back home, he would make himself forget. And there were plenty of other girls that would help him forget. She busied herself making the hour pass, and then she heard his car.

"I'll show you where I go when I want to get away to the country without leaving the city," she said as she directed him to a dry river which cut through the commercial and industrial section of East Los Angeles. He parked and Mariana led David by the hand as she picked her way across the wide, rocky stretch of sand, dry except for the tiny trickling stream in the center. Reaching the stream, she picked a large boulder to sit on and removed her shoes, letting her feet dangle in the water.

"It's wonderful to be barefoot. If I had my way, no one would wear shoes." She looked at him as he stood watching her. "Take your shoes off, David. The stream feels good." He hesitated, and she smiled. "Are you afraid it won't look dignified? Come on. You can be undignified with me."

He found another rock and sat on it, unlacing his shoes.

"By God, I will. No one can call me stuffy and get away with it."

The morning sunlight was gathering impetus. Shimmering heat waves above the river bottom warned that the cool rocks and sand would soon be fiery hot. The homes, buildings, and streets of the cities surrounding them were hidden by the dense shrubs and trees lining the river banks several hundred yards away on each side of them. No sounds could be heard except that of the tiny stream and fiercely hissing insects, whose noise seemed to magically jump from one hiding place to another. He watched her as she smoothed her hair, straightened her dress, the while gazing around at the white sand and white boulders and it occurred to him that had he not known her well he would have sworn her every movement was calculated to accent her gracious beauty.

"Don't you just love summer weather?" she said quietly, still scanning the surroundings.

Stiver undid the next button down on his shirt. He could feel drops of perspiration forming on his skin.

"I didn't think anyone liked hot weather."

"Oh, yes. It's the best time of all. The happiest times of my life were in the summer." She seemed pensive.

"Tell me about the happy times."

She regarded the river bed around them. "As far back as I can remember, when it was summer I'd put on just a pair of boy's trunks each morning, and that was all I'd wear till bed time. We'd find a lawn with a sprinkler and run through it all day. Squirting each other with a hose, filling paper bags with water and throwing them." Her face reflected the fond memories, then clouded a little. He was observing her closely.

"Then there was some unpleasantness," he guessed.

"No, not really," she said, gathering her thoughts to put into words. "It was just . . . well, growing up. While I was little, it was just a lot of fun, nothing but fun, each summer. Running from one little lawn to another. Sometimes we'd find the kind of sprinkler that squirts water around in a circle, sometimes one that throws a shower straight up. We'd fight, wrestle and play all day. Then one day, I don't think I was much over ten, I started to . . . grow up. Mom came to find me and I was wrestling with a boy a year or so older. He had his hands on me in places he shouldn't have, I guess," she smiled a little self-consciously. "Mom became furious when she saw. She ran right into the water and jerked him off me. She almost twisted his ear off. He howled and she called him a 'cholito.' Then . . ."

"A what?"

"A 'cholito'." She thought a moment. "That means . . . well, a cholo is a dirty name for Mexican. A dirty little Mexican. That's what it means. Then I remember she took us both, the boy and me, to his parents and told them what she'd seen him do. His father whipped him right there in front of us. Then Mom took me home and began lecturing me about how my body was developing and from now on I'd have to watch every boy who came near me, or they'd put their hands on me to try to take my pants off and even worse. I wondered for a year or two what 'worse' was. She took me to a store and bought me a one-piece girl's bathing suit. And ever after that, I could never go into the sprinklers, or hardly anything else, without Mom or Dad being along." She smiled a little wistfully. "I guess that was the end of a beautiful age. When I started filling out. The world changed. Sometimes I wish I wasn't considered beautiful. Some girls I like who are homely, they don't enjoy being around me." Her voice trailed off as she sat reflecting.

"You're the first woman I've ever known to complain of being beautiful," he said half jokingly.

"But it has been difficult. And so unnecessary and . . . un-fair. Do you know what it's done to Sammy?"

He was curious. "No."

She went on. "Always, Dad has waved him aside and paid attention to me. Not only Dad, but everyone else. To look at him now, you'd never guess it but he's been hurt so deeply that I think he really hates us all. Worse than that, I think he hates himself. When you're attractive, people pay attention to you. All people. Teachers, relatives, family, friends. And you learn faster. Once I got a head start on everything over Sammy, it was quite impossible for him to catch up. When I reached out to help him a few times, he'd almost start sobbing and just refuse to have anything to do with me." She looked up at David earnestly. "Are you psychologist enough to figure that out?"

He looked down humbly. "No, I'm afraid not. But I don't think you can lay the blame for what's happened to Sammy completely on yourself. And even if you can, it serves no purpose. But go on. Tell me more about the problems of being gorgeous."

She smiled shyly. "Oh, I suppose I should be thankful. But, it was in grade school I started to be sort of the representative of the class, or the school. In high school I once refused and I got the reputation of being a terrible snob. So now I accept. Like next week. I've been chosen to represent the business school in the 'Days of the Dons' fiesta."

" 'Days of the Dons' fiesta?"

"Yes. You know. It's one of those things they always have everywhere here in California. They close off a few streets by the old mission and have a two- or three-day celebration, early California style, to give everyone a glimpse into the days of the dons. I have to dress up in ranchero clothes and be in a little parade and pose for Chamber of Commerce pictures. Listen to speeches about 'our heritage,' greet newcomers and well-known personalities."

"This'll be next week? You didn't tell me."

"I'm sorry. But you'll enjoy it. There'll be booths all around selling Mexican food, art things, dancing, strolling mariachis. You've never been to one of these things?"

"No, it sounds like fun."

"I suppose it is. All the local Anglo politicians and officials talk on how picturesque is the heritage of 'our Latin friends,' and how great has been the Latin contribution to present-day society." She smiled. "I know most of it by heart, having been in a half dozen of these things." She rose. "Which reminds me. The school is paying for my costumes and I have to have them fitted today. The least I can do is have them fit well. We wouldn't want anyone to think my early California ancestors were poorly tailored. Come on." She took his hand and pulled him up. She walked ahead as they returned to the parked car, carrying her shoes in her hand. He watched her creamy-tan calves, and it seemed to him she had an outdoor girl's legs . . . and arms . . . and body . . .

"By the way, I don't think I told you, I've been doing a little research on early California history. And your California ancestors *were* well tailored and well dressed."

"Oh?"

"Yeah. And I'll bet you didn't know there's an old California family still here by the name of Sandoval."

"Uh huh. I met them once. At a days-of-the-dons festival. Or rather, I met the old lady—she's about seventy—and a Sandoval grandson. I was crowned Fiesta Maid, or some such thing, by the grandson."

"What kind of a guy was he?" He was aware of a stab of jealousy. Why? Simple. This Sandoval character would have an inside track with an impressionable girl like Mariana. He no doubt had looks, wealth, manners, spoke Spanish, had prestige . . .

"He was the usual kind. He'd been drinking too much and

had trouble keeping his hands to himself. The likes-to-play-with-peasant-girls type. I straightened him out in a hurry."

He held the car door open for her and when he was driving he pursued the subject. "How'd you straighten him out? Don't tell me! You cussed him out in Spanish."

She laughed. "No, what I did was a little more effective—and subtle—than that. When I spoke to him I used the familiar form."

Stiver pondered a moment. "Familiar form . . . how do you mean?"

"In Spanish there're two ways to talk to someone. Formal and familiar. It's kind of complicated, but in a situation like that I certainly should have used the polite, formal way. I said nice things, but in the familiar. It's . . . too complicated to explain. Doing that could have been a compliment, as you use it to talk to children, brothers and sisters or close friends. Improperly, it can show . . . what's the word I want . . . contempt. And it's pointed."

They drove without talking a while. Then he said, "Well, anyway, I've researched a little and found out the town your grandparents came from in Mexico was formerly called Agua Clara. That means clear water, doesn't it? And I've sent off some inquiries to see if I can find out anything about your ancestors. Who knows, you might be a lost heir to a giant land grant, or something. Hope you don't mind."

"No. Be kind of interesting. But I doubt if there's any record of us anywhere."

"You'd be surprised. When you start looking into indexed archives you can usually come up with a mention of just about anybody's ancestors anywhere."

He braked to a stop in front of the business college and let her out. "I'll be in touch," she said with a quick kiss.

D avid Stiver moved over to the slow lane and took the off-ramp when he saw the green sign ARBOLEDA. He came out onto a broad street with heavy traffic, traffic signals at each corner. On either side were wide sidewalks with an occasional square missing out of which grew trees. A large banner streamed across the street overhead as he entered the city. It read:

4IST ANNUAL DAYS OF THE DONS CELEBRATION
Presented by the City of Arboleda Chamber of Commerce.

He noticed signs and decorations along both sides of the street, placed to lend a festive air. Driving on toward the center of the town he noticed many pedestrians dressed in early California, Mexican, or Spanish costume, all headed in the direction he was. The evening sun was still hot and bright and the rush-hour traffic was tapering off somewhat. Only occasionally, Stiver mused, could he detect a trace of California flavor: an old post office building with red tile roof and arches, a tavern with walls of simulated plastered adobe. In one block, dominating everything around it, was a giant Tahitian cocktail lounge and dining room, with crude lumber making a great pyramid over the roof, flaming torches set at angles above the sidewalk, outrigger canoes suspended above the windows.

Traffic grew heavier and slower as he approached the center of the town where he knew the fiesta was in progress. He found a parking place on the street and walked down the sidewalk. Foot traffic was in general moving in the same direction. He saw an old sedan laden with dark men pull up and park at the curb. The occupants jumped out carrying suitcases and instrument cases. These were musicians, he knew. They jabbered in Spanish as they hurried toward the fiesta, each wearing uniform work clothes with SANITATION DEP'T lettered on the back.

As he came to the next intersection he saw the street to the right was roped off. Throngs milled about dozens of booths and concession stands. The heavy odor of steaming Mexican food hung in the warm evening air. Large trees of various kinds grew on either side of the street, their foliage meeting overhead in the center to give a vague tunnel-like feeling to the fiesta street. He walked along leisurely, looking at the booths with art work and hand-crafted items, stands offering tacos and chili, clothing, displays of carretas and wagons built by school children for the occasion. In a tiny corral was tethered an ox, and David read with amusement the posted information telling of the use of oxen in the days of the dons. Groups of children walked about, waiting to take part in their particular facet of the fiesta. Some were sandy-haired and freckle-faced, some had the brown skin and smooth black hair of the Latin, some were Negro, but all were in costume; the girls in flowing ankle-length skirts with lace blouses, mantillas over the head and rebozos around the shoulders, the boys in tight colorful trousers which flared at the ankle, leather jackets with small balls at the wrists and sombreros.

Amidst a crowd gathered in the center of the street David saw the half-dozen sanitation department workers, now in the full regalia of mariachis, a mixture of Spanish dance costume and the garb of romantic Mexican ranch hands. All sang, while four played guitars and one shook gourds and one clapped rhythm sticks together.

Stiver walked past a display where children dressed as early Californians were pretending to be engaged in various nineteenth century occupations. Two girls were operating a grape press, while two boys cured hides. A girl was reading from a paper to the bystanders: ". . . following the overthrow of Spain in 1822, the vast holdings of the missions in California were secularized—that is, the lands were transferred from ecclesiastical use to civil or lay ownership, and great land grants were awarded to private citizens . . ." He walked on. Then he heard her say his name, softly, as though she knew that the unique gentle quality of her voice somehow could carry over almost any cacaphony. He turned and saw her seated within a mockup of a ranch veranda. She wore a flowing leather riding skirt, tight blouse with lace and close-fitting sleeves, a pearl comb in her hair with matching earrings. She sat on a rustic porch bench while a youth in skin-tight caballero attire pretended to serenade her. David had to laugh at her expression of polite boredom. He walked to the veranda rail and noticed the youth observe him sharply for an instant before making his face become blandly inscrutable.

"Hi," he said, "you're a lovely señorita being courted, aren't you?"

She smiled genuinely, seeming to take refreshment from his presence. The serenading youth's eyes darted briefly from Mariana to Stiver, then he walked down the steps and into the crowd.

"But I don't feel like being courted right here. It's too hot." She had a delicately carved ivory fan with which she fanned herself. David realized he was staring as he watched her take a small wadded kerchief and dab at the dampness on her neck. He felt himself transfixed as she tossed her hair and shrugged, and he thought no movie queen with the best of directors could have done those simple movements with more surety and feminine independence. Then she looked at him and he knew that if he hadn't been before, he was lost in love.

"Please don't be too bored . . ."

"I'm not," he insisted, "I think this is terrifically interesting." He glanced about at the fiesta.

"I only have to sit here another hour or so. Then the mayor of Arboleda will give a little talk on Latin heritage and legacy, I will present an award to the best children's display, and then," her voice lowered sincerely, "we'll go to a nice air-cooled apartment."

As soon as they were in his car driving away from the fiesta she started talking.

"I'm glad that's over. It's all so phony. That mayor and his 'our good Latin neighbors!' He'd been drinking. Could you tell? I came within one inch of telling him to keep his God damned gringo hands off me. I can't stand that, him trying to appear fatherly, or something. He even asked me how old I was and if I dated much. I told him my father was very strict with me. That always scares them. He would have tried to date me even though he introduced me to his wife. 'Isn't she a lovely little Spanish girl?' he said. Makes me sick. Let's go to your place. I have a change of clothes in my case."

He noticed she seemed peculiarly preoccupied as he drove. He tried to study her without its being obvious and thought he saw sadness, joy, wistfulness and anxiety cross her face. A gnawing worry returned to him. As they entered the apartment he tried to get a good look at her shape, but could detect nothing. What the hell, he said to himself, my intuition's working overtime. She went to the bedroom and he went to the kitchen for a bottle of beer. She called him.

"David?"

He came into the bedroom. She stood there in a bra and half slip, but he saw the seriousness in her face and he knew.

"David, you love me, don't you?"

He stood looking at her. No, this couldn't be happening. She wasn't going to say she was pregnant.

"You have something you want to tell me, don't you?"

She smiled, and he thought it was a pretty good carefree smile.

"Maybe. But afterwards." She moved toward him. He stiffened as she put her hands on him.

"Tell me now."

"No, it can wait. We don't have very long. Don't you want me anymore?"

"Tell me now."

"No. Nothing's more important than us being together."

"No. You're going to have a baby, aren't you?" His mouth was dry, he was trembling.

She stood in front of him, arms folded.

"Yes. I almost didn't tell you. You didn't have to know. You're leaving soon . . ."

"What do you mean, I didn't have to know? Thank God you told me while there's still time . . ."

She waited. "Time to what?"

He paced the bedroom now. "If you hadn't then I'd really

get a shock when I'm back home. 'David, you're the proud papa of a bouncing baby boy.' Wouldn't that be glad tidings."

She suddenly sat on the bed and slumped. As he looked at her he thought she looked completely lifeless. Lifeless . . .

"Well, thank God, there's time to do something about it."

She looked up at him and he saw her strength there.

"No," she said simply.

"Don't give me that 'no' stuff. You know what has to be."

"No, I don't know what has to be. I won't have an abortion."

"Look, Mariana, I know you people and your religion . . ."

"We *people!* What kind of talk is that?"

" . . . You know what I mean. I mean, I know how you believe, but I knew a kid back in Illinois who had this . . ."

"David," her voice was soft, "it's not a matter of religion. That has nothing to do with it. I want your baby, so it can remind me . . ."

"Remind you?" He was thinking fast. "Look, you think I'm going to run out on you? That I don't want you for my own? Well, you're wrong. But it has to be the right way. You don't know this sort of thing can ruin everything. Everything, for us. A baby now and we'd never have a life together."

She was looking at him. "You mean, there's a chance for us? We could be together?"

"That's just what I mean. But not if we go louse things up like this. It has to be right, the proper way. Proper plans, and all that. We just can't have a baby and then go back home and expect to have a life left for us."

"Oh, David. I never thought the day would come when I didn't believe you. But I don't. You're lying to me."

"I'm not lying. Look, Mariana, just leave things to me. Like I said, I knew a kid this happened to. He got the girl to a doctor who fixed her up like that. Nothing to it. Then they were able to have their life together and people never thought anything about it."

"I don't care what people think."

"But I do. It's important. And if you could realize what all we'd be throwing away by what everyone would call 'a moment of indiscretion' it'd be important to you too."

"So that's really what rules your life. What other people think. Maybe it's important what *I* think."

"What you think has nothing to do with having a meaningful life together. We can't just throw all that away. I promise you, I'll be able to get a doctor to fix it up. We'll have lost nothing . . ."

"If I could just believe you, David. If I knew there'd be more babies. But I don't. Can't you see? This is my only chance to have a little bit of you, to keep me close to the thought of how it would be if . . . things . . . the world, were a little different . . . then I'd say, yes, this one doesn't matter."

"Well, you *can* believe me. But for God's sake let's do the right thing so we can have a life together." He sat beside her and took her in his arms. She started crying. "Just say you will, Mariana." He held her away so he could look at her face. She continued to cry. "Nowadays it's a safe thing to have done . . ." and he heard himself recite statistics on how many women have abortions and how it was safer than childbirth.

"All right, David. All right. You have the right to expect to be believed. Maybe I'm all wrong about what means more to you than anything. Maybe I was right in letting you know, instead of letting you go home without telling you."

They sat on the edge of the bed as she dried her tears.

"That's better," he said. "Now, how about me making some hot chocolate. Feel like a cup?"

She nodded. He went into the kitchen and heated some milk in a pan. When he took it in to her he was surprised that she had gotten in bed instead of dressing.

"David," and her voice was low and uneven, "I want to stay all night with you."

He felt anger flare. "God! I still . . ." but he didn't finish. Mentally, he framed the sentence he'd almost spoken. *I still have a little decency left!* Now why would he say a thing like that? How would sleeping with her be indecent, and what made him think he'd *lost* some decency. *Good God, I'm screwed up,* he thought. "What about your folks?" he asked as he set the chocolate down and sat beside her, taking her hand.

"Yeah, what about them?" she said.

O n Sunday morning a week later David Stiver awoke and enjoyed only a few moments of rested, luxurious peace of mind before his weighty problem settled on his consciousness like a wet wool blanket. He got up and, still in his pajamas, made a pot of coffee. He took a cup into the bedroom and began dressing. He looked over at the bed. "Where she has lain," he thought, and then smiled when he realized it sounded like a love-stricken high school boy.

But he remembered vividly that first night. Mariana had been a living trap. A tender, living trap. Wasn't there a play by that name years ago? Yes, and he remembered thinking the name sounded positively obscene.

He glanced with apprehension at the phone. Unless he got the hell out of here soon, it would be ringing. "Find out anything yet?" Mariana would ask. No, he might say to her, but be patient. Finding an abortionist isn't my forte.

He remembered the disappointments of the previous day, when he'd gone to the home of two faculty members, a woman sociologist and a man anatomy and physiology professor, and made a big show of taking them into his confidence. Each had known what he wanted when he'd said he wanted to talk over a problem off-campus. Each had said, separately, they sympathized, that a dozen or so students, male and female, came to them each year with the same problem. Each student said many lives would be shattered unless a pregnancy was terminated. What a sap he'd been to expect help from that direction. What had he expected them to say—"Need an abortionist? Sure, here's the number of the one I use. Tell him I sent you."

Then too, learning Sammy was a dope addict didn't contribute to his peace of mind. If Sammy found out his sister was pregnant by a gringo, no telling what he might do in a drug-crazed stupor. How'd he ever get into this mess, anyway, for Christ sake? He heard the phone ringing as he locked the door and walked toward his car.

Although it was only 9 A.M., he felt weary. Today he was going to try to establish a contact with an abortionist in East Los Angeles. He had no idea where to go, or how to go about it. But he'd try.

He cruised the streets on the east side until he saw a particularly run-down barroom. He parked, went inside and ordered a beer. Looking around, he saw a half dozen Mexican-American men drinking and playing a coin-operated game. Their conversation was half English, half Spanish. He was aware he drew curious glances as he sat alone, well dressed and looking out of place. He spent an hour sitting alone before he realized that in this place, at least, he was not going to be able to become friendly enough with anyone to ask where the nearest abortionist was. He drank up and left, and was sure the singsong jabber he heard as he walked out was a discussion about his presence. He drove a few blocks and found another bar.

This place had a different atmosphere, he saw as he entered. There were seven or eight men seated at the bar and nearby tables watching an attractive woman in her middle thirties dance to the roaring juke box. One of the men would say something to her in Spanish and they'd all laugh. Then she would say something tart back and they'd roar again. She saw Stiver and came up to him.

"Ay, a handsome young gabacho," she said. "Come dance with me." David began dancing with her, much to the delight of the men. They seemed friendly and shouted in English such things as, "Watch out, kid, she'll trip you and then beat you to the floor!"

"Don't pay any attention to them," the woman said to Stiver as they finished dancing and sat at the bar. "But you can buy me a drink."

"Sure," he replied good-naturedly. He spent an hour or so dancing and talking with her. The men were friendly and he sensed no animosity toward him. They joked, bought him a drink or two, and he bought them a round. Finally he sat her down and looked serious. Before he could speak, she said, "What'd you come down here for, handsome?"

He showed a little surprise. "A doctor," he said casually.

"Buy me a drink," she said. When she had it, she continued: "Your best bet's the Tortuga. That means the Turtle."

He looked blank. "I don't understand."

"It's a swingin' hype joint out on Fourth Street past Indiana. Go down there for an hour or two and you'll have everything in East L.A. offered to you." David thanked her and walked away. "Good luck" she called gaily. The juke box roared.

The Tortuga was a dirtier hole than the other two joints he'd been in. The crowd was young, about his own age, he guessed. He sat at the bar, ordered, and looked about.

At the rear, seated and standing around tables, were young women in tight jeans, with jet black hair, pancake make-up thick on their faces, hair piled ridiculously high, and boys about his age, casually dressed, unwholesome-looking, he thought.

Again he was aware he was conspicuous, but he sat at the bar minding his own business, waiting for some opportunity to develop.

After about a half hour Stiver heard a voice beside him.

"Hi, man."

Seated next to him, watching him, was a youth of twenty or so, in need of a shave, a long-sleeved shirt on, wearing slacks that needed pressing. David nodded to him, waiting.

"You ain't fuzz, man, so you must have an itch."

Stiver interpreted this correctly. "Know your way around the east end?" Stiver asked, trying to sound confident.

"Name it, man. If I can't deliver, I'll find you somebody who can."

"I want a doctor," Dave said evenly. The youth didn't bat an eye.

"Don't split," he said, getting up, and was gone.

Looking around, Stiver saw no one had noticed the encounter. Couples were dancing, the bartender was huddling with a friend in some conspiratorial conference, the juke blared a Mexican number. David waited. Presently he sensed someone beside him. He turned and faced Sammy Sandoval.

If Sammy felt any surprise at seeing Stiver, he didn't show it. He stood there looking at Dave, his emaciated, pretty-but-weak face expressionless. David noticed he too wore a long-sleeved shirt buttoned at the wrists, and suddenly he understood why. He also understood the meaning of "a swingin' hype joint." This was a hangout for addicts. He tried to retain his composure and was about to speak when Sammy said, "You want a doctor?"

Stiver was more astounded than afraid. Isn't he even going to ask who the girl is? he wondered. He noticed Sammy seemed more nervous and restless than ever.

"Yeah," he answered.

"You got four bills?" Sammy asked evenly.

"I can get it."

"When?"

Stiver thought a moment. A phone call to back home, urgently needing the money for a field trip and incidentals. His father would rant, but the money would be sent immediately.

"I can have it in the morning."

"For positive?"

"Positive."

Sammy thought. "Be here at noon. Both of you. Give the money to him," indicating the seedy youth outside the window. "He'll take you to the doctor." And Sammy turned and left.

At noon the next day David and Mariana walked into the Tortuga and sat at a table. Almost immediately, the grubby-looking youth appeared. The same crowd was dancing and drinking that had been there the day before. David felt the girls looking at Mariana and knew they knew.

"Got the four bills?" the youth asked. Stiver reached in his pocket and took out a roll containing four hundred dollars. The youth took it without counting it and rose.

"Follow me," he said, starting toward the exit at the rear. Mariana and David followed. All eyes in the place were on them as they marched through the couples near the rear. One of the girls with hair piled high said something to Mariana, and Mariana smiled weakly and said, "Gracias."

"What'd she say?" Stiver asked nervously as they stepped out into the alley.

Mariana looked at him, accusingly, he thought. "She said, 'Good luck.' What did you think she said?"

He didn't answer. The youth led them to a panel truck parked in the alley. He held the door at the rear open while they climbed in, then he got in with them. When the door shut they were almost in complete darkness. Stiver heard the engine start and felt the truck moving. The driver's compartment was sealed off from the rear, and there was no window.

He felt Mariana's hand find his as they rode. The truck seemed to be moving slowly. He felt it turn and gain speed. He heard traffic around them. He heard Mariana's breath catch every now and then, and he tried to remember to pressure her hand reassuringly.

The truck turned right, then left then right, then left, winding around. He could just make out the hands of his watch and saw they had been riding twenty minutes. Then he felt the truck slow and go over a bump, as though crossing the gutter into an alley. Slowly, the truck proceeded, and Stiver could tell by the echoing sound they were again in a narrow alley. The truck stopped.

The driver opened the door at the rear, and the seedy youth got out. David and Mariana followed. Looking around, Stiver saw the alley was crooked and it was impossible to see the street in either direction. Foolproof, he thought. He could never find this place again in a hundred years. Even if he ever wanted to.

The youth took them to a rear door of a building and went in, holding the door for them. It was an abandoned office building, evidently. Looking down the hall, he could see the windows on the street were boarded up. The youth led them to a stairway, and they ascended three floors, then went down a hall to a doorway. To all appearances, the entire building was deserted. Opening the door to an office, the youth showed them in and left. Mariana and David were in a small office. A desk with two chairs in front were the only things in the room. A side door opened and a man dressed as a doctor came in. He was in his early thirties or so, Stiver thought, and looked Mexican-American. He looked educated and was well groomed.

"I'm the doctor," he said in broken English. "Please have a seat." His manner of talking was that of an educated man. Mariana and David sat down, and the doctor sat behind the desk.

During an awkward silence Stiver saw Mariana looking at him, and her eyes said, *David, please! Please!* But he forced himself to look away and appear calm and steel-hard.

The doctor said: "I don't want to know your names. You came here for an abortion. I haven't much time. I'm a graduate of the School of Medicine at the University of Mexico City. I specialize in obstetrics. Are you sure you both want to go through with this?"

"Positive," Stiver said quickly. He wouldn't look at Mariana. God! he thought, if only nothing goes wrong. He'd never get himself into anything like this again.

"I'll have to ask you some questions, miss," the doctor said to Mariana, taking a pencil and pad. "How old are you?"

"Eighteen," Mariana answered quietly. The doctor made a note.

"And how long do you think you've been pregnant? Approximately?"

Without hesitation: "Seventy-four days." She was looking straight ahead. Stiver kept his eyes on the doctor.

The doctor made more notes. He glanced up. "Would you stand up please, so I can see your build?"

Mariana stood up. Stiver could see from the corner of his eye she was holding her head high. The doctor wrote some more.

"Thank you," he said. "You may sit down now. What's your birthday?" Mariana told him. "Do you recall just how old you were when you started menstruating?"

With a catch in her voice: "Just past twelve. Twelve years and three months."

He continued taking notes. "And when did you have your last period?"

"On the fifteenth. Three months ago." She started to sob and Stiver gave her a hard look. *No, by God,* he said to himself, *I won't weaken.*

The doctor wrote on his pad a few moments. Then he looked up. "Anything else you think I should know? Any . . . female trouble you've had in the past?"

Mariana tried to squeeze back the tears. She shook her head.

"No . . . no," in a small voice, "except maybe . . . well I only did it with him, if you need to know that. I was a virgin . . ." Her voice trailed off.

The doctor sat thinking for a moment.

"I see. Well," he got up, "if you'll come this way please." He indicated the side door through which he had entered. Mariana rose and walked to the door. The doctor looked at David.

"You may observe if you wish," he said. David's and Mariana's eyes met squarely for the first time since they'd arrived, she standing just inside the doctor's operating room, he in the waiting room.

"No, I'll wait here," David answered. Mariana cleared her throat to speak. She mustered an incredible amount of courage and her voice was firm, but just a little hoarse: "David, it should have been so different." Then just before the doctor closed the door, David had glimpsed a white linen-covered table.

Stiver waited.

He glanced at his watch as he lighted a cigarette. He listened and could hear traffic somewhere outside. He heard a click from the operating room. Five minutes went by and he heard another click. Was the doctor picking up and setting down his instruments? Maybe he turned on a valve or something. Silence from the next room. He quietly paced the floor, lighted another cigarette and waited. He refused to allow himself to think about the things that could go wrong during an abortion. It seemed hours, but his watch told him less than twenty minutes had gone by. No noise from the operating room. Supposing she died, and the doctor left through another exit. Here he was, waiting while her corpse cooled fifteen feet away.

Presently the door opened and the doctor emerged, removing the surgeon's mask. He had a little smile of triumph that told Stiver what he wanted to know.

"It went fairly well," the doctor said. Beads of sweat stood on his forehead. David noticed he was holding a white porcelain pan, and now the doctor held it up for David to see.

"I thought you'd like to see proof you are getting your $300 worth," he said, and David found himself staring into the pan at the butchered fetus.

The doctor smiled wordlessly, accusingly, at David's reaction of shock and horror. "Come in and see your friend," he said. "She's fine. Congratulations."

Stiver stepped into the room and saw Mariana's still, white unconscious form, still spraddle-legged, on the table. Her face looked a ghastly yellow-white, her hair coal-black. He stood still, watching, and saw her breasts rise and fall with her breathing.

The doctor waited until David had recovered enough to listen.

"I have to leave now," he said. "She'll be waking up in ten or fifteen minutes. She'll be drowsy. Help her get dressed and they'll take you back to where they picked you up."

"Are . . . are you sure she'll be all right?" Stiver croaked.

"We can never be quite sure. But listen. This is very important. She must have large doses of antibiotics. Here is enough in these capsules," he handed David a prescription bottle filled with gelatin capsules. "I can't very well write you a prescription, but this should be plenty. Have her take one as soon as she's able. Then another one tonight. One in the morning and another tomorrow night. Keep that up until they're gone. Then there should be no danger."

CHICANO

David stared stupidly at the bottle. He repeated the instructions so he would remember.

"Also," the doctor went on, "here is another medicine in case there is bleeding. If there is not bleeding, she needn't take these." He handed David another little bottle of capsules.

Stiver stood staring at Mariana while the doctor took off his smock and put on his coat and tie.

"I must leave now. Good luck." And he was gone.

He stood watching her, looking at her body. How different he felt now compared to that night—when? seventy-four days ago, she'd said. Then a flood of relief began to sweep over him. They had come through it. It was all over. Almost.

She stirred and presently opened her eyes.

She looked at him and said his name.

"You're fine, Mariana," he said quietly. "It's all over. Just take it easy."

After a minute or so she sat up and looked at her nakedness.

"Hand me my clothes," she said. As he helped her dress, she kept looking at him. "Was it a boy or girl?"

He didn't answer. The vision of what was in the pan would remain with him for life, he knew. When she was dressed he found a glass and filled it with water from the sink. He gave her one of the capsules and she swallowed it. They sat saying nothing for a while as she gathered her strength.

"Let's go," she said faintly. He helped her into the office and into the hall. The grubby character was waiting. He led them down, she making her way slowly down the stairs as Stiver helped her. He told the escort where his car was parked and got into the waiting panel truck with Mariana.

The ride back was devious. When the truck stopped they

393

got out and blinked at the bright sunlight as Stiver helped her into the car.

"Take me home," she said without looking at him. By the time they arrived in front of the Sandoval home she had regained a measure of strength. "I'll go in and rest. I'll tell Mother I don't feel well."

David handed her the bottle of medicine, repeating the instructions the doctor had given. He noticed the Mexican label and the name and address of a Tijuana pharmaceutical house on it. Fleetingly, he doubted, then felt guilty; just because it was Mexican was no reason to think the medicine might be bad. He walked her to the door and found himself hurrying back to his car.

He felt great guilty relief as he drove back toward the west side of town. *Thank God! I'm out of this mess,* he thought. He realized his shirt was soaked with perspiration and his throat felt dehydrated. Beer. That's what he wanted. The great pressing weight off his mind exhilarated him. He drove to the little beer tavern near the campus where his friend Amelio tended bar. Entering, he took a seat at the near empty counter and ordered. He drained his first glass immediately and ordered another. Several beers later he was loose-tongued and lightheaded. He tried to put the events of the past several months into perspective and order. The Mariana Episode, he decided, he would classify all that. He tried to place it as an era in his memory banks. Something that began at a certain place in his life and ended just as abruptly. And with finality. Yes. It was an experience now. Why should he regret it? We were all richer for any experience, good or bad, pleasant or unpleasant. He let his visions flit ahead into the future. He saw himself in upper-class suburbia, Illinois, dating smart, intellectual debutantes, who understood the problems of the day and took liberal positions. He pictured himself at the country club he'd been too young for four years before. How worldly he would be now, how much more experienced, broadened. He grinned to himself as he envisioned a social gathering of elite acquaintances as he said, in the course of a conversational argument, "I went with a Mexican girl while I was in California, you know." But slowly through it all she came drifting back to him. The maddening charm of her quiet strength. The primitive wisdom (was it really unpolished intellect?) she showed in all her observations and decisions. Her modest good taste in all she did, said and wore. At that beach party, how nervous he'd been about what kind of bathing suit she would emerge in from the dressing room, and when she finally had come to sit by him on the sand, she'd said, "I hope they're not staring because too much of me is showing." *No, no, Mariana. You aren't capable of showing too much of yourself. And if you did, others would not stare so.* Her face came roaring back to hover a foot in front of him over the counter. Fleetingly came the memory of her flesh, and the sudden onslaught of intense longing for her made him grasp reality and attribute it to the beer, or to his guilt at what he had caused, or a combination. His throat felt numb to the sting and coldness of the beer as he drained the glass.

"Amelio!" he called. The bartender approached. There was little business at this time. "Give me another glass," Stiver said thickly, "and then I want to tell you a story you won't believe." The ho-hum look on Amelio's face as he drew another glass of beer was lost on Stiver.

The phone was ringing. It seemed it had been ringing a long time. His mouth felt thick, his mind hazy, as he reached for it and put it to his ear just in time to hear it click and buzz. They'd call back, whoever it was. He was in bed with only a hangover and his shorts on. But there was something he should feel happy about. What was it? Oh, yes. It was over. But somehow, having pinpointed this, he felt as though his elation was contrived. He remembered with a pang of regret his talking to Amelio, telling him the whole story. He remembered how confused he'd been in trying to say whether he really was in love or not. That God-damned Amelio. He'd probably blab it all over. Well . . . the phone rang again. He picked it up. "Hello?"

He recognized the sound of her breath before she said anything. Softly, almost a sob, "David? . . . I need you . . . now . . . Please?"

His frayed nervous system jangled all over. *What the hell now?* "Mariana, listen to me. I know it's . . ."

Her voice cut in with quiet urgency. "You don't understand. I . . . I need you . . . now. *Please.*"

He replaced the phone and stood up, shaking slightly. He forced his head to clear as he dressed, trying to imagine the various possibilities of what might be happening, yet fearing to. He had an impulse to forget the whole thing. It was over now. There could be no child now to intersect his life's path. Whatever was upsetting Mariana would be no concern of his. She would have to solve her problems, whatever they may be, as best she could, without him. And any other problems that came along, also. He made a cup of coffee as he pondered and fretted, then threw it out as it felt uncomfortable to his raw throat. Another beer would fix him.

Still arguing with himself, he drove to Amelio's bar. As he took a place at the counter he saw the man he'd seen before here talking to Amelio. Amelio was oddly silent as he came to wait on him. Stiver downed his beer and went out to his car and drove to the Sandoval home in East Los Angeles.

He saw that Pete's truck and the family car were gone and knew she was probably alone. It took her a long time to answer the door, and he refused to gasp when he saw her. The paleness was gone and her face had a reddish hue. A combination of great sadness and pain was in her eyes. He realized she was near collapse. As he stepped in he put his hand to her face and felt the burning fever.

She took a breath. "Oh, David. I don't feel well. What should I do?"

"God! Mariana, here sit down. We've got to call a doctor."

"But . . . I took the medicine, like the doctor said . . ."

"Something must have gone wrong. You have a doctor that you call?"

She motioned to the telephone stand. "In the address book. Doctor Yamaguchi. He's not far . . ."

David found the number and dialed it. In a moment he was talking to the doctor, saying it was an emergency at the Sandoval home. He hung up and returned to her. "He says he'll be here in five to ten minutes. How you feel?"

She leaned back in the overstuffed chair and shuddered from a sudden chill. "Not very well. I didn't want to call him. Now Mom and Dad will know . . ."

"I don't care what they know. You may be in serious condition. I'll get you a blanket and some water."

Within minutes Dr. Yamaguchi arrived. He walked into the house without knocking, and Stiver had the impression the doctor would have been indignant had anyone questioned his right to do so. "It's Mariana," Stiver said, indicating the couch on which she rested. The doctor's bag was opened before he knelt. He listened through his stethoscope as he waited to read the thermometer. He forced one of her eyes open. Her breathing was heavy. Stiver was surprised as Dr. Yamaguchi read the thermometer and then rattled off something in Spanish. When she refused to answer, he repeated it emphatically. Then he looked at Stiver.

"What happened?"

Stiver looked at him evenly. "She had an abortion yesterday."

Quickly: "Illegal?"

David nodded. The doctor's hands went into motion inside his bag. "Get her onto the bed," he motioned toward the adjoining bedroom, "quick." Dr. Yamaguchi hurried to the bathroom and as Stiver helped her into the bedroom he heard the doctor running water into the basin and scrubbing his hands. Soon the doctor came in. "You can wait in there," he snapped, indicating the front room. Stiver stood still a moment as the doctor noticed the bottle of medication clutched in Mariana's hand. He removed it and studied the label, then took out a capsule and separated the halves. He tasted the powder. "You drink coffee?" he asked Stiver. David nodded. "Then here," he handed the medication to Stiver, "you can sweeten it with these. They contain powdered sugar."

Tingling at the implied severity of Mariana's condition, David walked into the other room and sat down. He felt through his pockets until he found a cigarette. He lit it and waited. Within a few minutes the doctor came hurrying out.

"Get some ice," he ordered, picking up the telephone. From the kitchen Stiver heard him ordering an ambulance. "No, I'll accompany the patient. I'm with her now. Just have that unit ready and Dr. Corb standing by. This is his specialty."

David took the ice cubes into the bedroom. The doctor wrapped them in a towel, muttering. Stiver made himself listen. ". . . try to keep the temperature down until we get to . . ."

Mariana lay on the bed. The doctor had taken most of her clothes off, and now she was still, her breathing deep but even, eyes closed but her face showing pain. Beads of perspiration stood on her face and neck.

David cleared his throat. "I guess you'll want details . . ."

"Not now," Dr. Yamaguchi said in his quick way. "Time for that later." He placed the thermometer in her mouth again and listened more with his stethoscope. Faintly, they both heard a wailing siren. The doctor looked at him. "Better get out in the street and flag them so they won't chase all over the neighborhood looking for the right house."

The ambulance came around the corner slowly, the driver trying to see the house numbers. Stiver stepped into the street and signaled with his arms. The driver saw him and roared to the driveway. The doctor came out of the house and Stiver heard him telling the ambulance men they'd need a stretcher because he'd just given the patient a shot of something with a long name.

He saw the Sandoval car turn the corner and slow, then shoot ahead and brake to a quick stop. Minnie jumped out, looking ridiculous, he thought, with her tight dress and thick make-up. She walked slowly, then saw the attendants carrying Mariana from the house. She ran. Dr. Yamaguchi intercepted her, shaking her by the shoulders to stave off the inevitable hysteria.

"Minnie," he said coldly, "now listen. Thank God you're here. Mariana's very sick. But I think she'll be all right. Do we have your permission to do anything necessary to make her well?" He glanced to see if the attendants could hear, knowing the possible importance of this at a later date.

"What happened to her? What happened?" The doctor shook her again and repeated the question. Mariana was now in the vehicle.

"Yes, yes, do anything. Where are you taking her?"

"To County Hospital. Get hold of Pete and bring him. We'll be in Emergency." He let go of her and started to climb in, but paused and looked at Stiver. "You'll be there too, won't you?" he said. It was more of a statement, and he didn't wait for an answer. The ambulance door slammed and Stiver watched it glide away. The noise of the siren broke out as it reached the intersection where traffic was heavy. Stiver found himself in the middle of a small crowd that had gathered in front of the Sandoval home. He asked a man nearby, "The County Hospital, is that the big one just off the freeway . . ." The man nodded.

The emergency entrance seemed like an ant hole in the side of the huge, sprawling fortress-prison-like building that sprawled among and dwarfed the dozens of other buildings in the hospital's adjacent complexes. Stiver entered, aware of the many persons there in the waiting room who wore dazed or bitter expressions. Most seemed to be quietly, hopelessly, content to wait unknowingly, until someone with knowledge good or bad came to them. The information desk told him Mariana was with the doctor now in a room down the hall, nothing else.

Through one door he could see the corridor, with rooms leading off on both directions. Through another set of glass doors he could see ambulance after ambulance arrive to disgorge its hideous cargo.

He took a seat where he could look down the hall, with the door to Mariana's room in view. Waiting, reflecting, the sounds of the hospital, the muted bell softly sounding, the half whispers of the relatives and friends of the sick and injured, the filtered wailing of departing and approaching sirens, lent a backdrop to this scene of climax. He had an impulse to walk away, turn his back on what was happening. No one involved here, Mariana's parents, her brother, she herself, could realize the importance of what was at stake. His family reputation, the position in society that awaited him, the relationship with his circle of friends at school, friendships he would have all his life, were jeopardized now if he became involved in a scandal.

He mentally pursued the idea of walking out on the situation. No one could prove what had happened. Every year thousands of young girls from the lower social stratum get pregnant and accuse a man from a well-to-do family of being responsible. How quickly his parents would come to his defense, with moral and financial support. The word "moral," as it flitted through his consciousness, faltered and stopped. The situation as it really was suddenly jelled, in focus. The one great immorality here was not in what had happened. It lay in his betrayal of this girl who wanted so desperately to believe in him and love him. He saw now that the immorality had nothing to do with abortion, or sexual license. He was a personal traitor.

Well, now that that was settled, he knew he was a no-good bastard. The question now was, how much of a no-good bastard? If he could betray her like this, jeopardize her life, screw her, consider her and her family as obnoxious obstacles in the pursuit of his happiness, it would be in complete character to continue. Like the villain in a movie who arrives at the point where a façade of conscience and morality no longer serves his villainy, he could now tear off the mask that said he ever cared about anything but the social safety and security, the loss of which he so flippantly had flirted with as a liberal. He saw that his challenging his family by going with her, becoming involved with her, was really like a boy seeing how far he dared swim from the shore, knowing or at least believing all the while he was never too far out to make it back to safety.

A chill grew in him as he saw a priest walk hurriedly in, talk to the information girl, and go down the hall, Bible in hand.

Stiver felt the blood returning as the priest continued down the corridor to the room just beyond the one Mariana was in. Not quite, he thought. Missed by one door. As he watched he saw Dr. Yamaguchi come out of the room. The doctor saw Stiver and came to him. He was small, quick, alert.

"I take it you're involved in this to one extent or another," he said. Stiver stammered, erecting defenses. The doctor laughed, and a little bit of compassion showed. "You're not on the witness stand. Come on where we can talk. Coffee shop's open. Hungry?" Stiver followed him down the hall, past Mariana's room. He looked hard at the door, refusing to think. Another hallway, larger, intersected the corridor. Stiver looked to the right and saw two stretcher beds, the occupants covered completely by a white cloth. He was aware he looked startled as he recognized the familiar attirement of death, and he saw the doctor give him a half-amused look.

The long hall emerged briefly onto a vestibule, where a half-dozen bloody and battered men, manacled, waited for the elevator while a policeman guarded them. Results of a brawl? he wondered. From somewhere behind them came the sound of a girl screaming, and for a moment Stiver stiffened. No, that voice sounded too young. A middle-aged couple came toward them, the man helping to support the woman as she tried to control spasmic sobs. What tragedy befell them? Stiver wondered.

White-frocked Negroes joked among themselves as they pushed along huge-wheeled carts laden with linen. A nurse hurried along on rubber soles, her purposeful, professional attitude somewhat at odds with her well-made-up, pretty, feminine face.

"You know," Dr. Yamaguchi said as he sipped coffee and munched a sandwich, "we have to make a report to the police if we think criminal action is involved in a case."

Stiver, idly stirring a cup of coffee, looked up. "No, I didn't know that. Stands to reason though."

"Whether she lives or dies, the cops will look into it."

David looked up again. "Dies?"

Yamaguchi looked grave. "Yep. She's in bad shape. I've done all I can until we know just how far the infection's gone inside her. Tell me, did the doctor who terminated the pregnancy give her this?" He held out the medicine bottle he'd taken from Mariana.

"Yes," Stiver said. "He said it would prevent infection."

"Well, it would have, if the contents of the capsules hadn't been removed. See, these guys are in a spot. Whatever they buy, if it's bad, or contaminated, they can't do a thing. They can't complain to the FDA, or the cops, or anybody else." He paused. "That's why we've got to get them."

Stiver shook his head. "I can't tell you who he is, or where to find him. They took us there in a sealed panel truck. Into a back alley somewhere."

"At least you can identify your contact. How'd you get to him?"

Stiver thought. God! What a mess. The contact was the girl's brother, only, he's too much of a hophead to realize the girl was his sister. And she didn't know it was her brother who fixed her up with an anonymous abortionist. Her parents don't yet know she was pregnant, by whom, or that she had an abortion, or that their son, the girl's twin, arranged for that abortion.

He felt himself spinning. He knew suddenly that there was too much to face. Pete and Minnie would know shortly about all this. He feared their reaction. What would that crazy hophead Sammy do when he found out his sister might be dying?

He looked at the doctor through dull eyes. "Are you going to name me as one of the people responsible in your report to the police?"

Dr. Yamaguchi regarded Stiver a moment, and it was impossible to tell if there were contempt or disdain or pity in his mind. The inscrutable Chinese, David thought, then remembered he was Japanese. "I don't know. So far all I know for sure is this girl is suffering from severe septicemia as a result of an abortion. Until we talk to her, we don't know for positive that it was an illegal abortion or if she did it herself. If she dies without talking, we may never know."

Stiver rose slowly, shaking his head as though he'd been studying all night. "I've got to go," he said, stumbling away.

"Wait a minute," the doctor said following him. He handed David a card. "You can get through to me most of the time at this number. If you want to."

Stiver stared stupidly at the card and put it in his shirt pocket. He walked out, making his way back to his car without going near the waiting room.

Entering his apartment he set Dr. Yamaguchi's card near the telephone. He looked at it a while. Then he went into the bedroom to lie down. It was too warm. He got up and opened a window and took off his shirt, then he lay down again and finally slept.

Feeling exhausted, David Stiver dragged himself from bed and made a great effort to look in the mirror. Yes, it was telling, terribly. For three days now Mariana had been in an intensive care room in critical condition. When, oh God, when, would it end? and how? Tossing in bed every night was more tiring than sitting up, he decided. And soon would come the knock on the door. He had been making a pretense of attention in his classes, but always he watched the door. Would it be Mariana, or Sammy, or Pete, who pointed the finger at him when the detectives started on the trail of the abortionist? Did they know now all about it? Were they waiting until they could come armed with a charge of murder, tracking down and accusing all who had a hand in her death?

A ray of hope came through. It was just possible, but highly improbable, that Sammy had not known it was his sister for whom he acquired the abortionist. And just barely possible Pete and Minnie were not at all sure Mariana hadn't been seeing other boys, that they wouldn't suspect Stiver, or at least would not be sure or suspicious enough to send the police on his trail. What was it Elizabeth Jameson had said when she telephoned last night? *Sammy's in such a perpetual narcotic fog, he couldn't remember whether he'd taken money for a doctor or not. And he's beyond caring about anything but his habit.* But Stiver wasn't sure of that. If Sammy really didn't care about anything, if he was now more vegetable than man, Stiver feared him the more.

David jumped as his phone rang. He answered it and jumped a little more when he heard Sammy say, "I got to see you, man." He told Sammy to come to his apartment.

Both Stiver's hands trembled as he let Sammy in. Sammy didn't speak a word until he'd gone into the bedroom and bathroom and kitchen. Then he nervously took a seat on the couch in the parlor. Stiver noticed Sammy's trousers were fairly new but wrinkled, his shoes polished but run down, and he wore a type of shirt that needed no pressing and had long sleeves. *Is it my imagination,* Stiver thought, *or does he have that glazed, contented look because he's higher than a kite on something?*

"Did you get fixed up okay with the doctor guy?" Sammy asked. *Good God! He doesn't know!* Stiver thought wildly.

He struggled to keep his voice steady. "Oh, the doctor. It wasn't for me. I guess the people I put him in contact with came out all right." He was observing Sammy closely, and when Sammy gave a little laugh, it could have been anything from self-consciousness to sarcasm.

"Well, man, I been thinking, you know, I don't make much on these things. But I got a real opportunity now. I . . . uh . . . wanted to tell you about it."

Stiver was wary. Was this blackmail? He felt nauseated.

"What kind of opportunity?"

"Well, you know my uncle, Julio? Sure you do. Well, you know he got busted the other day on a narco rap, don't you?"

Stiver was honestly surprised. "Uncle Julio? Arrested for narcotics?"

"Yeah. Busted but good. Aunt Angie's all shook up about it. Nailed on pushing. He'll go to the joint for that."

Stiver was still incredulous. "But . . . tell me about it. How'd it happen? Is he really guilty?"

Sammy laughed. "That don't matter now. But it's kind of connected with what I want to see you about. I figured now that you know a little bit about me, my business and stuff, I figure I can spill some more to you . . ."

David felt the bite coming. "So what is it you want?"

Sammy was a little hesitant. "Well, before Julio got busted, I was working for him . . ."

"I know."

"Well, I was helping him with some other stuff, like junk. Did you know that?"

"No, I didn't." David felt a creeping uneasiness at hearing this, as though he were being contaminated. But he was afraid.

"Well, to make it short, Julio passed on to me all how he did it. His contact and everything. It's foolproof. All I need is a little financing to begin with and I'll make it big."

Stiver noticed as he said these last four words his attitude changed a little and he realized he suddenly had an insight into Sammy's make-up: an introverted, crushed ego of little if any self-esteem, with a chance to maybe play big time. He also knew that this was the shakedown.

His mind raced. He had an urge to suddenly make a clean breast of it all, go to the doctor, the Sandovals, the police, and tell everything he knew. Even implicating Sammy. Or else he'd have to knuckle under to the little bastard's blackmail. Yes, maybe that's what he should do. This waiting, not knowing who knew what, was killing him.

"Okay. So you need financing. How much?" All his life he'd heard that once you pay a blackmailer, it never ends.

"All I need's about three hundred," *to begin with*, Stiver thought, "and I'll be in business. I can buy a load of pure stuff. Cut right, it'll bring about two Gs on the east side."

"And what if you get busted?"

"I can't, man. This is Julio's contact."

"He got busted."

"Yeah, but that's 'cause this old junkie of a whore I was dealing with found out too much. I didn't know it but she'd been looking for Julio for years 'cause he dumped her once or something. That's the big danger in this business. Getting turned in 'cause somebody's mad at you. It won't happen to me."

"Where will you buy it?"

Sammy's voice was conspiratorial. "I take my dad's truck, drive to Tijuana to a certain gas station. They'll be expecting me, 'cause Julio already gave 'em the license number. I don't know the connection, but he'll know the truck. I say I need a tire fixed, and he fixes it. The money's inside the hubcap. Then I come back to town. Meantime, he's put the H inside the wheel. Even if something goes wrong, I can claim I didn't know nothing about it. Lots of peddlers put the stuff into someone's car who don't know nothing about it, then get the square's address from the registration, and pick it up in L.A."

Stiver thought a while. He had an idea. "And what happens to me if you get caught?"

"I can't, man. Even if I do, you ain't involved. You loaned some money to a guy you knew. Why would a rich paddy like you want to get mixed up in this? You're clean, man. A user always takes his own rap. If I do get caught, I'm a first-timer. I'll get a year, maybe, at an honor farm, or maybe a rehab center, 'cause I'm a minor."

Stiver felt that he should shudder, but he didn't. He was becoming hardened. The tragedy of this boy ready to forfeit a year of his life as part of the game, as sort of an occupational hazard, was so far from the world of his own ideas and ambitions it was difficult to grasp. Surely he wouldn't be able to fathom it had he not known this family first hand. Yes, it would be interesting to reason out and analyze the forces and systems that had brought this about, the family attitudes, the underlying feelings of self-worthlessness that each of these people was born into and few disputed. But right now he had his plan to work out. So Sammy thought his life was worthless. Well, maybe it was. But Stiver's life had value, potential. If Sammy was out of the way for a while . . .

He told Sammy to come back the following day, and the next morning Stiver borrowed $300 on his car. When Sammy showed up, Stiver watched as the money was taped inside the hubcap. Stiver memorized the truck license number. He asked Sammy the details of the trip, when he expected to be returning, what routes he'd be taking, and as soon as Sammy left he went into his apartment and made an anonymous phone call to the Los Angeles County Sheriff's narcotic division.

· 4 ·

Traffic was light as Sammy approached the border stop. A few cars in front of him were waiting. The Mexican official spoke briefly to the drivers in turn and then waved them through. Sammy put the pickup in gear and drove slowly up to the official. He stopped, confident that his nervousness didn't show. The official stepped to the window of the cab and looked casually at him.

"Where are you going?" he asked Sammy in Spanish.

"Just into Tijuana for a while," Sammy answered.

"Plan to stay long?" the guard asked.

"No. Just a little while. Just to fool around."

The guard glanced at the bed of the pickup and then motioned Sammy through. Sammy pulled out and drove across the bridge into Tijuana.

Tijuana was filthy. Tourists, seeming not to notice, streamed up and down both sides of the street. Some were couples with children, thrilled at being outside the borders of the United States for the first time. Some were young girls, looking for cheap trinkets. Some were young men, looking for the women they knew abounded in the rickety hotels and patched houses everywhere in the city.

Dogs lay on the sidewalks or slouched along insolently, their mangy coats dangling shocks of loosened fur. A dog obviously dead for several days was in the cobblestone gutter, flies fighting greedily for the choice spots on the carcass.

Sammy had never been to Tijuana alone. The only times he'd come through he'd been with his father and mother, and they wouldn't allow him or Mariana to walk down the streets. Always, Pete had hastened through Tijuana, telling Sammy and Mariana there was nothing for them there. And Sammy understood that somehow Pete identified with the filth and corruption that was Tijuana, as though the Anglos would look at a *Chicano* and think, "He's like Tijuana."

Sammy drove down the main street and soon saw the service station he was looking for. He looked in the mirror, but couldn't see how anyone could possibly be following him. He pulled into the station and parked at the rear. Two attendants were filling cars. A big sign near the street announced gasoline was tax-free and considerably cheaper than a mile across the border.

Sammy sat in the pickup and waited, watching the attendants. Soon he saw one glance at the pickup briefly. The man finished serving the car and then came over to Sammy.

"You want something?" he asked. Sammy noticed the man had looked at the license number.

"I need a tire fixed," Sammy said nervously.

"Which one?" the attendant asked, and almost imperceptibly motioned Sammy to get out of the car. Sammy alighted and followed the man around the pickup, where the attendant stooped to look at a tire. The man then glanced up to see if the other attendant was watching, then quickly he stooped to loosen the valve core on the tire. It began hissing faintly and the man stood up.

"Yes, it's leaking," he announced loudly. "But I won't have time to fix it today. It will be ready in the morning."

Sammy started to panic. "But . . . I have to have it today . . ."

The attendant glared and whispered through his teeth.

"Shut up! I said I couldn't have it ready today. I didn't know they'd put another attendant on this shift. I can't get around to it until he's gone. Besides, how do you know the Customs didn't follow you right here?"

"But . . . I can't wait . . ." Sammy was aware suddenly his nose was running and he started to ache all over. He pulled out his handkerchief and blew his nose. The attendant correctly diagnosed the symptoms.

"I can tell you where you can get some stuff, if you've got to have it. How long can you last? Couple of hours?"

"I . . . guess so," Sammy stammered.

"Listen carefully. I'll say it once. Go to the Descanso Bar. Ask for Memo, La Chota. You got money?"

"Yeah."

"Well, if you can't wait, do what I said and you'll get fixed up. Now beat it."

Sammy walked away, puzzled. He headed back down the street, staring almost with awe at this world which was a stranger to him.

To any tourist, Sammy seemed a native of the environment. But to any Tijuana native, he would be instantly spotted as an American, considered "gringo."

As he crossed an intersection he saw a woman selling newspapers in the street. She stood between the lanes, dodging traffic from both directions. Her newspapers were under one arm and in the other she carried a baby no more than two weeks old. A bandanna was around her hair. Her dress was a large rag and she was barefoot. She screamed the headlines whenever traffic came to a stop, and she tried to get to every driver, saying "Paper, Meester?" The baby looked out uncomprehending at the world around him, squinting and blinking when he faced the bright sun. The woman's swollen breasts indicated she had not borrowed the baby as a device to gain attention.

Sammy walked on. Tamale and taco carts lined the broken streets, with sad-eyed burros harnessed, waiting patiently. The burros were painted with stripes, he noted, evidently to look like zebras, for some strange reason. Symbolic of the people of Mexico, they stood, utterly defeated, without hope, resigned to whatever fate their masters decided upon for them.

Sammy drifted to where a crowd had gathered on the sidewalk. A pitchman was busy demonstrating a magic kit. He laid a cigarette on the sidewalk and then made it apparently stand on end and do a somersault. "You too, can mystify your friends with this trick. The kit is yours for only one dollar."

In the milling throng Sammy stood still, unnoticed, between the crowd watching the magic show and a trinket stand. He saw a young couple, Anglos, approach the trinket stand. The girl looked over the jewelry and picked up a turquoise ring.

"How much?" she asked in English. The man in the stand looked her over only briefly.

"Twenty dollars," he said flatly.

The girl gave her escort a sidelong glance and then shook her head.

"Muy mucho," she said, meaning too much. "Ten. I give you ten."

The shopkeeper smiled politely. "They cost me more than that," he said sincerely. "For you, eighteen."

The girl shook her head again. "Mucho," she said. "I give you eleven." The shopkeeper shook his head, as though the offer was so ridiculous there was no need for further bargaining. With a knowing smile, the girl took her escort's arm and started to leave.

"Just a minute," the man said. The girl and the boy turned back with quick smiles. "I pay eleven for them myself. Make it twelve. It's yours. But if anyone asks, you paid seventeen."

The couple agreed and gave the man twelve dollars. Sammy got a good look at the ring. He had seen the identical thing for sale in East Los Angeles for two dollars. As the couple walked past he heard the girl say, "And that, dear boy, is how you can save eight dollars, simply by understanding these people."

Sammy picked his way through the crowd toward the Descanso Bar. He noticed the American tourists taking him for granted as part of the scenery, while the natives spotted him for a tourist.

He entered the bar and stood, waiting for his eyes to adjust. Americans, mostly servicemen, jammed the place. He took a place by the bar and looked around. Nearly a hundred people were seated around the stage while a shapely young girl stripped. Sammy had never seen a strip before, and he was surprised as the girl took off all her clothes and then did a suggestive dance, going through motions suggesting various normal and abnormal sexual acts. The servicemen screamed with excitement. Then a blond giant of a young man in his early twenties came from behind a curtain. He too stripped until he was nude, and then the two began a routine which was shocking even to the servicemen.

Only unconsciously did Sammy regret having a much greater lust than the one the show was designed to excite. As he watched he was mainly aware of trying not to show withdrawal symptoms. His running nose, he knew, looked as though he had a bad head cold. He jumped as he felt someone tap his shoulder. It was the bartender. He realized in Mexico no one cared the slightest whether you looked nineteen or twenty. He ordered a drink, hoping any peculiar actions would be interpreted as intoxication.

He didn't want the drink, but he stood there looking at it, forcing himself to pick it up and drink it. His hand shook as he raised it. The taste was bitter and the alcohol sickening. But this was a front.

He forced the drink down his throat and set the empty glass back on the bar. Then he noticed the bartender still there, looking at him knowingly.

"Everything okay?" the bartender asked. Sammy thought a moment. He remembered what the service station attendant had said. Ask for Memo, la chota. Memo, the cop. He wondered if Memo was really a cop, or if it was a nickname.

"I'm looking for Memo, La Chota," he said.

Without looking around, the bartender said, "He's the one sitting on the third stool from the end."

Sammy looked in the direction indicated. He saw a medium-sized man in his middle thirties talking to a girl. Sammy studied the man carefully. He looked typically Mexican, mustached, black hair. Sammy walked over to him and found the man facing him expectantly.

"You Memo?" Sammy asked shakily. He was shuddering now from want of heroin. The man nodded.

Sammy was afraid he would try to hold him up, demand an outrageous price for a fix, so he tried to appear casual.

"I was told you could get me fixed up." There was no fear of being overheard in the noise-filled room. The girl next to Memo had turned back to the bar.

"You need a jolt?" Memo asked point blank.

Sammy hesitated only a second. This was Mexico.

"Yeah," he replied.

Memo looked him up and down briefly. "How much money you got?"

Sammy shrugged. "Enough."

"Can you last an hour or two?" Memo asked, looking at his wristwatch.

"Sure."

"Give me three," Memo said almost flippantly.

Sammy pulled out his money and peeled off three one-dollar bills. "Put the rest inside your shorts," Memo ordered. Sammy complied. Memo finished his drink and stood up to go.

"Come on," he said, taking Sammy gently by the arm. He led Sammy outside and down the sidewalk, keeping a hold on his arm, gently but firmly. On the corner was a police call box. Keeping his grip on Sammy, Memo unlocked it and spoke briefly into the phone. Then he hung up and locked the box.

Sammy became apprehensive. "What's going on?" he asked, glancing at Memo's hand on his arm.

"You want a fix, don't you?"

"Yeah, but . . ."

"You'll have it soon. Just keep your money where it is. Use it only when you need it. Don't be afraid."

Within a minute or two a paddy wagon came around the corner and stopped. Two uniformed policemen got out and came up to them.

"Sí, señor?" one of the officers said politely to Memo.

"Take him," Memo said, thrusting Sammy gently to them. "Drunk."

"Sí, señor," the policeman said. One held the rear door of the wagon open while the other guided Sammy inside.

As the wagon pulled away, Sammy glimpsed Memo returning to the Descanso Bar. Within a minute they arrived at the station and Sammy was led out. The policemen led him to a desk where another officer sat.

"Drunk?" the officer said to the two with Sammy. They nodded.

"Empty your pockets, please," the officer said. Sammy did so. He could feel his money under his shorts. The policemen looked disappointed when they saw he had only change in his pockets, but they did not search him.

"Come this way," one officer ordered. Sammy obeyed. He was again apprehensive as he followed the man through the rear door into the alley, and then toward the oldest, most rickety building he'd ever seen. A heavy door was at the entrance, and the officer banged on it. Sammy heard what sounded like padlocks being unlocked and the huge door swung wide. The officer pushed Sammy through.

"Drunk," he said to a man seated at a desk, then the officer walked out. Another officer closed the door and bolted it. Sammy looked around.

The desk was situated directly in front of a jail door. Several prisoners lounged behind the bars, watching curiously.

"Your name?" the officer seated asked. Sammy told him.

"Now," the officer said pompously, "you have been searched. You claimed you have nothing of value on you. We cannot be responsible if you have lied. Is there anything you want to turn over to me?"

Sammy shook his head. The officer made a gesture and another policeman unlocked the barred door. Sammy stepped in.

Sammy was reminded of a scene in a movie he once saw showing the prisoners in a medieval dungeon. It was a huge brick and plaster circular room, with small barred windows almost at the top of the twelve-foot walls. About a hundred men were there. There were no chairs or bunks. A single table stood at one wall near a two-burner stove and water faucet. Half the prisoners were American Anglos. Their faces were drawn and desperate. The others were Mexican, evidently of various stations. Some were well-dressed, some looked like beggars. Almost all, except a few Americans, lounged around lying on the floor, which was concrete. Sammy had enough presence of mind to act like a veteran. Two Mexicans approached him hostilely.

"Where you from?" one demanded.

"Screw you," Sammy said, walking past them. They shrugged, unconcerned their bluff had not worked. Sammy walked across the floor to the far side and sat down against the wall.

He waited further developments.

Three Anglo-Americans, obviously servicemen in civilian clothes, stood by the barred door.

"No word from my buddies yet?" one of them called out plaintively to the officers seated outside the bars.

The officer rose and came to the bars, looking angry. "No!" he *spoke* in broken English. "When someone comes to pay your fine, we'll let you know. Now shut up." The serviceman looked chagrined. He stood still, looking miserable as he stared out through the bars.

A youth Sammy spotted immediately as a Mexican-American picked his way across the floor and sat down beside Sammy.

"What you busted on, man?" he asked in familiar English jargon.

"Drunk," Sammy explained. The youth reacted a little. Just a slight, knowing, narrowing of the eyes. But also Sammy sensed a retreat, a rejection.

"Got a monkey, huh, man?" he asked.

"Don't know what you're talking about," Sammy said, trying to control the butterflies he felt starting up in his stomach.

"Don't give me that, man," the other said. "Let me see your arms?"

He took Sammy's arm to roll back the sleeve, but Sammy jerked away. The youth smiled.

"You're in the right place anyway," he said.

"Yeah?" Sammy asked uncertainly.

"Yeah. You want to score?" he looked around. "Hey, Manny! Come here."

Across the room a dark, ragged man, perhaps in his early thirties, rose slowly to his feet and came toward them. He deliberately picked a spot nearby and casually sank down. Sammy instantly spotted him as a mainliner.

"Yeah, man?" he asked.

The youth spoke to him, not caring who heard. "This guy wants. How soon?"

The man looked lazily at Sammy. He spoke in English, in the dope addict's dialect. "Gotta have bread, man," he said. "Scratch me twice, you'll score in a half hour."

Sammy thought a moment. "Where's the john?" he asked.

Manny laughed loudly. "Over there, man," he said, pointing to a corner. Sammy rose and walked toward the corner, looking for a door. Near the corner he saw a small hole in the concrete where a toilet had once been. A water tap extended from the wall nearby and he saw this was how the "toilet" was flushed. He was aware of other prisoners watching him with amusement as he looked at the toilet. He turned and walked back toward the youth and Manny. As he did he absently tucked his shirt into his trousers, and when he got there he had two dollars in his hand. He handed it to Manny.

"Don't cross me, man," he warned.

Manny laughed. "Hear that, Enrique? He don't trust us. Where would I split to, man?"

From across the room someone shouted, "He thinks we're dishonest," and the other prisoners roared. But Sammy noticed the American Anglos didn't laugh. They just stood or sat around looking worried.

Many rose lazily and walked toward the wall where a large bullfight poster hung. He pulled back the poster and Sammy saw a hole in the wall about six inches across. Manny shouted in the hole.

"Hey! One more." He held the two dollars in front of the hole. "Hey! Anybody home in there? Or are you out for the evening?"

The other prisoners again rocked with laughter. Except the Anglos.

Sammy looked at Enrique. "What's so funny?" he asked.

Enrique explained. "That's the felony tank in there. You think this is bad. It's worse in there and they're all doing at least two years."

Manny was still holding the two dollars in front of the hole. Suddenly a long slender dark arm reached out and grabbed for it. Manny jerked it back.

"Uh huh. Not so fast. Didn't your parents teach you to say please?" The room again rocked with laughter. Like a living thing itself, the dark arm relaxed and sank down. Manny turned to the others.

"Now we will see a lesson in manners," he announced to all. "First we must teach ignorant animals . . ." As he looked away, his hand holding the two dollars moved just within reach of the dark arm, and in a flash the money was gone. Again all laughed as Manny looked bewildered. Glancing around, Sammy saw even the American servicemen smile. Manny returned to Sammy and Enrique, gesturing helplessly.

"They are beasts in there," he said. "I have tried to teach them to be civilized, but to no avail."

Sammy sat surveying the tank.

"How long do we have to wait?"

"Not long now, baby," Manny said.

"Is it good shit?" Sammy asked.

Manny looked a little offended. "Baby, it's the best shit in the world. You probably never had it so good. Just be patient. I'm sweating it too." And for a moment his face lost the lackadaisical nonchalance and Sammy saw the desperate lines there.

"How soon can I get out of here?" Sammy asked.

Manny's casual attitude had returned. "Why, baby, you can get out of here now. All you gotta do is pay your fine."

"How much is that?"

"For drunk? Four bucks. You got that much left, don't you?"

"Yeah," Sammy said.

Suddenly Sammy heard a loud voice calling his name.

"Sandoval!" It was the guard outside the bars.

"They're paging you, man," Manny said.

Sammy stood up. "Here!" he called.

The guard looked at him. "You're guilty of being drunk. Fifty pesos fine or four days. You got the money?"

Sammy looked down at Manny.

"Tell the man no, Junior," he said quietly.

"No," Sammy hollered.

"Well," said the guard, "either you get it or I'll let you out in four days." He sat back down at his desk.

Sammy sat back down and waited. Manny lay back on the concrete floor and tried to look blasé. Looking around, Sammy saw the dozen or so American servicemen sitting in a circle around the jail door. All looked with anticipation, as though any moment their liberator would arrive.

Others sat around or paced, talking in low voices. After a few minutes he noticed several of the prisoners who were dressed more in rags than the others were looking up toward the ceiling. Glancing up, he saw a trap door directly above the center of the room. More of the ragged prisoners were gathering beneath the trap door looking upward. Presently the trap door opened, letting in a blaze of sunlight. Silhouetted against the bright sky was a figure of a man.

"Muchachos!" the man called. "Here you are!" The man

held a handful of loose cigarettes in one hand, and then he flung them down. Instantly, the prisoners beneath dropped to the floor and began grasping and snatching the cigarettes. Manny raised his head with half interest and watched.

"So lucky they are," he said to Sammy. "Those beggars. They have simple wants."

Within a few minutes the men had picked up all the cigarettes. Some had gotten four or five, others only one or two. They all sat down on the floor and lighted their smokes. The man above had left. And Sammy sat and waited.

The sun was starting to set, and the feeble light admitted by the high barred windows diminished. A meager light bulb on the ceiling reluctantly glowed. Suddenly the bullfight poster jumped. Manny, seemingly almost asleep, heard it rattle and instantly rose, walking toward it.

"Our ambrosia is here," he announced. He raised the poster and a hand protruded from the other side of the wall, holding a condom. The neck was tied. Manny took it and returned to Sammy. Looking around, Sammy saw all heads turned in their direction. A half dozen prisoners from around the room came toward them and squatted while Manny untied the condom. Another prisoner produced matches, a can of water, and a spoon.

As the heroin was prepared in full view of all, Sammy looked around. The Anglo-Americans watched in fascinated horror. The ragged Mexicans watched casually.

"Our newcomer is first," Manny announced, loudly. He took a hypodermic needle and filled it from the spoon.

"Your arm, please sir," he said to Sammy. Sammy looked around once more, hesitantly, then offered his arm. Expertly,

Manny injected the fluid. The half dozen others who had come up crowded closer, arms held forward.

Manny looked them over. "Lalo, you only paid half," he said accusingly to one.

"All right, then," Lalo said desperately. "Give me only half. But quick!" His face quivered.

Manny smiled. "I'll give you all this time. I know you're saving money to get out of here. You better bring some more money tomorrow if you get back in."

Soon the only light in the tank came from the lonely light bulb on the ceiling. It was eight o'clock. The heroin had taken effect and Sammy was calm, relaxed and feeling at peace with everything. He thought about paying his way out, but then reconsidered.

Manny was lying down, his head cradled in his arms.

"Manny," Sammy called softly.

"Yeah, man," Manny answered dreamily.

"How early in the morning can I get another fix?"

"Early, man," Manny said. "Stick around. A guy who don't know his way around Tea Town has it tough scoring. Stick around for an early morning jolt and then split."

Sammy thought a while. "Okay," he said softly, "but do I have to sleep on the concrete?" Manny laughed and sat up.

"No. Give me two bits. I'll rent you a mattress."

Sammy produced a dollar bill. Manny took it and rose, going to the far end of the room. One of the prisoners who had taken heroin sat on a stack of cardboard that had once been large boxes.

"Our friend wants a mattress," Manny told him. The prisoner removed the top sheet of cardboard, took the dollar and gave Manny change. Manny returned to Sammy, gave him the change and laid the cardboard on the concrete.

"There you are, man. There's your mattress."

Sammy looked at the cardboard. Then he lay down on it, propping his head on one hand. He surveyed the jail. The servicemen still sat in a half circle by the door, looking out expectantly. The ragged prisoners lay down on the concrete, tossing, trying to find the most comfortable position. The ones who had taken heroin seemed asleep already. The jail had grown quiet. On the other side of the bars the guard sat with a bottle of wine and a magazine. They were all bedded down for the night.

Glancing at the clock on the dash, Sammy saw he had been driving nearly four hours. He would be in Los Angeles in a short time, he realized, and he cautiously eased the pickup to the right of the slow lane onto the shoulder and let it coast to a stop. Traffic, as usual, was very heavy along the freeway. He waited a few minutes, looking in the rear-view mirror closely. There was only the steady stream of cars going by. He got out and went to the wheel he knew contained the heroin. He pried off the hubcap and removed the plastic package taped to the wheel. Replacing the hubcap he got back into the pickup. The effects of his last jolt were now wearing off, and he pondered a moment whether to prepare another fix. Just a small one, to hold himself until he was in a safe place where he could really pop.

It took only a few minutes, and he used a tiny tin spoon which he threw away after filling the hypodermic.

He let the effects of this shot brace him, jar him to what he considered a sharp level of reality. He eased the truck back into the slow lane and continued on into Los Angeles. Still driving carefully, yet not too much so, he stayed on the freeway and at the downtown interchange he took the Harbor Freeway out past the Coliseum to Century Boulevard. He took the off-ramp there and turned left heading into Watts. He stayed on Century to Avalon, then parked and walked north a few blocks, then he turned right and continued walking. He paid little attention to the thousands of black faces along the way. They paid scant attention to him, seeking something else to be mad at, he thought. If he sensed hostility in this community, he had a comforting, secure feeling he was not the object of it.

He walked, still enjoying the effects of the drug, until he came to a gasoline station on a corner. Behind the station were a series of apartment buildings. Across the street, on all sides were shops and stores with living quarters or offices above. He knew that from one of the hundreds of windows that over-looked the service station, a pair of field glasses was probably trained on him. At the edge of the blacktop at the rear of the station property, near the sidewalk, was a telephone booth. He went to it and stepped inside. He slipped in a dime and dialed a number. A trained, professional woman's voice answered, re-peating only the number he had just dialed, in questioning voice.

"I'm trying to reach Mr. Jordan," Sammy said.

He could tell the girl at the other end was consulting notes or records. "One moment, I think I can put you through to him," she said. Then he heard a click and the line was ringing again. It rang a long time, but Sammy was patient. Then the phone was answered.

"Sammy boy, you got a tail a mile long," said a deep, reso-nant Negro voice. Sammy started to panic.

"You sure?" he asked, and almost turned around to look.

"Positive," the voice answered. "They just pulled up and parked fifty feet from you. See that station wagon with the driver who looks like he's drinking beer?"

Sammy turned his head a little. From the corner of his eye he saw a station wagon parked near the service station exit. A Negro sat at the wheel, surreptitiously swigging from a beer can.

"Yeah, I see," Sammy answered.

"Well, what you can't see from where you are, is Big Ed crouched beside him. You're on, Sammy baby."

"What'll I do?" Sammy pleaded.

"If I was you, I'd try to make it to the can there at the station. When you hang up, make a break for the can like a bunny. Happy flushing!" and the line clicked off.

Sammy waited another minute or so with the receiver at his ear. He could see now the Negro in the car was only pretending to drink. He could make out what looked like perhaps someone crouched down beside the driver. Jordan was right. In a flash, he dropped the phone, threw open the door and made a dash for the men's room at the station thirty yards away. He'd only gotten a few steps when he heard the door of the station wagon open and slam, and heavy footsteps chasing him. The door to the men's room loomed in front of him and he grabbed and twisted at the knob, throwing his weight against it. It was locked. The women's room was just a few steps farther, slightly ajar, and he dashed into it. The footsteps were almost upon him, but he made it to the commode, whipping out the little deadly package from his jacket pocket, throwing it into the toilet and flushing it all at once. The package disappeared, and Sammy stood up and faced Big Ed, narcotics officer, who was just coming into the rest room.

Sammy held up both hands. "I'm like a whistle," he said. Big Ed grinned.

"Not this time, Sam," Big Ed said. He put his hand into his coat pocket, and crudely concealing what he removed, he pretended to search Sammy's breast pocket. "Look what I found!" he exclaimed, seeming to remove a hand-rolled cigarette. At that moment the Negro who had pretended to drink beer arrived. "George," Big Ed said to him, "look what I found on Sam baby!" He held up the marijuana cigarette. George smiled and clucked his tongue at Sammy.

Hello?"

"David? David Stiver?"

"Yes."

"This is Elizabeth Jameson."

"Oh . . . Hi, Liz . . ."

"You knew . . . Mariana died Monday, didn't you?"

"Yes, I knew."

"At three o'clock. I was there."

"Oh. I'm . . . glad you were there, Liz."

"Where were you?"

"I was in class . . . at that time. I guess."

"Well," a deep, uneven breath, "she died."

A long, long pause. A heavy sigh. Almost a whisper. "What can I say, Liz?"

Her voice was low, controlled anger. "What can you say? I'll tell you what you can say. The only thing that would make me feel better would be if you said you're taking strychnine at this minute . . ." Her voice rose. ". . . but then ten of you wouldn't be worth one of her, you no-good, low-down dirty snob of a . . ."

"Elizabeth! Elizabeth! All right, all right. You're hysterical, now grab hold." In the silence he could hear her labored breathing.

Then, in a small voice, "I just wish I was hypocrite enough to say I was sorry for that outburst. But I'm not. You know what she said, David? Before she died? You want to know?"

He did not want to know, but he heard his own unspoken voice saying, *You must know what she said, because you've got to suffer a little bit for what you are.*

"What did she say?"

A great measure of control seemed to come to Elizabeth.

"Dr. Yamaguchi wanted you to know just what happened. I waited three days outside her room but couldn't see her. She kept saying, whenever she was conscious, 'Is he really here? You're just saying that, Doctor, 'cause if he was you'd let me talk to him,' and Dr. Yamaguchi would say, 'Sorry, relatives only. Hospital's rules. But he's out there, pestering me as much as you are.' Finally, near the end, I was sitting in the waiting room. Dr. Yamaguchi had sent her mom and dad home saying he'd call them if there was a change, and he came to me and said, 'She's awake now. She feels fairly well. But the end's not far off.' I begged him to let me see her, and he finally said, 'No. If I let you in to see her, she'll know he's not really here.' He started to walk away, and his face had a terrible look. I ran after him and stopped him. I said, 'She knows anyway, doesn't she, Doctor?' And he said, 'She's not quite positive. I want to keep her that way.' He started to walk away, and then he stopped and turned and said, 'I'm really quite powerless to do anything more for her.' She died about three hours later. But you don't have to worry, David. One of the first things she made clear on the first day was that you and she had broken up because she'd been fooling around with another guy."

David's mind had been reeling, but suddenly it snapped to. "What's that? You said . . . she said that?"

"Yes, David. She said that. You didn't know her very well, did you? Or you wouldn't be surprised. She made sure you were out of it before she died," Elizabeth's voice was raising hysterically again. "She didn't want her death to inconvenience you, David. In fact, her whole god-damned race is a terrible pain in the ass to all you . . ."

"Liz! Liz! You're not even making sense now. For God's sake, Liz, I'm human too. I know, I know, you'd never guess, but please, *please*, I can't take anymore." He broke into great sobs and could hear Elizabeth crying also.

Finally she said, "I hope your classes won't interfere with the funeral . . ."

Through clenched jaws: "Please, Liz . . ."

He listened as she made an effort to stop crying. He heard her start to say something several times, and then, "I guess I'll see you there," and she hung up.

Stiver replaced the phone and sat still for a long while. Then he stood up and went to the kitchen and started to make coffee. Now was the time, he thought, for the ghosts to appear. To hear her voice, fleetingly feel her hand on his arm. Yes, he deserved any such hauntings. But they didn't come. He sat sipping coffee. Would he be able to go to the funeral and then forget her? He had to know. No use speculating. Someone, perhaps the God he wasn't sure he believed in, had made the decision whether he would be with her. He realized with a start there was no decision left, no use debating, cursing himself or wondering what it could have been like. He heard mail fall in the chute.

After some minutes he walked sluggishly to the front door and saw several letters. He was about to turn away, leave them lying, when one caught his eye. It was a foreign envelope and from Spain. He picked it up. The answer to his query on the Sandoval family tree. Did it or did it not matter now? He couldn't decide. He read.

Dear Mr. Stiver:

I am answering your query concerning an early Sandoval family in the village of Agua Clara near the city of Hermosillo in the state of Sonora, Mexico. As you no doubt know from your studies, a mission was founded and a town established at Agua Clara in the eighteenth century. It is fortunate and customary that the early Spanish clergy and explorers were in the habit of keeping accurate and extensive journals; thus it is with pleasure that I am able to send you a copy of a translation mentioning a Sandoval at Agua Clara. Mention of the party in whom you express interest is somewhat brief, but remember that here in the Museum of Archives we have over a million documents, journals and letters dating from the Spanish Empire period which we have not yet had time to examine. It may well be there is a great deal more written about the Sandoval soldier.

Best of luck with your studies at your magnificent university in Los Angeles, and a copy of your completed term paper, thesis, or whatever it is you are preparing, for my files would be greatly appreciated.

Antonio Beltran

Historian
Museum of Archives
Madrid, Spain.

July 7, 1785

"... *By the Holy Mother, the life of a missionary is one of great effort and requires patience and endurance. Today in the Village of Agua Clara three newborns were found, obviously of Spanish lineage, with native, heathen names. The mothers swore by Mary they had not been informed by the soldiers who sired their infants that each must bear the surname of its father. More and repeated instructions necessary to the soldiers of the garrison. The new lot, all Barcelonians, are having difficulty adjusting to the heat and rules. One corporal, Leonceo Sandoval, with threat of his weapons, drove a family from its shelter in the village and took the daughter, a young wench of less than fifteen years, for his own. He is a bad one, that Sandoval, and talks of obtaining land title in California to retire on, as he has served with the military many years in many campaigns. He has requisitioned passage for his wife from Spain to California that he may live the life of a family rancher ...*"

May 1, 1786

"*Blessed is the Mother of God, for the ship has arrived, bringing to us, I hope, spices, fabrics, dyes, and the little luxuries which reward life in this remote outpost so far from the homeland. The soldier Leonceo Sandoval will accompany our caravan of tallow, hides and wine to the sea to ship to other places. Sandoval will not be returning to us. The ship bears him two-fold gift. His wife, from Barcelona, and an official land grant, making him the owner of countless thousands of acres of land in California, near some pueblo called Nuestra Senora la Reina de Los Angeles, which I understand is near our two California missions, San Gabriel el Arcangel and Mision de San Fernando. The native girl here who bore Sandoval two children will move into the mission quarters. I have much work for her and she shall be taken care of by the Church. One child, the boy, looks strikingly like his father, the strong, Spanish features and intellect being particularly conspicuous in this child. I think he belongs in the Church, and I will prepare him for such."*

He put the paper down on the table and thought. Yes, even this would have made the difference. It was hideous, but it would have. It was all mixed up, wasn't it. A brute of a soldier, with a family, but his Indian mistress having a child out of wedlock. The very same illegitimacy which had cost a girl her life would have been overlooked, he thought, if he could have said, "Oh she's from a fine old Spanish family that settled in California before the turn of the past century." Being able to say that—just that, *only that*—would have given him the courage necessary and made the difference. Now he heard voices, exaggerated, like Hollywood stereotypes of phony society matrons: "Her aristocracy is quite apparent." "The Castillian comes through, doesn't it?" "Closely related to one of the California Spanish families that retained possession of holdings to this day . . ."

He caught himself thinking—*No wonder she played the part of Days of the Dons fiesta queen so well*—and then he realized what this thought meant and he screamed to himself, *It's no use. You can't teach ideas out of people.*

Stiver didn't go into the church, but waited outside. He saw the scores of people enter, dressed in their best. He guessed at least a hundred and fifty people attended, counting the dozens of children and teen-agers. Finally they began coming out, a priest leading the way down the wide steps to the sidewalk beside the busy street and almost across from the vast cemetery. He started to follow the crowd, and saw the immediate family group leaving the church by a side entrance, getting into waiting limousines. He recognized Pete, and Minnie, as she held both hands over her face and Pete half-supported her, his face comically like the tragedian of the drama emblem. Minnie was dressed in a shiny black dress, too small for her, really. Pete had on a suit and hat. He recognized some of Mariana's uncles and aunts. They all would ride the short way to the grave site. He walked, following the much larger group of cousins, relatives by marriage. Traffic halted on First Street as the crowd crossed, not walking particularly slowly, but without talk. He followed.

They gathered at the open grave, the many dark faces and black eyes. Those arriving in the limousines went to the front of the group beside the open grave and sat in folding chairs placed there for them. The hearse arrived, parking as close as the narrow road in the graveyard would permit, and the pallbearers— he didn't know who they were—carried the casket containing Mariana's body to the grave and placed it on two pieces of lumber laid across. The priest stood beside it and began a last ceremony.

The words were drowned out as Pete and Minnie began sobbing aloud, and soon others nearby did likewise. And suddenly it was over and the crowd was drifting away. David looked for Sammy and then remembered with a chill. And Julio. He saw Angie but Julio was missing and David felt his stomach jerking. Now Minnie was refusing to leave, trying to go to the coffin. He heard her say, "Let me see once more, I just want to see her once more," but a host of brothers and Pete forced her away toward the limousine. Slowly, they left, and slowly the rest of the crowd began drifting away. He saw the old man, Neftali Sandoval, moving around the crowd, coming toward him. David stood rooted, watching him approach. His uncut white hair came past his ears, his great mustache dripped the tears that ran from his eyes. Slowly he moved, bent, looking at the ground carefully where he placed his feet. He wore a plaid flannel shirt beneath a brown, worn sport coat, and his shoes were black and white saddle shoes, spotless. He came up to David and stood beside him, facing the grave. He began talking in Spanish and David looked at him. Was he saying something to the grave or to him? The old man's voice cracked, but he turned toward David and continued talking, his mustache moving as his lips did. David thought he caught the interrogative intonation of a question, but he wasn't sure. Then the old man wasn't talking, but simply looking at David, as though he expected an answer. David just looked back, shrugged and then started crying. The old man nodded and briefly put his hand on David's arm, and David was surprised at the gentle masculine strength he felt in that touch. Then Neftali Sandoval walked away and David realized one of the old man's sons was standing nearby. He couldn't recall which one it was.

"What did he say?" David asked.

Victorio's voice was cracked as he answered. "He asked you if you ever knew a more beautiful girl in your life." David looked down, shaking his head, and Victorio went on, "And he said she looked exactly like another girl he knew long ago, but that girl never really existed."

Stiver looked at him, puzzled. "What'd he mean by that?"

Victorio started to walk away slowly. "I don't know. I guess the old man's getting really old."

David realized he was the last one to linger near Mariana's grave. He started to walk slowly away and then glanced at his watch and walked faster. If he hurried he could still make it to graduation rehearsal on time.